EAGLE

BAY

Other Titles by

KEN CRUICKSHANK

The Emerald Cross

Stand Up: a memoir of disease, family, faith & hope

EAGLE BAY

KEN CRUICKSHANK

Glendoveer Press LLC

Phoenix, Arizona

For information about this title or to order other books and/or electronic media, contact the publisher:

Glendoveer Press LLC
24654 N. Lake Pleasant Pkwy.
Suite 103-220
Peoria, AZ 85383

Cover and interior design by The Book Cover Whisperer:
OpenBookDesign.biz

978-1-960981-01-1 Paperback
978-1-960981-02-8 Hardcover
978-1-960981-00-4 eBook

Printed in the United States of America

FIRST EDITION

*To my loving wife, Karen, who believes in me.
You deserve more praise than an entire
library of dedication could express.*

PROLOGUE

1534

The skies filled with masses of birds as Capitán Juan Francisco Montoya, his mapmaker, and two conquistadors descended a coastal mountain on horseback. Violent tremors shook the earth, causing their horses to snort and shuffle wildly.

Struggling to calm their mounts, the horsemen watched in horror as a great wave stretched across the entire seaboard, approaching the bay at speeds unimagined. The wall of destruction charged into the anchored *Santa Sofia* and her three hundred Spaniards on board. A raging sea engulfed the galleon and swept it into a forest of towering pines.

"¡Mi barco! ¡Mis hombres!" cried the capitán. My ship. My men.

Weeks later, gazing north from a ridge overlooking his marooned galleon, a somber Montoya reflected on the carnage and death. He regretted not sailing back to Seville with his bounty of incredible treasures. His decision to chart New Spain's northwestern shores delayed their homecoming, dooming the expedition and his conquistadors.

Capitán Montoya studied the natural wonder of the mysterious place that fate delivered him. Stunning shores and rock formations. Rivers and valleys like none other. A land filled with abundance.

A land that would one day be called Oregon.

EAGLE BAY

CHAPTER # 1

1986
Eagle Bay, Oregon

Thomas Westbrooke considered it strange that a tired relic of a bygone era was the busiest lunch spot in his thriving hometown. The Lighthouse Inn was a nondescript rectangle with shingle siding painted an unsightly pale blue, but what it lacked in curb appeal was countered by sweeping vistas of Eagle Bay and Cape Nahteenwa. The place was an institution serving a devoted clientele of dealmakers, fishermen, and seafood lovers.

Glancing over his shoulder from the host station, Thomas watched John McCloud saunter through a sun-drenched parking lot with a pleasant expression that mirrored his personality. As he entered, their mutual smiles reflected bonds formed in grade school and maintained into their mid-twenties.

They clasped hands in their familiar grip and embraced. "You're still all muscle, buddy," Thomas said as he thrust his palm into John's rigid shoulder.

Amused and voicing agreement, John patted his sleeved bicep, and they followed a server to the right. Ambling through a maze of patrons to an open table, they seated themselves in sturdy wooden chairs crafted from local Douglas firs. Black and white photos of anglers in their dories at sea covered three walls. An antique ship wheel highlighted the room, and nautical artifacts lay displayed in dark wood cases.

John removed his Vuarnets with calloused hands and exposed inquisitive brown eyes. Thomas looked and acted like the busy executive he was. The handsome duo sat and conversed, oblivious to onlookers' eyes.

A ponytailed young woman arrived with a pen and pad of paper, and they ordered their usual plus two half-pints of house porters. Midday light poured through twenty oak-framed windows, illuminating their faces.

Upon laying a cotton napkin in his lap, John said, "It seems like you or someone from your company is in the news every week. Whenever your ugly mug shows up on TV, the kids point and scream, 'There's Uncle Thomas!' I'm guessing your business is booming?"

"Things are going well," Thomas said after silencing his vibrating pager. "We just broke ground on a new building." He spent five minutes updating John on the happenings within his family's eponymous firm, Westbrooke Coastal Industries.

"Impressive," John said with a nod and smile. "We'd be just another dreary beach town if it weren't for you Westbrookes." He took a sip of water. "How are your mom and dad?"

"Robert's fine. After the board elected me CEO two months ago, he moved to chairman," Thomas said. "We're meeting with Goldman

Sachs next week—they want to take us public." He paused. "Regarding Emma . . . well, her condition never changes. But you know that."

"Yeah, of course. It just feels right to ask," John said, reminding himself of Thomas's burden, having a mentally diminished mother who was once vibrant and capable. "Hey, I saw that *Forbes* ranked you as one of the top hundred execs under thirty. Quite the achievement, you mover and shaker. Congrats."

"Thanks, but it's really not a big deal. And it was due to Robert's reputation more than anything I've accomplished."

"I seriously doubt that," John said. "I'm always impressed by your modesty. If I had your skills, I might not be schlepping drywall and boxes of nails across dirt." Thomas appeared unmoved. "Come on, smile. You know I'm right." He clutched Thomas's wrist. "You're an extraordinary man. Princeton grad. Westbrooke business maverick. The vaunted 'Pillar of Eagle Bay.'"

"You done?" Thomas said before beaming. Because Robert raised his son never to challenge his supremacy within the family dynasty, Thomas appreciated John's acknowledgment of his contributions to Westbrooke Coastal Industries. He couldn't recall a single instance when his father expressed anything similar.

They centered their woven placemats just as their server lowered two piping hot bowls to the table. The salty aroma of fresh clam chowder drifted upward, teasing their senses. Nothing felt more Oregon Coast than feasting on fresh chowder.

"Are we still on for tomorrow?"

"Of course," Thomas said, creasing his forehead as if it were an absurd question. "Nothing gets in the way of a day of fishing, *mon frère*. Wasn't that the pledge we made in high school? 'Not girls nor homework shall stand in the way of fishing in the delta or the waters of Eagle Bay.'" After reciting the words, he lifted his spoon with its pudding-thick soup.

"Unbelievable." John shook his head. "I'd pay a thousand bucks for your memory, maybe more."

"Be thankful you don't have it. Contrary to the adage, time doesn't heal all wounds. Not for me, anyway; I can't forget anything. It's a curse."

"Then be happy you haven't done anything *truly* batshit crazy. Recurring memories of blowing up mailboxes with M-80s in high school shouldn't weigh on your conscience too much." John simulated an explosion with his hands. "Besides, that was my idea, not yours."

They reminisced about a range of pranks and shenanigans before Thomas glanced at his watch. "Enough about our teenage exploits. How's Skye? You know, I'd give anything to find a woman like her."

"She's doing great, thanks. But get real—you've dated more accomplished and beautiful women than I can keep track of." John leaned closer. "Of course, none of them were Skye McCloud material. You just keep looking." Thomas grinned and nodded.

A more animated John teasingly redirected the conversation after swallowing sourdough bread dipped into abundant clams and potatoes. "So, my friend, I've got some wild news." He stared with his brows arched but didn't elucidate.

"I figured something was up. You looked a little too eager when stepping inside. So what's the mind-blowing announcement?"

"This will come way out of left field. I drove up to Depot Bay yesterday searching for building sites. You know that dinky old museum, the Pioneer?" John received an affirming nod. "I noticed they'd strung a banner over the entrance reading Oregon Coast History Day." He shuffled his chair forward. "I stopped in and spent thirty minutes rifling through piles of old magazine and newspaper clippings."

"Sounds unbearably tedious," Thomas said.

"You'd think so but get this: I found a newsclip photo of our grandfathers standing together in 1928."

Time froze as they locked gazes. Thomas's blue eyes studied John, but he said nothing, sitting numbed and introspective: *He didn't just say that. No one blindly stumbles onto the truth. Impossible.*

John noted a twitch above Thomas's left eye. He measured how his friend's face instantly expressed confusion or doubt, and he understood: It was a stunning piece of information given their years-long friendship.

"Our grandfathers, standing on the beach in front of Cape Nahteenwa." John shook his head and wiped the froth of hops and barley from his mouth. "Pretty amazing, right? The Westbrookes and McClouds—*connected*—decades ago? How could we not know this?"

Twisting his neck, Thomas gazed out to Eagle Bay, transfixed. The drone of an airplane taking off nearby came and went. He inhaled slowly, deeply, his thoughts contradicting his composure. *No, John. Please, buddy, reverse course. I swore to Robert you'd never be a threat.*

John waited for a reaction, but Thomas remained silent. "Anyway, I asked for a copy, but the granny working there said to take the original. The museum's closing down—no funds or visitors—so I slipped it into my pocket." Thomas didn't respond. "You late for a meeting? Preoccupied? I thought this was pretty damn remarkable."

Thomas stretched a smile. "Sorry, you caught me off guard. Can I see the newsclip?" He took a swallow of beer, trying hard to convey calm.

"When it reappears. I could've sworn it was in the glove box of my

Bronco, but I checked when I parked—nothing. I left for work in a rush, so it's likely sitting in my desk drawer at home." John chuckled. "With all this buildup, I need to find it before we meet up tonight."

"You do indeed, Mr. McCloud," Thomas said with a half-smile and no hint of trepidation. "But I'm curious; why are you convinced it's our grandfathers?"

"It spells it out in the caption! Who, where, and when. Our two grandfathers and some dark-skinned stranger."

Thomas pressed back in his seat and wiped the lenses of his sunglasses with the clean edge of his napkin. "Hmm . . . 1928? What was Skye's reaction?"

"Haven't told her. I thought we could dig into this further before surprising our families. There's obviously more evidence somewhere." John's face expressed amazement. "Our fathers will be shocked."

"Indeed they will," Thomas said as unwelcome thoughts of interrogation dominated his psyche. *Evidence? Just what "evidence" are you looking for, John? Was Robert right about the dangers of our friendship? Have you been playing me all along?* That harsh thought disgusted him, and he sought consolation by chastising Robert for raising him to be relentlessly paranoid of people, even his closest friend. Feigning excitement, he said, "It's quite the discovery. Good work, Sherlock."

"*That's* what I was waiting for," John said, slapping the table. It took a while, but he was pleased to have Thomas on board finally. "Wild, right? I couldn't believe what I was staring at after I picked it up. I'm returning to the museum next week to tear through their archives. Come with me."

"I think I will. Did you find anything else? Articles? Records? Other photos?"

"Maybe I did, and maybe I didn't," John said as he pushed his empty mug away. He flashed a mischievous grin. "I enjoy frustrating you with snippets until what I call 'the full reveal.'"

"Yes, you always have." Thomas stroked his chin. "So find the photo and caption. I'm intrigued. And I agree—keeping this from our families gives us time to coordinate the surprise. Still have the code to our gate?"

"Sure do. You'll see me driving up your ridiculously long driveway in six hours." He beamed. "Make sure my bed has extra pillows; your guest mattress was hard as a rock last time I slept there."

"Duly noted," Thomas said, projecting benign disapproval. He stood and extended his arm for their departure. Thomas gently tapped John's chest with a closed fist in the parking lot, and each man peered into kind eyes. John jumped into his Bronco and saluted, then roared up Highway 101 toward his worksite.

Thomas slumped back in his Jag and stared out to Eagle Bay, struggling with dire thoughts and conflicted emotions. Ten minutes later, he rubbed his temples, started the car, and took a slow route back to the Westbrooke Coastal Industries campus, fixated on a single thought.

What have you done, John?

Punishing gusts roared up the hillside and whistled past Ford pickups and a construction crew throughout the afternoon.

John double-checked the framers' work using the tape measure clipped to his belt, ensuring the dimensions met his exacting standards. It grew clear that more two-by-sixes were needed to complete the upstairs framing, so he told the men to continue while he ran into town to pick up supplies. Time and productivity were money.

John fired up his Bronco, popped in a well-worn Aerosmith *Rocks* eight-track tape, lowered his window the old-fashioned way, and drove past project debris, hoping to avoid errant nails often drawn like magnets to his tires. His front windshield framed white-capped breakers pounding coastline rocks and tidal pools as he drove south toward Eagle Bay.

Upon graduating from the University of Oregon, John pursued a career he'd always relished: custom home building. Entering Benson Lumber & Hardware, a symphony of *Hello* and *Hey Johnny* drifted from aisles, check stands, and loading docks. He appreciated the town's friendly manner and shared a particular camaraderie with people in the building trade.

With curls of red hair flowing down her back, Suzy Kildare smiled as she rang up John's order of thirty pieces of lumber, two bags of nails, and three saw blades. "It's good to see you, John," Suzy said, her fingers tapping register buttons faster than he thought humanly possible. She charged his account and presented a receipt. "I saw that big house you're building on Northshore Drive. It looks mighty fine," she said with a wink. "Why don't you build me a place like that?" The other cashiers and a manager chuckled; it was the sort of banter Suzy had carried on for years. "I won't tell Skye," she said, a comment prompting hearty laughter from several locals.

"Let me chew on it, Suzy. And I'll run it by Skye tonight," he said with a nod. Hopping back onto the highway, John anticipated his daily homecoming with Skye and their children, Johnny and Dakota. He lived in a great town, worked the only job he wanted, and his wife and kids brought him more happiness than he probably deserved. Oh well, someone had to draw the winning ticket.

An elk suddenly sprang into his path from behind roadside blackberry bushes, forcing him to slam on his brakes and skid off the side of the asphalt. The massive instigator moseyed along as if nothing had happened. He appreciated its obliviousness.

Everything inside the car had smashed forward into the dashboard and seatbacks. As he picked up items from the floor in front of the passenger seat, he found the missing newsprint with the photo of his and Thomas's grandfather. "Yes!"

Minutes later, he stopped at a gas station to fuel up and add two quarts of Pennzoil. He remembered the library across the street offered printing and copying, so he asked the attendant to add the oil and a filter before darting over a crosswalk while clutching the newsclip.

Inside the library, he focused on the image transferred onto white paper and grew pleased with its clarity; anyone could easily discern that two of the three men pictured were a Westbrooke and McCloud. John folded the print-out twice, grabbed the original from atop the copier glass, and returned to the service station.

He paid for the gas and oil and added a tip that prompted a beam from the uniformed, shaggy-haired teenager sporting a shirt with blue stitching that read "Reggie." Stepping into his Bronco, he checked the time and decided to drop by his parents for a quick hello. Three weeks had passed since his last visit.

Upon arrival, John slid down his seat and strode into the house through the garage, just as he had for twenty years. He heard running water in his parents' master bath toward the back of the home. Turning left in the hallway, he nearly crashed into his father.

"How've you been, son?" They hugged, and John was again impressed by his ex-military father's muscular arms. His dad held up a folded piece of white paper. "This was lying on the driveway next to your truck. Without my glasses, it's just a blurry photo. Is it yours?"

John wasn't ready to divulge the fascinating discovery linking an earlier generation of Westbrookes and McClouds. He snatched the paper from his father's grasp. "Yep—it's just a copy of an old photo of the Cape taken decades before developers transformed Eagle Bay."

"Well, progress was inevitable for this slice of heaven. Hey, why don't you join me in the den?" They entered, and his father grinned while tapping the side of a brown cardboard box folded shut. "You've promised to remove this stuff for I don't know how many years." Patting John McCloud III on his back, John McCloud II said victoriously, "Today's our lucky day."

The younger John laughed while unfolding the four top panels. "I think it's one of those things I want but don't want. I mean, look at this junk: prom pictures, yearbooks, baseball cards, and magazines. Oh, and Grandma's mysterious pendant."

John lifted a strange piece of jewelry depicting a fiery sun. Someone had looped a leather strand through a hole above the crudely made silver and gold medallion. He placed it around his neck and smiled at his namesake. "I've always thought this thing was cool. Still no idea where Grandma got it?" He held it between his thumb and forefinger, focused on its detail. "It looks somewhat authentic, in an antique-ish kind of way."

"My mother told me it showed up just before my father's departure for Alaska, sometime in the 1920s."

"But you're positive it's worthless crap?" John asked.

"Yep, according to that jeweler downtown—Van Dykes—it's a fake relic. They offered me twenty bucks for it."

"Didn't they go bankrupt?"

"You think that means they misvalued it?" He chuckled and offered a knowing expression. "Go ahead and get it reappraised. If it's worth anything, consider it an advance on any inheritance. That is *if* your mom and I don't spend all our meager savings."

"Deal," John replied while fitting the pendant's leather necklace over his head. He placed the folded copy of the news clipping inside the front cover of his high school yearbook, dropped it into the cardboard box, and lifted the contents. "I'll transfer this stuff right now. No more cluttering your house." He turned and found his mother approaching, dressed in sweats and Nikes, her dark hair still damp. John set the items down, and they embraced.

"How's my favorite son?" she asked. "Can you join us for dinner? Where are Skye and my darling grandchildren?"

As an only child, John grew used to his mother's excessive attention. Since her diagnosis of Parkinson's, he relished a devotion that might be difficult to express one day. He noticed the trembling of her left hand had worsened.

"Sorry, Mom, I need to go. Skye and the kids are waiting at home, and then it's off to the Westbrookes. Thomas and I are fishing the delta tomorrow. We'll see you and Dad for Johnny's birthday, right?"

"Of course."

Sensing his mother might insist on an extended visit, John pecked her cheek and walked briskly toward his truck as he called out reassuring words to parents he cherished. He leaped inside and put the car in reverse.

"Give the kids our love!" she yelled as John gunned down the driveway. "And say hello to Thomas!"

John leaned over the passenger seat toward an open window. "Will do!" The heavy pendant tugged uncomfortably on his chest hairs as he sat back. He adjusted it, honked twice, and roared away. The visit extended his good mood.

Driving over twisting country roads to what he sometimes referred to as his "poor man's estate," it wasn't until he turned up his driveway that John realized he had, once again, left the box of his teenage nostalgia in his parents' den. Smiling, he questioned whether his father would stick it back in the closet and forget about it for another five years.

John and Skye's light brown residence was a single-story, L-shaped ranch home clearly in the throes of renovation. John and his friends recently installed new siding, windows, and doors that dramatically improved its curb appeal.

Six-year-old Johnny and four-year-old Dakota waited for him while straddled atop a corral fence, their hands and heads in constant motion. He turned off the ignition and placed the rediscovered original newsclip in the glove box to share with Thomas later that night. Stepping from the Bronco, the kids screamed and grabbed his legs as he palmed each of their heads; it was a ritual he relished. Skye stayed in the house, waving through a window.

The trio stepped through the front door, walked hand-in-hand toward the kitchen, past a sunflower wall clock, and greeted Skye. She kissed her husband, and John asked the kids how they'd spent their day. Then he beamed as Johnny and Dakota spoke faster and louder to ensure their account drowned out their sibling. The kids' incessant chatting continued through dinner.

John helped Skye with the dishes before spending twenty minutes in his office filing business receipts. It was Skye's turn to read aloud, a bedtime routine often lasting half an hour or more. Later, John kissed both children good night, and the couple plopped themselves onto the middle of a worn sofa.

Skye exhaled melodramatically and presented an adoring smile. "Well, honey, this is the life we asked for," she said, pointing down the hall toward the kids' bedrooms. "Honest to God, the two of them are nonstop energy. I'm exhausted."

When John leaned in for a kiss, the pendant's outline grew visible through his sweatshirt. Skye squeezed it through the gray cotton. "What's this?"

John leaned back and pulled the relic from under his shirt. "Just a remnant of my youth that I grabbed from my parents' house. This thing mesmerized me as a teenager." Skye studied it, front and back, and projected intrigue while lifting her shoulders. "I agree," John said. "I'm not sure what to make of it either. Dad had it appraised—says it's worthless."

"Well, it's certainly unusual." She released it. "But I'd never wear it."

"And you don't have to," he replied with a thumbs-up. "I'm hoping it'll bring us luck tomorrow; we got skunked the last time we fished the delta." He placed the pendant beneath his sweatshirt while staring into green eyes that reminded him of springtime in coastal forests. "God, you're beautiful."

"Why, thank you, Mr. McCloud. So why don't you cancel your fishing trip and join me for some adult playtime?" She lifted her brows and squeezed his hand. "Make a choice: your beautiful wife or your best friend."

He laughed. "Sorry, I'm committed. But twenty-four hours from now, your stinky husband will need a shower and might be too tired to lather himself up. So don't make any plans."

"Hmm, sounds interesting, but I'll have to check my calendar." Skye caressed his shoulder. "Thomas needs another distraction besides you. Tell him I think he should settle down with an amazing woman and raise a brood of little Westbrookes."

"I have, but he says he hasn't found a woman as great as the one I've got." John put his arm around her, buried his face in brunette locks, and inhaled. "And he never will. Skye McCloud is one-of-a-kind."

Thomas accepted that he should have assumed fragments of the Westbrookes' dark history could eventually surface, though he never considered that his dear friend might be the trigger. But if John had indeed stumbled onto links between their two families, it would be naïve to assume he didn't know more than he'd revealed. Robert always demanded caution: *Trust no one*. So despite John having been the epitome of loyalty since grade school, Thomas forced himself to consider that he might have dangerous intentions. His heart reasoned that John was incapable of such scheming, but Robert raised him to presume the worst.

Thomas's hesitations eventually faded—as they always did—allowing him to justify the harsh verdict. If John knew more than he let on and shared that information with Skye, his parents, or close friends, it could invite scrutiny and cause the downfall of the family dynasty. Robert programmed Thomas from an early age to eliminate such possibilities. The astonishing secrets lying in a vault below Robert's estate enabled everything three generations of Westbrooke men had achieved. Thomas knew if John learned the origin of those secrets, his reprisal would be swift and thorough. Strict principles guided John McCloud's life, and that was now a problem, regardless of how little he knew.

Thomas attended his meeting with Westbrooke Coastal Industries' vice president of marketing before clearing his late-afternoon schedule. The young executive needed time to think. Staring out at three Douglas firs, he watched squirrels and blue jays scurry over trunks and branches, peaceful images contrasting his disturbing thoughts.

Rational people would have summarized reasonable options, but Thomas's next step felt preordained. His dread struck like physical pain. He again challenged whether the decision needed to be binary and necessary. Perhaps he and Robert could compromise.

Thomas turned and absorbed a photo of John and him in a dory boat fishing for lingcod. They were smiling with arms stretched around each other's shoulders. Should he have shared the burdens of his childhood with John during those teenage years? Would his friend have intervened and redirected Thomas's future? And his own?

At five-thirty, Thomas stepped out the front doors of the family's corporate headquarters. He walked to his Jaguar, acknowledging an employee's greeting with a faint smile and flick of his chin. He opened the door, sat down, placed his briefcase on the passenger seat, and turned the key. The rumbling sounds of the sports car's exhaust pipes typically enthralled him. Not today.

Driving through the north side of downtown Eagle Bay, he recalled pedaling his Schwinn alongside John to a '40s-era malt shop on 2nd Avenue that served Tillamook ice cream. Restored buildings and bungalows lined every street, most of them between seventy and one hundred years old. All newer construction complemented the historic structures. The city center bustled with a thriving business, arts, and entertainment district due to the Westbrookes' influence.

As he sped past a herd of elk he'd often seen grazing between the city and his family's estate, Thomas reminisced about his many hunting trips with John. The two friends would drink whiskey stolen from Robert Westbrooke's bar while seated next to a roaring fire encircled with stones John yanked from a stream bed. Before bedding down in their tent, they would place two or three of the heated rocks inside their goose down sleeping bags to counter the biting chill.

Pulling over to a bluff, he studied views of Eagle Bay, Cape Nahteenwa, and the coastline. Stunning nature and the comforting smells of a warm fall day could not diminish his burning unease.

He got back in his car and drove three more miles. Upon pushing the remote on his Jag's sun visor, the wrought iron gates to his family's estate opened; he lived in the property's guesthouse. Thomas had called from his office an hour earlier, advising Robert they needed to speak.

Thomas parked and entered the den of his parents' residence. He found Robert smoking his pipe, wearing silver-rimmed bifocals, and turning the pages of a book chronicling the adventures of Spanish conquistadors.

Thomas stepped toward a bottle of Scotch lying atop an English antique and asked his father if he'd like an ounce of the aged whiskey. He declined. Thomas filled his glass and studied the deep wrinkles etched between Robert's brows; they projected the intensity of a hawk.

Marking a page, Robert set his book next to a desk lamp and asked for a recap of his son's lunch meeting with John. Thomas sometimes wished his father would show as much interest in him as in matters affecting the family's secrets. He repeated his conversation with John, after which he hoped to see an expression of sympathy, but Robert conveyed nothing. It was an unreasonable expectation.

Thomas stared away as Robert offered his opinions on the troubling development, including courses of action. Something needed to be done, and he understood his father's words were more of a directive than a discussion. Thomas had hoped their chat might lead to sharing the burden, but he knew better. That had never been Robert's style.

Having swallowed the last of his second drink of whiskey, Thomas set his etched glass on a silver coaster. Robert's final words halted him: "You always knew your friendship with John was a risk. You and Emma supported it; I never did."

Thomas remained still, recalling when he'd first met John in grade school fifteen years earlier. Though he'd stopped seeking comfort in God since Robert forced him to kill as a child, Thomas nonetheless pleaded for intervention that might prevent what remained disturbingly inevitable. He made his way down the hall.

Entering the home's impressive library, where over three thousand books lined the shelves, he scanned those with science and medical titles. He selected one on the history of anesthesia, supposing he had time to mix the chemicals required to create chloroform. It turned out it would take too long. The book also explained that chloroform does not quickly induce unconsciousness as he had presumed; that's a Hollywood myth. He checked his watch and moved outside.

Low clouds obscured any light. Thomas stopped his march down the path, telling himself he should rewrite the family's future, ignore Robert's tutelage, and protect a friend who could never understand his fate. The son was more capable than the father in every way. *Do it*, he argued, *defy the patriarch. Establish new rules.* He resumed his walk outside, tormented by a truth.

Thomas isolated himself in the barn for sixty minutes. He gazed out a window and saw John's Ford idling at the estate's gates, then lowered his head and rubbed the bridge of his nose. Wasn't there a less excruciating choice? No, of course not. Nothing about his life had ever been easy—that was another myth.

Sounds from John's approaching truck indicated the stone driveway was barely wet from the settling mist. High beams swept around a corner of the barn. John parked near a side door and stepped from his vehicle dressed in jeans, a sweatshirt, and boots. He smirked. "Thomas, still wearing your suit? Seriously? We're going fishing, not to an interview." John pulled something from an envelope. "I found the newspaper photo! Here are our grandfathers standing together. Incredible, right?" John moved below an outdoor floodlight and read aloud the print proving their identities. He looked up and stressed, *"They knew each other."*

Thomas forced a weak smile, then asked for the photo and inspected it. "Who would have guessed? Let's get inside."

His tone surprised John, who recalled Thomas's similarly subdued reaction when first told of the newsclip at lunch. Why hadn't he grown spellbound?

They entered the dimly lit century barn, and Thomas switched on more lights. "Something to drink? Coke, 7Up, beer?" He flicked his chin at a restored '50s-era refrigerator. "The fridge is full."

"Sounds great," John replied. He opened the door and scanned the variety of cans and bottles lining the shelves.

While John was deciding what to drink, Thomas asked, "Is this the only original clipping you have? Are there any other newspapers in the museum?"

"That's our only link to history, Mr. Westbrooke. If we lose that, no one will believe us." John chose not to mention the photocopy he'd printed at the library; he considered it immaterial. "Ah, man, this hits the spot," he said after taking a swig of a cold brew. Upon his second sip, clarity struck: Discovery of the family links had genuinely unsettled Thomas.

John sensed movement over his right shoulder before powerful blows crumpled his body to the floor. He blacked out.

Thomas glanced at the mallet, released it, and felt repulsed by what he'd done. With glassy eyes, he bound John's wrists and ankles together with duct tape. He dragged the unconscious body to the middle of the barn. Thomas hoped his instincts were correct, that John knew more, and this wasn't all for naught.

As he positioned John's back against a thick wooden post, Thomas noticed something protruding from underneath his sweatshirt. He reached down and exposed it. His instincts were proven correct, and he turned at once elated and devastated.

Minutes that felt like days passed. John began to stir, hurting and moaning, confused and barely able to sit upright against the post. "What happened? What's going on? Why . . . why am I bound up?"

Thomas stepped closer but said nothing.

"God, my head's throbbing." He stared at a rubber mallet lying on the floor that he hadn't noticed upon entering the barn. "Thomas? What the hell? Tell me you didn't hit me with that."

He lifted the mallet. "I did, twice, in the temple. I didn't want to, but everything has changed." He removed his suit coat and rolled up his sleeves.

"You bashed my head? Tied me up? What the hell are you talking about?"

"Meddling in my family's affairs has grave consequences. I've got two pieces of evidence that prove you're conspiring." Thomas held up the old newsclip photo. "First, you shouldn't have gone looking for *this*."

John extended his bound arms from the floor and glared. "A damn press clipping. So what if our grandfathers were friends? Like you and me? Why's it matter?"

"You've made yourself an unacceptable risk."

"I'm lost, Thomas. I thought you'd find the family bonds intriguing."

Thomas stared at him with an extended hand, dangling the pendant. "Secondly, this convinces me you lied about everything." He swung the medallion like a pendulum as if trying to hypnotize. "You've been scheming behind my back."

"That's a bullshit piece of fake jewelry. It belonged to my grandmother. End of story."

"Impossible. It's one of *the assets*. You must have others. Where'd you find them? Where are you keeping them? And who else knows? My gut was right—you've discovered the past."

John shot back, "'The assets' means nothing to me. You need to get your shit together, Thomas. Tell me this is all some sort of bizarre joke. Deliver the punchline and untie me."

"I thought about our lunch discussion. I think you're planning to blackmail us." Thomas laid the pendant on a workbench. "But you've uncovered things no one can know. You should've left well enough alone before it was too late."

John stared and leaned forward, rubbing his temple with the top of a taped wrist.

"You've left me no choice." Thomas opened a cabinet and grabbed a twenty-foot leather bullwhip. He expertly swung the lash like a fly fisherman, snapping its frayed end to deliver a sharp, firecracker-like pop.

"Now you're threatening me like a wannabe cowboy? Get a grip."

"What about your lies?"

"I've never lied to you."

Thomas lowered the whip. "Even worse—you've betrayed me. You went digging for information about my family and the assets. You've sealed your fate."

"You've suddenly become unhinged. None of what you're saying makes sense, and I could never blackmail you or your family, even if I knew what you were talking about."

The woven leather whip sprung to life, and Thomas snapped the loose threads of its tapered end against John's chest. An angry yell preceded a light stream of blood oozing from a slice through his sweatshirt.

"*Damnit, Thomas! Stop! Go get Robert!*" John pleaded, assuming Thomas was suffering a mental breakdown, even though he'd never seen him act oddly. Perhaps his mother's condition was genetic. "You're torturing me?"

Thomas lashed at his friend again, leaving a welt on his bicep. "Tell me everything you know and this will end. Reveal your plans, and I'll forgive you."

Wordlessly, Thomas simultaneously begged John for forgiveness. He stepped away, his shadow etched by the glow of an antique gas lantern wired with electricity. Rain tapped on the roof's wood shingles, filling the barn with a dull hum. Leaking water dripped from a ceiling beam and patted gently on the floor twenty feet away.

John struggled to rub his cheek with tightly constricted forearms, offering every protest he could muster. Nothing he said snapped Thomas out of his confusing state.

Thomas swung the whip a third time. John was ready and moved his duct-taped arms to a defensive position, causing the last two feet of woven leather to coil around his forearms. Thomas attempted to yank it away, but John maneuvered his hands to clutch the weapon, preventing its release.

Thomas dropped the bullwhip to the floor. "Still claiming innocence?"

"Look into my eyes. You know I'm telling you the truth."

Thomas left the barn and returned minutes later carrying a brown case. He walked to a workbench near the cabinets, opened the container, and stared at its contents for a long pause. He removed a Sig Sauer pistol and inserted two rounds into an ammo clip while keeping eye contact with John. "You and me, we're cursed," Thomas said while removing the suppressor and screwing it onto the threaded barrel of the handgun.

"*A gun?*" John said with panic. "Stop and help me, Thomas. This isn't you."

"My father raised me to distrust people. To accept that others might challenge the past. Try to steal from us." He crumpled his brows. "Bad decision, John. We both know you're guilty."

"Of what? You're paranoid."

"This didn't have to happen."

"*Nothing's going to happen!*" Images of Skye and their children bore into his consciousness. He shivered. "You could never pull the trigger . . . never. You know that." His efforts to loosen his restraints failed; bulging veins appeared through reddened arms.

Thomas strode forward and crouched down. "Last chance to come clean."

"Take a step back. Get a hold of yourself. You once told me I was the only true friend you had. I've always loved you like a brother."

Thomas hesitated. "You're my only real friend, John." In a desperate voice, he added, "You had to know something like this would happen after your sleuthing."

"Put the gun away," John said, his face begging. "You're not well. You look and sound possessed."

"Perceptive words."

"Free me. Or get Robert."

"Robert knows you're here." He adjusted his grip and pointed the weapon at John.

"*Damnit!* You can't just shoot me, for Christ's sake!"

"I need information. You're making me do this." A tear gathered at a crease on Thomas's face; he wiped his eye with a sleeve.

"Family secrets? Assets? I swear I don't know what any of it means." Still seated, John's back and neck pressed back against the post. He tried to slow his breathing.

Familiar scents of burning pine and maple from the valley below wafted through the air, typically comforting smells now at odds with the tension. "Let me walk away," John said, believing he'd glimpsed a flash of sympathy. "Thomas, we can get past this. It's okay."

Thomas stepped away and rubbed his forehead with the suppressor barrel, then turned and peered into frightened brown eyes. John watched the weapon get aimed at his chest, now believing this could actually happen—someone he considered family might kill him. With the gun still aimed, Thomas's facial muscles seemed to relax, and hope began to build.

A single shot rang out.

The bullet entered the right side of John's chest. Pieces of bone and tissue splattered behind him. John's constricted body slumped sideways, with his skull suspended inches above the floor. His gaze settled on Thomas.

Shock numbed his pain. Red oozed from the wound. John's raspy breathing pierced the air. He could smell his blood, and warm sensations cascaded down his chest and arm. It had all become too real.

"Sorry for . . . for whatever you think I've done. Let me live." John twisted his neck and gazed up. "Help me. Please." The whip remained wrapped around John's arms.

Thomas yelled through tears, "Tell me what you've found! Stop pretending!"

John mumbled, "Everything I know, you know." His breathing grew more labored.

Ten-foot doors rattled as a gust of wind tested century-old hinges. The clanging of a metal coupling against a flagpole outside mimicked the remote pings of a buoy in Eagle Bay. John grew lightheaded.

Thomas cocked his head and studied the weapon in his hand. Moistening dry lips with his tongue, he moved his gaze to a random depression on the floor.

John peered up. "I'm innocent."

Thomas's pistol tilted downward as if it were heavy.

"One day, you'll accept . . ." John caught his breath, ". . . what I've said." Blood stained his teeth and trickled down the edge of his mouth. "Tell Skye I loved her to the end. Figure out . . . how . . . to do that."

Anguish covered Thomas's chiseled face. He stepped forward and fired the second round, grazing John's heart.

Lying still as his blood pooled, the adrenaline that provided resistance to an execution waned. His lips moved, but no words were released.

Thomas bent forward. "I'm sorry. You've always been a better man than me."

John fought hard to speak. He whispered, "What . . . are you?"

"I'm everything and nothing people think I am." Seconds passed. "But by tragic design, John. Not by choice."

John's vision faded to black.

CHAPTER 4

Thomas crouched with his Sig Sauer gripped atop his knee. He watched heat from the burning slug create wisps of smoke that swirled into the cool air. Aromas of spent ammo and scorched flesh were intense. Moist eyes blurred his vision. Slowly, they dried.

Staring at John's lifeless body, he considered slicing and peeling away the gray tape but realized it would serve no purpose. He strode to the jagged pendant of the sun and picked it up. It was heavy, maybe four ounces of gold and silver. He caressed and studied the centuries-old piece. "Our family histories repeat. You'd discovered the truth."

Thomas tugged at an oval brass cuff around John's still-warm wrist; it was too tight to remove. He returned with bolt cutters he'd grabbed from a workbench drawer, sliced through its edge, and removed it. Climbing a ladder into the loft, he hid the cuff behind a beam.

He descended and walked to the far end of the barn, where he opened an oak door. Observing dark hills surrounding his family's estate, Thomas leaned against a jamb and listened to an owl's hooting. He felt sick.

Minutes later, his father entered and grimaced. A two-foot crimson arc spread from John's chest, whose body lay at the base of a thick, rough-hewn post of Oregon Coast Range timber. Robert said, "Well, this is a mess." With pursed lips, he turned to Thomas. "You'll need to scrub that area down."

Thomas didn't move.

"So, he was figuring things out?" Robert asked as aromatic cherry drifted from his burlwood pipe.

Thomas stood expressionless during a long stretch of silence. "He claimed ignorance," he finally replied, his cheeks flushed.

"Hmm . . ."

"He was wearing this." Thomas handed his father the pendant of a fiery sun.

Robert walked to brighter light and admired. "*I'll be damned.* You know what this is?"

"Of course, it's one of the assets."

Robert smiled. "It's much more than that." He patted Thomas's shoulder. "Good work. It looks exactly as described in the journal."

"What journal?" Thomas asked while shaking his head with squinted eyes.

"I'll enlighten you soon enough." Robert glanced again at the ancient jewelry. "This single piece could have supported John's family for a generation. Where did he find it?"

"I don't know."

"Had he ever talked about it?"

"No."

"Not sure if that's fortuitous or problematic. I lean toward the latter. It's good he's dead."

Thomas didn't reply while removing his red and black silk tie. He walked with his head bowed.

"And you said he found the newspaper photo in the Randolph

Museum? I'm surprised. I had that tiny place scrubbed clean ages ago." Robert drew steadily through the warm stem pressed to his lips, then said, "Show it to me."

Thomas stepped to a table, closed the case holding his Sig Sauer, picked up the newspaper photo, and handed it to Robert.

"Is this the only copy?" Robert asked, in a tone implying it had better be. Thomas didn't answer, so his father repeated the question.

"Yes, it is."

"You're absolutely certain? This isn't something you can be wrong about."

Thomas exhaled loudly. "I *think* it's the only copy, and I don't *think* anyone else knows about it. Your questioning is annoying. At this point, things are what they are. I've once again protected your precious Westbrooke legacy, Robert."

"Most people would consider killing John unwise if you weren't positive you had every version of this." Robert extended the newsclip as pipe smoke billowed and floated across the barn.

Thomas flashed ire at the condescending tone. "Most people don't kill. Don't get me started. You sit in the house, smoke tobacco, manage Emma's care, and read about your expanding business empire—the one *I've* expanded."

"Calm down."

"Listen carefully, Robert. You've become ungrateful. It's a mistake taking me for granted."

Robert flashed disappointment before lifting the pendant. "I'll put this in the vault."

"Don't—I'll take it."

"No, you won't. Such decisions lead to sloppiness. It's valuable, and we've got too much at risk for you to be careless again." Robert placed it into the pocket of his dark tweed jacket.

Thomas's gaze bore into his father's. "One day, I may not ask for permission. I'll simply take what I deserve."

"My son, the prodigy, spreads his wings. Relax. The assets enable everything important to us, but you mustn't get lured into worshiping them. You've become emotionally attached. They're a tool, not the end."

"They mean something different to me than to you. That was *your* doing," Thomas said, letting his words settle. *React, you bastard. Acknowledge your role.* He continued, "Wealth is an easy pursuit, as I've amply proven. I don't need more money. The assets have always enthralled me. Consider my passion a threat?"

"I don't. I'm steps ahead of you in ways you can't fathom. You're intelligent to a fault. Let's finish this." Robert inspected John's body. "He was a stationary target. Why'd you shoot him twice?" He looked at the bullwhip and glared at Thomas. "This looks excessive."

Thomas teared up, something he hadn't done in his father's presence in over ten years. "I don't have to justify anything to you." He wiped his eyes, looked up to the ceiling, and nodded. "You're the one who taught me that pain is justice, Robert." There was no response. "I think I was twelve at the time." Thomas scratched a forearm while his father remained quiet. "Yes, I've memorized a lifetime of your absurd wisdom."

"These situations should never get emotional," Robert said. "Whatever's eating at you, let it go. Emotion leads to poor decisions. Poor decisions lead to scrutiny. Scrutiny is our greatest threat."

"Eating at me? I just killed my best friend." Thomas took a deep breath as he surveyed the scene. The surreal image took him back fifteen years to a twisted rite of passage that still tormented him. He stepped away and seated himself on a weathered pine bench. Pulling his Cartier from his wrist, he placed it on an armrest. He removed his custom dress shoes and laced up work boots.

"Burn those when you're done," Robert said.

"You think?" Sarcasm dripped from his lips. "I know the routine. I'm the one with a photographic memory."

"You're sensitive tonight. That's curious," Robert said. "I hope it's just the adrenaline talking. Regardless, we have a dead man in our barn and need a plan of action."

"Yes, I'm sensitive. You should be, too." A long moment of silence passed, then Thomas explained his strategy for the cover-up of John's murder. He spoke unflinchingly, but his body and mind felt pained.

His father internalized the plot. "Risky, but it should work. There's a lieutenant we can buy off." He motioned to four empty horse stalls in a corner of the outbuilding. "You know where to dig."

The Westbrookes hadn't boarded horses in the barn for years. Flooring that matched the rest of the restored structure had been extended over the original dirt stalls years earlier. Thomas began removing pieces of a craftsman's grid of wooden planks. Having exposed the dirt, he walked toward a rack of shovels.

Robert raised his hand and pointed a finger. "Wait. Before it gets too late, reinforce your alibi with Skye."

Separating himself from Robert, Thomas stretched the long cord of a green wall phone and dialed the McCloud's home.

Strolling from the table in her breakfast nook to the end of the kitchen counter, Skye glanced at a sunflower wall clock before picking up the white receiver. "Hello?"

"Hey Skye, it's Thomas."

"Howdy. You guys all set for the delta?"

He hesitated. "Almost. John's outside, tuning up the boat. He said to expect one or two salmon tomorrow."

"Yum. Is he going to hop on to say good night?"

"He's covered in grease and asked me to call." Thomas considered John's final words. "He said . . . he says he loves you."

"Of course he does." She smiled at her reflection in the kitchen window. "Have a great time. Good luck, and stay safe."

"We will. Goodnight, Skye."

Thomas rubbed his brow with a forefinger while approaching his father. "John's blood is on you, too. I hate you for this." Despair sought the comfort of shared complicity.

"Don't point at me. This was *your* decision, *your* murder."

"You've turned me into the killer I never wanted to be."

"I've helped you become great," Robert said. "Don't relish what you've done, Thomas, but don't regret it. Killing John was prudent."

"Prudent?" Thomas asked. "As I said, you're indebted. The assets will one day be my reward." Thomas drove a spade into the soil with his boot. He stopped to gaze at Robert, who stood next to a collection of restored antique gas pumps in the middle of the barn—three red, one yellow. On the wall beyond Robert were road signs from the 1920s that Thomas and John had hung during college. On the verge of more tears, he tightened his grip on the shovel and kept digging.

Thomas emptied twelve fifty-pound bags of barnyard lime over John's body and covered him in the dirt he'd excavated from the gravesite. Finally, he laid the wooden planks back down, concealing his work.

Thomas stood dirtied in a two thousand dollar suit he'd worn to bury his best friend in the corner of an old Oregon barn, in a gravesite he and Robert had previously disturbed. He considered the dichotomies of his life as his father casually repacked his pipe bowl, then ambled toward a cabinet that stored cleaners he'd use to mop John's blood from the floor.

An incinerator ignited. A red glow emanated from the furnace's belly, and expanded metal began pinging. Thomas would burn everything he was wearing. They considered incinerating John's body but grew concerned about the odors of death drifting through the hills.

Robert offered a nod, exited the barn, and walked toward his residence.

His father's shoes crunched over a gravel path while Thomas measured the ruthlessness of John's slaying. Robert had never personally killed a man, but he'd still managed to destroy lives. Thomas asked himself whose acts people would judge most wicked. The thought faded; the conclusion was irrelevant.

Thomas recalled his family's darkest secret. The night his grandfather killed the first John McCloud sixty years earlier, then stole the assets.

The night a dynasty was born.

Pitch darkness and chill settled. The boat ramp was empty and still. Rods, bait, and beverages for two leaned against the boat's console. Two life vests hung from hooks on board.

Only one man stirred.

Thomas launched the dory into tranquil water before leaping back onto the riverbank with a length of rope he fastened to a small pine. He parked his truck and trailer on the pitted dirt lot and pushed his feet into John's boots. Walking to and from the dirt lot and across the graded boat ramp, he ensured the tread marks of both men's boots lay embedded in the surrounding mud. He untied the rope from the pine and slipped while shoving off, drenching John's boots and his feet in a 51° chill. A Chinook salmon broke water ten feet out just as he gained control of the boat.

The twenty-two-foot wooden dory was painted blue on its sides; its flat hull and trim were bright yellow. The bow section arched upward. Five-inch horizontal oak capped the perimeter. He stepped behind the center console housing the captain's wheel and throttle controls. He would've ordinarily attached the "kill switch" cord hanging from a toggle next to the ignition, which would stop the motor if an impact threw the pilot. Today it was an unnecessary safety feature.

Upon stretching a thick cap around his head, he fired up the Merc 120 and puttered out to the delta. He stared overboard into the still-dark waters. The Dungeness crabs, running salmon, and seals common to the area were not yet visible. He and John had shared similar moments many times. Now one of them was dead.

While moving past dunes and toppled trees, Thomas scanned ahead, carefully avoiding sandbars that could ruin the dory and his plan. He reached the unobstructed delta and tried to expel agonizing images from his actions seven hours earlier. It was futile.

The sun rose beyond gray skies, illuminating an estuary shrouded in mist. The brackish water appeared eerie at slack tide, and the shoreline remained barely visible. Memories came rushing back. He turned off the engine and closed his eyes. Thomas recalled Robert forcing him to kill a man on a different body of water when he was twelve years old.

He removed John's boots and laced up his own before gazing at the channel. The consequences of his actions today and years earlier, and their permanence, engulfed him. "I didn't want to hurt you, John." The words dissipated across the broad expanse of water, dunes, and pines. He shook his head. "But you made a terrible decision."

Restarting the motor, he continued his slow advance. As the haze lifted, he passed deer seemingly staring through him, judging him. "You were poking around. Conspiring. You forced my hand. You knew about the assets. Left me no choice." The whirring of the motor muted his words.

He gauged the wind-swept whitecaps where the river met the Pacific while steering in tight circles. Gusts of wind picked up as the boat moved closer to the jaws. A combination of high tides, swollen river, and strong surf created a violent gateway to the ocean, a deadly mixture of natural forces. He, too, might die this day.

Needing more space, he piloted toward the cliffs, then back to the river's mouth. Without hesitation, he pushed the throttle forward to full tilt. He'd timed it well; a ten-foot wave crested just as he charged into it. He turned hard at the point of impact.

The dory shot skyward as if constructed of balsa wood before flipping over amidst the breakers. Thomas and everything aboard got tossed into a raging sea.

Wild surf battered him; the smacking of a wayward oar pained his legs. Few men could survive the conditions, he realized. Pushed below the surface and swept out to deeper seas, he questioned whether this was his end.

Frigid water inhibited his movements. His boots made it difficult to stay afloat; he pried them off. He debated removing his life vest but didn't, disgusted by a decision that would likely save him. He deliberated swimming further out to ensure his demise, but that was never part of the plan. Instead, the natural athlete stroked northward, away from danger, then toward shore. He could kill John but not himself.

The closer he made it to sand, the heavier the burden of truth became. John was gone forever, the victim of a tragic "boating mishap."

"Ahh!" he screamed, struggling to stay afloat. "Ahhhh! Kill me. Kill me, too!" Minutes passed. His shrieks waned. He swam to safety, overcoming the swells and currents.

Standing waist-high in seawater, Thomas pondered being alive. If people understood the truth, they'd wish him a lifetime of torment for what he'd done. He again chastised his friend for unnecessarily sealing his fate.

Stepping onto the beach, he measured his contempt for Robert and the life of turmoil he'd orchestrated for his son. He debated how best to overcome demons his father had instilled, to become the decent and generous man people believed Thomas Westbrooke to be. *I'm exceptional. I can transform myself.*

"I loved you, John, but—" He stopped, having grown weary of justifying his deed, of struggling with his essence. He studied the horizon and whispered, "I'll take care of Skye." It was the single thought that eased his mind.

His constricted muscles shuttered, and walking grew difficult. The light breeze exacerbated the effects of his fifteen minutes in chilly waters. He embraced his misery as purging. Goosebumps grew conspicuous as he sought the shelter of undulating, grass-covered dunes blocking the winds. He sat and waited.

Twenty minutes of solitude along beaches littered with white-washed timber and dead sea creatures passed. He watched a bright orange and white HH-3F Pelican helicopter make its second of four daily passes. The Coast Guardsmen discovered the overturned dory with its bright yellow hull. Moments later, the copter made a beeline to Thomas.

CHAPTER **6**

Glimmering sunshine had broken through the fog.

A police lieutenant drove over rolling hills and up a gravel driveway past timber, corrals, and an old barn under renovation. The McCloud residence was a simple, sturdy home typical of the era of its construction—sometime in the 1920s. Panoramic views from its hilltop perch were stunning, capturing Eagle Bay, breakers of the Pacific, and the Coast Range to the east.

The doorbell rang as Skye cleaned the house. Her mood mirrored the beauty outside. Bono and U2 were blasting in the background. She turned down the volume on a Kenwood receiver and stepped to the front door. Gripping the brass deadbolt knob, she placed her other hand around the door's handle. The hardware felt unusually cold.

She hesitated to turn the knob and twisted around to glance at Dakota and Johnny, both happily occupied by their toys. She swung the door open and saw a green and white police cruiser parked thirty feet away. The expression on the officer's face unsettled her; she wished she hadn't answered.

"Can I help you?" *Don't complicate our lives*, she silently implored.

"Mrs. McCloud? John McCloud's wife?"

She nodded but said nothing.

"My name is Lieutenant Boseman, ma'am," he said while removing his brown trooper-style hat. The police officer's appearance struck her: stocky build with dark fur sprouting from his nose, neckline, and arms. His pleasing hazel eyes appeared misplaced on a face one might otherwise judge as uninviting.

Resisting the officer's intrusion, Skye rubbed the underside of her left wrist with her right thumb, a life-long habit and unconscious expression of anxiety. She replied ambiguously, "Yes, hello. I'm busy, officer. And my husband's fishing." *Turn around and go away.*

The officer provided his initial report. "Ma'am, are you okay? Did you understand everything I've just informed you of?"

She watched his lips move, and his words reached her ears, but nothing registered. Time seemed suspended. Her face turned blank as she stared at horses trotting through a corralled field. She turned to the officer but couldn't hold eye contact and lowered her head. "What?" she finally asked, as if in a daze.

"Do you mind if I step inside?"

Snap out of it, Skye. "Yes, of course, come in." She turned to the children. "Johnny, Dakota, you two go play in the den, okay?" She glanced at the lieutenant and added, "Mommy won't be long." Her arms tingled.

The siblings ran to the small room laughing. Moments later, a door slammed shut. Their shrieks of joyful laughter got ignored.

Lieutenant Boseman resumed, "There's been a boating accident involving Mr. McCloud, based on information from Thomas Westbrooke. Was your husband expected to be fishing in the Bear Point Delta this morning?"

"Yes. He's okay, right?"

"An extensive water and land search have begun. We haven't found your husband yet, but please—"

"*What?* Are you searching the delta or ocean? Please tell me he's not in the ocean." Getting dumped into the delta offered a decent chance of survival, but the ocean could be unforgiving. She muted any screams and clutched a coat rack in the entry hall for balance.

"We've assembled resources in the area. Their boat flipped over in the jaws, and Mr. Westbrooke swam to shore. We're searching for your husband in the Pacific. We'll utilize every boat, aircraft, and technology available for this operation."

"Dear God," she whispered. Her mouth fell open. Glancing at the sunflower clock, she noted the time: 11:30. The guys typically launched at 5:30 a.m. It took thirty minutes to motor through the river and delta. If swept out through the jaws, John may have been struggling amidst merciless seas for five and a half hours.

"We have a grief counselor and another Eagle Bay officer arriving soon." His police radio sounded; he silenced it and settled his gaze back on Skye.

She spoke through gathering tears, "A counselor? What are you suggesting? My husband's alive. *Find him!* I don't need a grief counselor." She shook her head. "I need my children's father. You understand?"

"Ma'am, a counselor will help you deal with the uncertainties of the situation. I want to locate your husband as much as you do. We all do."

Twenty minutes after their daughter-in-law's call, John's parents stepped through the front door, appearing confused but acting resolutely. Skye updated them on developments, and John's mother walked down the hall to occupy Johnny and Dakota. Skye's father-in-law, wearing his standard U.S. Navy polo, wasted no time pressing authorities for information regarding the search for his son. Observing him interrogate officials and demand answers reassured Skye. It gave her hope.

Another police officer and a woman approached her front porch, which only added to Skye's horror—this was all really happening. She nodded at the two faces and waved them in. The pair looked injured by the image of a young mother trying to make sense of a situation considered unimaginable minutes earlier. Skye stepped toward the female counselor and spoke, trying but failing to sound strong and fearless. Skye remained quiet for a long stretch. "Please help us."

"There are over forty search and rescuers, ma'am. All are highly skilled and committed to finding your husband. Is there somewhere you and I can sit and talk?"

Skye nodded yes but quickly changed her mind. "I can't just sit here. I've got to get to the beach near the jaws." She left the counselor stranded in the family room. With Johnny and Dakota still oblivious and occupied by her mother-in-law, Skye grabbed John Senior and requested that he accompany her to the accident scene. It was now 12:30.

Lieutenant Boseman drove the anxious wife and father-in-law to the confluence of river and ocean. The officer glanced at Skye's grief-stricken face as they meandered over coastal roads. She stared out her window and mumbled what he assumed were prayers.

Stepping from the car, she noticed the surf and swells were strong. Too strong. Clouds were moving in, and the skies were darkening. She scanned the waters repeatedly, counting and recounting the number of rescuers and other authorities on the scene. John Senior's muscular, tattooed arm pulled her close. He said nothing, which further unsettled her.

Three hours on the sands beyond stretching tides passed, and the demeanors of those hunting for John appeared gloomier. Or was that only her imagination? Skye eventually asked Lieutenant Boseman to drive her and John's father home, assuming the children were by now questioning their parents' absence.

Upon their return, the further updates Skye received meant nothing. They were full of clichéd grandstanding about the broad scope of the search and exercises. What was missing was an announcement that they'd rescued John. Panic and doubt consumed her.

Late that afternoon, Thomas stepped through the kitchen door, expressing anguish and shaking his head with compassionate eyes. He hugged Skye tightly. "I'm so very sorry." As he held her, he looked toward John Senior and nodded.

"But how can he be lost, Thomas? It makes no sense. He must have swum to shore as you did. Right?" Reddened eyes begged for an affirming *yes*. She clutched her father-in-law's hand as he stepped forward to hear Thomas's words.

"It was terrible. We got attacked by pounding waves." He scanned the faces in the room before gazing at John's father. "But he's a strong swimmer. It's not hopeless."

"Oh Thomas, of course it's not hopeless. He's going to make it." She waited for someone to agree. John Senior's expression appeared transformed into pain or disbelief, unnerving her.

As two officers asked to speak privately with Skye, Thomas walked to the living room, sat on a sofa, and covered his face with his hands. Onlookers watched his quivering body rise and step outside.

Day turned into night.

Skye understood that staying alive in the frigid Northwestern waters would be difficult after twenty minutes during any time of year. She cursed herself for employing logic to weigh John's odds of survival. She tasted blood after worriedly biting her lower lip for hours.

Hopes for a joyous ending faded. Officials hinted it might be time to accept the unbearable, to begin mourning. Hour by hour, person by person, the McCloud house emptied. At 3 a.m., John's parents, Johnny, and Dakota lay sleeping down the hall. Skye rested in bed, exhausted. The concept of sleep felt absurd. She reenacted what most believed were John's final hours and found herself focused on two thoughts. If he was gone, he knew she loved him. And he left this world enjoying one of his outdoor passions with his best friend, Thomas Westbrooke.

Dear God, no. Bring him home.

7

CHAPTER

Emergency personnel insisted it was fortunate that even one man had survived. Overhearing such comments tormented Skye.

The Westbrooke family offered everything within its scope of influence to ensure the hunt for John was one of the most comprehensive in the history of Oregon Coast rescue operations. Once again, the dynasty had cemented its reputation as a staunch benefactor of everything decent within Eagle Bay. Robert gripped his omnipresent pipe while perched on the Bear Point Spit, observing maneuvers. Citizens were impressed by the Westbrooke patriarch's commitment to a just cause: finding the body of a fine man, his son's closest friend.

Then two days passed, and still, nothing. Skye remained certain John's body would eventually float ashore; it was the conclusion she felt made sense.

Thomas's younger sister, Sarah, a recent graduate of Wellesley College, clutched Skye's hand on the sands of the delta. Other friends and family found it difficult to approach the grieving wife; there were periods when spectators uncomfortably observed Skye's isolated silhouette.

On the day of the accident, Thomas provided the Eagle Bay Police Department with a statement:

We were having a great time fishing. John hooked a big Chinook just as the sun broke through. I saw it flash by, and it must've been fifty pounds. I throttled the main engine to follow the fish as it darted for the ocean. We were getting too close to the turbulent jaws, but he begged me to move out just a bit further to land the fish. I got caught up in the excitement and did as he said. A large wave pushed the front of the dory up almost vertically, drenching the engine with water and killing it instantly. I tried to restart the main engine and then the kicker—they just wouldn't start. The rough waters ate us up, one huge wave after another, flipping the boat and tossing everything inside, including John's life vest. He insisted it was too warm to wear, so he'd taken it off, against my advice. I loved the guy, but he could be very stubborn. There was no way for me to see or do anything once the boat flipped. I almost got swept far out to sea and barely survived. I knew deep down John was gone.

Skye wanted to scream at John for not wearing his vest, to ask him how he could be so foolish. Berate him for what he'd done. For leaving her alone. For leaving their children fatherless. For scarring Thomas with guilt. Seconds later, she tearfully begged him to forgive her harsh judgments.

The oars, vest, and other contents floated up to beaches within a mile of the calamity. Locals continued to yearn for the natural beauty of their coastline to be disrupted by the discovery of John's body. Anything that might provide closure. But days became weeks. Even the Westbrooke family pulled its resources. Services were held, and hearts slowly mended. People moved past their anguish.

Skye McCloud did not.

Thirty days after the tragedy, she stood on the spit jutting into the confluence of the river and sea. Near sunset, she noticed what appeared to be John's remains tumbling in light surf. Johnny was building a sandcastle behind her; she turned and screamed at him to stay put before rushing to the water's edge.

Her heart pounded, and tears were full as she approached John's lost remains. "Thank you, God," she moaned. But then, twenty feet from the rolling form, she collapsed to her knees. A six-foot section of a partially devoured oarfish, with its spine exposed and faded to grayish-white, its rough outline mimicking a human body, particularly to a grief-stricken wife needing closure, had drifted to the beach.

Skye plunged her face hard into the sand. A sickness of despair gave way to literal sickness. She raised her head and peered through blurry eyes at a weakening sun, tasting the tears, mucus, and sand stuck to her mouth and chin. *Am I such a bad person that I deserve this torment?*

Johnny grew frightened and disobeyed her command. She found him staring blankly when she lifted from her knees and twisted. Rushing to hug his tense body and caressing him without speaking, Skye swore she'd always love her children as much as she loved John. A warmer breeze unexpectedly embraced them, or did she only imagine it? She pulled Johnny's head to her chest.

A strengthening wind tossed the six-year-old's thick brown hair about his face. He turned to the turbulent jaws that consumed his father's dory and whispered, "I love daddy."

Skye squeezed his hand and suppressed yet another stream of tears.

CHAPTER 8

Skye mourned, but she also took control. While John's dream of becoming a successful spec homebuilder had begun to materialize before his disappearance, the widow's combined savings and investments currently totaled only $55,000. A portion paid for John's funeral and life celebration; she invested the remainder in stocks.

Thomas sent her a card offering further condolences and included a check for $10,000. She tried to return it, but he insisted it get spent on pressing obligations. John would've been proud of his best friend's support.

Skye sometimes smiled while contemplating Thomas and John's friendship. The publicly respected benefactor and CEO of WCI didn't look or act like he belonged in Oregon. Thomas bought tailored suits and casual clothes from Boston and New York, attended Princeton, and maintained relationships with influential people in the Northeast. In those ways, he was the antithesis of John.

Because of the Westbrookes' wealth and power, sycophants constantly sought relationships with the family. But Skye and many locals understood John was the person Thomas most admired and strived to be around, the only friend that truly mattered.

Skye had become a jack-of-all-trades in maintaining her property, not wanting to waste money having professionals fix every electrical, plumbing, or maintenance issue. She also leaned on her farmhand Diego's horse stabling and ranching knowledge—deeming him a godsend.

Because Skye couldn't afford to employ Diego full-time, he would arrive each day at sunrise and leave by noon, which left plenty of work, sometimes too much, for Skye. But she was figuring it all out.

Drivers on the outskirts of Eagle Bay would occasionally recognize Skye jogging on the weekends over winding roads. She found that a brisk pace over miles of countryside helped alleviate her stresses. Riding horses through meadows and streams adjoining her poor woman's estate—it was no longer John's oft-described poor man's estate—she'd invariably find solace in her beloved equines.

She grew closer to Thomas. Skye's friends assumed their strengthening bond was due to loneliness or because he was handsome and wealthy. That wasn't the case. She didn't need a trophy male to function independently. Thomas had merely proven himself to be a decent person. He doted on her children and remained interested in her well-being for all the right reasons. Despite their relationship, she felt it unlikely she'd ever remarry. It wasn't necessary.

In late June, vibrant green and blue hues framed the Oregon coastline. Skye relaxed and appreciated a quiet afternoon after working in the stables all morning. Thomas's Jag wound up her long drive, and he parked and walked over a fresh-cut lawn.

Three one-gallon jars sat perched on the front porch's white railing, each filled with five Lipton tea bags and four hours of radiant sunshine. Skye moved two rocking chairs closer together and pulled off her straw hat. "Howdy, stranger. Have a seat. I'll be right back with sugar for the tea." They caught each other up on recent happenings while drinking from sweating iced glasses on a warm day.

"So, things are okay?"

Skye expected Thomas would ask the question, as he regularly monitored her welfare. She nodded, smiled, and explained that life was pretty darn good for the McClouds.

Thomas eased into joking and reminiscing about John, their days at Eagle Bay Academy, and how much he missed his best friend. He apologized for making her eyes glisten before removing sunglasses from his perspiring head to wipe dirty lenses with the hem of his polo shirt.

Skye took a deep breath. "Oh, never apologize, Thomas. I miss him, but I know he's happy, looking down, watching us have this conversation. You don't know how much I appreciate your fond memories of him. It warms my heart."

"I'm glad." He refilled his glass and shifted his gaze to a pasture. "Wow, look. Now that's a rare sight. Check out its wingspan." A golden eagle had used its massive talons to lift a snake from thick grass. It soared to the top of a pine, where it remained perched as the reptile struggled for life.

"Get them all, eagle," she growled. "I hate snakes."

Thomas smiled. "There she goes, off to her nest with a fresh kill. It's inevitable, right? Survival of the fittest."

Monte Cristo and Crater, the McClouds' dogs, showed up with wagging tails, seeking scraps from whatever the two humans were consuming. With only liquids on the table, they lost interest and scattered.

"So, where were we?"

"Skye, you know how the details of big events seem to get hard-wired into our minds? Weddings, funerals, birthdays, holidays, and so on?"

"I guess so, but I don't have a photographic memory like some of us." She winked before swiping twice at an annoying yellow jacket. "Why?"

"It's interesting. With all the havoc and heartbreak the day of the accident, I still remember John leaning against the side of the boat and showing me this strange gold and silver pendant of the sun strapped around his neck."

"What?" She squinted as if avoiding the sunlight, even though the canopy of a giant maple tree blanketed them in shade. "Oh wait, that thing? It was just a random piece John's grandmother passed down. She'd kept it for fifty years. John's grandfather had picked it up sometime during the 1920s. That's all he told me. Why do you ask?"

Thomas adjusted his glasses. "It's just unfortunate that a family heirloom, real or fake, was also lost that day."

"Well, maybe. I guess. Who cares at this point? I only saw it once, the night before the accident." A light tingling on her skin prompted her to slap at a bug—she missed it. "Darn these pesky things." She held up the jar of tea to Thomas and raised her eyebrows.

"Yes, please, bartender." Thomas extended his arm and kept eye contact as Skye refilled his glass. "Thanks." He continued, "So it was one-of-a-kind?"

"Excuse me?"

"I mean, the McClouds owned no other similar pendants or jewelry? John was wearing the only piece?"

Skye released a sigh of annoyance. "I have no idea." She stood abruptly. "I don't see that it matters, although you seem preoccupied with it. I should hunt down the kids and pull dinner together."

"Hey, I'm sorry. It was a random thought. None of it matters." He set down his drink and placed his hands on her shoulders.

"The question felt forced and unnecessary," she said. "It's not a memory that's special."

"It was an idle recollection. Forgive your number one fan?" He tilted his head downward and peered over the top of his sunglasses.

"Yep. But I really should figure out what to feed the kids."

"Got it, but first, I've got something to show you. Have a second?"

"Uh . . . okay, sure." She followed him to the trunk of his Jag.

"I picked this up at the meat market. I hope you like it."

"A slutty girl in tight leather pants and too much makeup? I'll pass."

"You're a funny lady." He laughed. "I meant from the slaughterhouse in Carlton." He opened a cooler holding ten cuts of beef, chicken, and lamb. "This should last you a while."

"You don't need to do this."

"You're right. I don't. Have a good weekend."

Skye carried the meat inside and placed it in the freezer. When she unpacked vegetables from a brown paper bag, she found a new Barbie doll and two Ninja Turtles. She stared out the window and beamed.

ON THE MORNING OF her twenty-eighth birthday, Skye awoke to the sounds of Johnny and Dakota moving about earlier than usual. She was disappointed they'd chosen this particular day to investigate the whereabouts of the elusive crowing rooster or the wonder of a rising sun. Couldn't they go back to bed? As approaching sounds of sibling chatter grew louder, her pulse jumped. She detected the interspersed voice of a man—an intruder.

Act quickly, she told herself, just as John had taught her. She bounded out of bed, spun the dial on the safe, and grabbed her pistol. She gripped the cold weapon with both hands and turned to enter the hall. Her bedroom door flew open.

"Happy Birthday!" Behind the children was a man holding a silver tray, matching coffee pot, and breakfast for one. He stared into a loaded Ruger P89 with a twitchy finger on its trigger.

"Whoa, gunslinger." The man froze.

"Darnit, Thomas!"

"Shoot him, Mommy, shoot him!" Dakota was laughing and jumping about, assuming the pistol was a toy.

Skye returned the gun to the safe. "Sorry, but you need to be way more careful, Thomas. This thing is loaded." She nodded with her mouth agape before realizing she was standing in front of a beam of revealing morning light highlighting her body. Wearing only a thin knee-length T-shirt, she flew back under the covers.

Thomas reset his wandering eyes to peer into hers.

"We tricked you, Mom," Johnny said. "I knew you'd never guess." He twisted around to Thomas. "See? I told you it'd work."

Dakota hopped into bed with Skye, who bit her lip and peered up at Thomas. "This was sweet."

"You're remarkable, Skye. You deserve a lot more than breakfast in bed. Happy twenty-eighth."

She suppressed the urge to cry and yanked up the rose-colored comforter to cover her barely concealed breasts.

"Enjoy it before it gets cold." Thomas moved the tray from the nightstand to her lap. "Kids, treat your mom special today. Have a great day, Skye. I'm off to an appointment." He turned and tousled Johnny's dark hair with his hand as he stepped toward the door.

"Goodbye," Skye replied with a tightened throat.

He winked. "Thanks for not shooting me."

Thomas strolled through the narrow hall to the front door, passing a sunflower clock showing 6:27. He let the dogs inside and strode to his car.

Diego toiled nearby, lifting bags of crop seed from the bed of his Ford pickup. The cowboy offered a friendly face. "Hola, amigo."

Thomas leered and drove away.

9 **CHAPTER**

The glow emanating from candle wicks helped Robert imagine Juan Francisco Montoya's writing in his journal aboard the *Santa Sofia*. He realized that the Westbrooke dynasty could get scrutinized and exposed if the manuscript fell into meddling hands, let alone any authorities.

Robert had spent the previous twelve months translating each page of Capitán Montoya's extraordinary account. He'd become addicted to the incredible adventures penned onto thick parchment pages. Every bit of candle melted away some nights, dripping downward to cover the base of a small antique brass candelabra. He wondered if Capitán Montoya burned wax or oil for his nighttime writing.

Robert's father had yanked the journal from the clutches of a man he'd murdered in 1928: John McCloud, grandfather of Thomas's dead best friend. The elder Westbrooke had passed the manuscript to Robert when the future heir turned thirty. Robert kept the writings locked away for too many years, he thought, but building the family empire had always been more important than understanding the fascinating events that delivered their immense fortunes to the shores of Eagle Bay. So far, he'd translated eighty of the one hundred twenty pages. It was a slow process for a man who'd never studied Latin and needed to decipher sentences while reconciling for faded ink and the scribing nuances of a Spanish conquistador who died centuries earlier.

Robert grew fascinated by Montoya. He yearned to know more about the man whose gallantry seemed more Hollywood than historical nonfiction. So far, he'd learned the *Santa Sofia* was the largest galleon ever constructed before its maiden voyage in 1533. Over three hundred men, most of them warriors, some of them friars and monks, a few of them both, were under Montoya's command as the *Santa Sofia* sailed from Sevillian shipyards on the banks of the Guadalquivir River into the Gulf of Cádiz in Spain. Before departing, Capitán Montoya's endpoint was "the land of the Azteca," Robert had learned.

Robert reclined in his leather chair, took a sip of his port, stared at a dancing shadow, and imagined other events awaiting revelation on unread pages. While sipping his Graham's 1952 vintage, Thomas entered the den.

The prodigy sat down with crossed legs as his father described for the first time how the journal made its way into the Westbrooke family's hands. Robert spoke as if his ancestor hadn't stolen the leather-bound manuscript from the McClouds. That assertion prompted Thomas to narrow his eyes and nod with an expression of ridicule. Robert countered the unspoken judgment by stating numerous rare books and works of art in private hands had been similarly possessed through intellect, guile, and vision. Were the Huntingtons, Vanderbilts, or Carnegies any different than the Westbrookes? Robert answered his own question: unlikely. Regardless, he added, none of that mattered.

More animatedly, Robert described the exploits of Montoya and his men as they engaged in one astonishing adventure after another.

He spoke of his deep admiration for Montoya's chivalry and moral leadership amid astonishingly challenging circumstances.

Thomas took a deep breath, swirled the last few drops of port for a long while, set it down, and leaned forward. "The man you're speaking of, the oh-so-gallant Capitán Juan Francisco Montoya, would have despised people like you and me. People who pilfered their wealth from those better than them. Don't you see the irony in your effusive praise of a man who is the antithesis of everything you and I represent?" Thomas stood, grabbed a bottle, and refilled his glass. He softly chuckled. "I guess one could argue that the Westbrookes and Montoya might not be so different *publicly*."

"What's eating at you?" Robert wiped his forehead with the palm of his hand and used a bent finger to rub below an eye. "Not long ago, you seemed more loyal to the family, our legacy, and Eagle Bay's future."

"Cut the sanctimonious crap." Thomas walked to Robert and extended his arm. His father glared before handing over Montoya's journal, then Thomas flipped on more lighting to scan the pages. "Loyalty," he said as he passed the journal back to Robert. "That's a theme you've pounded into my head from an early age. Your version of loyalty taught me to kill. Your version of loyalty taught me to lie in undetectable ways. Your version of loyalty turned me into the good soldier I am, a man so committed to his twisted father's guidance that he never strikes back, even when he knows he should."

Robert lifted his imposing physique from a chair and approached him; their faces were now uncomfortably close. "Don't you dare dismiss my undying devotion to our family or community. Never lose sight of what we've collectively achieved since claiming ownership of the assets."

"Claiming ownership? Stop speaking in code. *We've killed and cheated to build our empire!* Let's tell it like it is." He took off his suit coat and tossed it on the back of a chair. "You can't tell me you're the man you want to be, Robert. I know you're as disappointed in your legacy as I am in mine." When they shared a room, Thomas occasionally felt like he grew smaller in his father's presence.

"That's patently untrue. Don't try to share your burden of self-incrimination with me, Thomas. And don't lose your resolve, or you'll lose my respect. If you lose my respect, you'll lose my trust. If you lose my trust, you lose everything." Robert held his glass up to a light, turned it to inspect the sediment, and finished the tawny drink.

"I'm not going to be your surrogate anymore," Thomas replied. "It's pathetic that I haven't yet broken free from the bonds you placed on me as a child. Our family's secrets exist in two minds: yours and mine. I control important parts of this precious dynasty. Every business we own is now legitimate, thanks to me. Who or what am I protecting anymore? It's time to dial back our paranoia."

"We can never let our guard down. And what we're protecting—history, extraordinary wealth, reputations, and our family—is more important than any guilt-tinged insecurities you're struggling with." Robert pushed the cork back onto the Graham's, tugged on a brass lamp chain, and exited. "I need to get rest. I've got a busy day tomorrow."

Seconds passed before Thomas stepped into the hall. "I'm interested in Skye."

Robert stopped, turned, and stared.

"I've fallen in love with her."

Robert creased his forehead and paused, staring indifferently at a wall, then back to Thomas. "Oh, you're serious." He pursed his lips and scratched his temple. "Falling for her would be foolish and dangerous."

They measured each other. "Don't look at me like that. It's a ludicrous fantasy. Do you think bedding the wife of the man you murdered will help you deal with what you did? That's frighteningly pathetic."

"You relish giving me advice that runs counter to my ambitions. I have a right to seek happiness, and you should support that end. I've been loyal to every inane obligation you've handed me."

"Damnit, Thomas, enough of the blame game. You're acting like an injured puppy. You made every major decision in your life—*including killing*—yourself."

"Including drowning a man in our pond? On your command? Before I'd reached puberty? I'm not an injured puppy, you bastard. I'm a damaged man you've beaten down with a lifetime of psychological abuse. You can go to hell." He grabbed his coat and their shoulders bumped sharply as Thomas moved angrily down the hall.

Robert called out, "*You* murdered John. *He* knew too much. It was the *right* decision. Get over it."

CHAPTER 10

Skye Renée McCloud

&

Thomas Edward Westbrooke

request the honor of your presence

to share in the celebration of their marriage on

Saturday, 24 September,

Nineteen Hundred Eighty-Eight

at three o'clock in the afternoon

St. Michael's Church

2657 Salmon Run Dr.

Eagle Bay, Oregon

Skye understood better than anyone that John had been an exceptional man. But time and the unwavering persistence of another gentleman, Thomas Edward Westbrooke, had stripped away the thick veneers of resistance to sharing her future. Few people in Eagle Bay could recall a wedding with such anticipation.

Thomas was handsome and fit, a young business tycoon, and a member of the most visible family on the Oregon Coast. The Westbrooke Coastal Industries empire included vast agricultural and forest land holdings, dairy operations, and real estate. Family members were generous philanthropists. But Skye never grew awed by wealth. Thomas's gentleness, steady commitment to helping her family, and unrelenting pursuit of her heart had won her over.

Thomas insisted on installing ADA equipment in John's ailing mother's home; her Parkinson's had advanced. He'd also paid for a new snack stand on the Eagle Bay Eastern Little League grounds. He'd proved himself to be the sort of man any mother would hope her daughter could marry, personifying the moniker the press had propagated: The Pillar of Eagle Bay.

Thomas replaced dilapidated corral and border fences on Skye's current and Thomas's future residence. Before their impending wedding, Skye demanded their united family live in the only home her children had known, the one they'd shared with John. Thomas tried to tempt her with more extravagant properties, but she'd remained unyielding.

John's death left a void in both of their lives, and that shared bond was important to Skye. Thomas once showed up at her door inebriated and wracked with guilt. She consoled him with the truth that no man could have saved John that tragic day in the delta and ocean.

One month later, while Johnny and Dakota went to friends' houses for the weekend, Skye invited Thomas for a romantic dinner. They finished their wine, and she pulled out a bottle of Bailey's to pour into small glasses of ice. They talked for hours sharing dreams of their future. Now staring more than speaking, Skye stood and dimmed the lights. She sat back down, and their bodies pressed against each other. Two aromatic candles burned atop the coffee table. As she studied his face and pondered his most profound thoughts, he laid his arm over her shoulders. Her body grew alert.

Thomas leaned forward and kissed her, then put his palm on her cheek and glided his thumb across her eyebrow. Skye felt her breathing deepen; her heart rate increased. She set his hand on her thigh, pressing it into her soft, warm skin. Surprised by how aroused she was, she stood and said, "Not here." She clutched his hand and led him into the master bedroom, where they undressed and made love.

With their perspiring bodies entwined, Thomas whispered, "I love you, Skye."

She rolled over and laid her head on his muscular chest. "You *better* love me." She released a long, steady exhale as Thomas caressed her skin.

"You're the most amazing woman I've ever met. We're going to have a wonderful life together."

His comments pulled Skye from the moment. She'd heard eerily similar devotions from another person years earlier.

It was 1988; they were to be married in one month. Thomas entered Skye's front door wearing khaki shorts, an untucked polo, and loafers over sockless feet: Hamptons in the Northwest. He removed his Ray-Bans as he sauntered with one arm behind his back. "I come bearing gifts, pretty lady." He handed Skye a small, wrapped box.

They hugged, and Skye felt intoxicated by a Calvin Klein fragrance she now considered Thomas's signature. His sturdy body felt reassuring. She told herself that her friends had been right; he was an easy man to appreciate. She guided him into the living room, her green eyes glistening in reflections of afternoon light. They sat on the loveseat in front of a coffee table adorned with a horse figurine. Her mind anxiously debated what might lay inside the pentagonal box. Upon opening it, she peered trancelike out her great room window framing the lush hills of Eagle Bay. She said nothing, absorbing the pines, grasses, weathered brown barn, and regal horses trotting through wood-fenced pastures.

"I had it custom-made by Van Dykes. I know how much your gift to John moved him, and I just wanted to express my love in a similar way. You mean everything to me, Skye, and represent all that's good in this world."

Inside was a gold bracelet adorned with three carats of brilliant diamonds. The inscription on the underside read *"Skye and Thomas, Forever."* She struggled to overcome her daze. "Oh, Thomas, I don't know. It's beautiful, but it prompts so many memories. It's just . . ." Her thoughts whirled with conflicted emotions. She couldn't think straight. Part of her wanted to ask him what the hell he was thinking. She fought back the urge to scream.

Seven years earlier, Skye had given a bronze cuff to John. Its inscription read: *"John, Love Forever, Skye."* Thomas had admired the couple's expression of affection. The original design could be easily fastened to and detached from John's wrist, but he'd surprised her by having an artisan enclose the band during a three-hour ordeal. After encircling the piece, it became impossible for anyone to remove it without sawing through or clipping the metal. John had often called it his most cherished possession.

"Thomas, it's gorgeous." Skye knew her fiancé possessed an authentic love for her, so the best part of her couldn't muster the strength to tell him she didn't want the darn thing. Sometimes, she convinced herself, when intentions were genuinely decent, it might be best just to let things be. "Thank you," she said, offering a slight smile.

Lying in bed that evening, Skye reminisced about the original simple brass band John had worn. Not eighteen-carat gold, not fitted with expensive diamonds, but exceptional in other ways.

Thomas adores you. He's a wonderful man. Let it go, Skye. She extended an arm and switched off the lamp atop her nightstand.

12 **CHAPTER**

"I'm eager to see your father again. We hardly spoke during the search for John." Skye smiled at Thomas from the passenger seat of his blue convertible. "I'll never forget everything he did to help. All the time and energy. The money. You must be proud of him."

Thomas kept his eyes on the road. Moments passed. "He's excited you'll soon be his daughter-in-law."

"And even though Emma isn't well, I'm thrilled we'll be sharing a room where we can share our hopes and dreams for the future," Skye said. She checked her makeup in the visor mirror and continued, "Who knows how much she'll understand? Maybe more than you think."

"Keep your expectations in check, Skye. Emma will probably just stare ahead. Sometimes she'll lock onto you, but it's as if she's looking through you. We never know what to expect. But I agree, it's great we're getting together." He extended his arm and squeezed her thigh.

She could sense his trepidation; this would be the first social gathering with both of Thomas's parents. Most citizens of Eagle Bay had learned of the local legend of Robert Westbrooke. Like others, Skye had observed Robert from a distance during her lifetime. The esteemed citizen seemed unapproachable for reasons she couldn't express. While she'd voiced disappointment with Thomas not introducing her future in-laws sooner, his explanation reduced anxieties. He clarified that his parents were private people and Robert's constant care for Emma was his *raison d'être*. Skye accepted the justification; she could never challenge seclusion driven by a man's devotion to a compromised wife he adored.

The Westbrooke residence was a classic colonial structure not common in the Northwest. Magnificent madrones and oaks graced the five landscaped acres abutting their home. The total estate holdings spanned over three hundred acres, spreading from their hilltop sanctuary to rolling knolls, verdant meadows, picturesque ponds, and streams. The couple drove beyond a pillared entrance, rounded a circular drive, and parked feet from the white mansion's steps. A nurse exiting the front door smiled; she appeared to recognize Thomas but proceeded straight to her car without comment.

"Does Emma require homecare visits?" Skye asked.

"Yes. A nurse shows up every morning to medicate her. That woman's the second RN to be part of the routine. She's been doing it for six years. Another woman walks Emma around the property regularly, a sort of physical therapy. That's why she appears fit. Robert arranged a precise care regimen after her meltdown."

Skye hoped Robert walked with Emma, too. "I don't mean to resurrect difficult feelings, but what's her exact diagnosis? What triggered her breakdown?" The idea that an energetic young mother could suddenly become incapacitated unnerved her.

Thomas paused to stare at his reflection in one of the home's front-facing windows. "One day, she was fine. The next, she was a stranger." He removed his sunglasses. "She left me—left *us*—during a tough time. We all suffered."

"I'm so sorry," Skye said, clutching his hand.

"I remember it like it'd happened yesterday." He shook his head slowly, absently staring. "It's been fifteen years." Thomas's thoughts drifted to the Emma of his childhood. She'd been a capable woman, a committed philanthropist, and an influential public cheerleader for community causes. Before marrying Robert, she'd double-majored in English and French at the University of Portland and earned a master's in English literature from the University of Washington.

Emma's father, Winston Packer, was the grandson of one of the original lumber barons of the Northwest. A charity event in Eagle Bay had brought her and Robert together. Thomas assumed a marriage of love for one had merely been a bond of strategic convenience and logger baron inheritance for the other. He considered the genesis of his union with Skye to have been nobler than Robert's duplicitous pursuit of Emma.

"Any chance she'll recover?"

"The doctors say no. Something in her mind just completely broke down." Thomas turned away and rubbed his forehead, not sharing his belief that his actions at age thirteen had driven Emma into mental oblivion. That fateful afternoon, Thomas had accidentally killed a girl, his classmate Gabriela, in their barn. He remained still, weighed down by painful memories and the burden of truth.

Skye snapped him from his trance. "You okay?"

"Yep." He grabbed her hand and smiled. "Let's get inside."

Thomas led her down a vast hall with black and ivory marble tiles set in a checkerboard pattern. He stepped to the side and held out his right arm, guiding Skye into a splendid room where Robert and Emma sat in wingback chairs. A cherry wood antique coffee table stood before them. The sweet smell of tobacco permeated the room, though Robert's pipe rested unlit in a hand-carved holder on the table. Emma sat impeccably dressed in a gray skirt and matching jacket over a white blouse. Her expression appeared blank.

Skye epitomized style in a white knee-length skirt and peach-colored silk blouse. Robert stood up and smiled, extending both arms and embracing Skye's left wrist and hand. "Thomas has been enamored with you since your days at the Academy. Now you're engaged." He shifted his gaze between the couple. "We're thrilled you'll soon be family, Skye."

"Thank you, Robert." She beamed and turned her head to Emma. "It's an honor to meet you both. You have a wonderful son." She placed her arm around Thomas's waist. "You must be special parents to have raised such a fine man."

The elder legend turned to Thomas, winked, and smiled while peering into Skye's eyes. He motioned toward a sofa that looked simultaneously centuries-old and brand new and asked her to sit. "Let's get to know my future daughter-in-law."

She thought it unusual that Robert hadn't yet introduced his wife; Emma stared straight ahead and had not attempted to speak. Skye was uncomfortable that no one had acknowledged the mentally ill woman.

Robert glanced from Skye to Emma and back to Skye. "My wife would be so pleased with your pending nuptials if she could comprehend the news. She was once an active, intelligent, and inquisitive young woman. Like you, Skye." He smiled warmly. "I've dedicated my life to her care, as I hope Thomas has explained."

"He has, and a wonderful testament to you, Robert." Skye reached and grasped Emma's hand, sensing a flash of energy exchange between them. It was a remarkable moment. Was it a transcendent bonding? Or was Skye only hoping for one to exist?

While Emma sat trance-like, the ensuing banter was welcoming. Skye noted similarities between Robert and Thomas—two remarkable men. Gratitude for her blessings engulfed her.

Her enthusiasm slowly waned. Two hours passed, and Skye watched Robert's expressive conversation grow forced. It was justifiable, she surmised; he was a busy man, and caring for Emma was a full-time job. They'd already talked longer than she'd expected.

As Robert turned to sneeze, Thomas nudged his elbow into Skye's side, and the couple shared agreeing glances. Thomas rose and clutched his future wife's hand, gently lifting her from the sofa. With final small talk concluded, Robert moved past Emma. Thomas kissed his mother's forehead and patted her shoulder as he stepped away.

The men gathered in the hall, stared out a window to the valley, and held a private conversation. Skye moved to Emma's side. "It's been wonderful visiting with you, Emma. I look forward to becoming part of the family. Thomas treats me like royalty."

Skye again felt surges of energy emanate from the matriarch's hand. Emma's stare grew more focused, even engaged. She tilted her head. Finally, a whisper was released, "No . . . No."

A moment later, she appeared mentally vacant. Her blue eyes seemed to fade to gray, to turn lifeless. Her mouth opened and didn't close. She had disconnected.

Strange, Skye thought. The poor thing.

Robert peered through a soaring arched window as Thomas and Skye drove off the estate grounds. He returned to Emma's chair and stroked her thick, graying hair.

CHAPTER 13

Sarah arrived at Eagle Bay Regional Airport two days before the wedding. It was her second trip home since the drama of John's disappearance two years earlier. She was pleased Thomas picked her up at baggage claim; it would allow forty minutes of private conversation on their drive to the Westbrooke Estate.

"I'm happy for you, Thomas. You seem more content than you've been in years. I guess that's what the right woman can do for a man."

His eyes stayed focused on the road. In a soft and genuine tone, he said, "I am happy, Sarah. Thanks for recognizing that. Skye's a special woman."

"Indeed." She squeezed his right arm. "And in an unexpected way, John's still in your lives. Perhaps it was destiny . . . following the tragedy."

"You know, in many ways, it does seem preordained." He glanced at her. "I hope you'll find what I have someday."

"Maybe I will," she replied, looking out at many shades of new growth emerging from the forest. "I want you to know I sensed the burdens Dad handed you after Mom grew ill. It wasn't right or fair. He forced you to grow up too fast."

"It's true everything changed after Emma's meltdown. And yes,

Robert and I have an unusual relationship. Nevertheless, I respect him." Sarah was oblivious to the dark horrors that defined Thomas's youth. Her upbringing had been more traditional, more normal. The siblings' lives diverged before they'd reached their teens.

Sarah viewed her reflection in his sunglasses. "But you can't even call our parents *Mom* and *Dad*, Thomas. That's so tragic." There was no response. "I know Dad's a strong personality, but he loves you."

He inhaled.

"You know that, right?"

More silence.

"Okay, enough of that."

"Yeah. New topic," Thomas said as they passed two fly fishermen casting for steelhead. "How's your job going? Any plans to leave the East Coast?"

"I love my job more than ever." She lifted her coffee from the console and took a sip. "The Northeast fashion scene fits this Oregon girl just fine." She laughed. "I'll likely stay in Boston or New York long-term."

"I hope you do. I'll miss you, but it's the best place to advance your career." An ODOT flagger cautioned of a stop ahead; a work crew cleared debris from one of many winter landslide stretches still under repair.

"To be honest, for years, I'd intended to move home to help with Mom. Dad wouldn't let me. Upon graduating from Wellesley, I tried again. He kept telling me she wouldn't want me to spend any portion of my burgeoning career as her caretaker. But I'm not so sure."

Thomas nodded as the flagger waved him through. "Robert likes to control things, Sarah. Just let it go. And he's probably right about what Emma would want."

"Maybe. Sometimes I think he's oddly committed to Mom's routine. You know? Don't get me wrong; it's a wonderful thing. But when I ask questions about which doctors recommended which care protocols, Dad grows silent. I don't get it."

"I don't know what you want me to say."

"I'm sorry. You're saying 'I do' in two days, and I'm harping on Dad's idiosyncrasies. In case I forget to say this later, let's try to stay in closer contact moving forward. It seemed like we were drifting apart before the boat accident."

"It's a deal."

As they continued over twisting creekside roads, Sarah thought Thomas looked preoccupied. He inexplicably acted less interested in discussion, and they stopped speaking.

Early that evening, uneasy quiet extended throughout the Westbrooke household, no one taking control of conversations or expressing excitement over the looming wedding. Sarah found it sad and unsettling.

Later, Thomas hugged his sister. "I'm so glad you're here with us." He kissed her forehead and retired to the guest house for the night.

With little success, Sarah spent thirty minutes seated with Emma and Robert, trying to engage her father in meaningful conversation. She held Emma's hand, yearning for the family she'd remembered from childhood. No one noticed her misty eyes.

14

CHAPTER

Skye floated in the clouds. She would soon marry a genuinely decent man who adored her. She'd long ago convinced herself Johnny and Dakota would benefit from having Thomas in their lives. Weeks earlier, Skye grew deeply touched by Thomas's heartfelt request to adopt Johnny and Dakota in the future. A hairdresser snapped her fingers to pull Skye back to the moment after applying hairspray in a bride's room adjoining the church.

"You look incredible," Sadie said. "Nothing like that bucktoothed tomboy I first met at the St. Paul rodeo. Thomas is one fortunate *pretty boy*."

She enjoyed delivering her oft-repeated judgment. At the rehearsal, Sadie had arrived with a Texas-sized hairdo and an outfit Skye considered comically revealing—a loose-fitting top and a too-short skirt. Today, with her hourglass figure encased in a bridesmaid dress, she appeared beautiful *and* appropriate.

"Calling me a bucktoothed tomboy brings back great memories. But if you call Thomas a pretty boy once more, he may find another place to buy flowers. So tread lightly, dear maid of honor." Sadie was not only giving away her closest friend; she had earned one-quarter of her floral shop's annual profits by supplying arrangements for three engagement parties, a bridal shower, the rehearsal dinner, and today's wedding and reception.

Skye understood how the moniker "pretty boy" might have originated; Thomas personified Ivy League preppy: Ralph Lauren button-downs, sweaters over shoulders, penny loafers, impeccable grooming, and a model's body. Had he not been athletically gifted or a member of the renowned Westbrooke family, he may have suffered the consequences of his peculiar Yankee ways.

"You know it's so true! Sometimes I'd swear your future hubby grew up with Northeastern elitists. But you know I love him. I'll only mock him behind his back." Sadie flashed a big smile and a mischievous wink Skye typically interpreted as "trouble's brewing."

The two women had shared twenty years of their lives. They'd confided in each other regarding schoolboy crushes and, later, the men in their lives. During Skye's bachelorette party, a drunken Sadie blathered on about how her best friend had nabbed such a remarkable man. "And you'll be able to buy *anything* you want!" she exclaimed. Skye grew relieved after Sadie's pangs of jealousy subsided.

"Well, it's time." Sadie clasped the bride's hands between her own and squeezed. The wedding party entered the room, and one presented Skye with a bouquet of white roses.

Two years after her John's disappearance, six-year-old Dakota beamed while tossing rose petals down the aisle. Guests turned mesmerized when Skye commenced her procession in a simple but elegant dress. Onlookers would've been startled to learn the future Mrs. Westbrooke bought it off the rack at Nordstrom, a fact Skye noted with pride, but that Thomas lightheartedly considered unnecessarily pedestrian.

As Skye began her wedding march, she noticed Johnny sitting on Grandpa McCloud's lap, an unexpected development. Confined to a wheelchair due to advanced Parkinson's, Grandma McCloud sat on the outside aisle of a front pew. The elder McCloud's attendance honored their son John, his best friend Thomas, and the daughter-in-law they'd never stopped loving. Skye wished her parents could've joined the celebration, but her father died one year after John's disappearance, and her mother struggled with advanced dementia.

During rehearsals, the priest informed Skye and Thomas that he had a knack for accurately forecasting unions and told them their future together would be amazing. Skye was caught off guard by the claim, so she only smiled without commenting. Husband and wife then exchanged their vows, and the festivities began.

Music blared until eleven inside the clubhouse of the new Bayview Dunes Golf Club. No other family in town would've been able to schedule such a raucous bash at the recently-inaugurated private club; the tentacles of Westbrooke influence stretched far and wide.

As the exhausted bride and groom prepared to depart for Portland, sinking into the leather seats of Thomas's classic '71 Jag XKE, with its streaming colors and *Just Married* shoe polish, Skye's new husband spoke his first private words.

"Why was Johnny sitting with the McClouds?"

"What?" Her expression remained fixed as the comment settled. She gathered herself. "That bothered you? Johnny sitting with John's family?"

His gaze transformed after seconds. "I'm sorry—what a stupid thing to say. The McClouds are fine people. Johnny loves them, and that's beautiful. I'm just tired." He offered a tender smile.

"Thanks. I don't have the energy to deal with silly surprises. I forgive you, Mr. Westbrooke." She brushed rice out of his hair.

He tapped on his chest. "I'm the luckiest man in the world." Settling his eyes on a contented face, Thomas put his car in gear and jetted past the celebrating guests. A good-natured shriek echoed as he pinned them back into their seats with a quick acceleration out of the club. They enjoyed the three-hour scenic drive and checked into Portland's landmark Heathman Hotel.

"Thank you, Thomas," Skye said as the elevator lifted from the hotel's grand lobby. "Even though my dad's gone and Mom is sick, they would've been so proud of you today. It was just as I'd dreamed it would be."

"You deserved it." He placed his palms on her cheeks and wiped away a tear of joy. "My job's to make you happy." A bell rang, and the brass doors split apart, offering views of elegant halls from a bygone era.

Thomas felt exceptionally worthy after making love to Mrs. Skye Westbrooke for the first time. As his wife slept, he appraised the orchestration of their futures together. Yes, a man had perished to put the wheels of their union in motion. A good man. A man they both loved. But Thomas had long ago concluded that giving Skye a life of commitment, adoration, and privilege would compensate for the horrors he'd inflicted on John. It wasn't the script anyone would have written, but it was a love story that would end well for a remarkable woman and her two children.

He could've won over any woman, but Skye was the one he wanted. Of course, he realized the citizens of Eagle Bay considered him quite the fortunate groom to call Skye his own. Those people were right, and he was thus committed to becoming the man Skye deserved.

Lying on his side, Thomas appreciated Skye's soft skin against his fingertips. Comforted by the cadence of her breathing and the profile of her face outlined in fading light, the room's heater kicked on just as he settled into a deep slumber.

The full moon illuminated a forest of towering firs and magnificent ferns. Thomas the Witness followed a path of golden stones that glistened onto the flora lining his path to an unknown destination. Upon entering a clearing covered by spectacular glowing wild-flowers, two yellow and white birds arrived, fluttering about as light from a mysterious source enhanced the scene. Below the two birds lay something non-existent moments before: Thomas and Skye's bodies slumbering contentedly upon a suspended cushion of embroidered silk. Thomas the Witness smiled at the sleeping couple that had adoration fixed upon their faces. The two birds became dozens, then hundreds, their feathers displaying colors known and unknown, their collective splendor astonishing. Thomas the Witness stared at his resting likeness with an otherworldly bliss. He watched the serene, contented Skye begin to stir and rise; the Witness grew mesmerized as she caressed the face of his ethereal image. Her eyes narrowed as she tenderly stroked his jaw and temple. Thomas the Witness watched her grasp a loose bit of his skin on the face of his slumbering likeness. Skye's expression turned disturbed. Pulling upward, the mask of skin stretched before snapping away, exposing a black face with gray eyes. Skye shrieked in disbelief, and Thomas the Witness pleaded for calm as he rushed forward to clutch the flesh mask and struggle to stretch it back over the grotesque image of his likeness. Skye's anguished cries grew desperate as the macabre Thomas disintegrated into slithering swarms of insects. Thomas the Witness released horrified screams while trying to embrace and comfort Skye, but she transformed into a translucent apparition, slowly fading into nothingness. He begged for her forgiveness but knew that the charade of his life justified the horrific illusion before him.

"Thomas, Thomas, please!" Skye grabbed his shoulder and shook him. "Honey, wake up. Wake up! I'm right here." She twisted to turn on the lamplight.

Thomas stopped twitching, opened his eyes, and returned to the real world with grief etched across his face. He wrapped his arms around her tightly, his body moist. "I love you, Skye. Please know that. It's all that matters."

"Of course. And I love you."

15

CHAPTER

On their second morning in Portland, they'd awakened to views of rain-splattered windows framing an unusual summer downpour. They'd managed just seven hours of sleep during their forty hours in the city. Three dozen red roses filled a crystal vase in the middle of a round table; their sweet smells permeated the hotel room. New brown and tan Louis Vuitton luggage lay stacked against a wall, Thomas's gift to Skye the week before.

They changed out of their white cotton robes and into island colors for the two flights to their honeymoon destination: St. Croix, in the US Virgin Islands. Skye eagerly anticipated ten days on the warm sands of the Caribbean. Life was good. Expectations were high.

John and Skye spent their first honeymoon in the sleepy town of Bandon on the Southern Oregon Coast. It was all the newlyweds could afford as recent college graduates, but she couldn't have cared less about their finances or any associated constraints. That rain-drenched affair was the most fabulous week of her life, matched in unbridled joy only by the births of her children.

The home Skye and Thomas rented on the East End of St. Croix was a luxurious peach-colored, contemporary, one-level residence with unobstructed views of the lapping blue-green tinted Caribbean from every vantage point. As she strolled to the outdoor foyer connected to the kitchen, which stood eighty feet from the water's edge, the agent who'd coordinated the rental yelled, "Quick, look out to sea, just to the west of Buck Island. Humpback whales are spouting! It's quite uncommon. Let's consider it a symbol of good fortune for your marriage."

Thomas placed his arm around Skye's waist and squeezed.

An eight-pound Spiny Caribbean lobster—natives called it a langouste—was boiled for their dinner prepared by a local chef. Though not part of the famous Maine lobster family, langoustes look similar with one glaring exception: long antennas instead of claws. Earlier, Thomas coaxed Skye to hold the lobster by its whiskers for a honeymoon snapshot; the creature measured a remarkable thirty inches.

The chef sliced the crustacean's meat into large three-inch squares. Because she knew no one back home would believe such claims, Skye would return to Oregon with photos as proof. A bottle of 1982 Château d'Yquem complemented their meal. Thomas was a stickler for fine grapes, so Skye knew it had to be an exceptional wine.

The privacy of the property enhanced the moment. Later, they snuggled on a wide chaise lounge crafted from the island's famous but depleted dark mahogany woods. Fonseca Vintage port washed down Austrian dark chocolates. Disrobing and stepping into the sea, where the wonder of an infinite sky enhanced their romantic interlude, Eagle Bay became a faded contemplation.

Skye melted in the warm waters as Thomas caressed the outline of her body. He stared down at her tanned skin, firm and tantalizing breasts, and her thick mane of brunette hair falling beyond her shoulders. His soft touch hypnotized her. The heat of desire far exceeded the temperature of the warm, shallow surf. Her legs grew weaker as they leaned into each other.

"Let's move inside," was a delicate whisper falling from her lips.

Entering their bedroom, she felt a powerful surge of emotion erupt from her body. He laid her on top of the four-post mahogany bed. Sounds of the ocean carried through their room and added passion to an already heated moment.

She arched her back, and her moaning grew pronounced; she wondered if it bordered on melodramatic. She shuddered, recovered, and hoped for more of the same, pleased that Thomas had grown visibly stirred.

Their bodies twisted together under a single sheet; it was too warm for blankets. Skye lay on her side, peering into Thomas's eyes. She found herself uncomfortably reminiscing about John and forced that perturbation from her mind.

People often commented that Thomas was steady, measured, and rarely out of control in business and sport. Skye was struck by how that discipline also carried over to his lovemaking. It didn't matter. They'd now laid together several times, before and after the wedding, and each moment had fulfilled her. She loved him, and her unbounded adoration enhanced every touch, kiss, and climax. "I adore you, Thomas. Everything feels so right." She meant everything she'd said, though she wondered if a tinge of guilt had prompted her words.

Thomas stroked her arm. "I'm no longer just an ardent pursuer of the prettiest girl in Eagle Bay. I don't deserve you, but I will forever be your loyal husband, madame." He leaned closer and met her inviting lips.

CHAPTER 16

Omelets were an excellent use of leftover lobster from the previous evening. Sitting at a table on a patio beneath a covered structure, they enjoyed their breakfast and cold mimosas as sailboats traversed the bay. Turquoise and blue seas sparkled as whitecaps came and went.

"You're fine with me fishing?" Thomas said. "We could cancel, and I could spend the day here." Thomas was an avid sportsman, and it was Skye's surprise for him to enjoy a half-day of fishing. She'd secretly reserved a boat and crew through Cruzan Sportfishing upon arrival, a decision motivated by memories of John and Thomas enjoying their angling trips years earlier.

Skye wore a rose-colored bikini, teal sarong, and a wide-brimmed straw hat. "Nonsense, go have a great time. That's the whole idea, Thomas. The owner said there's a strong run of yellowtail ten miles out, so go catch us dinner. We can use the belly as sashimi and the rest for tacos or *poisson cru*. How's that sound?"

"Poisson cru? Yes! I love that stuff." He added, "But remember, fish are fickle. Keep your expectations in check. Who knows, I might even get skunked." He smiled at a gecko doing push-ups on the white stucco wall beside him.

"I know, I know. I won't *expect* big fat fish, but if you can deliver, you'll make me very happy. Which can lead to all sorts of favors." She smiled coyly. "Remember, they drive like lunatics here and on the wrong side of the road. Pay attention. Be safe." She blew him a kiss.

He winked, grabbed the keys, and departed.

Thomas instantly grew conflicted. Part of him considered doing the rational thing, but moral struggles were always his companion. Minutes later, he pressed the brakes and pulled the car to the side of the road. He stared at his reflection in the rear-view mirror and shook his head. *What are you thinking? You love Skye! You're a new man. You've evolved. It's only been three days! Stop this shit. Don't call this woman.*

He felt nauseous, confronted by his duplicity after working hard to earn Skye's hand. He'd overcome Robert's objections to his marriage and inspired himself through his transformation since "that night in the barn." He had defied the very thing he'd once considered unconquerable: the effects of his twisted upbringing.

Instead, he removed a note from his wallet: Zhara 340-555-6281. Leaning against the arc of the steering wheel, he pushed his forehead hard into the plastic, seeking pain. *Here's your chance, God. If you exist, reveal yourself. Please help me. Someone, something, help me.*

He turned off the ignition, got out, and stood on the asphalt edge overlooking the ocean. Dirt, brush, rock, and cacti surrounded him. The smells of sea salt were strong. He battled the urge to call Zhara as his thoughts moved to Robert: *You did this to me, you sonofabitch.*

He stood next to the car and measured elongating shadows caused by a traversing sun. Walking to the driver's side, he shut the door and dialed Zhara. She answered, sounding just as he'd remembered. Aroused, he fought back vigorously against waves of harsh self-judgment. He hated himself and instantly scorned Zhara for taking the call. But he didn't hang up.

They'd engaged in a days-long sexual tryst four years earlier during a Caribbean Islands sailing competition. He'd kept the sexy Puerto Rican's number in his wallet since then, the same leather now sharing photos of Skye and the children. Despite silently condemning himself as a worthless piece of shit, he asked Zhara if she'd be available for a day sail. An expert deckhand, she sounded interested but informed him it was the height of tourist season and that her company had her booked out for weeks. He promised to double her employer's boat rental fee and give her a $2000 tip—she quickly committed to changing the schedule.

He started the car and drove west toward a catamaran skippered by a beautiful woman who wasn't his new wife. He tried but failed to excise Skye from his thoughts temporarily. Upon arriving at the marina, he stared one last time into the mirror, genuinely hoping the man peering back at him would convince him to stop, turn around, and return to their vacation rental. Seconds later, Thomas shut the door and strode toward the water. Flags on land and sea fluttered southward. Well-fed fish hovered in schools beneath the white dock planks he stepped across. As he approached a slip, he spotted a voluptuous dark body preparing for the day's adventure.

"Well, if it isn't that incredible sailor from Puerto Rico. How've you been, Zhara? It's wonderful to see you." Her exotic appearance titillated him.

"I've been well. I'd almost forgotten your name since you disappeared without a trace. You said you'd call me after the competition. Do you remember that?"

He adjusted his sunglasses. "I came down with a bout of mono after the regattas, then got buried in work and, honestly, didn't have time for anyone. Still don't." The response was lame, he told himself. No matter.

She stared into Thomas's lens-covered blue eyes while untying the dock lines before catching a reflection from his left hand. "You're married?" She inhaled deeply. "Your wife knows you're sailing with me, right?"

He stared back impassively and eventually smiled. "So what do you say we shove off?"

Zhara shook her head. "You're in charge, captain. Where are we headed this fine morning?" The winds were pushing the catamaran from the dock.

"To Buck Island. We can anchor up on the North Shore for good food, even better alcohol, and . . . relaxation." He told himself he'd detected complete understanding, perhaps even mutual desire.

Blue and yellow sails stretched into gorgeous arcs during the trip to their private escape. Zhara looked like a well-endowed swimsuit model. Thomas turned more excited, knowing her large, soft breasts would soon be his domain. He deliberated the differences between Skye's body and hers. The comparison made him uncomfortable, but it was a hesitation he easily purged from his mind.

They dropped anchor, and Thomas wrapped his arms around her from behind, stroking her stomach and thighs. Zhara stood stiffly but was tolerant of the handsome, wealthy Continental. Minutes ticked by, and she eventually turned passionate. They shared their bodies throughout the day while saying little. Two miles away, across

a narrow channel on the other side of Buck Island, Skye was contentedly sunning herself.

Thomas poured himself an island concoction and lay down on the
deck after they'd had sex again. Zhara sat quietly for ten minutes but
stood abruptly. "We need to pull anchor and get back to the marina."

"Why'd you put a T-shirt on? You've hidden those beautiful assets."

"That sounds pathetic."

"Come on. Everything's going to be fine."

She began packing things up. "Just don't talk to me."

"Whoa, what's gotten into you? Please, don't let a silly thing like
guilt weigh you down. Take a seat. I'll pour you a sedative."

"I can't do this," she shot back. "We had fun in the past, but things
have changed. I've suddenly been struck by how different we are. I've
got to get off this boat, and you've got to get back to your wife." She
mumbled, "By the way, I'm . . . engaged." She shook her head. "So
let's go. I mean it, right now."

"Zhara, take a breath. First off, you're not wearing an engagement
ring. Secondly, you're having a Jekyll and Hyde moment."

"The ring is getting sized. I fell for your suave bullshit again—
shame on me. But I'm the Jekyll and Hyde? Whatever. I'm surprised
I didn't figure you out before. You've just become very transparent."

"Please don't pretend this isn't who you are." His tone changed.
"It is, and that's okay. You're engaged. I'm married. Let's enjoy the
day before moving beyond it. It'll be our secret little rendezvous." As
he studied her face, he wondered whether Zhara considered herself
an equal to Skye, a thought he found repulsive, so he leered and said,
"My wife is a better person than you'll ever be."

"What the . . . ? I feel sorry for her—she's married to a con man. Pull up the anchor, or I will. You're right; we're adults. My adult decision is to get the hell out of here. You can jump overboard if you'd like, but I'm returning this cat."

He walked up behind her, attempting to soothe her by placing one arm around her tense body. She pushed him away several times before shoving him. His drink spilled, and he tossed the plastic glass into the cooler.

She started pulling up the anchor.

"You're not one to judge me, Zhara. You're a worthless whore. *My* worthless whore." She stood frozen, too shocked to respond. Her lips moved as she silently repeated everything he'd just said.

"You think you've abruptly become a virtuous woman? I've just paid you $2000 for sex. I'm guessing your fiancé wouldn't consider that honorable. You're a prostitute, Zhara."

"What? Oh my God!" She shook her head with furrowed brows. "Go to hell, asshole!" She slapped him. "I'm going to tell your wife who you *really* are."

He struck her with the back of his hand; he'd never hit a woman before. She stumbled against the starboard railing and tripped, and her body lay partially aboard with one breast exposed. He advanced again with an intense gaze.

She tasted her blood. "Okay, okay, Thomas. I'm sorry. Just leave me alone. Please. Let's return the boat, and we'll go our separate ways."

Seeing real fear in her eyes, he halted his advance, turned away, and rubbed his forehead while staring at islands on the horizon. He turned back. "I'm sorry. You don't understand."

She stepped back, nearly tripping over a rope and the cooler. "I . . . Please don't hurt me, Thomas."

"I'm not going to hurt you, Zhara, even though I want to. But listen carefully. You'll receive $2000 for your work today, plus $10,000 to keep your mouth shut. Don't ever go to the authorities. Never attempt to contact my wife or me because doing so would be bad for all of us. Stare into my eyes and tell me you understand." He removed his shades.

"Okay, but I don't want your money," she said, looking pale and terrified. "I won't talk to anyone. Ever."

"No, you'll take the money." He narrowed his eyes and moved his tongue across his bottom lip. Her comments and threat to speak with Skye prompted dark thoughts. He stood conflicted, disturbing himself by contemplating the differences between hurting and killing her. "Let's get back to the marina. We'll part ways, and that'll be the end of it. Don't forget your promise."

She yanked hard and set the jib, licking the fresh wound on her mouth. Goosebumps covered her forearms, and she said nothing.

Thomas stared away on their return, listening to nylon sails flapping in the breeze. He felt like the monster Zhara surely condemned him to be. No woman would ever accept apologies for such threats and violence.

17

CHAPTER

Zhara and Thomas returned the catamaran without further incident. She informed her boss that a slightly swollen lip was due to a slip and fall on the boat's deck. As Thomas drove back to Skye and their waterfront rental, he stopped at the Christiansted Marina to buy the nicest tuna available. He placed the fish inside a white Styrofoam cooler filled with ice and put it in the trunk.

"Boo!"

Skye jumped. He'd placed the head of the tuna inches from her face, jolting her senses after hours of peaceful Caribbean slumber.

"Oh, my God! That ugly thing freaked me out. Don't ever do that!" She grinned and raised a threatening fist.

"How was your day, pretty lady?"

"Warm and beautiful." Her half-read book, sunscreen, iced tea, and lip balm lay on the chaise's pull-out shelf. "I see you caught a nice one. We'll be eating tuna for weeks—that thing is *huge*." She stepped beneath the outdoor foyer's roof and pulled off her Vuarnets, but even in the shade, the sun's reflected rays from the ocean, pool decking, and lightly colored walls forced her to squint. "Wow, you didn't wear your sunblock. You better put a thick dose of aloe vera on right away."

Skye understood a reddened face wasn't unusual after a full day of fishing, drinking beer, and telling exaggerated stories with a boat full of stinky fishermen.

"How was the crew? Good guys?"

"What? Oh, yes, good people." He removed his sunglasses, leaned over, and kissed her forehead.

"*Yay.* I was hoping so." She squeezed sunscreen onto one hand and rubbed it across her forehead, cheeks, and nose.

Thomas said, "Hey, I feel all sweaty and smelly like that tuna. Let me shower before helping you cut it up for dinner. No chef tonight— the pressure's on us to create a meal worthy of our second night in paradise. Can we pull it off?"

"I have no doubts. It's tough to screw up with hours-old fish. Now please go rinse off—you stink."

Dinner tasted amazing. Pinkish clouds floated amidst a pink and blue sunset, and five multicolored sails dotted the bay.

Skye stepped away from the table to move behind Thomas's chair. She massaged his shoulders and chest. "Something about this island heat makes me feel sexy. Up for skinny dipping, Mr. Westbrooke?"

He'd grown further repulsed by the horrors inflicted on Zhara. The effects of his failures engulfed him.

Skye stepped around and sat in his lap, clasping her hands around his neck and meeting his gaze. "So, what do you think?"

"I'm sorry, Skye. The fishing wore me out. Would it be okay if we just lay here listening to the surf and waited for the stars?"

"Oh, my goodness, that sounds like one of the most romantic things ever. I'd love to share your chaise lounge."

An hour later, she remained curled on his body, her face awash in serenity and adoration. "You're a fine man, Thomas."

Soon after, with Skye close to sleep on the chaise lounge, Thomas traced the satellites traversing the skies. His eyes welled. He'd hoped things could be different, that he could be different. But he'd now shattered his expectations. He committed to regaining control over his troubled soul.

Skye made her way to the spa for a massage the following morning. Thomas took a dip in the ocean before walking to a hillside church he'd seen nearby. He read the brass plate affixed to its stone façade. The church was over two hundred fifty years old, built by enslaved people and later renovated by their emancipated descendants.

It was architecturally magnificent, styled after the San Juan, Puerto Rico, churches of the 1700s. Thomas was captivated by the entry columns, elaborate cornice moldings, and Neo-Gothic architectural elements. Entering the empty structure through an unlocked front door, he sat in a dark mahogany pew. He appreciated the relics, crosses, and crucifixes, impressed by their artisanship.

He grew sufficiently inspired to feign belief in God. He heard a door shut before a Black man in street clothes moved toward him.

"Good afternoon," the man said. He was inches shorter than Thomas, with a sturdy build, and looked about sixty-five.

"Good afternoon." Thomas nodded.

"I'm afraid I'll have to ask you to leave," the man said in a thick African accent. "I need to lock up until tomorrow's service. I hope you understand."

"Of course," Thomas said. "Just killing time. I'm guessing the priests are out saving the flock?"

"Well, there's only one priest for this small parish." The man chuckled. "You're looking at him. So unless you need saving, the answer at present is no." His smile came naturally, and he appeared sincere.

"What I need may be more than an ordinary saving. Good day." Thomas wasn't interested in having to overcome a cultural divide. His issues would be challenging enough for any Westerner to listen to, comprehend, or renounce. And he still wasn't sure why he'd been drawn there in the first place. He respectfully tipped his head and exited through the faded entry door.

Just as he'd reached the bottom of the outside church steps, the priest called out, "Excuse me, sir. Do you have a moment?"

Thomas turned and debated whether to walk away, but the affable man had dulled his apprehensions. Without further consideration, he replied, "I do."

"Would you like to discuss something? I have time to listen."

"Where are you from, if you don't mind my asking?"

"Tanzania," he replied. "I was initially assigned to the diocese of Philadelphia." With an exaggerated Rastafarian inflection, he added, "I've been a Cruzan for over five years, mon."

Thomas grinned. "I'd imagine this assignment to be a pretty nice gig."

"It has been therapeutic. My diocese essentially forced it upon me." He relaxed his smile. "My name is Father Joseph." Extending a massive hand, he barely squeezed when they shook. "I drank too much trying to cope with the responsibilities of a large parish stateside."

"I'm sorry. I'm Thomas. It's a pleasure to meet you. What was your birth name?"

"Akili. It is rare that someone asks me that question."

"I believe it's Swahili," Thomas said.

"Yes. You are a learned man." He sat down on the church's original stone wall. "Let us talk."

"I'm not a Catholic," Thomas said. "My wife is. My mother's a devout Protestant, but mental illness has robbed her of the ability to express her faith. I don't believe in your god or any gods. I say that with respect for what you do for a living. I admire the sacrifices you religious make." He relished unloading his sentiments.

The priest barely reacted while peering into Thomas's eyes. "You sound as if you are trying to justify something. What is on your mind, friend?"

Thomas was surprised by his quick judgment and candor. "People consider me a fortunate man. I come from an affluent family, and I've lived a privileged life. I've never wanted for anything."

"Never wanted for anything material? Or for anything more substantial? Like love, integrity, and goodness."

Thomas lowered his head, removed his glasses, and rubbed an eye. He dissected Father Joseph's words. "Love, integrity, and goodness are relative qualities for people like me. Even if I possess them only slightly, if you knew me well, you might consider it remarkable I uphold them at all." Thomas sensed Father Joseph was analyzing him. He didn't care.

"Why might I draw that conclusion?"

"Because I've persevered through what I've seen, been forced to do, and chosen to do. But those trials have tainted me."

"I'm sorry," replied the balding man. "I witnessed great misery during my youth in Africa. We have all endured hardship—even you privileged. I sense pain and remorse. You strike me as a capable man. Do you know how to reform?"

"Any pain I feel is justified. And yes, regret is often my companion." Thomas watched sweat accumulate on the man's face; the day had grown unseasonably hot.

"Those are troubling statements. Tell me more. You can be blunt. After years on the islands and twenty on the mainland, I have encountered every conceivable indiscretion or misfortune."

He judged his behavior with Zhara to be so deplorable that he surprised himself with his frankness. "I'm a killer, an adulterer, and a fraud." Thomas gazed out to Buck Island. "I feel irredeemable."

Father Joseph frowned. They looked at each other for a long pause, neither man speaking. Finally, Thomas asked, "Have I surprised you?"

"Those are damning words. I pray you are embellishing, especially about killing. If you are not, can I assume you have paid your debt to society?"

"I have paid a great price for my most heinous acts. This I promise you."

"I see . . . then you are on the path to redemption. God has given us free will and a conscience. You have used both to seek me out. You can conquer your failings. It is a choice."

"But only if I believe in your god? I'm solipsistic. We see the world through different lenses."

"We all have a conscience. You know which choices are necessary, whether you believe in my god or not."

"So the burden's all mine. That's unfortunate—for others. Whether I reform, I'll still have respect, affluence, my remarkable wife, and a family. Others pay the price if I don't."

"The burden isn't all yours, but the choice is." He wiped the moisture from his brows. "Those who love you will support your transformation.

If that's what you want, and if you let them. You can differentiate good from evil. You must pursue good. No one can serve both light and darkness, and no one should want to." He placed his hand on Thomas's. "I will not care much if you lose prestige and affluence. I do not want you to lose your family."

"I won't lose my family unless I intend to."

"Another harsh and tragic statement. How many years have you been married?"

"Four days."

"Please, friend." The priest halted. "This is unfair to your new wife."

"I'll give her a good life."

"Through deceit? No," he said, shaking his head. "May I ask why you married?"

Moments passed.

"I was there when her first husband died. He expressed his undying love for her. I am fortunate to be married to this remarkable woman who represents everything good in humanity. Your sermons on love and compassion reflect people like her."

"Yet you lie to her? And are unfaithful?"

"I love my wife. I'm trying to evolve into the person she believes me to be. I've made great strides. But I live in conflict. You have decided to believe in something that transcends family—your god. I, too, believe in something extraordinary."

"May I ask what that is?"

"You'd never understand," Thomas replied. "I serve multiple passions. I've enjoyed our discussion and hope you haven't grown distressed by your glimpse into my world. Pray for me if you think it'll help. Good day." He turned and walked away.

The priest ran to catch up with the puzzling stranger. "You must take responsibility for your actions. Nothing justifies you deceiving others as you are, especially those you profess to love."

"I meant what I said. I do love my family." Thomas smiled and patted the side of Father Joseph's shoulder. "You're a worthy man by our world's standards. Thanks for your time."

"I do not know if your list of transgressions was a fictional boast or a confession," he said. "You must find the strength to pull yourself from the edge of darkness."

"And if I don't?"

"If you choose darkness, you may fall off a cliff." He added, "Into an abyss that might be difficult to pull yourself from."

"For the sake of others, let's hope that doesn't happen. I must go." He departed while deep in thought, uncomfortable with a reminder of the truth: Nothing justified his despicable deeds—past, present, or future.

When Thomas returned to the house, it was empty. He poured himself a drink and sat in the foyer, watching the occasional fishing boat motor across the bay. Reviewing his conversation with the cleric, he realized he'd never opened up to anyone like that before. He wished he'd toned down the bravado and pleaded for help. It was unsettling having someone he connected with predict the likely consequences of his actions.

Skye arrived home in an upbeat mood. Thomas catered to her every desire throughout the remainder of their honeymoon, taking her to spectacular beaches and coves, the finest restaurants, and romantic sites for relaxing conversations. He surprised her with a sunset jaunt on the island's southern beaches straddled upon a chestnut mare. Thomas carried a blanket and bottle of chilled Nelthropp Rum Cream. They splashed through mild surf illuminated by a full moon on their trot back to the stables.

The Terrace Restaurant at the famed Buccaneer Resort, with a table reserved on the rail overlooking manicured grounds and the Caribbean, was the surprise location for their final dinner. Thomas chose a reservation time that guaranteed a colorful horizon and soft breezes. Conch fritters and callaloo complemented charred filet mignon and lobster tail. They shared a bottle of 1980 Petrus and local desserts.

Skye missed the company of her children more than she'd admit, but her calls home informed her they were happy and healthy. The kids were content; she was blissful; Thomas was in high spirits. It wasn't fair that she'd been granted such good fortune.

Her honeymoon was perfect, but as she peered out her window on the final approach to Eagle Bay Airport, observing the familiar shades of green framed by rivers, lakes, and the ocean, she appreciated the emotions that could only emanate from a place called home.

CHAPTER 18

Skye and Thomas returned from St. Croix and quickly settled into their routines. Both grew excited about the progress made on their home renovation; the property was evolving into another spectacular Westbrooke country estate. However, Thomas had another gnawing priority requiring his attention. He'd become fixated on removing unwelcome reminders of John's legacy. People or things prompting memories of the man he'd loved but killed served no purpose and burdened him with unwanted guilt. Thus, the McClouds' trusted farmhand needed to go.

More than a friendly Mexican cowboy, Diego Estrada was a fixture for the McCloud family. Skye was comforted knowing he'd remain a constant of their ranching, farming, and horse boarding operations. The *vaquero* left home at age sixteen, searching for opportunities and a better life. He was a talented hand who exemplified the work ethic common to immigrants from all countries pursuing their dreams in America. Skye had informed Thomas that Diego married a woman from Sea Cliff County named Lupita. The young couple expected their first child when the challenge of delivering a breech baby resulted in the deaths of mother and daughter. Diego mired himself in despair for not having insisted Lupita get transported to a hospital at the first signs of labor. Though homebirth had been a joint decision, the choice now wracked him with regret. Diego never remarried and told Skye he never would; she hoped he'd change his mind one day.

Thomas left the office early, knowing Skye and his soon-to-be-adopted children wouldn't be home until after their school's ice cream social. The executive insisted he was too busy with work issues to join them. Winding up the driveway, Thomas noticed Diego's Ford pickup parked next to the barn. The worker was toiling away on broken fencing at the far end of the Westbrookes' acreage. Thomas approached the barn and intercepted Diego as he walked back to his truck.

"Hello, Diego. Have a minute?"

"Sí, Mr. Thomas. What do you need?" Diego took off his hat and wiped the sweat from his brows with his sleeved arm.

Thomas delivered the news in Spanish, which he spoke fluently. "I'm afraid we won't need your services in the future." He measured the confusion written across Diego's face. "We appreciate everything you've done in the past, but my wife and I have decided to manage the farm operations ourselves." Thomas realized banishing Diego would significantly increase Skye's workload; if it were too much for her, he'd find new help later. "I've got a check for what we owe you, plus three extra months' wages. I hope you agree that's generous."

Diego's clenched jaw shifted as he dissected the news. "But Mr. Thomas, just before your wedding, Mrs. Skye told me she wanted me to work more, not less. She wants more acreage planted. And she's planning to board many horses." He squinted. "Have you talked to her? I'm surprised."

Thomas extended his arm with the check. "Yes, of course, we've spoken. Please don't make this difficult, Diego."

"I've worked for Mr. John and Mrs. Skye for six years. It doesn't make sense."

"I understand. But Mr. John is gone, and this isn't a negotiation, Diego. I'm telling you this is your last day, and I'm giving you extra money to ease your transition to a new employer. You won't have any trouble finding work." Thomas noted what he thought was the face of defiance, so he added, "Also, I'm assuming you're here illegally. I'm not interested in breaking the law by hiring aliens."

"You haven't spoken with your wife yet, Mr. Thomas. She would have told you I've been a legal resident of the United States for three years. I'm wondering if maybe you don't like Mexicans. I've worked hard for the McClouds, and I'm an honest person."

This task was supposed to have gone more smoothly, Thomas thought to himself. "I do not dislike Mexicans. Unlike my father, who despises people like you. And you now work for the Westbrookes, not the McClouds." He stepped toward Diego, close enough to study the pores of his face. "Take the money and leave. Please, Diego, don't ask me to explain. Don't try my patience."

The cowboy instinctively brushed his thick mustache exceedingly slowly with a forefinger. "Where is Mrs. Skye? Let's discuss together."

"*¡Jesucristo!*" Thomas exclaimed. He turned exasperated and switched to English. "Get off the property."

Upon breaking their stare down, the sturdy worker strode to his truck bed and turned back to Thomas. He paused, put his hat back on, and said, "This isn't right. Everyone in Eagle Bay tells me you're a good man. Honest. Generous. Loyal. I think those people are wrong."

Thomas noticed shadows drifting over Diego's dusty boots. He glanced up and saw vultures soaring, but there would be no human flesh to pick apart this day. He pondered if perhaps the ugly predators hoped to feast on his decaying soul.

Twisted resolve and purpose enveloped him. Thomas realized that after finishing this disgraceful act and booting the Mexican from their property, he could rededicate himself to the honorable life he'd lived during his courtship with Skye. His encounter with Zhara, and Diego's heavy-handed firing, would prove to be aberrations. He reached inside his coat, revealed his Sig Sauer, and raised the gun to Diego's head. "Leave and never return. This is not how I wanted our conversation to end but stay the hell away. The police are my friends, Diego. You comprende, amigo?" Thomas swung his aim to a hand-painted image of Our Lady of Guadalupe on the truck's back window, a religious tribute to Diego's dead wife and daughter. He pulled the trigger. A 9mm bullet shattered the glass artwork before embedding itself in the dashboard.

Diego stood stunned, silent. His eyes glistened. He stepped haltingly to the door of his truck and gripped the handle. There was no more eye contact with Thomas. "You will never see me again." He started the engine, lay his palm atop shards of painted glass on the truck's vinyl bench seat, mumbled something, and rambled off the estate.

Thomas prepared to inform Skye of the difficult emotions he'd confronted while firing a respected farmhand who'd betrayed his family's trust by stealing one of his Cartier watches and several pieces of Skye's jewelry. He'd also tell her that because Diego had offered deep remorse upon being caught red-handed with their possessions, he'd decided not to call the authorities to have him arrested. He hoped she would consider that a noble, forgiving act.

CHAPTER 19

Sixteen years earlier: 1970

Six men had completed their work. Thirty heavy wooden crates had been carried from a fortified trailer into a cement-walled basement beneath the new Westbrooke residence. The laborers had no idea what they'd transferred and were promptly shuttled off the estate when finished.

Hours later, after Robert, Emma, Sarah, and twelve-year-old Thomas had finished eating, Robert returned to the basement. As he descended the stairs into the room holding the crates, he saw a faint light shining through the second entry—the access point used to haul the cargo inside. He inserted his arm into a shelf below the stairs and grabbed his pistol.

"I know you're in here. I'm armed. Show yourself."

He heard shuffling and what sounded like a heavy piece of metal scrape the floor. Scanning the room, he readied to fire.

"Come out now, or I *will* shoot you."

"No, don't shoot." One of the crew members hired to move the containers, a young man with dark skin and shoulder-length black hair, stepped out from the shadows clutching a crowbar.

Robert walked forward, pausing to flip two switches with his gun extended. The room brightened.

"I'm sorry. I was just curious."

"Curious about what?" Robert recognized the man.

"These boxes. They're so heavy. I wasn't going to take anything."

"Of course you weren't. How'd you get back up the hill to our property? You left with the other workers." As he moved to the crate the intruder had hidden behind, Robert kept the weapon pointed.

"I parked outside your gates and walked. Honestly, I wasn't going to take any of those things."

"'Those things?' For your sake, I hope that doesn't mean you've seen what's inside."

"But it's all still there. I swear I was just curious."

Robert inspected the crate. One of the lids had been pried open. The trespasser had viewed its contents.

"So you *have* seen what's inside. You were going to steal from me. Where do you live?"

"I was curious," the man said. "That's all. I live in Barton, thirty minutes from here."

"How old are you?" Robert asked. "Are you a Mexican?"

"I'm twenty-two. I swear to God I wasn't going to rip you off. I was born in Barton. I'm an American."

"Hardly."

"Please, don't call the cops. I'll never come back here. I'm sorry."

"You should pray I *do* call the cops. The alternative is much more frightening. What did you think of the contents?"

"The contents?"

"Don't fuck with me. Tell me what you saw." He aimed the gun more deliberately.

"Okay, okay. I saw what's inside, but I didn't take anything."

"Only because I walked in on you." Robert patted him down with his free hand.

"Sir, go ahead; you can call the police. I'm okay with that."

"But they'd set you free, and you'd tell all your *Chicano* friends what you've seen here, then five or ten of you would be scheming against me. No thanks."

"What are you going to do? You can't hurt me. I didn't do anything."

"But you tried. Remember that everything happening from here on out is your own doing."

"Call the police. I'll tell them the truth."

"Precisely," Robert said. "And therein lies the problem. You've stumbled upon one of the greatest secrets in history. You've changed your future, sorry to say."

Spinning around, the young man bolted for the door. As he twisted the handle to gain freedom, the butt of the gun cracked loudly against his skull. He dropped unconscious.

Robert bound and gagged him with rope and tape before walking upstairs. He found Emma and Thomas laughing at an episode of *Cheers.*

"Thomas, I need your help on a project."

Robert's tone halted Thomas and Emma.

"Come on, let's go. We'll be back in an hour or so."

"What's going on?" Emma asked.

"Don't worry about it." Robert sounded combative. "Thomas, let's go, damnit. When I say I need your help, I'm not asking for permission."

"Stop that, Robert. Please don't talk to him that way. What's gotten into you?" She stared steely-eyed.

He paused and peered out a window. "You're right." He exhaled loudly. "I'm sorry. A pasture fence broke. We need to repair it before the horses scatter. Excuse my tone."

"Let's go fix it, Dad."

"I'll help you guys," Emma said.

"Thanks, hun, but we've got it. Let's feast on that fresh blueberry pie when we get back."

"Yeah, a la mode. Bye, Mom." Thomas smiled.

Father and son walked outside and jumped in a pickup. They drove around the residence to the rear door of the basement. Still under construction, the room would become the permanent storage space for what lay inside the containers. In one month, the finished vault would be impenetrable.

"This is an important day for you, Thomas. You need to trust me and do as I say. You understand?"

"Okay, Dad."

"It will be confusing and uncomfortable, but it's necessary."

Robert opened the basement door and quickly put his hand on Thomas's shoulder. A young man was bound and lying on the floor; his eyes darted frantically.

Thomas squealed, "Who's that?"

"This man was hiding in here. He tried to kill me with a crowbar and wanted to steal from us."

"Really?"

"Yes, and he'll try again. He'll try to take things from our family.

He'll never stop. He'll try to kill all of us—you, your mother, your sister, and me."

"But why? Why would he hurt us?"

"Because we own something astonishing that makes our family special and powerful."

"Huh? Like what? What is it?"

"I'm going to show you, but not before we do something frightening." He studied Thomas, then continued. "It's necessary, and you must trust me. Can you do that?"

"Um, yes. I guess so."

"Help me get this man into the bed of the pickup."

"Why? To drive him to the gate?"

"Just do it."

Thomas sat in silence as Robert drove for five minutes to the far end of their estate. His father put his hand on his knee and squeezed. They parked near a dock extending into a large pond.

"He wants to hurt us, take things from us. He will always want this. And son, he's not the only one. Someday, others may try the same thing." Robert began to weave a metal chain through weights he'd taken from his gym.

"Dad? Dad? *No!*"

Robert walked over, stooped down, and put one hand on each of his shoulders. "Yes, Thomas. I know this must seem horrible to you, but it's not. It protects our family. Trust me."

Thomas began crying. "But, but . . ." He lowered his head.

The bound man struggled against his constraints. They dropped him twice while carrying him across the dock's wooden planks and laid him down near the boat, where he began grunting.

"Kick him hard."

"*What?* Dad, no! I can't," Thomas said, stepping away. "*No!*"

"Pain is justice, son. He deserves it." Robert kicked the man in the head.

"*Stop. Stop!*" Thomas screamed.

"You're disappointing me," Robert said as he delivered a second blow.

Thomas's face twisted up; his lips trembled. He mumbled, "What's happening?"

"Get in the boat," Robert said.

Robert attached a chain from the boat to the man's bound and weighted body lying on the dock. He accelerated. The chain stretched tight, yanking the trespasser into the pond. The prisoner dangled against the outside hull of the boat, his head and shoulders barely above the water. He turned frantic.

"It's going to be alright, Thomas."

"But . . ." He looked at Robert with desperation. His nose, mouth, and chin oozed tears and snot. "Please stop, Dad. Please."

The chains remained woven around the man's body, who stared up to the skies from the cool water, no longer squirming with panic.

Robert grabbed a pair of wire cutters. A single link kept the man from dropping into a watery grave. "Cut it, Thomas. He will never be able to hurt us, never be able to steal from us. We will be safe."

"I can't," he sniffled. "I just can't, Dad."

"You can, and you must. You'll understand one day. You'll realize this was necessary. It's his fault. He's dangerous. Illegal. A thief. A bad man."

"I can't, I can't," Thomas pleaded. "This isn't right."

Robert slapped him across the cheek.

"I can't. *No!* We need to stop!" The prisoner defeatedly shook his head. *"Look! Look!* He's sorry, Dad. He's sorry! Please help him. *Please!"*

"Look at me, damnit. It's okay. Now cut the chain. Be strong." Robert slapped him harder, and snot flew into the water.

Thomas's expression turned blank. He gradually reached for the wire cutters, stared at Robert, waited, and clipped the man's lifeline. The intruder closed his eyes as he sank into the muddied water.

"It's okay, Thomas. It's okay. You were brave. I'm so proud of you, so very proud." Robert hugged him.

The boy sobbed.

"You must never speak of this to anyone. Not to your sister. Not to your mother. It is *our* job to protect this family. That's what we just did. We protected our family and a great secret. You understand?"

Thomas quivered and nodded up and down.

"I'm passing important responsibilities of family protection on to you, just as my father did to me. We now share a common bond, Thomas. This great honor will be our legacy."

The boy hardly reacted.

"Now I'm going to show you something remarkable. The great secret. You'll see why this man broke into our home." They drove back to the house, entered the basement, and stood next to the crate that had been pried open. Robert removed the lid.

Thomas lowered his head. He refocused on what lay before him and wondered if it was real.

"These are what I call *the assets*," Robert said.

Thomas extended an arm and caressed what lay inside, grasping and carefully inspecting the artifacts that most intrigued him. The agony of the previous hour slowly abated, and he knew that was wrong. He felt guilty, frightened, and dirty but grew strangely consoled by the curious, remarkable relics.

"What do you think, Thomas, about the assets?"

"They're interesting." He was particularly intrigued by a strange male figure which stood three or four inches high. "Where are they from? How did we get them?"

"I'm pleased you're fascinated. You should be. I will reveal the answers to those and other questions over time. Remember, this secret is *only* for you and me." Robert turned around to grab the hammer.

Quickly, Thomas grabbed the object captivating him. He placed it inside the pocket of his sweatshirt, his father unaware.

Robert stepped to a shelf and grabbed a handful of four-inch nails, squeezing several between his lips. He drove each one into the thick wooden lid of the crate, securing the contents awaiting transfer into the vault under construction.

"Let's head back to the kitchen." He placed his hand on Thomas's shoulder, guiding him toward the spiral staircase leading from the basement up to the den. Thomas's fingers remained inside the pockets of his sweatshirt, tightly clutching his fascinating treasure.

Emma beamed as they entered. "There you are. How are my two workers? Fence repaired? Horses corralled?" She placed two plates on the table, each filled with heaping portions of blueberry pie and Tillamook vanilla ice cream. "Just as you requested, Thomas," she happily announced.

Thomas moved cautiously. He met his mother's blue-eyed gaze, pulled a chair away from the table, and sat in front of his dessert. He began eating without addressing her or glancing her way.

Emma raised her brows.

Robert smiled and sat down, patting Thomas on the back. "Big Thomas was an immense help. We repaired the fence, and I was proud of his hard work. He's earned this delicious reward. Haven't you, son?" Robert flashed an expression Thomas considered unmistakable in its intent.

"Thank you, Robert." He finally turned to his mother. "It's a delicious pie, Emma." It was the first time he'd addressed his mother and father by their names.

"Emma?" She half-smiled at Robert. "Well, I guess our little boy's growing up."

"He's a little tired," Robert said. "But yes, I think he's growing up."

Emma assumed Thomas would return to his fun, obstreperous self the following morning. Instead, weeks later, she'd grown concerned; he had recovered little of his jovial essence. She gradually realized the cherished son she'd known had inexplicably vanished forever.

20

CHAPTER

If it had been easy, it wouldn't have been necessary. Thomas transformed himself after his disturbing fling with Zhara and banishing Diego. He now considered both events faded beacons of the past. Five years of tranquil marriage had since ensued. Living a life that met Skye's hopes and expectations was his gratifying achievement. He hadn't been so happy since adolescence. Thomas officially adopted Dakota and Johnny, so they now shared the Westbrooke surname, an honor Skye felt her husband had earned. The couple had settled into contentment.

Despite the better life Thomas forged, he never forgot what he'd done on St. Croix or what he was capable of. He assumed the shadows of any disturbed man's past lurked just beyond consciousness, eager to reappear. Thus, he worked hard to be the man Skye believed him to be.

Recently, horrific nightmares of standing over John's body—two bullet holes blasted through his chest—haunted him. John was sleeping in each hallucination, his stomach barely rising and falling. Thomas would kneel and peer into a peaceful face. John's head would suddenly twist sideways, and his lids would open wide. Hugely dilated pupils with glowing red and yellow veins stared menacingly. Thomas relived this horror at least one night each month.

Subliminal contemplations had prompted the visions, Thomas concluded. But he struggled with the question, "Why now?" He welcomed the disgusting reminders of a life he'd left behind. They reinforced a purpose: Keep walking the path to redemption.

Soon other disturbing thoughts surfaced.

He fantasized about wild sexual encounters with other women. It made no sense; his adoration and admiration for her had grown stronger than ever. She was the talented, compassionate, and only woman he genuinely revered. He struggled mightily to push the unwelcome urges aside but dreaded failure.

Thomas processed these thoughts while driving toward his parents' estate. He would say hello to Emma, though she'd express nothing beyond a wisp of recognition of her son in return.

As much as Thomas eschewed his father, he admitted Robert's commitment to Emma might be termed impressive. And even though Thomas recalled few expressions of love from his father toward Emma—all of them occurring before her meltdown—he wondered if there might paradoxically be elements of good within Robert.

The house was quiet. Classical music typically greeted him from one of the many rooms in the sprawling residence. He stepped inside the den; it was empty, but a glow emanated from the staircase that spiraled downward from a corner of the room. As Thomas's dress shoes clacked onto the cherry wood floor at the base of the steps, Robert spoke from inside the vault. "You've caught me doing inventory. Business is good?"

"I think you mean, 'Good evening, Thomas, is your family well?'" He found Robert standing with Montoya's journal in one hand and his reading glasses in the other. "Yes, Robert, my family is well. Thank you for asking."

"Why do you do that? It's aggressively confrontational." Three similarly sized and crafted assets were sitting atop a metal container. Robert put his glasses back on, turned to a page marked in the journal, and glanced back and forth between the manuscript and the three relics of history before him.

"I mock your disinterest in my family because it's just that—disinterest. Skye and the kids recognize your lack of genuine curiosity about their lives. But I've told you that before, and it's made no difference."

"Have you told your wife that you murdered her husband?" Thomas froze; he was typically more adept at anticipating his father's crushing barbs. "No? Okay, then. You tell Skye you splattered John's guts onto our barn floor, and I'll be a better grandpa." Robert removed his glasses and set his eyes on Thomas's. Neither man blinked nor moved for a long pause.

"You bastard," Thomas eventually said.

"You're a murdering fraud, but that's an issue between you and Skye. As for me, I'm grateful. You put the family first—*our* family first—when you killed John. It's what you should have done. My comments aren't mocking you, Thomas. I appreciate you in significant ways." Robert put his folded bifocals in his shirt pocket, returned the three bejeweled artifacts to their containers, and turned off the lights in the spacious vault. He closed the door. Though steel and titanium dominated the vault's interior and door, its outside walls and door façade were exquisitely trimmed in wood by a craftsman. It was nearly impossible to discern whether the entry even existed upon closing the door.

"Follow me," Robert said, leading Thomas back up the spiral staircase to his den. "I think you'll find this interesting. Have a seat. Grab me two fingers of port as I look for something." Robert spread out Montoya's journal and dozens of pages of Robert's hand-written notes. "I've learned Montoya was initially after Aztec gold for the king of Spain." He smiled expressively, like a child who'd discovered something special, something important. "But there wasn't any gold. And Montoya claimed Hernán Cortés might have stolen it! If true, we're talking a complete rewrite of conquistador and Aztec history."

Thomas wouldn't tell Robert, but he was genuinely intrigued by his father's revelations. He again committed to claiming the assets one day and possessing Montoya's historical account of his journeys. While he wanted to ask Robert where he kept the journal, he knew that would trigger suspicions. Not a problem; he wasn't yet in a hurry.

Robert raised his hand, clutching a white sheet of paper covered with his notes, holding it high as if he were bidding at an auction. "It took me quite a while to translate this passage, but I think I've got it straight now:

An honorable man claims Gonzales, leader of yesterday's scouting party, assaulted a native woman. He testifies thus as truth, on oath and Bible, that Gonzales ran her through with his saber after the woman screamed and attempted to flee to her people. The evidence is strong, and Gonzales has offered no denial. God help us.

"Sounds rather damning," Thomas said, again trying not to appear fully engrossed. "Was that in Mexico?"

"No, modern-day Peru. The woman killed was an Inca. After finding no gold among the Aztecs, Montoya saved the life of a remarkable stranger who led them from Mexico to Inca treasures thousands of miles away. Every page of this damn journal is astonishing." Robert grabbed a different page of translations from his pile of notes. "This last part reminds me of you, Thomas. You scoff at my words about loyalty, but Montoya's fealty to the king was no different than yours to our family and me. Gonzales had put their mission in jeopardy by raping and murdering that woman. And this is how Montoya responded, which I'd like you to correlate to what you did to John for the benefit of our family:

> *Upon gathering the truth as best able, I informed the ship of my judgment. The monks acted as faithful men of God, comforting the despairing accused who begged for forgiveness. I was saddened to see Gonzales's body hanging from a rope, swaying across the deck, tears in the eyes of his countrymen. Justice is often painful.*

Thomas said nothing but reflected on a critical difference: John McCloud was innocent. He stood, grabbed his coat, and returned to his family.

CHAPTER 21

Dakota relished sixth grade and couldn't care less about her appearance. Her five-six frame consisted of twigs for arms and legs, with big knots functioning as knees and elbows. Her head was too big for her rail-thin body, and she'd recently ruined her long mane of brunette hair by letting a girlfriend play hairdresser. Her mouth protruded with shiny metal. All that considered, it was easy to recognize that her halting green eyes would one day grace a beautiful woman.

With dark hair, broad shoulders, and immense energy, Johnny walked his junior high school halls as a lanky thirteen-year-old. He'd spent countless hours with Thomas since their family union under a shared roof, but Skye had recently noted their father-son time had dwindled. She broached the topic and asked Thomas to give the boy more attention; he enthusiastically committed to doing so.

Both children drew strength from seeing their mother so happy. She believed her teenage son possessed what most parents would consider an unusual sense of duty to his family. Lately, Johnny was desperately missing his birth father, more than Skye realized, a truth she'd have found unsettling if she were aware.

Westbrooke Coastal Industries' business empire continued to expand rapidly. Thomas secured Oregon Departments of Energy and

Environmental Quality support for turning thousands of acres of harvested timberland into the largest wind-turbine operation in the Northwest. WCI also acquired a competitor based in Phoenix and relocated half its operations to Eagle Bay.

It was nothing short of remarkable that the Westbrookes had been able to convert their early nondescript investments into a sprawling company spanning sixty-five years. To those traveling through Oregon on Highway 101, the scene of the WCI Business Campus, incongruously set into the midst of hundreds of acres of flat grazing land at the base of the Oregon Coast Range, was unlike anything else observed along the state's coastline.

Because WCI was a private company, it was challenging for outsiders to calculate its value. *Fortune* magazine recently estimated the family's net worth to be in the $1.5 billion-$2.5 billion range.

A Pulitzer Prize-winning investigative reporter for the *Oregonian* spent two years probing the history of WCI, a challenging pursuit because of the company's obsessive privacy. While he lauded the organization's philanthropic contributions to Eagle Bay and the state, he concluded he'd need a staff of five and two more years to dissect and fully understand the company's formative years.

Skye had grown increasingly conscious of how little she knew of Thomas's family businesses, so she grew captivated by the *Oregonian* reporter's suggestion that the founder of the WCI, Thomas's grandfather William Westbrooke, was a violent man of ill repute. She smiled at the idea of Thomas being such a character; the humorous prospect would be fodder for ribbing him. Thomas had proven himself to be a doting father and husband fully engaged in all their lives—precisely as she'd expected.

Johnny and Dakota were no longer excited to see their father on television because it occurred too often. His reputation as a business maverick and generous donor grew in lockstep with the expansion of WCI. That success inevitably led to a progressively advantaged lifestyle for the Westbrooke family, which Skye pretended not to notice.

She remained deeply in love with Thomas, though sometimes disappointed that their romantic life had lost a bit of its luster since their courtship and honeymoon. Otherwise, their marriage was healthy, and she believed passion in bed would be a poor barometer for her life's fulfillment. That said, she remained occasionally conflicted by memories of a love that had seemed to grow daily during her union with John.

Skye, Johnny, and Dakota had just completed a ride through the forest abutting their property. While Thomas appreciated the family's fillies and mares, Skye and the children shared more enthusiasm for the horses. As they cooled down and shampooed the animals, she couldn't help but smile while measuring her children's happiness.

The remainder of their day involved preparing for a big occasion. "We need to decorate the kitchen before he gets home. Where are the balloons and streamers? Mom? You look spaced out." Skye sat absorbed in views of white corral fencing and lush green meadows that were often her private solace, but she snapped alert as she felt her left arm getting tugged. "I'm sorry, honey. Your mother was daydreaming."

"No, duh," he said, grinning. "But Dad will be home soon."

Thomas anticipated celebrating his fifth anniversary with Skye in the Pearl District of downtown Portland in four days. Once dominated by warehouses and industrial relics, the Pearl had been gentrified and offered art galleries, award-winning restaurants, and a distinct cultural vibe. It was Skye's favorite part of the Rose City. But since today was the actual date of their 1986 wedding, she had planned a fun surprise around Thomas's arrival home.

"Okay, kids, Mom says *yah!*" She theatrically motioned as if snapping a bullwhip. "Let's get busy and make this place party central."

Thomas had been gone for three days to a small riverfront lodge along the banks of the Metolius River in Sisters, Oregon, a region renowned for brown trout fly-fishing. Skye and the kids had grown accustomed to his outdoor adventures with buddies. After decorating inside, the family heard their dogs barking, indicating Thomas was winding up their aspen-lined driveway. They rushed out to meet him.

Blaring rock and roll exploded from the truck's cabin. Thomas turned down the volume and hopped out of the Ford diesel pickup, looking disheveled. He beamed for a period before speaking and tripping over his words. "How's my amazing goddamn family!" He burped obnoxiously and continued, "Gimme some hugs!" His eyes were beet red. "The king has returned!"

Skye glared as she awaited an apology and her more familiar husband. Johnny glanced up at his mom and said, "The king?" Dakota yelled, "Dad, why are you talking like that? You sound like that old jerk at the restaurant." One month earlier, Thomas had grabbed an inebriated patron and escorted him out of the building.

"Come on, chop chop—I need a hug from my kids and hot wife. *Hold on—I fucking love this song!*" He jumped back into the truck's cab and turned up the volume to Ted Nugent's signature anthem about sex, *Cat Scratch Fever.*

"*Thomas!* Turn! Off! Your! Radio! What do you think you're doing?"

Skye stepped forward while pointing at the children and grabbed Dakota's arm, yanking her away from the truck.

"Mom, I don't think Dad can hear you." Johnny struggled to make sense of it all. "He smells like—"

"Sweat and alcohol, Johnny. Your father smells like a drunk. And he *can* hear me."

Skye rushed forward, pushed Thomas away from the steering wheel, and aggressively turned off the stereo. "What's gotten into you?" She yanked out the keys and tossed them onto the driveway before ushering the children away.

"You go, Skye!" Thomas yelled as the trio marched toward the front porch.

Skye stopped and turned around, glowering with furrowed brows and clenched teeth. "Why don't you sleep outside tonight? You don't deserve time with your family!" Dakota put her arm around her mother's waist and squeezed.

"Watch out, young Westbrookes—your Mom's a goddamn buzzkill today!" He disregarded their horrified expressions.

Skye's skin bristled. She placed an arm over each child's shoulders and picked up the pace of their retreat. "I'm sorry your father's acting like this. He's not feeling well, but that's no excuse." *He's a drunken ass on our anniversary*, she thought. *Unbelievable.*

Before entering the front door, she pointed at Thomas and blurted, "Go unload your gear! And your conscience!" The siblings waited for their father's reaction, hoping for conciliatory words.

Thomas laughed aloud. "Yes'm, rodeo queen!"

Johnny pushed the front door open just as Skye was closing it.

He stepped onto the porch and screamed, "You . . . you . . . you . . ." He pointed and stared at Thomas with burning rage and scorn.

"Me what?" Thomas yelled back. "Spit it out, Johnny."

His mother grabbed him by the arm and jerked him backward. Just as she was about to slam the door, Johnny stepped forward and bellowed, "You're acting like an asshole, Dad!"

"*No!*" Skye grabbed her son and gazed intensely into his eyes. "Don't you *ever* talk like that around me again, Johnny. Just because your father's acting dreadfully doesn't mean you should." She silently appreciated his trying to protect her. "You kids head to your rooms for a bit," she said. As they strode briskly down the hall, she added, "Everything will be okay."

Skye needed time to internalize events. She felt injured and confused and dissected every second of the previous ten minutes. Dakota lay on her bed and began writing in her diary. Johnny was pissed off, bewildered, and feeling bad for Skye.

Thomas climbed into his pickup and drove to the barn. He unloaded his gear and meticulously cleaned and stored each item. The barn, like the garage, was fanatically well-kept.

Ninety minutes later, he stepped inside and moved to the kitchen. His face no longer appeared frozen in a vile expression, and the whites of his eyes had cleared considerably. Skye was drying a black skillet she'd used to cook lingcod. Her jaw muscles remained strained and sore. Johnny and Dakota rejoined their mother for dinner before returning to their bedrooms.

"What's with all the party favors?" Just as he'd spoken, Thomas figured things out. "Oh, wow. Damn, I'm sorry. This was an anniversary surprise. What a terrible entrance I've made."

"You think? It was despicable. You returned home drunk on our fifth anniversary, spewing terrible, hurtful words. Cussing up a storm. You scared our children. You weren't their loving father, but an intoxicated and mean—"

"You're right. And I'm so sorry."

"I'm not done!" She continued, *"Your wife* anticipated your arrival on an important day only to be—*like her children*—sorely disappointed. That man in our driveway was a mean-spirited, condescending ass." She tossed the skillet into a cupboard; it delivered the clanging desired. She leaned over and ripped down streamers while releasing indecipherable mumbling. "You could've killed someone on the road. You were dumbass wasted when you arrived."

"Come on. I said I'm sorry, Skye. You don't need to keep preaching."

"*What?* I'm not preaching! You've been in the house less than five minutes! I'm only telling you the truth. Give me a break—preaching? That's pathetic."

Thomas stood next to the kitchen counter and watched Skye move about agitatedly. "You're right. Of course, you're right. I drank too much with my friends and ruined a special occasion. I'm so sorry. You're an amazing woman—my amazing woman—and I should never treat you that way." He remained still.

"'My amazing woman' sounds disparaging after you've shown up as a drunken ass. You don't," she flashed air quotes, "'own me.'" They stared at each other. "I'm hurt. You hurt the kids. None of your behavior made any sense. None of us recognized you. This whole thing was bizarre."

"I get it. I screwed up—big time. But you know that wasn't me. We drank too much." He embraced her. "I love you. Please forgive me."

She remained rigid. "I love you, too, Thomas. Deeply. That is why I would never do what you did to me." She pointed down the hall. "To us."

He held her at a distance with *sorry* etched across his face. "Can I fix this? Let's get the kids."

"No way. They're in bed, and I'm spent. You've ruined the evening." She nudged away, needing space. "Your disturbing behavior came out of the blue. I'm shocked you could act like that. Talk to me like that. Belittle our son like that." She set one hand on the counter. "I *never* want to see *that* person again."

"Skye, please. I'm the same person you knew before I left for Sisters. The good man you married."

She gazed out a window. "Good men don't act that way. Don't you get that?"

"Of course I do. But please don't let my stupid behavior give you real doubts about who I am or what you mean to me."

She remained silent for an uncomfortable stretch, then said, "How could I not?"

"Let me fix this. Please. I've got something special for each of you. Let me try to put things back on the right track." He stepped forward, clutched her hand, and kissed her forehead.

Skye stared out a window and glimpsed a bright moon peek above the Coast Range.

"Let me do this. I don't want the kids going to sleep thinking their dad is the man they witnessed." Skye stayed quiet. He said, "I have to make this up to them. And to you."

She eased a bit. "They were looking forward to an evening of celebration. If they're up for it, I'll do it for their sake. Not for mine.

I need more time to process all of this." She scowled. "Don't you *ever* pull a stunt like that again. I mean it." She checked the time. "I'll ask the kids if they're up for it. You certainly owe them a better end to their day."

Thomas returned with three boxes as the family gathered around the hand-crafted table. He passed the largest to Skye and two equal-sized packages to the children. Dakota appeared relieved by recognizing her "real" father.

"Go ahead, kids, open them up." Thomas smiled cautiously. Dakota's joy pleased Skye; before her stood a hand-carved mirrored image of her mare. "It's Biscuit!" she announced while clutching the likeness and gazing at Thomas. "She's beautiful, Dad."

Johnny responded less enthusiastically about his gift. "Thanks."

Skye leaned toward the kids. "Dakota, Johnny—your father wasn't feeling well earlier. He's very sorry." She expected and received an affirming nod from her husband.

Thomas spoke genuinely. "I shouldn't ever act like that. Or use language like that. Mom and you two amazing kids mean the world to me."

"It's okay," Dakota said. "I know you're a great dad, unlike the stranger using the F-word in the front yard." She stared at Thomas as her parents glanced at each other.

"Mom, open up your present," Johnny urged. He didn't care about the gifts, but he wanted Skye to receive an apology, even if he considered it a guilt-inspired gift from Thomas.

Skye smiled and opened the box. It contained a superb imitation of River, her Appaloosa she spent hours with each week.

"Happy anniversary, Skye. I love you."

Unexpectedly, her eyes moistened. It was a response she assumed

Thomas would misinterpret. *These are tears of uncertainty, not gratitude,* she thought to herself.

The evening wound down with the couple sitting in the glow of their fireplace. Thomas spoke of great moments from the last five years. Skye said little and refused to feel guilty for her angry outbursts. Thomas's bumbling entry and lashing barbs were beyond troubling, even if she'd never heard him lash out like that. Desperately hoping his behavior hadn't been profoundly revealing, she tried but failed to disregard the exhausting possibilities.

Thomas caressed her body as they lay in bed, but Skye gently pushed his arm away, foreseeing an evening of anxious thoughts. Lying on her side with her back to Thomas, her arms pulled tightly to her chest, she rubbed her wrist with an expression of hurt.

The following day, and for three weeks, things trended toward normal in the Westbrooke household. The children were active and happy, pushing Thomas's bizarre behavior to the back of their minds. Skye and Thomas shared time with their horses on local trails that cut through rolling hills with views of the Pacific coastline. Thomas behaved like a model husband; his actions backed up his apologies.

Because life had stabilized and time had lessened Skye's hurt, the phone call caught her off guard.

"Mrs. Westbrooke, so listen, I don't want you to panic. This is something we can, well, eradicate. It's an unwelcome circumstance, of course, but with the right—"

"Dr. Bedford, please tell me what you're getting at."

"The pap smear came back positive. You have gonorrhea."

"You can't be serious."

CHAPTER 22

"I can't even think straight. I thought I had a urinary tract infection. This is bullshit. I'm livid. I must be a naïve idiot for not picking up the clues. He slept with some slut. Now I've got her STD. Unbelievable."

"I get it, Skye," Sadie said. "I'd be livid, too."

"*Livid?* I'm way beyond that. It's disgusting and humiliating. I ran for miles this morning, trying to clear my head. No luck." She pushed her tea away and fell back onto the sofa. "I've got to pick up special antibiotics at the pharmacy . . . that'll be fun. Damnit." She shook her head with a contorted face.

"Let me grab more tea," Sadie said, stepping into her kitchen and returning with a steaming kettle.

"Life was approaching normal just days ago. Now, this." Skye leaned forward, put her elbows on her knees, and pressed her palms to her forehead. She exhaled and raised her head.

Her strawberry blond confidante, Sadie was always the first person Skye sought refuge from during times of crisis. The two ladies sat on a blue sofa in Sadie's small country home. The floors, like the furniture, were well-worn. Sadie occasionally diverted her eyes away from Skye to the former WWII naval airbase across the street; private aircraft took off and landed.

"Skye, look, you need to shoot straight with Thomas. Ask him if he's sleeping around. I'll admit I say that with reservations—he's always been such a gentleman. At least, I thought so." She took a sip of her Earl Grey. "I strongly doubt he's a serial cheater."

"Wrong answer. He's sleeping around. How else do you get gonorrhea? Honestly, I'm leaning toward telling him to move his ass out. I feel so violated, so suspicious." She stared away, rubbing her temple. "Think about it. He may have slept with that slut *on our anniversary.*" She sounded defeated. "It's painful. Our marriage may be over."

"God, I hope not. Here's my opinion: I think he's essentially the man you thought you married. If he were a regular cheating sonofabitch, we'd both know it. He could never go undetected in this town—*especially* not him. Demand the truth and measure his words. I don't know what else to advise. Sorry, I'm hardly helping." Sadie wore a low-cut blouse and tight jeans, her typical outfit.

"You're helping a great deal," Skye said, trying to smile. "Thanks for listening. You're the only friend I could've turned to." She'd been unconsciously swirling her tea with a spoon as if mixing an elixir. The whirling sounds of stainless steel on glazed ceramic filled the room.

"You can stop stirring. Come here and give me a big hug." They embraced. When they separated, Skye's eyes conveyed hurt but also defiance.

"I should go. The kids get out of camp in forty-five minutes. I told Thomas I needed to discuss something important. He got the message; he knows I will not laud him as The Pillar. Should I hide the Ruger in my purse as a backup plan?"

"You're amazing," Sadie said. "Able to squeeze out humor amid all this hurt."

"I was serious about the gun." Skye's smile faded. She grabbed her red leather purse and reached inside for a heavy key chain with its enameled green and yellow Oregon Alumni medallion. She looped the purse straps over her shoulder and moved to the front door with its peeling paint.

"Depending on what he tells you, packing your gun might make sense. Aim for his, well, you know."

"His *huevos rancheros*?"

It was an easy set-up, but they laughed like teenagers, as they had at Eagle Bay Academy.

They parted, and Skye spent the thirty-minute drive mired in silent deliberation. What honorable man does something like this? Her cerebral debate ended as she pulled into Camp Coho.

Two animated children jumped inside the car. Johnny had spent most of his time at the archery range and carried a blue ribbon for winning a camp-wide competition. He won the "under fifteen" contest at twelve years old. Dakota chattered about the "fun and crazy girls" she'd spent the day with, failing to mention she'd defeated a cocky boy in a sprint challenge.

Cruising home through rolling hills provided more time for Skye to think and dissect. As she rolled up the estate, her heart rate accelerated. Surveying their property and the majestic horses grazing beyond the freshly painted white fencing, she told herself to stay calm and focused.

Skye knew women in Eagle Bay who would have advised her to let bygones be bygones. "No way. Hell no," she whispered. She'd made it on her own before they were married; she could still fly solo. She didn't want to be single again; her goal was reconciliation with concessions. Sincere apologies. No more surprises. Love, respect, and truth. She'd demand it.

She stepped out of the car and realized Thomas hadn't yet arrived home. She strolled inside, and her anxieties mounted. The kids ate quickly before getting picked up for overnighters. Finally, Thomas's Jag wound up through their manicured grounds.

He stepped cautiously from their expanded six-car garage to the kitchen. Skye thought he resembled someone carrying a great weight of shame. He should feel like crap, she reminded herself. His right hand clutched a fresh bouquet of red roses, but the flowers wouldn't cut it. She hoped he'd gauged the depth of her anguish. Mid thought, Thomas walked in the door.

"I love you. You know that." His eyes were begging. "I'm sorry for whatever heartache I've caused or the stresses I've put you under." He laid the roses on the counter after Skye expressed no interest in them. He gave her a long squeeze. She stood stiffly, arms at her sides.

Rehearsed words were too easy, she told herself. Does he already know about her diagnosis? Is he apologizing in advance for something else he's done? She found the strength to confront. "What are you apologizing for?"

Turning to glance outside, he took a deep breath before meeting her gaze. "I'm not positive. I have an uneasy idea, but I don't even know if I have the guts to blurt it out. Whatever it is, I'm deeply sorry. You mean everything to me."

His words prompted suspicion. Was he apologizing for multiple transgressions? She hated herself for holding such thoughts. If they persisted, her marriage was doomed. Regardless, she needed to move forward on her terms.

"Thomas, again, why are you apologizing? Tell me now."

His jaw unclenched. "I believe you know I was unfaithful, Skye. These tears reflect my regret. I know nothing I say will remove your pain. It was a selfish decision. I'm sick about it. I hope you allow me to prove my love for you."

She measured his earnestness but wanted to slap him. Suddenly, her composure dissolved. "*I have gonorrhea!* That you got from a slut you slept with!" A broken dam of tears rushed down her cheeks, spotting her light blue silk blouse. "Look what you've done to me. I'm a good person, a good wife. *You pursued me!* Now, this? Damn you. I feel victimized having to explain a pain that *you*, Thomas, *you* inflicted." She grabbed tissues while shaking her head.

"Skye, I'm so sorry. You're an incredible person and a perfect wife. You didn't deserve this, of course. I swear it'll never happen again."

"*Once was too often!*" She hated playing the part of the emotional wreck and struggled to regain equilibrium. Be stronger, Skye.

He approached again cautiously.

"No, give me space. Who was she? Or who *is* she?"

"I got drunk at The Log Stop in Sisters in the middle of our trip. We were joking around, playing pool and darts. I was weak, and she was persistent. I stopped by her place, and . . . one thing led to another." His forehead creased. "And now you're sick. She's disgust . . ." he said with disdain. "I'll never see her again."

"What a stupid comment! And she didn't get me sick—*you did.* 'One thing led to another' sounds trite. I'm not clueless. Did you follow her to her house just before our fifth anniversary? Or on it

. . . Damnit. I don't deserve this!" She gritted her teeth and slapped the counter before grabbing an antique candelabrum to hurl, then gently set it down.

"She's nothing to me. I was a drunken ass who ended up hurting the wife I love. Give me a chance to prove myself, Skye. I *will* be a good husband." He stepped toward her, but she retreated. He stared at the floor for seconds, looked back up, and said, "I'm truly just so damn sorry."

"You lied and cheated, but you're blaming her. You've embarrassed me. You got me sick. If I decide to stay, you're right—you'll be a better husband. *If* I stay." She turned and shook her head below the sunflower wall clock that read 7:05. The banging from a chair she thrust into a table provided no relief.

"You must know I love you," he pleaded.

"I don't know anything anymore."

She told him she'd mull things over and decide their future. As she walked down the hall, she'd already begun reviewing every sentence from their conversation. Was he sincere? His words appeared genuine. Or was he lying? She headed to bed, exhausted.

Thomas stood in the hall after turning off the lights. He locked the front and back doors with their antique brass deadbolts. Stepping in front of the hallway mirror with its thick beveled edges, his eyes narrowed, and he mouthed, "One of you disgusting whores did this. I swear you'll pay for it."

CHAPTER 23

Monica West tested negative for gonorrhea. That news from Sisters, where the single mother lived with her two children, satisfied Thomas. She was paid $10,000 for any distress caused by the testing process—hush money. Two weeks later, she moved to Florida to raise her children near her extended family.

Jo Lynn Brown sounded relaxed when he called. Until Monica's test returned negative, Thomas wasn't sure which of the two women he'd slept with recently had infected him. There was no longer any mystery: Jo Lynn gave him the disease he'd passed on to the wife he loved.

"We're big boys and girls." Jo Lynn was terse over the phone. "Bad things can happen when you sleep around. But it wasn't me—I have no symptoms."

"It's asymptomatic," Thomas said.

She hesitated. "Excuse me?"

"Never mind."

"If I got an STD and passed it on to you, as you say, then somebody gave it to me, and somebody gave it to him. Life goes on. Deal with the hand you're dealt. Your wife's the only innocent here. Unless she's . . . well . . ."

"My wife doesn't sleep around," he said, cringing. He instantly detested her.

"That was unfair of me. I'm sorry."

"I'm aware of the consequences of adultery, Jo Lynn. I must admit I'm intrigued by your lack of regret. I'm torn between applauding your acute sense of reality or viewing you as a despicable bitch who's complicated my life." He checked the time.

Jo Lynn stiffened, standing between her back porch and the river. "Oh, go to hell. Cry me a river, rich man. You see, this is why I'll never get married. You guys pull this holier-than-thou crap. You told me I had the nicest tits you'd ever touched. Remember, Thomas? I do. And you're right; I have an amazing body. It's served me well in the past and will in the future. What do you want from me?"

"I think you've given me everything I need, Jo Lynn."

"Ooohhh. You sound more pompous than mysterious. You should be embarrassed. Anyway, Thomas, I took the next two days off to work in my yard. I've got things to do. By the way, how do I know you didn't infect me? My advice is simple: Remember the good times we had."

Thomas had moved well beyond the implications of discovery. Thirty seconds after what he perceived was a tacit acknowledgment of her guilt, he'd already outlined their futures. Any more time spent on the phone took away from executing his plan and managing his busy life.

"Thanks for taking the call, Jo Lynn. Take care of yourself. Goodbye." He picked up his coffee, licked his lips, and glared out his office window to the business campus's park-like setting. He studied a towering Douglas fir as he collected his thoughts.

The rest of his day involved meetings where senior staff delivered business strategies for his review. The prospects of presenting to the CEO of WCI made even the most seasoned executives anxious. Not because he'd berate management for offering something he viewed as flawed but because his strategic thinking was so far superior to theirs that it was awe-inspiring and humbling to receive his feedback.

Thomas called Skye, who was vacationing in Seattle for three days with the kids. He wished them well and reminded her to buy Pike's Market food and Emerald City mementos for Johnny and Dakota. Skye appreciated his efforts to get their marriage back on solid ground; things were slowly improving.

"I love you, Skye. You're the good in my life."

"Thank you, Thomas," she replied from inside a café while stroking Dakota's hair. The healing process included one cautious step at a time. "See you tomorrow night." Both kids sensed traces of contentment in their mother's tone; they looked at each other and smiled as Skye hung up.

Thomas left the office and sped home. His day wasn't over. He parked in the garage and changed into his riding gear, pleased to have found the opportunity to break in his new Ducati Monster. He replaced both tires with a brand-new set that was wider and stamped with a different tread pattern. He'd read reviews of his bike reaching speeds of 190 miles an hour and anticipated a great stretch on Highway 22, between Eagle Bay and Sisters, where he could test the bike's performance boundaries. The motorcycle was jet black, his leathers and boots were similarly dark, and he wore a charcoal gray helmet.

Exploding out of the backroads, he reminded himself of his conference call with WCI's Chinese agriculture division in six hours. He needed to be efficient with his time.

The ride at dusk through the Santiam Pass was divine. The trees had just begun changing hues. He relished their beauty for thirty minutes before the skies turned dark. His Ducati passed cars as if they were standing still, though he paid little attention to the police detector on the bike's dashboard. The air felt unseasonably warm for an early fall evening.

Upon finishing his conversation with Jo Lynn, his mind was at peace, and he was satisfied he now possessed the truth regarding the gonorrhea's path of transmission. He expected a less complicated and more just future as he traveled down a rarely used forestry service road and parked his throaty bike on a bank above the famous river. The sounds of a dry breeze pushing through noble pines, combined with the spring-fed waters' constant dull roar, were ethereal. He considered how this perfect nature contrasted the inevitabilities wrought by his increasingly twisted soul.

Jo Lynn stood in her kitchen. Thomas knew she'd be home alone, just as he knew there would be no neighbors within six hundred yards. He'd visited her primitive, classic log cabin property twice for drinking and sex. Winter's heavy rains and snows had not yet arrived to swell the meandering waters. Thomas intentionally wore boots that would leave footprints three sizes larger than his typical tread. He cut his way through gathering darkness to knock on Jo Lynn's back door.

She answered with a hesitant smile. "You must be kidding me. I didn't expect to see you, well, ever again. Now you and your killer blue eyes show up at my door after a morning of damning insults. You're here to apologize?"

"If that's what you want to call it. I'm here to set things straight after our difficult conversation."

"Difficult? I'm blown away that you're here, Thomas. So I'm assuming you've stopped blaming me for your problems?" She reached to turn up the flames below a pot of water.

"In a matter of speaking."

"Whatever that means. You are a difficult man to understand."

"I've been told that before." He flashed a half-smile. "I thought we might enjoy each other's company one last time." He winked.

She arched her brows, wrinkling her forehead. "That sounds unnecessarily gloomy. But it also must mean your STD is all healed up." She wore a loose green blouse, skintight Wranglers, and a pair of ostrich-skin cowboy boots. Her dyed-blonde hair contrasted with unusually red, full lips.

"Yes indeed, healthy and happy. We can relax tonight and fade into the sunset tomorrow." Thomas added, "Go our own ways."

"Come on. You drove three hours to deliver that message?" She walked up and stared through her green eyes into the sort of face typically gracing the covers of magazines. Facing him with alluring, slightly buck teeth that added to her attraction, she bit Thomas's lower lip and massaged it with her tongue. "We can live our own lives, so to say, after a nice dinner and an extraordinary dessert." She tossed him the peeler. "But first, you need to work on those potatoes."

He had long ago memorized the layout of her home and surroundings. Knotty hickory walls accentuated the moonlit forest views framed by the cabin's windows. His favorite spot inside was the sitting area next to her river rock fireplace.

"I guess you can't pitch in until you take off your riding gear." She moved sensually up against his body. "Want me to help you out of these leathers?"

"Whoa, not so fast."

He pulled handcuffs from inside his jacket and lifted them with a smile.

"Not quite time for that, honey." She demurred, then said, "But later? Might be fun."

Thomas snapped the strands of the cuffs around her left wrist and secured the other end after lashing them around a sturdy wooden post running from the countertop to the ceiling.

"Really, cowboy, dinner first." She smiled.

His actions weren't aggressive or unnerving, just unexpected. By the time Jo Lynn humorously protested, she'd been shackled to the post.

"You having fun? I'm hungry, so it's time to free your date."

He stared back blankly.

His silence suddenly unnerved her. "Thomas, seriously. What part of *not now* didn't you understand?" Bewildered concern gradually stretched across her face; Thomas had subtly transformed, she told herself.

"The joke is over. *Get these damn things off me.*"

He stepped away to pull the blinds and curtains across every window before dimming the indoor lights.

Jo Lynn panicked and thrashed to pull from the handcuffs, hoping to slip her narrow wrists through the couplings. Abrasions produced droplets of blood that spread across her skin and got flicked onto the grooved pine flooring. She yelled out, questioning whether his intentions were wicked, not just bizarre. That thought pushed her to struggle more violently. She'd never seen *this* Thomas, and that terrified her.

Thomas's gaze remained unemotional, but his movements expressed purpose. He disregarded her fears, moving coolly and precisely. Pulling his leather riding gloves tight around his fingers, he stopped to glance at the horrified woman before wiping down anything leaving prints. He pushed kitchen appliances, cutlery, and Jo Lynn's phone beyond her reach, a precaution he understood was unnecessary. *Leave nothing to chance.*

Shrieking in pain and fear, she pleaded. "Whatever you're doing, whatever you want, just don't hurt me."

He moved about as if he weren't listening.

"Please!" she implored. "I'm sorry we got your wife sick."

"It wasn't *we*, you worthless slut. You, Jo Lynn, *you* got her sick."

She thrashed again desperately. "Okay! Sorry I got her sick." Her face and body contorted.

Thomas moved briskly around the pantry and toward the front door. He listened to her sounds of terror as he strode through the kitchen and out the back. He re-entered, and gasoline vapors filled the room.

"Pain is justice. You're going to pay for hurting my wife and nearly costing me my marriage. I'm setting your home on fire, and I'll watch you struggle and die. Please remember this is justified. Are your swaggering words from our delightful morning chat regrettable now? Tragically for you, it's too late."

"I'm not a bad person," she cried. "I'm begging you. Help me."

"There must be ramifications for our actions in life—that's called reality. It applies to everyone but me."

"No!"

"You're going to burn, Jo Lynn."

"No, no! Please, Thomas, I'm begging you!"

Within minutes she could feel the heat from two roaring blazes. Her skin warmed as a flood of tears fell from her eyes. The only chance to escape was to tear her hands through the cuffs, break the large back patio window, and throw herself onto the deck. She tried again but failed to free her wrists. It was hopeless.

Thomas peered into the inferno from the back window. He wondered if Jo Lynn had resigned herself to dying a horrible death, as he had hoped. Flames darted in every direction, licking the walls and ceiling as if they were alive. Thick smoke swirled inside the room.

Jo Lynn's facial expression unexpectedly transformed into what Thomas measured as some level of tranquility. *How the hell could that be?* Her movements no longer appeared frantic. He grew mesmerized, disbelieving, and enraged. Then he noticed her chest expanding as she deliberately inhaled as much of the dense, suffocating smoke as possible. She met his eyes after her final gasp, and he saw defiance.

The cabin exploded into a yellow and red inferno. Jo Lynn blacked out and collapsed, dangling unconscious with handcuffed wrists wrapped around the post and suspending her body above the floor. She had outmaneuvered him. The brilliant Thomas Westbrooke would be vanquished because his insentient victim would stop breathing before any red and yellow tentacles from the blazing cabin met her body. She would not experience the agony of getting burned alive, the only punishment Thomas and his twisted mind had deemed worthy.

He stopped watching a demise he'd expected to be more painful and terrifying. Justice had not been served. He made his way back across the river with the cabin fully engulfed. His Ducati reflected the intense blaze, and he climbed aboard the bike as distant neighbors released anxious shrieks. Twisting the throttle, he accelerated over desolate country back roads.

Speeding toward home while analyzing the evening, he dissected the absurdity of killing Jo Lynn. It solved nothing, yet he had felt obsessed with pursuing the act of warped vigilante justice. He remembered the priest on St. Croix warning him about one day being completely overtaken by darkness if he didn't change his ways. Had he reached that point? He twisted the throttle further, every curve becoming a precarious balancing act of life versus death. Black skies layered by distant galaxies shone through his helmet's shield.

Inside their barn, Thomas removed the extra-wide treads from the Ducati's rims, the oversized boots he'd worn, and his leather gloves that left no evidence. Flames rose quickly after tossing everything into an incinerator he'd often used to burn debris from stable and field projects. He was steps ahead of the authorities and unconcerned about ever getting questioned, let alone implicated.

He dialed into the call with his China team after showering, during which he acted engaged, composed, and easy-mannered. He settled into a leather recliner in the home's den and recalled the evening's details as he tasted 1958 Fonseca-Guimaraens port.

The killer scrutinized Jo Lynn's final moments while inserting his classic rock CD. He set the volume low and poured himself a second glass. Staring at a photo of Skye set inside a dark wooden frame, the depth of his love for her offered hope. While he knew he should feel repulsed by his actions hours earlier, he just didn't.

In his mind, he had overcome a lifetime of inconceivable burdens orchestrated by an evil father. Jo Lynn's demise was the inevitable consequence of Robert's wickedness, not his. If people knew how the son had persevered after an abusive childhood, they would agree those years of torment and misery would predictably lead to acts of horror.

Roger Daltrey's haunting rock anthem, *Behind Blue Eyes*, continued playing in the background. Thomas absorbed every word. He accepted that people might label him a bad man for today's gruesome crime, but Jo Lynn was guilty on many levels. The anticipation of his future with Skye permitted him to lash out now and redeem himself later. He was exceptional, a prodigy, capable of things other people could never consider, like moving beyond any malice he had inflicted. Today, a complicated man let his tortured conscience exact damning vengeance against a despicable woman. He wasn't proud of it, but it was done.

It struck him that the intriguing lyrics of *Behind Blue Eyes* paralleled the life of Thomas Westbrooke. Leaning forward, he buried his face in his palms and whispered, "Damn you, Jo Lynn."

CHAPTER 24

Skye's financial advisor career ambitions bewildered Thomas. Nonetheless, he complimented her pursuits. Skye assumed he was bothered by the unspoken underlying message: She was putting herself in a position of independence lest their marriage ever crumble. Thomas's infidelity months earlier and Skye's humiliating STD diagnosis had likely inspired her burgeoning career aspirations—he owned that truth. However, Skye was not pursuing divorce; their marriage had recovered better and faster than she'd expected. Ironically, self-analysis related to the cheating saga triggered the realization that a fire of achievement burned within.

Skye sat in a leather chair inside a wood-paneled office in downtown Portland, next to a large window framing a sun-drenched view of the vibrant cityscape. "You scored in the top five percent on both tests," the regional manager informed her. After glancing at his two associates, he stood and pushed his chair away from the table, straightened his red tie, and shook her hand. "We've decided to award you the franchise. We believe you possess the skills and drive necessary for success."

"You're kidding," Skye replied. "Just like that? I thought you said it would take months to make a decision." She was proud of what she'd already accomplished. She'd been studying long hours in preparation for the Series 7 & 66 exams required to become a licensed stock trader and financial advisor. She'd decided to leverage her economics degree from Oregon, to add the dimension of a demanding career to her life with Thomas.

"Typically, these decisions take longer," he continued, "but we've got a good feeling about opening a Hastings & Hawkins branch in Eagle Bay and an even better feeling about you being at the helm."

"I'm thrilled, and you made the right decision. I'll commit to a simple philosophy: If I prosper, so will Hastings & Hawkins." She knew why the decision had been fast-tracked; the company wanted to tap into the Westbrooke family's influential network of contacts. She didn't care. There were no reservations about leveraging Thomas's family name; after the trials and heartache she'd recently endured, it was the least he owed her.

Hastings & Hawkins held lofty expectations. They wanted Skye to develop a portfolio of $200,000,000 in clients' funds under management within five years. The century-old, Seattle-based firm built its reputation by delivering impressive rates of return for clients with net worths of at least $5,000,000. Skye had aimed high and hit the mark; a great opportunity stood before her.

Business soared from the evening of the grand opening. Thomas invited many of his well-heeled connections to the event, and Skye booked eight clients and $22 million under management in her first month. She delivered presentations to business, retiree, religious, and social organizations. Six months later, her client base totaled twenty-one and represented $46 million under management. It wasn't easy, but it wasn't difficult, either. Skye had a talent for understanding financial instruments and effectively presenting opportunities while building trust with wealthy clients.

⟿

TWO YEARS PASSED. STRAINED emotions settled, and family members eased back into their routines. Skye shifted her business into high gear, and it consequently exploded. She would sometimes excitedly calculate her income with a pen and notepad: One and one-half percent of sixty million was $900,000. Hastings & Hawkins took sixty-five percent. The combined costs of her office and equipment, administrative assistant, and a junior associate were $110,000 per year. She'd make $250,000 in this, her second year. Sixty percent of her business came from Westbrooke family contacts, but so what? She'd achieved something significant.

For over seven years, she'd been Mrs. Skye Westbrooke, the homemaker mother of a merged family. She had thrived in that role and was now proud to reinforce to Johnny and Dakota a valuable message about how motivation and a strong work ethic can change one's life at any age. If their mom could build an exciting career from scratch in her thirties, the kids were more likely to believe their possibilities were boundless.

Skye remained convinced that staying married and working through their issues had been the best decision for the family. She'd still occasionally find herself reliving the hurt of his infidelity and crushing barbs, but two years of reconciliation paved the road to renewed optimism and diminished heartache. It calmed her to remember Thomas had unhesitatingly acknowledged she would leave him if there were any future indiscretions.

⌒

SEVEN YEARS GAVE WAY to a decade of marriage; it was now 1996. Thomas remained an involved father and husband. The family was active in the community, both children were doing well in school, and each seemed happy at home and with their teams, clubs, or friends.

Johnny and Dakota occasionally questioned how well they understood their father. Thomas was more private than their friends' parents, and neither expected that would change. But they didn't feel unloved, unsupported, or disrespected. Seventeen-year-old Johnny never disparaged any expression of genuine love and commitment to their family from his father. If Thomas's words and actions appeared heartfelt, they probably were, he told himself. Skye considered Johnny's faith in his father essential. Without trust, families don't function properly.

Skye and the kids believed good days lay ahead.

CHAPTER 25

Thomas began including seventeen-year-old Johnny in outdoor adventure trips. The teenager had proven himself a capable shot with a powerful thirty-aught-six hunting rifle. When they practiced shooting, Thomas grew impressed by how Johnny handled the potent kick of the gun.

Johnny was excited about the hunting outing they'd just started in the steep elevations of Northeast Oregon in the Wallowa Mountains. He appreciated the evening campfires shared with his father's friends. Being there made him feel relevant to Thomas and the world.

"Johnny, did you know Thomas and your birth dad were a couple of hell-raisers in high school?" Bill Dunphy made Johnny smile. He was vice president of marketing for a beer distributorship who carried forty extra pounds of hops and barley on his sturdy frame.

"Well, I guess I shouldn't be surprised. Do you have stories to share?" Johnny saw an opportunity to gather intel on both of his fathers. "Anything embarrassing I should know about?"

Bill laughed. "There are plenty of stories to tell," he said as he scanned the faces around the fire. "I don't want to be the one blamed for spilling the beans. Most of us would have gotten expelled for the shit Thomas and John pulled." He glanced at the other men. "Am I right?" They all nodded with agreeing quips.

Bill continued, "But they got away with everything because nobody in the school wanted to mess with one Robert Westbrooke. He instilled fear and commanded respect." Bill brushed his jet-black hair straight back with his free hand. His rosy cheeks glistened in the glow of the embers. "Thomas, you guys never even got detention."

Huddled around a fire that burned hatcheted logs culled from dead forest limbs, the three other men laughed at the image of Robert Westbrooke showing up at school to "set things right," as he liked to announce. Johnny listened and wished Robert weren't such a mystery to him and Dakota, but he looked forward to learning more about his father during their hunt.

"I'd have to agree," Thomas replied, grinning. "John and I got away with murder." He instantly regretted the morbidly truthful remark, sure that the other men would set intense eyes upon him, attempting to sear his soul. Nothing happened. He told himself that any alarm was irrational.

"Nope, no one could emulate your legendary grandfather." Bill took a swig of his stout ale and continued, "Not that I'd suggest you should want to. It's best to sit back and be entertained by him."

"What the hell is that supposed to mean?" Thomas asked coolly.

Bill said, "Only that he's a complicated man who lives by his unique code. Powerful and successful? Absolutely. But he gets shit done by intimidating. By threatening."

"That's ridiculous," Thomas said more forcefully. "Guys, if you don't mind, I'll mentor my son—thanks. My father's advice helped make me successful. And Bill, Robert's achievements were driven by his strong character." Thomas again questioned why he often felt obliged to defend a patriarch he quietly abhorred. He also knew all the residual angst he confronted almost daily, scars from his father's mentoring, was taking a toll on his psyche. He continued, "It's offensive you'd speak critically about him. He's done more for *your* city than anyone else in the state. It's even more offensive that you'd do this before his son and grandson. Seems inappropriate and ungrateful. Agreed?"

Johnny rubbed his eyes as the smoke danced, wondering what to make of the banter. Grandpa McCloud had always advised Johnny to be forthright, honest, and decent. Grandpa Westbrooke, on the other hand, remained a mystery. Johnny hoped the unsettling discourse would subside as he churned hot embers with a stick, waiting for one of the men to lead the way to less acrimony. Johnny grew unsettled by his father growing even slightly riled. Fair or not, it provoked memories of his fifth-anniversary outburst and the harsh words he threw at Skye.

Bill chuckled and opened another beer. "Let me say this: In your magazine interviews, you always mention integrity and, let's see, stewardship and responsibility. Oh, and charity. That's your mantra, Thomas. And you live it. I'm just saying I doubt Robert lives it the way you do. It's just an opinion. No offense."

Thomas said, "And you'd be dead wrong with that opinion."

Johnny thought the back and forth was ruining a perfect evening. He hoped Thomas would ignore Bill's comments. When he raised his eyes, Thomas's untroubled gaze met his; he wondered what his father was thinking.

Thomas turned to Bill. "You've never been shy about sharing your opinions." He continued, "You want Robert to be the person you claim, but I think I'd be the best judge. Either way, it doesn't matter. We're all just friends sharing a fire and stories in the Wallowas. It doesn't get much better than that, does it?" He swallowed a draw of Weinhard's, tossed a log into the fire, and shot a wink at Johnny.

Thomas's words improved the mood. Bill handed Johnny a beer, who gripped it while shooting a hopeful glance at Thomas. His father extended a thumbs up. Smiling, Johnny twisted off the cap. Bill picked up telling stories about Thomas and John's escapades in high school, and Johnny wondered if he had a friend who was as close as his two fathers appeared to have been.

As the men shared exaggerated stories, Johnny thought Thomas looked uncomfortable. It made sense; he missed John. Johnny realized he and Thomas were each weighed down by painful loss.

"John was a remarkably good man," Thomas said after the recollections subsided and camaraderie pulled the men together. "We all miss him."

"Thanks, Dad. I do, too. People think I don't remember him well, but they're wrong." His brown eyes reflected a sincerity that mesmerized the adults. It wasn't what he'd said but how he'd said it.

Johnny glanced at the dark lab-retriever mix curled up beside him. John and Skye had adopted Crater on his thirtieth day inside a shelter; a veterinarian would've euthanized him the following morning had nobody claimed the skittish canine. Johnny enjoyed the mutt's disposition and loyalty but especially his link to John. He stroked the animal's head and body.

"You love that dog," Bill said.

"I do. Crater's getting old, but he's still the best. We got him just before my fifth birthday. My mom jokes that he's my second guardian angel after Dad. I mean, my first dad—John."

"I love him, too, Johnny. Make sure he stays close to us during the hunt. There are coyotes everywhere. Even reports that wolves are returning to this corner of Oregon." Thomas twirled a twig between his fingers. "Let's keep Crater safe." Bill recommended they kill the fire and get shut-eye before what they all hoped would be a successful day of elk hunting.

The morning was clear and crisp. Five of the largest Roosevelt elk ever taken had come from the surrounding mountains. Nobody was more excited than Johnny, who dreamed of shooting a trophy he'd mount that could also provide a year's supply of steaks and sausage.

Thomas grew impressed by Johnny's enthusiasm and preparation. The teenager had stepped from his tent before everyone except Thomas, who'd taken a break-of-dawn hike alone. While his dad was gone, Johnny started a fire, boiled water for coffee, made orange juice, and assembled all his and Thomas's gear for the hunt.

"My, my, son, you're welcome to join us any time you'd like." Thomas returned in a great mood. "If you'd have tagged along the previous ten years, I'd have eaten better and maybe scored more elk."

"I wouldn't have helped you much when I was six or seven years old." Johnny's still-uncombed brown hair was sticking out in several directions; his eyes appeared partially glued shut.

"*Au contraire*, big Johnny." Thomas straightened and waved his arms at the groggy men stirring before him. "I'm convinced you would've brought me much better fortune than this motley crew." Thomas's goose-down vest and Pendleton shirt mirrored the brown and green of their campsite.

It took the band of hunters another hour to test the cold morning dew and prepare for a trek to their favorite hunting meadow. Hiking away from camp, they heard bull elk bugling in the distance, heightening expectations as they marched in search of the largest species of deer in the world. Mature Roosevelt bull racks measured as much as four feet across.

Father and son settled at the base of the meadow. Frost covered everything, but Johnny was too excited to allow the cold to constrain him. After two hours in the blind Thomas and Robert had constructed twenty years earlier, a harem appeared north of their position. Behind the females, standing tall and proud, was a bull of enormous proportions, the largest Thomas had seen in years.

"Dad! Dad, look." Johnny's eyes grew twice their normal size. Fortunately, the bull was too distant to get spooked by the boy's enthusiasm. He and Crater studied the majestic animal, whose warm breath created billows of mist.

"Sshhh, be still." Thomas began to instruct Johnny. "Now, slowly move to the right, kneel, and use that brace for your rifle. This is your bull, but he's much too far away still. Get set up, and he should move across that section of meadow. He's headed to the creek." Thomas tracked the elk with his binoculars.

Johnny couldn't believe Thomas was letting him attempt to shoot the majestic bull. The elk stepped through lush green grasses toward the rushing creek. Three towering but dead evergreens stood prominently on the far side of the water.

"Aim for the shoulder and chest. You're trying to take out its lungs or heart. You could also target its neck. It depends on your confidence." There was no response; the young hunter grew hypnotized as he tracked the trophy. He wanted no more coaching; he myopically focused on the prize.

Johnny fired off a single round without warning and one hundred yards before the prescribed target zone. Thomas turned livid that he hadn't followed his instructions until he watched in awe as the bull dropped in its tracks. They both stood astounded that Johnny could make that shot, at that distance, through those trees.

Father, son, and Crater moved to the fallen target, thrilled that they'd taken a prized wapiti only fifteen hours into their three-day hunting trip. Thomas's friends had been tracking the elk themselves, assuming it had moved out of range of the Westbrooke duo.

Approaching the downed animal, Bill said, "Wow, Thomas, unbelievable shot. Look at the size of that damn thing. I'm blown away. Congratulations." He was jealous. They all were.

"Well, gentlemen, I hate to deflect your praise, but we've all been outgunned this day. Johnny shot that bull from 250 yards. I couldn't believe it myself. It's his kill." Johnny had never seen Thomas act so proud of him.

Walking as a merged group the last three hundred feet, they approached the fallen elk. Thomas placed his arm around Johnny's shoulders, squeezing and good-naturedly punching him, slapping the bill of the teenager's cap over his eyes.

Circling the beast, the hunters inspected the situation. "Dad, he's still breathing," Johnny said. "He looks like he's panicking. I think he's trying to stand. What do we do? We can't let him suffer."

Bill, his face covered by an unshaven shadow, didn't give Thomas a chance to respond. "Shoot him in the head, Johnny. It looks like your bullet missed his organs and ricocheted into his spine." Bill pointed to a wound on the arc of its back. "He's paralyzed, but he won't die for quite a while. And you're right. He's suffering. Put him down."

Johnny hesitatingly positioned himself for a shot into the elk's head. Thomas interrupted.

"Hold on. If you do that, it means you didn't take him with a single shot. And if he's paralyzed, he's in no pain. Leave him be." The command was precise, unequivocal.

"I can't just leave him like this, Dad," Johnny said. "I don't care if it takes two shots. It's the right thing to do." He squinted. "Bill's right."

Thomas measured Johnny's discomfort as the elk shifted unnaturally, unable to stand and flee. "We can't pack him out of here right now anyway," Thomas said. "Let's go grab the Polaris. He'll die, and we'll load him up and drive him out." He paused. "If you shoot him again, you've diminished the achievement, Johnny."

"Jesus, that's macho bullshit. Let him finish him off, or I'll damn well do it. The thing is suffering, paralysis or no paralysis. I'm serious. Take him out—*now!*—or I will." Bill inspected the loaded bullet in his rifle for emphasis and stepped forward to ready his aim. "I don't even recognize you right now, Thomas."

"Relax. This needn't be an emotional decision." Thomas's blue eyes bore into Bill's, and he put his hand around the barrel. But then he silently told himself to end the debate. It was a good day: His seventeen-year-old son had taken down one of the largest elk he'd ever seen. Disbelieving the advice he was about to impart, he said, "Bill's right. Shoot it in the head."

Thomas then noticed something the other men had observed minutes earlier; Johnny's eyes were moist. With an expression tinged with compassion, the teenager took a purposeful stance, steadied his aim, and fired a killing round.

CHAPTER 26

Early the next chilly morning, before the adult hunters and Johnny had awoken, Thomas quietly prepared to hike up a steep trail while it was still dark. Like many extraordinarily successful individuals, he needed little sleep to be productive. Few people could keep his hours and not hit the proverbial wall.

As expected, Crater heard his rustling and was at his side as he began trekking up the trail. Thomas appreciated the beauty of Northeast Oregon's terrain: stunning valleys, majestic crags, undisturbed streams, and abundant wildlife best viewed at daybreak.

At the crest of a peak, man and dog settled to enjoy the revelation of blankets of sunshine stretching beyond mountain faces and meadows. Thomas petted the handsome canine and found himself further impressed by his disposition.

But then, he slowly grew disturbed by what the dog represented.

Thomas stood conflicted by his decision. Hesitations born of morality presented unwelcome burdens. He understood that any consternation with the impending moment would soon pass. He knelt and peered directly into Crater's brown eyes before kissing the dog's silky coat. Its warm breath soothed his leg at the cliff's edge high above a valley. "Your only crime, buddy, is of being a constant reminder of the man you represent. I'm sorry."

Nightmares of killing John had been stalking him recently. And even though he'd fully renovated the home John once shared with Skye, transforming it into a shell of its former appearance, he'd been unable to extinguish his friend's eerie presence. Thomas's thoughts grew foreboding.

Peering eye-to-eye with the man removing his collar, Crater exploded into a wild frenzy, baring teeth and preparing for battle with an enemy exposed through millenniums of evolved instincts.

Amidst the sounds of fury, Thomas clutched the loose skin on Crater's underside and muscled their bodies to a steep granite face. The crazed animal flailed viciously at Thomas's arm, but the dog was old and the human too strong. Thomas flung Crater over the cliff, hearing nothing else but knowing the result. Then he stepped forward to peer down and recognized the dog's silhouette partially obscured by the brush he had rolled into after crashing into massive boulders. No animal could survive such a plunge.

Ten minutes later, after time spent in his unique manner of personal reflection, Thomas began his descent to base camp, disgusted by his actions. He leaned over thick brush and vomited. Further down the trail, he tasted tears.

When Thomas returned, the other outdoorsmen were slumbering, so he built a fire and boiled water for coffee to coax them into the frigid air. He reached into his vest pocket, grabbed the dog tag, and tossed it into the middle of the rising flames before pitching more logs into the blaze.

One by one, with tired eyes and faces not yet handsome, Johnny being the exception with his chiseled good looks, the men made their way to the aromas of fresh brew. Coffee brought them to life.

"Well, Johnny, is that dog of yours trying to finagle his way into the meat locker to feast on your fresh kill? You know, I only eat elk steaks untouched by canine paws—or any other canine parts. I'm funny that way."

The other campers were not yet sufficiently awake to laugh at Bill's humor; they only smiled and nodded in agreement. The burning pine crackled, and smoke rose straight up, eliminating the need to rotate around the fire pit to relieve burning eyes.

"I don't know where Crater is," Johnny replied. "I assumed he was out here peeing on trees or chasing birds. Did you see him when you got up, Dad?" Johnny was holding a tin of hot apple cider.

"Actually, no," Thomas replied. "I haven't seen him yet. I assumed he was still sleeping after the excitement of the hunt and kill yesterday. Don't worry, son. He'll show up within a couple of hours. He always does." He threw another log into the pit.

"What about the coyotes and wolves you mentioned?" Johnny asked. "I mean, they wouldn't be hanging around our camp, would they? Watching him, tracking him? We should search for him, don't you think?" The prospect of leaving the wilderness without Crater was too much for him to consider.

"I'm sorry," Thomas began, "but if he wandered far from camp during the evening, there's a chance he could've encountered predators. These mountains are chock full of coyotes, wolves, cougars, and wolverines. But let's assume he'll show back up."

"He slept with me last night," Johnny said firmly. "We need to look for him."

"*Stop, please*. I don't know what else to tell you," Thomas said. "He'll probably show up. If he doesn't, you'll need to accept that these can be dangerous mountains for a dog. Let's all hope he's okay."

Johnny realized he'd irritated Thomas with the conversation, which confused him. None of the campers said or did anything to lessen his anxieties. Rubbing his eyes and scanning the forests and meadows surrounding them, he looked for a wagging tail. He walked the area while listening for clues.

The other hunters assumed the wayward pet would return in a heap of dust at any moment. But one day later, the experienced hunters accepted Crater was likely gone forever. They hated knowing that the loyal friend who'd served as an emotional bond to Johnny's biological father had vanished. The men unsuccessfully attempted to lift the boy's spirits as they packed up. The group reached their SUVs in the late afternoon of day three, transferring their supplies and securing the ATVs to the trailers.

Back at base camp, buried below six inches of accumulated ashes from days of fires, lay a scorched black plastic tag. Barely legible were portions of a phone number and letters that had once spelled out "Crater."

Johnny remained stoic during the long drive home. He grew uneasy knowing that his faith in Thomas, which he'd cautiously resurrected over the previous few years, had just suffered a massive setback. As the truck rambled up their estate's driveway, Johnny stared out the rain-streaked window, burdened by grief and the weight of distrust. Was his father capable of hurting his dog?

CHAPTER 27

Weeks had passed since the hunting trip. Johnny was helping Skye with yard projects on a sunny and dry fall day. He entered the garage looking for a spaded shovel.

Like most young people, he was curious and recognized an opportunity while making his way to the other side of the six-car garage. The bottom drawer next to Thomas's custom workbench remained ajar. It typically remained closed and protected by a keypad security latch. His father had been called away minutes earlier for an urgent business call. In his haste, Thomas hadn't fully closed the drawer.

Johnny inspected the contents. Lying inside were sixteen bizarre drawings. They looked to be depictions of old, perhaps ancient, relics. Johnny initially assumed his father wasn't the artist, but he found boxes of high-quality colored pencils. He wondered if the images represented an occult obsession. Lying beneath the art, he found the detailed professional blueprints of a chamber or vault. None of it made any sense.

"Hi, honey; what are you up to?" Skye had quietly strolled up.

Johnny tossed all the pictures and blueprints back into the drawer. He reflexively wiped his palms on his shirt and bit his lower lip.

"Johnny, your father wouldn't be happy knowing you were rifling through his private things. How could you think that was okay?" She removed the leather gloves that protected her hands as she cleared brush from behind the stables.

"I know, I know," he replied. "But the drawer was cracked open, so I just pulled it out. It's no big deal. He'll never know."

"I'll never know what?"

Johnny twisted awkwardly.

Skye flashed her husband a look of disappointment.

"I'm sorry, Dad. I was only checking it out. Curious, that's all. Everything's just the way it was." He found it impossible to interpret his father's reaction.

"It's okay, relax," Thomas said. "Do you have questions about any of it?" He reached down, pulled his colorful designs out of the drawer, and placed them on the workbench, leaving the blueprints alone. He put his hand on Johnny's shoulder and smiled.

Johnny said, "Well, they're sort of strange. Weird animals, tiny people, weird objects. The only one resembling anything normal is the sun. Did you draw these?" Johnny looked at Skye, expressing confusion.

Skye glanced at the image on top of the pile. "Is that John's sun pendant?" She wiped the sweat from her forehead. "Did you draw that? It's remarkable . . . but why do it? You've never mentioned any of this." She stared, genuinely confused, careful not to act accusingly in front of Johnny. "Didn't you ask me about that thing years ago?"

"Yes, I told you back then I thought it fascinating. I still do. Then I just decided to draw it, along with this other stuff. It's a hobby. Keeps me out of trouble." Thomas grinned and winked. "All these images are Thomas Westbrooke originals. Any critiques?"

Johnny sensed Thomas was hiding something; he believed he'd

stumbled onto something important. Something telling. He wondered if Skye held similar thoughts.

"You're talented," Skye replied softly, appearing preoccupied.

Johnny thought he could read Skye's dismay. He concluded it would've taken his father days to complete just one of the detailed drawings.

"Let's respect one another's privacy in the future." Thomas patted Johnny's back and handed him his shovel. "Right now, why don't you help your mom finish clearing the brush?"

Skye flashed a strange look and began walking toward the stables, putting her thick gloves on as she marched. She wore jeans, a white T-shirt, and brown boots. A cheap and weathered straw hat completed her manual labor outfit.

Johnny, similarly outfitted minus the hat, caught up with her. "I know I shouldn't have been digging into his stuff." They veered down a dirt path. "But it's bizarre, right? Sketching strange things in the garage? Never telling us he could draw like da Vinci? Locking it all up? And blueprints? Totally weird, don't you think?" He quickened his pace and craned his neck to interrupt Skye's assertive march straight ahead.

"Stay out of his stuff," she snapped. "It's none of your business what your father does with his own time. Do you tell him everything you do on the weekends or at night? Never you mind." She continued walking aggressively to the stables, not making eye contact.

"Okay, relax. I get it," Johnny replied. "Forget I ever brought it up." Having reached the piles of debris, he kept his mouth shut and transferred the weeds and clippings to a black trailer. Mother and son spoke few words to each other the rest of the afternoon.

Today's episode was just the latest experience Johnny put under scrutiny. He assumed his mother believed Thomas had reformed since his cheating and belligerence five years earlier. Maybe he had; she'd know better than anyone. But Johnny was skeptical.

He lay in bed dissecting years of observations: Thomas seemed oddly distant from his parents. Neither Westbrooke grandparent showed genuine affection for Skye, Dakota, or him. Thomas cheated and gave Skye an STD (he'd overheard that news as Skye discussed it with Sadie in the kitchen). Diego vanished days after his parents had arrived from their honeymoon; had he really stolen from them, as Thomas claimed? His father wanted to let an elk suffer and seemed unaffected by Crater's disappearance. And finally, he discovered the strange drawings and a set of blueprints. *What the hell was going on?*

Thomas had to be orchestrating layers of deception. Skye would draw the same conclusion if she'd witnessed what he had. But Johnny paused to challenge himself: Was he *positive* Thomas was a damn liar and schemer? Such claims could ruin his parents' marriage; was he willing to influence that outcome?

Johnny spent weeks reflecting on his concerns. The more he examined, the more emboldened he grew. He felt the truth lay behind the veil of Thomas's insulated image. Embracing one of his father's oft-repeated phrases, he agreed that *knowing is controlling*. He would uncover the truth and then act—whatever that meant.

What he didn't realize was that Skye was steps ahead of him. Thomas's drawing of the sun pendant John had worn the day he'd disappeared and his resolve to keep the image locked away triggered an avalanche of suspicions. Things weren't adding up.

CHAPTER **28**

One week after Johnny discovered the strange etchings, Thomas's business travels took him to Buenos Aries, Lyon, and Geneva. When Skye inquired about which business interests required visits to those cities, he answered politely but vaguely that the travel was necessary due to "intricate financial matters." When she pressed for more detail, reminding him that she understood financial matters quite well—*I am, after all, a wealth advisor*—his clarification remained ambiguous. Thomas's recent tentativeness and the peculiar etchings incident pushed her life back into uncomfortable doubt and uncertainty. It was time to force a conversation.

Thomas stood with an expression of annoyance.

Skye had made no progress.

He checked his watch. "I have no idea what you're talking about. I've had a long day and have a meeting in the morning. Please, Skye, can't this wait? It doesn't seem important."

"You've got a meeting on Saturday morning?" Skye asked. "And are you aware of how condescending you sound, Thomas? After the discovery in the garage with the drawings—including John's sun pendant—I'm shocked you aren't making more of an effort to communicate. To explain things." She waited for a response but received none.

"This can wait."

"No, it can't wait. That's what I'm talking about. I suddenly feel like there's a growing divide between us. I want to talk about *us*, and you act as if it's no big deal. It's our marriage, our future, that's all. Can you spare a moment to speak with your wife?"

"What's with the antagonism? Did a girlfriend put you up to this?" He removed his suit jacket and loosened his collar. "Or are you just in a bad mood?"

"Thomas, please. Stop for a moment and think about what you just said, how you're talking to me. This isn't you. At least, it hasn't been you."

He didn't reply and scrolled through missed calls on his cell phone.

"Put the damn phone away!" she snapped. "And yes, my *girlfriend* agrees that you and I need to talk. I confided in Sadie because she's always been there for me." Growing furious as he remained staring at his phone, she derided, "Including when you cheated with an unnamed slut and gave me gonorrhea."

"Not tonight." He slowly lifted and shook his head. "That was five years ago. I was sorry then. I still am."

She persisted. "Sadie's the one who's helped me move past it. To forgive you. You should send her a 'thank you' card on our anniversary. Give her and me respect. I'm just trying to improve our marriage." Her face begged for compassion while she silently pleaded for him to realize how hurtful his words had become.

"You're tired and looking for an argument, Skye." He moved closer and spoke dismissively. "I'm not taking the bait. You need to calm the hell down, okay? Don't do or say things you'll regret. That's the best way to harm a good marriage. Don't push my buttons."

"Where's this heartless machismo coming from? I'm confused. And heartbroken."

He exhaled and rolled his eyes.

She glared. "I'm bothered by your growing apathy about me, about us. Show commitment and have an adult conversation. Like you used to, not so long ago. Don't dismiss me like I'm an ill-conceived business idea."

Thomas frowned, turned to grab his coat, and bellowed, "Damnit, Skye. I'm not having any more of this. You sound neurotic."

"Neurotic?" she said, her voice cracking. "What's happened to you?" Any hopes for reconciliation evaporated. "You pompous Princeton ass. Why have you decided to disrespect me *now*?"

"I respect you, Skye. You are successful. I'm impressed. Even if most of your flourishing business came from my family's contacts."

"Wow," she said. Her shoulders drooped. "You're becoming un-caring . . . and mean. What have I done to deserve this?" She wiped her eyes. "Poor Emma, I wonder if Robert treats her like this. That *Oregonian* reporter said the Westbrooke men have all been unusually mysterious. Maybe they've been much more than that—none of it good." She glared, hoping to pierce his invulnerability.

"Robert's a better man than anyone you know." He switched off the kitchen lights. "My father and I are complicated people. That's how we achieve things. And never forget your place, Skye. You're just along for the ride."

Her mouth fell agape, and her expression froze in astonishment. *"Are you kidding me?* So cruel and heartless. What about the beautiful things you've been saying about me for the last decade?" Tears streamed down her face. "Are these your true colors? Were they repressed for too long?" She tried to prevent it, but bursts of sobbing interrupted her words. She forced herself to get composed. "Yes, you and Robert *are* complicated. But newsflash: John may have been less accomplished by Westbrooke standards, but he was a far better man than either of you could *ever* be." She had hoped she'd never utter such a snarky comment.

Thomas let the words settle. "So, John still rules the roost in your pretty little head. Interesting. You know you're fortunate, right? I mean, I could've married any woman I chose. Agreed? But the thing is, Skye, I wanted to marry you. It might be more accurate to say I *wanted* you and got you. Just as I wanted the company we acquired in Phoenix. I wanted it, and I got it. See how this works?"

She stepped forward in her dark slacks and red silk blouse. Clenching her jaw, she raised her hand as if ready to strike but lowered it. "Oh my God. How patronizing can you get? Get out of my house! Get the hell out *right now!*"

Silence.

"I mean it," she continued. "I was praying my feelings about you changing were wrong. I swear I was. You've just removed all doubt about what you've become. Or who you've always been. Listen to yourself, Thomas. So unkind, so deplorable. *Get out!*"

"You can't mean that."

"I can and do, damnit."

"Are you this pitifully misguided about your current standing? Do you believe you can demand Thomas Westbrooke leave *his house* on your command? Please don't act confused. You're embarrassing yourself. The kids are happy and understand how privileged they are. As you should. Now, I'm going to my bed, in my bedroom, in my house. Good night."

She stepped in front of him, her body quivering. "You bastard. John bought this house for *me*." She slapped him hard across the face with her right hand; her manicured nails scraped his lips and cheek.

His reflection in the Country French mirror revealed blood dripping down his chin. His styled light brown hair had become disheveled. He grabbed her by the neck, pinned her against one of the hallway walls, and sneered. "I believe you're only tired and in a rare foul mood. Your gracious husband is going to let this pass. He's a good man."

"I, I ca . . . I can't breathe . . ." Skye's face turned red. Her eyes bulged.

"Tell me you're sorry." He spoke calmly. "You brought this on, and we'll end it on my terms. Tell me you're sor—"

Out of his peripheral vision, he caught a flash of movement and turned. A shadowy figure flew at him, dressed in nothing but white briefs. Johnny was airborne before Thomas could digest the threat. The son began pummeling the father.

"*You sonofabitch!* You freak. Leave Mom alone! Leave her the fuck alone!"

"Get off me, Johnny! I don't want to hurt you, but I will if I have to."

"Shut up. Go to hell! You were choking her!"

"Thomas, Johnny, stop! Both of you! *Please stop!*"

"Look at his face. He looks evil!" Johnny yelled. He swung at Thomas wildly, failing to land his punches.

Dakota dashed from her bedroom in a pink nightgown, screaming.

Thomas collected himself and hit back. He threw an elbow into Johnny's head and dazed him. He struck him in the solar plexus with such force that air exited his lanky body. Johnny rolled over, crumpled, unable to respond. Skye and Dakota pleaded for Thomas to stop, but it was already over.

"*Damn you!* You've hurt my son. I'll never forgive you for this, *never.* You're a terrible man, and I hate you right now. Get out of here. Leave us alone." Her words masked real fear.

Struggling to breathe as he got to his feet, Johnny moaned, "You choked Mom. You'll never be my dad again."

Thomas turned and stepped slowly into the kitchen. He sat down with his elbows on his knees, staring at the floor as his right hand rubbed his forehead.

Time felt suspended. Dakota cried in her mother's arms. No one spoke.

Thomas walked to a counter and grabbed Skye's set of keys. He returned to the hall where his wife and children huddled. "I'm sorry. I didn't mean anything I said." He handed her the keys. "It's probably best for you to leave for the evening."

"Kids, get dressed." Johnny and Dakota walked to their bedrooms in silence.

"You shouldn't have provoked me," Thomas said. "Let's work this out tomorrow after emotions settle." He removed his red tie and carefully folded it. "Again, I'm sorry."

"Work this out? We're *finished*, Thomas." She stepped forward assertively. "We'll never live under the same roof. You're despicable. Think about what you've just said and done. Our marriage is over on *my* terms, not yours." She attempted to slap him, but he grabbed her arm midflight,

Squeezing her wrist progressively tighter, he stopped just before she appeared ready to scream out and slowly released his clutch. "Please, Skye. I said I was sorry."

"Who the hell are you?"

"A man who loves his wife and children. I couldn't be more sincere about that."

"Right now, I feel that couldn't be further from the truth. I'm sure the kids would agree."

Johnny listened from his bedroom and unzipped his duffel bag to grip the pistol he'd packed, ready to bolt toward his parents with the loaded weapon. He heard Thomas walk across wood floors and step out the front door. Johnny shoved the gun back inside the bag. He and Dakota continued packing.

With moist eyes, the siblings walked silently toward the Land Rover. Thomas watched from the porch, expressionless.

Skye approached him. "I've seen through you. I'm devastated. But let me reiterate, this ends on my terms. Deal with it."

They drove off the estate peering through wiper blades screeching against the front and rear windows. Gusts of wind pushed birch and aspen leaves across the landscape, many stuck to the SUV's windows. As Dakota looked back at him, Thomas barely moved, his silhouette fading.

In a voice laced with grief, she asked, "Mom, what's happening? Why's Dad acting like this?"

"I don't know, honey." She haltingly added, "Everything's going to be all right."

"Are you and Dad getting divorced?" The words were as uncomfortable for Skye to hear as for Dakota to utter.

"I'm sorry you both had to overhear any of that. But we're a strong bunch. We'll get through this." She quickly turned over her right shoulder to offer her daughter a reassuring smile. When she turned to Johnny in the passenger seat, his expression was grim, jaw stiff, and eyes intense. "You okay?"

"I'm fine," he replied. "You should divorce him."

Skye struggled to remain composed while unsettling thoughts whirled in her mind. What had triggered the avalanche of crushing barbs Thomas had just delivered to the woman he seemingly cherished for so long?

CHAPTER 29

"Of course, Skye, head on over. Cody's here. See you in ten minutes."

Skye had discussed concerns about her marriage with her best friend only twelve hours earlier. Would Sadie be able to fathom Thomas acting as cruelly as he just had? He'd been unintimidating their entire marriage, minus one disturbing fifth-anniversary episode. Skye forced herself to embrace an unsettling adjective for tonight's behavior: frightening.

They turned off Highway 101 toward Sadie's home, which sat on a parcel of unfenced property and backed up to hundreds of acres of farmland. Headlights illuminated three cords of firewood stacked on the right side of the driveway, up against the side of the house. Flowers that brightened the yard and entry through spring and summer had wilted as the cool moisture of late fall had arrived.

Cody and Sadie were each nearing forty and had dated for eight years. Skye couldn't grasp why they hadn't married. They owned their homes and lived independently but shared each other's company several nights a week. Cody managed a logistics organization for WCI.

Cody's imposing physique was visible as the family approached "Aunt" Sadie's house. The gentle giant, a six-five First-Team All-State basketball selection out of Siuslaw High School, advanced with an expression of compassion.

Swinging Skye's door open, Cody whispered, "I'm so sorry." He glanced at the passenger seats and perked up. "Hey, Johnny. Hi Dakota. Grab your stuff. There's hot chocolate inside." He got both teens settled into bunk beds in a spare guest room. Cody understood they would've preferred their own space, but under the circumstances, he thought they might want to dissect the evening in each other's company.

Skye removed her raincoat and placed it on the hook of a wooden coat rack Cody had built by hand. Her hair appeared matted by rain. As she described the drama, she faced expressions of disbelief. "Everything's changed. This is the end of our marriage. I didn't recognize him."

"It all sounds . . . crazy. Impossible. I just expected you two would talk and work things out," Sadie said.

"He completely lost it when I forced the conversation." Skye shook her head. "He was so demeaning and hurtful."

"Did he make any threats?" Cody asked.

"He grabbed my throat and punched my son! Forget about threats." Skye glared at Cody. "He was just so perverse. He even smiled while choking me—a sinister smile, like Jack Nicholson in *The Shining*. I should make a police report. You guys agree?"

"You have to make that call," Cody replied. "We weren't there. I'm struggling with everything you've just described. It seems impossible." He poured Skye two ounces of Jim Beam and placed the bottle atop the blue Formica. His massive hand delicately presented the glass.

"Thanks." Skye lowered her voice. "That's just it, Cody. I swear Thomas isn't the person we all thought we knew. *He hurt me.* You know how something you witness changes a long-held outlook in seconds? That's what just happened. I don't think we know my husband."

Beams of light flashed through the front windows. They were surprised to see an Eagle Bay Police Department cruiser park behind Skye's SUV. The recently promoted Sheriff Boseman, a young lieutenant who met Skye the morning of John's disappearance, was soon tapping on the front door.

"Hello, folks. Sorry to bother you, but I'm looking for Mrs. Westbrooke." His green jacket and hat were dripping wet. "I noticed her car in your driveway and need to speak with her. Can I come inside?"

"Yes, of course, Sheriff," Sadie said, confused.

Skye overheard the entryway conversation and grew unnerved as he walked into the kitchen. "Hello, Sheriff. It's been a long time."

"Your husband called us, Mrs. Westbrooke." Sheriff Boseman wasn't halted by her beauty tonight, as he had been the day of the boating accident and John's disappearance. "He's accusing you of being verbally and physically violent. He's also concerned you might hurt yourself. I was hoping you'd come down to the station. It might be less confusing for your children if we did this in the precinct."

"Whoa, slow down. How about some fact-finding? And how'd you know my kids were here?" She grew annoyed as he continually glanced at the bottle of whiskey.

"Just assumed, ma'am." He added, "Do you want to hurt yourself, Mrs. Westbrooke? Or the children?"

"Oh wow, it sounds like you believe his lies. I'm not going to hurt myself. The kids? Get real. Look at my throat—*he* did this. I'm the one who needs to press charges. Take my statement. And go ask my husband for the truth." She'd often been impressed by how easily Thomas could redirect people and resources for good causes. Was he doing it now for vengeance? Is that why Sheriff Boseman showed up?

"It's your right to file a complaint, Mrs. Westbrooke." He added, "We'll need to take photos of any injuries. But with all due respect, I see no abrasions or trauma on your neck. Regardless, documentation of injuries should happen downtown."

She rushed over to a mirror in the hall bathroom. "It was much worse at the time, Sheriff. He choked me! Sadie, Cody, tell him."

The couple stared at each other for an uncomfortable moment, neither speaking.

"Hello?" Skye said, perturbed.

Johnny rushed into the kitchen. "Sir, I saw much of it. Don't believe anything my father told you. And I don't like how you're talking to my mom—*she's a victim.*" He stepped between Skye and Sheriff Boseman.

"Relax, son," the sheriff said. "I'm just trying to determine what happened."

"She told you what happened!" Johnny exclaimed with hostility.

"Young man, you need to leave this room," the officer said. "Is this going to be a problem?"

"Johnny, I'll be fine. Keep Dakota company. Everything will be okay." Skye admired his protective instincts. Dakota watched the exchange from the hall.

"Her neck was redder when she arrived, Sheriff," Cody interjected. "It's probably easy to choke a woman without causing abrasions. I mean, I'm guessing so. I can't speak from experience." He shook his head, realizing how stupid he sounded. "I'm saying I believe her, as you should. She was distraught when she arrived, and I'm sure her kids will back her story up."

"Then I recommend we get downtown to take photos and file your complaint," Sheriff Boseman said. "And to discuss Mr. Westbrooke's claims of domestic violence. We've already recorded your husband's injuries. He's receiving medical attention."

"*Ha!* And the evening gets stranger. He's one in a million. How pathetic." Skye lifted her brows. "Medical attention? He needs a shrink. Fine, let's go." She looked around. "Where's my purse?" She walked across the kitchen and grabbed it, wondering why someone had moved it to the other end of the counter. "How long should this take, Sheriff?" She grasped her raincoat, shrugged it on, and pulled her hair from beneath the back collar.

"There's no guarantee, Mrs. Westbrooke, but probably less than three hours."

She turned to Sadie and Cody. "Do you mind watching the kids? I'm so sorry about this, guys." Struggling to appear fully at ease, she squeezed Sadie's arm as she passed.

"Don't be silly," Sadie murmured. "I'll grab some snacks for the kids, and we'll try to settle their nerves."

Skye stepped inside the small bedroom with its low ceiling covered in years of white paint. She gave Dakota a firm embrace and forced a smile. Johnny told her the truth would prevail.

Dakota blurted, "But how can they do this to you, Mom?"

"It'll be fine, honey. Your mom's tough—just like her kids. You are in good hands, and I'll see you shortly." Skye blew a kiss as she left the room.

The sheriff informed Skye she'd need to be transported downtown in his cruiser. She was humiliated while being handcuffed and placed in the back seat. "Is this necessary, Sheriff Boseman? It seems ridiculously suspect."

He informed her it was standard protocol for transporting alleged domestic abusers. *I'm not a deadbeat criminal,* she silently proclaimed, shaking her head in disbelief. The stainless-steel cuffs were cold, bulky, and uncomfortable. She remained incensed but grew resigned.

As the car backed out of the driveway, sixteen-year-old Dakota stormed out the front door begging for her mother. The evening had destroyed the innocence of her youth. Cody rushed to comfort her, leading her back to the warmth of the ranch-style country home. After watching car lights fade into the mist, Sadie filled her fireplace with dry timber.

The car was cold and sterile. Passers-by peered into the rain-splattered side window as they moved through town, startled to see a beautiful woman inside rather than the typical young male. Skye stared straight ahead.

She walked into the Eagle Bay Police Department, thankful that the big drama of the evening would soon be behind her. It still seemed unbelievable Thomas could deride her as he had, let alone choke her.

"Mrs. Westbrooke, this is Sergeant Sweeney; she'll process you before setting you up in an interview room. Seat her in 6B, Sergeant. Get her something to drink."

Skye watched his ego get mollified as he barked orders. The fluorescent lights were so abundant that her eyes hurt from the reflected white. The metal detector she approached looked brand-new.

"Please pass through," the sergeant said. "I need to search your purse on this platform. You can wait right there," she motioned to a nearby table with three chairs, "to observe me pulling out the contents."

Skye obliged and took a seat, paying meager attention to the officer's rummaging for a weapon that was not inside.

"Marilyn." The sergeant grabbed the attention of one of the precinct administrators. "Get the sheriff back up here. A large bag of what looks like meth is in the subject's purse." She pivoted. "Can you explain this, ma'am?"

"What?" Skye wasn't sure what she'd just heard. "What are you talking about? I don't even know what meth looks like, and I certainly didn't walk in here with any. You're mistaken, or somebody's put it there. You understand?" She stood and stepped in the direction of the sergeant.

"Stop, ma'am. Please stay seated."

Skye wanted to cry, flail, and scream. She was astounded by the pace and gravity of developments. She inaudibly yelled out, *Help me! Someone make things right!* She stared at the sergeant. "I'm innocent. It's not mine. I'm a good person."

Sheriff Boseman overheard the exchange as he entered. "Get it to the lab." He stared into Skye's eyes with disgust, judgment painted across his face.

Her dilemma had grown intolerable. "That's not mine. I've never so much as smoked a joint. Ask around. It was placed there by someone. Sheriff, you returned my purse to me after I got out of your car." She pointed at the sergeant. "And that woman just rifled through it. You're the only people who've touched it since I left my home."

"Mrs. Westbrooke, I have no idea how the substance entered your purse. You can blame me if it helps you through this. You'll need to be drug tested. The number of narcotics in the bag warrants a distribution charge, not just possession. When did you get involved in illicit drug trafficking?"

She recognized he enjoyed patronizing her. The man who'd shown so much compassion during John's disappearance now seemed intent on embarrassing her. But soon, his ridiculous accusations and pompous expressions relaxed her. She'd been the victim of a perverse ruse and would simply have to prove it.

He snapped her back to the moment. "Can you explain the narcotics, Mrs. Westbrooke? If it proves to be methamphetamine?"

Becoming convinced her experience was motivated by a husband's revenge gave her strength in a way that only the truth can. She told herself to control her breathing and say as little as possible to a sheriff she'd now measured crooked. She gained strength. The sheriff sensed her transformation.

"I told you; I don't do drugs. I certainly don't sell drugs. This is ludicrous." Her eyes darted between the sheriff and sergeant. "I want to call a lawyer."

They'd played her as the fool. Had a lifetime of trusting those around her made her susceptible to the vagaries of a charlatan? It won't work, Thomas.

"As you wish," said the sheriff. "Sergeant, book our suspect on charges of distribution of methamphetamine and spousal battery. Allow her to call her lawyer. Forward me the lab results."

"Spousal battery?" she repeated as if the charge were comical, then chuckled. "How pitiful."

Minutes later, Skye quietly mouthed, "I'm going to expose you, you deceitful bastard." She sat back in her angular metal chair with plastic armrests, woven fingers in her lap. Locking her jaw, she glared at Sheriff Boseman and the sergeant, pondering how a single day had so profoundly altered the course of her life—yet again.

30

CHAPTER

Skye made two calls from the Eagle Bay Police precinct. First, she dialed Steve Collins, an old classmate from Eagle Bay Academy. He'd graduated with honors from Oregon State and Stanford Law School and got recruited by the top law firms in Silicon Valley, Chicago, and New York. But even in high school, Steve told classmates he could never leave the state of Oregon for too long. "God's country," he'd labeled it. Thus, he ultimately accepted a position at Steel River in Portland, the most prestigious firm in the Northwest.

"Steve, this is Skye Westbrooke . . . or Skye McCloud." She wasn't sure how to proceed. "I hope you've been well. I'm sorry for calling you so late. The thing is, Steve, I'm in jail. In Eagle Bay."

"Skye, it's great to hear your voice. Even at midnight. Take a deep breath and tell me what's going on." Sitting on the edge of his bed in blue and white striped boxers, he put his glasses on and grabbed a pen and paper.

"Steve, I'm being set up, or the sheriff's just mean and spiteful. Or both . . . I don't know. Somehow a bag of meth got into my purse. It's crazy. They have no right to—"

"Stop." *Meth? That's not the girl I remember.* "What are the charges?" He brushed back his black hair and rubbed tired eyes with a bent finger.

She surveyed the precinct. "I can't talk too loud; it's not private. They're charging me with domestic violence. Spousal battery, I guess." A homeless-looking man was watching her from his seat. She lowered her voice, "And the distribution of meth. They're crazy charges."

He smiled into a window reflection from his high-rise condo. "So the domestic abuse charge involves Thomas?" A view of Portland glimmered beyond the large pane of glass.

"Yes." Skye recalled that Steve and Thomas had never developed a close friendship at the Academy.

"Tell me what happened."

"I was trying to engage Thomas in a discussion about our marriage. He'd seemed indifferent lately after years of being a wonderful husband. He erupted into this heartless, vicious person. Like something I'd never seen before. I slapped him because he deserved it."

"Lady, I'm a nice guy," uttered the homeless man sitting nearby.

Skye turned her body away from the stranger, maintaining her grip on the wall phone. "My son tackled him while he was choking me. Thomas hit him—*hard*—and told us to leave. The whole thing was crazy."

"Anything else?" Steve didn't need another reason to dislike the mysterious Thomas Westbrooke. Nonetheless, he'd just found one.

She paused. "Now Thomas is telling the police . . . well, I don't know what he's saying. I think he's orchestrating some strange revenge, even though that sounds irrational when I say the words."

The Pillar of Eagle Bay, the heralded symbol of Eagle Bay. This was all quite interesting to Steve. He wanted this case. "Skye, one of my associates will drive down tonight to post bail. I'm tied up in court tomorrow, but I'll drive to Eagle Bay later in the afternoon. If you choose to have us represent you, I can promise you an active defense with the best legal team in the Northwest, if I may be so bold."

"Do you believe I'm innocent?"

Guilty people often ask lawyers that question. "Yes, but we've got other things to focus on." He checked his body in the window and sucked in his gut, then opened his nightstand drawer and pulled out a Butterfinger.

"But I swear I've never seen meth, never used it, never bought or sold it—nothing. Someone placed it in my purse." She waited for his response, not focusing on what he said but on how he said it. She needed an ally.

Just then, a drunken woman in a blue dress, high heels, a dirty fur coat, and reeking of sweat and cheap perfume was escorted past Skye by a policeman. The woman overheard part of her phone conversation and slurred, "We're all innocent, princess."

"I heard that," Steve said lightheartedly.

Skye shook her head.

"Steel River would like to represent you," said the lawyer. "The charges sound implausible. The ball's in your court. All I need is a green light."

"Green light given. I want to prove Thomas trumped up this whole thing. Something sinister is going on."

"You haven't changed one bit." Steve circled her name on the paper and smiled. "Intelligent and righteous, among other impressive traits." He quickly realized how inappropriate that had sounded. "Before you go, I want to say I was sorry to hear about John's passing. He was a special man."

"Thank you." She sighed. "He was a rare soul."

"So here's what happens next: Sean Kennedy, one of our top young guns, will drive down and bail you out. Hole up at a trusted friend's or relative's place. Please don't talk to Thomas until you and I have met. Clear?"

"Yes." She let out a deep sigh. "I'll see you tomorrow night." Her watch showed 12:45 a.m. "I guess that's technically tonight."

Her second call was to Sadie.

"It's so good to hear your voice," Sadie said. "The kids are asleep. What's going on? Cody and I have been sitting next to the fire discussing everything. It's all so—" She stopped herself. "I'm sorry. Tell me what you need."

"Thanks. I'm charged with domestic violence and the distribution of meth. A bag of it was in my purse, and a lab test proved it was indeed meth."

"Meth? What? Are you—"

"Wait, please. I've spoken with Steve Collins. He's agreed to take my case. One of his lawyers is on his way here. I'll be back at your place in less than three hours."

"Okay. Wasn't Steve the co-valedictorian of our class? The guy who split all the awards with Thomas? Sorry, I'll shut up. You can stay here for as long as you'd like. I know we're tight on space, but—"

"I'm going to call the McClouds to see if we can settle there. I've got to run; see you soon." Skye turned around to find the sergeant standing nearby.

"I'll begin processing your discharge. When your lawyer arrives with bail, we'll release you."

Skye glared. "I think you or the sheriff is corrupt." She realized the woman might not be guilty of anything, but her suspicions had indicted both. "I'm going to prove it." She finally followed Steve's instructions and shut up. Solving riddles would have to wait.

CHAPTER 31

Skye woke up wondering if it had all been a bad dream, but she recognized Sadie's home, not the master bedroom she shared with Thomas. The kids slept as she joined Sadie for coffee, and thirty minutes later, the landline phone rang.

"Hello, Sadie. It's Thomas. Is Skye free?"

Sadie felt uncomfortable having to speak with Thomas in Skye's presence. "She's busy right now and needs rest and space, okay?" She fumbled through the conversation with a man she'd always admired.

"Tell her I love her," Thomas said. "And give the kids a hug. Remind Skye I had to press charges because Johnny and Dakota shouldn't have to see their mother in that state." He paused for a long moment. "And tell her we can work through our issues. I'll be at her side as we confront her demons."

"Okay, Thomas. I need to go." Sadie hung up.

"What did he say?" Skye asked. She'd accepted her marriage was over, but she simultaneously and, she realized, foolishly longed for signs of genuine remorse.

Sadie replied in a monotone voice, "He said he loves, and he had to press charges for battery because you're setting a bad example for the kids. Says he'll be at your side as you work to overcome your demons." She lifted her brows.

Skye released a sad laugh. "I hope you don't believe any of that crap. Talk about removing all doubts about whether my husband's a fraud." As she spoke, a look of incredulous condemnation settled in. "He's conned me . . . but for how long?"

Cody arrived and started a fire inside the river rock fireplace; escaping smoke indicated the chimney needed sweeping. The evening's drama got circumvented through a classic Sunday morning of bacon and eggs, coffee and orange juice, newspaper sections passed around, and a football game on television. It smelled and felt like fall. Hours later, Skye thanked Sadie and Cody for their support and drove her family to the elder McClouds' home.

The initial week of news reports that Skye Westbrooke had gotten arrested for spousal battery and methamphetamine distribution stunned the community. It seemed implausible that the well-respected wife of the CEO of WCI, a successful Hastings & Hawkins financial advisor and a pinnacle of goodwill herself, could be charged with such crimes.

Oregon had a burgeoning problem with meth abuse, especially in the coastal towns. Analyses concluded the state had the country's highest meth usage per capita. Neighbors hotly debated how and when the epidemic reached every segment of society, even the noble Westbrooke family. Sadly, misguided or frightened locals were pleased to see the crisis unfold; it allowed them to cope with the problems of drug addiction permeating their own households.

Dealing with the fallout was particularly difficult for Johnny and Dakota. "Hello, princess, can you score me a hit of your mom's rock candy? What'ya say, sweet thang?" The popular Grant Stark caught Dakota off guard with his movie-star good looks and easy manner.

"Get away from me. My mom's never used drugs in her life, loser. Go hang out with your dumbass friends."

Eagle Bay Academy classmates considered Dakota attractive, intelligent, and independent. Like her mother, she was an outstanding barrel racer and excelled at soccer. But she was senselessly insecure and unaware of how many classmates envied her skills and aptitude.

Grant had half the female student body dreaming about him. "Here's my number." Dakota's hand trembled as she feigned disinterest but accepted the note. "If you wanna hang out sometime down by Squaali River or the bay, gimme a holler. I'm not the rebel troublemaker you might think. But you're definitely hot." He flashed his smile, and her knees almost buckled.

With Grant several paces beyond her, she snapped back, "Dream on." Then she breathed deeply and floated on air.

"Grant, there's no reason to be talking to my sister." Johnny had caught the end of their exchange and confronted the reputed Casanova. "Can't you find a loser skank to hit on? I don't want you talking to her. Is that cool? Just leave her alone."

"We're cool, Johnny. No problem," Grant replied, looking like a fashion idol in his jeans, blue shirt, and bomber jacket. "I won't chase down your sister. But it's not my fault if she calls me, right?" Grant smiled at Dakota as she put his phone number inside her backpack behind Johnny's back.

"I don't need to worry about that because she's smarter than you'll ever be, Grant. Don't expect a call. See you at practice." With their testosterone-filled pleasantries out of the way, Grant left the siblings alone.

Johnny turned to his sister. "Dakota, you don't want to know this guy. He seems okay, and I know all the chicks in school think he's quite the dude, but he's an asshole. Who knows what he's really about?"

"Don't worry about me. Worry about yourself," she replied. "I'm fine and can make my own decisions."

"No need to jump down my throat—just be careful. Grant's bad news." She didn't appear interested in anything he said, so Johnny changed the topic. "Hey, have you taken much heat about Mom's arrest? Holding up okay despite all the stares?" Johnny felt like the entire school had eyed his every move since he'd set foot on campus. They were standing on the edge of the quad, on a wide cement walkway surrounded by cut grass and towering pines. Robins and blue jays in the trees darted back and forth to gray metal lunch tables, their incessant chirping mixing with the students' conversations.

"Oh, you know," Dakota said. "The usual BS. Everyone thinks they know Mom better than I do. And everyone thinks you and I are spoiled rich kids. What about you?"

"Same BS. I hang with my buds and ignore the rest." He heard the bell ring; they had five minutes to get to class. "As Grandpa McCloud says, it's your family and friends who get you through life."

"God, I love Grandpa. He breaks things down to simple truths," Dakota replied in a sad voice, almost too quiet to be heard. She smiled, "Stop looking at me that way. I'll be fine."

Johnny had grown more concerned about how most guys stared at Dakota, though he understood why they did. She was a stunning sophomore: five-ten with thick brunette hair, huge green eyes, and olive skin. Grandpa McCloud called her Dark Irish. Johnny didn't want the Grant Starks of the world getting too close, believing she was vulnerable.

While Skye and Thomas had met once and spoken several times since her arrest weeks earlier, the two teenagers and their father would reunite for the first time later today. Steve Collins advised Skye that Thomas had ample legal rights to visit the kids. Johnny would attend solely because he didn't want Dakota to be alone with someone he could never trust again.

Thomas picked them up from school and drove them to the only home they'd lived in before the dramatic evening that changed their family. So far, the conversation in the breakfast room next to the kitchen was unemotional. "Well, it appears you kids are holding up well under the unfortunate circumstances."

The teenagers remained quiet.

"I'm very sorry, Johnny," Thomas continued, "for striking out at you. You're strong, and you were hurting me. You tried to protect your mother, which I admire, but you didn't see what had led up to that moment."

Johnny stared around the room, looking for the salt-and-pepper shakers fashioned after Oregon lighthouses he'd grown up with. He wondered where the wooden bowl that used to sit on their counter was; their father had made it with a lathe at the Academy. He turned disgusted; Thomas had gotten rid of memories of his birth father. Johnny assumed it was a calculated move meant to cause heartbreak and pain for him and Dakota. *What other reason could there be?*

Thomas said, "I love your mom, but she was unrelenting that evening, and I merely attempted to stop the violence. You understand?"

"Dad, did you grab her by the throat and smile?" Dakota asked, her voice cracking. "That's insane. How could you do that?"

"I needed to settle your mother down, Dakota. But who told you I was smiling? That's patently untrue."

Her eyes shifted to her brother.

"Come on, Johnny, let's be honest," Thomas said, pressing back into his seat. "The entire episode was excruciating. I put my hand on her shoulder to lower the tension. She continued to slap me. I reacted to protect both of us." He lifted his shoulders and turned his hands palms up.

"You're lying," Johnny shot back. "All you do is lie. You were smiling." He glanced at Dakota and in a firm voice said, "He was smiling."

"Johnny, please, it sounds like it was just an adult argument that got out of hand." Dakota set her iced tea down, determined to fix her broken family. "Dad didn't mean it. He loves Mom." Her eyes begged for agreement.

"You know why I've recently stopped calling this guy 'Dad'? Because he's not the person we thought we knew." He put his sunglasses on, stood up, and added, "And maybe never was."

Thomas waited for Dakota's reaction.

"*What?* What a terrible thing to say, Johnny. You don't mean it. Tell Dad you're sorry."

"No! Wake the hell up, Dakota. He's a damn liar," Johnny said. "Don't believe anything he says."

"Johnny, please stop," she cried.

"He was choking Mom so badly she couldn't breathe. Maybe he's always been like this. Maybe he's changed. Who knows, and who gives a shit? We done?" Johnny thought Thomas's expression affirmed everything he'd just said. He felt vindicated.

"Your brother thinks he has all the answers." Thomas let out a deep sigh and stood. "We should wrap this up." He handed Dakota her coat and said, "Perhaps in a day or two, you and I can hit a Dutch Brothers and chat in the car. I know you love their white mochas." He pressed his hand to her cheek and smiled.

"Fine, you two go chat," Johnny said. "There'll be no more chats with me. I don't recognize you anymore, *impostor*. You're no longer my father. I'm serious. You threatened Mom and somehow got her arrested on drug charges. And I think you know what happened to Crater. Maybe you even did something to him. You keep playing games and bullshitting us. My dad and father was and is John McCloud, who died in a boating accident with his best friend, but that friend turned out to be a liar whom I no longer choose to be around or call *Dad*."

"What are you saying? What do you mean? Of course he's our father. How can you say that? I love you, Dad. And I know Johnny does, too." Dakota wiped the sleeve of her sweatshirt across her eyes.

Thomas said, "It's okay. Pack up, and I'll drive you two back to the McClouds. Johnny, you know I love you, and my door is always open. I'm sorry you're feeling so disappointed in me. You simply don't understand. Adult relationships can be very complicated. I hope we can all work this out. Please give me that chance." He placed his hand on Dakota's shoulder and guided her to the front door.

"I'm a lot smarter than you think I am, impostor. Grandpa McCloud says I'm perceptive. I'm not happy about everything I said—it didn't feel good. But you're the only one in this family who ended up being someone different than expected. You said terrible things to Mom that night. You choked her and got her arrested. You're full of shit."

"Enough of the absurdity. Let's go," Thomas said.

Johnny stepped closer. "Our mom's amazing, the best. But you pull this crap? Why'd you even marry her?"

"I married your mother because I loved her, son. And I still do."

"Bullshit. You're a fraud. Never call me son. You're acting."

Thomas said nothing as he stretched his leather driving gloves over his fingers. Moments later, he stepped to Johnny, peering eye to eye. "Do you think the CEO of WCI could've guided the growth and success he did if he weren't a talented man? Would I have given millions to charities if I weren't a generous man? I'm certainly no charlatan. I'm exactly whom people say I am, Johnny. I'm The Pillar of Eagle Bay."

"Whoa! What a lame response." Johnny dared Thomas to lose his renowned cool and strike him. "He's insecure, Dakota. He knows I'm right. I don't care about any of the newspaper and magazine hype. You inherited a ton of money, so what? You pose for magazines. BFD. Mom earns her money. I know what you're really like. I've seen it. I didn't want to believe it for years—I swear I didn't—but I do now. I finally get it. You're just a nasty dude."

On the drive home, Dakota sat in the front seat, despairing. Johnny's jaw remained gritted, his muscles tense. He was sure he'd penetrated a thick veneer of deceit.

Thomas's fists gripped the leather-bound steering wheel. His knuckles twitched as his heart rate increased. He looked into the rearview mirror and met Johnny's eyes. Neither man blinked. An unwelcome urge built: Thomas wanted to hurt his son.

CHAPTER 32

Steve and Skye met six times in two months; the local Embassy Suites served as their gathering place. Steve considered Skye more focused when sitting in a room away from the elder McClouds' home and her Hastings & Hawkins office. Today it was Steve who found himself distracted by views of stormy skies and white-capped surf.

Like Thomas, Steve often wore impressive hand-tailored suits. Unlike Thomas, he was not in impeccable physical condition. His six-foot frame carried an extra thirty-plus pounds. Still, Skye considered him handsome, strong, and confident. She also thought he appeared more Italian with each meeting.

"Are your parents from Italy?" she asked. "It's an unrelated question, but I'm curious. Maybe on your mom's side? You never looked Romanesque while at the Academy." She paused to smile. "But today, you look like you might have gladiator ancestry." She assumed he'd lathered his scalp with a hair product; he combed his shiny black hair straight back, emphasizing facial features that now seemed strikingly Italian.

He spread Philadelphia cream cheese onto an onion bagel. "If you want me to be Italian, then I am." He lifted his brows, stood, and poured fresh decaf into Skye's generic white hotel coffee cup.

She opened her briefcase and said, "That sounds like a pickup line. I was just curious, bar guy." Peeling back the top of her coffee creamer, she mixed it in with a spoon and leaned forward, sipping ersatz caffeine.

"Fact is, my dad got stationed in Italy during World War II," he said. "He was a field surgeon who earned his stripes saving soldiers."

"Wow," she said. "Are you going to tell me he met a beautiful Italian woman in the village? They fell in love, married, and lived happily ever after."

"That's precisely what happened," he replied as he added even more cream cheese to his bagel. "They moved to Scottsdale after I graduated from the Academy. Mom needed a respite from the rain. They spend their summers at Lake Como, near her family."

"So, there it is," Skye said. "For once, I've guessed someone's heritage correctly."

"That you did." He turned sideways. "Look at this nose; it screams Roman gladiator, doesn't it?" He hoped the banter would continue.

Skye nearly inquired further when something told her not to. She'd enjoyed their time together preparing for the case, perhaps too much, she thought. Seconds later, she asked herself why that would be inappropriate, but then she concocted good reasons and refocused on the legal business.

A long, embarrassing moment of gazing into each other's eyes ensued.

Steve cleared his throat. "Skye, none of Thomas's bizarre actions make sense. There's typically something to point at. Were there significant changes to his work routine, lifestyle—anything?"

"I'm not sure how to answer." She stared through a dirty window and listened to studded tires roll over wet streets. "For months, I'd assumed something specific, like his health or work stress, was affecting his moods. But now I'm wondering if he'd always been like this but somehow concealed it. That sounds ridiculous when I say it."

Steve licked his lips, clicked his pen, and jotted some notes.

"You've known him for years," she said. "Don't you think his personality's changed? It sounds like another stupid question from a wife, but I'm at a complete loss to explain his behavior. Regardless, things have passed the point of resolution. The kids need less anxiety and more stability."

The skies grew darker, and sensors switched on streetlamps, though it was only mid-afternoon. Winds from a fast-approaching front pelted rain into the windows. They watched wet maple leaves sweep against glass panes, their fall hues sticking and fluttering.

"You know we weren't great buddies at the Academy." Steve offered a bagel and continued, "We were always cordial, but I found his father and him to be unnecessarily cryptic. I also thought he might be unscrupulous—I can't put the finger on why. I figured he'd flourish in professional pursuits because he's brilliant and cunning." He set down his pen and leaned back in his chair. "You asked. There you have it. But my opinions don't matter."

His expressions revealed more than his words: Steve undoubtedly disliked Thomas. Skye wondered if he considered her stupid for marrying such a man.

"Most people's sentiments verge on veneration, as you know," she said.

"Understood," he said dismissively. "About the case, it's going to be impossible to prove the sheriff or sergeant put the drugs in your purse. You're obsessed with that determination, but cases rarely get won by fixating on a single discovery. It's never that easy."

"It's your job to prove it," she shot back while pacing in a green blouse and white skirt and rubbing her hands together. "No one touched my purse at home the night Thomas choked me. Either Sheriff Boseman inserted the meth while I was in his squad car, or his female sergeant placed it inside after I arrived at the precinct." She walked over to a coffee cart, absentmindedly added more brew to a cup she'd barely emptied and noted that even darker clouds were moving in from the west.

"It won't fly. We'd be more successful proposing one of your children or Cody or Sadie put the drugs in your purse—establishing they weren't yours."

"*Are you nuts?* My kids sure as hell didn't place drugs in my purse. Neither did my two best friends. I don't mean to sound unreasonable, but I'm paying you serious money, Steve. One of those two officers, or both, placed the meth in my purse. You need to prove it. It's a key to the case. The truth is slipping away." She'd moved from charming to annoyed and aggressive.

"You hired me for a reason. Let me do my job."

"So you can suggest my kids set me up to get arrested on drug charges? Are you serious?"

"The point is, simply claiming something as plausible—but not being able to prove it—is a losing strategy. We need to build a convincing case for a jury if that's where this ends up." They locked gazes. "One that justifies the money you're paying me." He lowered his head and peered over his glasses.

Her nerves frayed. *Life* was taking a toll. She knew she was acting irrationally but wasn't ready to admit it, so she changed the subject. "I want to accelerate our divorce. You know, I took my vows with Thomas seriously. After our blowup, I even foolishly debated reconciliation. But the train has left the station. I'm also meeting with a priest to discuss an annulment. Anyway, I'm hoping you'll personally coordinate my drug case *and* divorce."

"I'm sorry you have two deal with all this, Skye. I realize it's difficult, but I admire your grit. Please know that." He was delighted to get the green light to handle her divorce from a man he considered dishonorable. He said, "So listen, I'm comfortable we can negotiate half of all the assets accumulated during your marriage. We'll initiate an in-depth financial discovery. Dissect the family's wealth. Make sense?"

"I'm not going to need *half.*" She nodded disapprovingly. "Only negotiate something that'll allow us to live comfortably, cover medical costs, education expenses, the horses—you know what I mean. My business has been going well; the 'drug dealer' headlines haven't affected my client list." She pursed her lips and nodded. "More than anything, the kids and I want *our* house back."

He rose from his seat and stepped forward. "Thomas has a considerable sum of wealth. You deserve what courts have established your share. As your friend and lawyer, I'm telling you it's appropriate to get aggressive." He continued cautiously, "Particularly considering your devotion to the institution of marriage, and his lack thereof, based on unearthing we've done. I'm assuming you already knew that."

"Knew what?" She appeared in physical pain with her lips pressed tightly together. A moment later, she asked, "What unearthing? Even beyond the fifth-anniversary fiasco? Oh, God . . ." She suddenly felt emotionally exposed. If Steve was going to rattle off a litany of affairs, she wasn't mentally prepared to confront them.

"We had to build a profile on Thomas to prepare for your drug defense."

She measured her anxieties in a window reflection. Acute clarity replaced unease. "Okay, go ahead. Get aggressive."

"It's the right decision."

"I'll call Thomas Saturday morning about the divorce and let you know how it goes." She offered a weak smile, grabbed her long brown raincoat, rummaged through her purse for keys, and stepped to the door.

"*Bon chance*," he said.

CHAPTER 33

Silence filled both phones.

Finally, Thomas asked, "Are you looking for a response?"

"I needed to let you know what I've decided. It's best for me and the kids," Skye said.

"It is? You've gotten ahead of yourself, Skye. You've got a drug charge that needs defending." He stared at a framed photo from their wedding. "I still love you. Did you spend any time considering reconciliation? Keeping our family whole? Committing?" They were sincere words, though he knew Skye would consider them preposterous.

"You're amazing. Frightfully so." She shook her head, squinted at the receiver in her hand, and said, "First of all, I didn't get myself into this *problem*. Someone named Thomas placed it in my lap. Secondly, you've become violent and mean. Do you honestly believe anything that happened that night was my fault? That would be ludicrous." She walked outside. Her in-laws' property backed up to a forest of maple trees; their trunks swayed in opposing directions amidst shifting winds. The smells of damp forest were palpable. The setting was soothing, but the conversation was not.

"Is that your defense? That your husband, who loves you eternally, has also set you up to get arrested for meth distribution? It's illogical and won't sell in court. You know that." He held the bottle of Scotch upside down, draining the last quarter ounce.

"Thomas, you've become talented at shifting facts and my words to suit yourself. It's wacky and unhinged."

He didn't respond.

"And my business may suffer from the bad publicity. Clients will grow uncomfortable investing with an alleged meth head. I've worked hard to build my client list, and you're building these damn roadblocks."

"Why would I try to destroy a business my contacts built?"

"Oh, please, not again. I hope I keep every client if only to prove they're investing in me, not the Westbrookes."

"This is my reward for giving you a pampered life?"

"You gave me a privileged life, not pampered—that's your ego talking. But you know, all I ever wanted was love and respect. And more recently, sanity. You became detached from the one thing you insisted you loved so much: me. You don't love me, Thomas. You love the *idea* of me, of possessing me—as you said yourself that crazy night you choked me." She wondered again what had pushed him to such behavior.

"Annulments are ridiculous. But pursue it if it makes you feel less guilty for ruining our marriage. I only acquiesced to a church wedding to appease you, to make my future wife happy. Religion brings a burden of unnecessary guilt."

She sensed his relief as he liberated himself from the bonds of yet another deception. She asked herself why a man with a previously unspoken contempt for faith would conceal his true sentiments for so long. Why exert the energy to pretend?

Skye sat on a cedar mortise and tenson hand-crafted bench, wiping moist eyes with her sleeve. "I genuinely loved you for much of my adult life. Now I pity you, Thomas." She struggled to accept that she'd married an appalling man. With the receiver to her ear, she wondered which phases of their life together he'd been duplicitous. Could it have been all of them? Her body shivered.

"I don't want to get divorced. I love you. I don't think I can be any clearer. You are hearing what I'm saying, right?"

"*Stop!* You. Do. Not. Love. Me." She heard him inhale deeply.

"The tragedy is, I do, Skye. So very much."

"Then you're pathetic, not just twisted. I need to go. Steve's going to beat my drug charge. We still believe you orchestrated the whole thing. Steel River will oversee my interests in our divorce. Contact Steve directly regarding anything about the matter. I don't want to talk to you moving forward. Goodbye." Skye waited for a response but hung up after seconds of silence.

Thomas scanned the family's stables. The horses huddled below the protection of a wood canopy. He'd made several notes pulled from the conversation and embedded them deeply into his memory. He walked to the hand-carved Asian bar with its inlaid Mother of Pearl, grabbed a new bottle of Glenmorangie, and slowly poured himself a small glass. He dialed Robert.

"Robert, it's me. I just hung up with Skye." He'd called him "Dad" only once as an adult, from Princeton, after he'd gotten drunk on a case of Heineken.

"And?" Robert was characteristically quick to the point, raising his polished wood pipe for a draw.

"She's committed to divorce."

"I figured she would be. She's a capable nemesis. Your lack of discipline has put the family in a bad spot. We'll address that later. Any chance you can get her back into the fold?"

Thomas recalled Robert once telling him Skye was an intelligent woman, like the younger Emma. It wasn't a compliment but a warning. Thomas had worked diligently to get any support for the idea of marriage. Robert's only guidance had been never to let any woman stand in the way of his duties of protecting the family's good name and the assets. Finally, he replied, "Back into the fold? Doubt it. She sounded resolute."

"Damnit, Thomas, I was right again. You used to be more predictable. Your carelessness is a huge problem for the family."

"I am my father's son. And my father is a contemptible man with a dark heart. You are the reason I'm losing Skye, the only good thing in my life."

"Stop with the self-serving pity. I've spoken with Sheriff Boseman. I know all about the ruse going on. Let's review. First, a reminder—you murdered your best friend. Then you married his widow. Now you've set her up to fight ridiculous drug trafficking charges." Robert's condescending laugh echoed through the phone. "And I'm responsible? I'm genuinely worried about you, Thomas. So much so that I've decided not to give you the codes to the vault, as I'd told you I'd do earlier this year. I don't know if you're under too much stress or if your marriage has affected your decision-making. Whatever it is, it's too great a risk to grant you unfettered access to the assets." He paused. "Never forget, I'm pulling all the strings."

Thomas wanted the vault codes desperately. But there were multiple ways to attain them, he thought. "You're pulling strings? That's delusional. I've overseen the family's business interests very well.

Don't irk me with any of your disjointed moments. And my issues with Skye don't affect our family's affairs." Thomas was confident a divorce wouldn't cause any harm to the dynasty or revelations of the Westbrookes' dark secrets.

"It's a good thing I've kept my mind sharp." Robert set his pipe on the table. "You don't impress me with your ability to assess risks. Who's going to represent Skye in court?"

"Steel River. Steve Collins. You might remember him from high—"

"Steve's a talented lawyer who will win a weak case. Steel River will want to look at our companies' books and bank records. That's a potential disaster, Einstein. For someone the business community considers a brilliant mind, such a visionary, you can sometimes be as incapable as your mother."

Extended silence.

"You need to listen carefully," Thomas said. He'd prepared his speech. "I'll never repeat this. My life has been an enduring commitment to your design and desires. I've tried for twenty-five years, since the day you turned me into a murderer at age *twelve*, to gain total independence with no success. I consider my loyalty to you to be peculiar. It remains oddly binding. I shamelessly laud your achievements and doggedly fulfill your aspirations. But my inability to resolve who I am versus who I could have been has made me more reckless, vile, and warped than even you can imagine, Robert. I'm advising you to stop with the insults and broken commitments." He awaited a response. The line went dead.

Robert placed calls over the next hour to two trusted confidantes: Luigi Bucaso in Sicily and Antonio Salazar in Buenos Aires. He delivered identical instructions. "Not urgent, but a heads-up. Sometime soon, I may be forced to allow cursory access to the assets. I want everything scrubbed and everything prepared for transport. Be ready, rehearse, and don't screw up." Westbrooke assets lay secured inside bank vaults in Geneva, Lyon, and Buenos Aires.

Thomas's cell rang thirty minutes later.

"Hola," said Antonio Salazar. "Your father just called regarding a potential transfer of the assets. What do you want me to do?"

Thomas had guessed right. Robert had grown profoundly unnerved by images of Steel River lawyers and accountants swarming the family's banks. Robert had put Antonio in charge of managing millions in non-US assets stored in Argentina. But Thomas had covertly offered him $500,000 a year to act as a double-crossing informant. The Argentine understood that aligning with Thomas could be a more beneficial long-term relationship. Though Robert was sharp of mind, Thomas was unquestionably the future of the Westbrooke dynasty and its secret assets.

"Interact with my father as if you'll carry out his demands, then call me with updates before any assets get relocated. Understood?"

"Sí, of course," Antonio replied. "It is a pleasure to assist a partner who fully appreciates my contributions and value. Buenos noches."

Thomas thanked him and hung up the phone, simultaneously calculating how to eliminate the Argentine pawn who knew too much. He also dissected numerous courses of action to free himself from a lifetime of shackles Robert used to control him. Of course, there was only one way to do that.

CHAPTER 34

July 15, 1971

Thirteen-year-old Thomas was busy sketching. Over the past year, he'd spent countless hours detailing images of the same object. Taking a moment to stare out at meadows from the barn's loft, he noticed someone walking next to the white fences crisscrossing his family's acreage. He gathered all the papers, tossed them inside a wooden box, and hurried down the ladder.

Thomas bounded across a lush green meadow with a smile pasted across his face. It had been one year since being forced to drown a man in a pond on their estate. Simple interactions with friends and schoolmates helped erase his nightmares. He would learn later that his demons were impossible to fully vanquish.

A pretty thirteen-year-old brunette in a white knee-length skirt and a blue top walked northward with a yellow daisy fashioned into the white ribbon binding her hair. She daydreamed while walking next to the fencing with a three-foot branch she slid up and down the pickets. A black and white puppy followed her, expressing the joys of a nature walk as only an unleashed dog can.

"Hey, Gabriela, what's up?" Thomas asked, his heartbeat increasing. He studied her face and grew mesmerized by her beauty.

"Hi, Thomas. Walking home this way saves Gonzo and me a ton of time. I'm not supposed to be on the"—she flashed air quotes—*'Westbrooke property,'* but it's stupid to walk another half mile to get home, right? Where's your sister?"

"Sarah's on a Girl Scout trip to Georgia for ten days. Gonzo's a funny name. What does it mean?"

"It's short for Gonzales, my uncle's name. I call them both Gonzo."

"Oh . . . So, do you like living on Johnson's farm, Gabriela?"

"It's awesome. My dad's in charge of everything now, so we get to live in the manager's house."

"Gabriela, your dad only works there. Mr. Johnson's in charge of the farm because he owns it." He spoke matter-of-factly, not considering his words insulting.

"Uh, nice try. Mr. Johnson told me yesterday that my dad's in charge of the *whole* farm. What a dumb thing for you to say."

"Whatever, it's not a big deal. Would you like to go inside our barn? It's pretty cool." The Westbrookes' capacious red Century Barn was the most impressive in Sea Cliff County.

"No, my dad would freak out. Crossing your fields is one thing. Hanging out in your barn would fry his brain."

"Why?"

"My dad and Mr. Johnson say your dad's a jerk. And a bully. They don't respect him."

Thomas drew his head back. "He's successful. Mr. Johnson's a crappy farmer; we'll buy his land for a low price one day. We'll own it."

"Says who?"

"Says my father."

"Well, I doubt it. My dad also says your dad hates Latinos. You know my family's Mexican-American, right?"

"Well, actually, I thought you were just a Mexican, but it doesn't matter to me."

Her mouth opened wide. "Don't you *ever* say 'just a Mexican!' I'm leaving." She marched away.

"Whoa, Gabriela—relax. Yes, my father's racist. So was his father. Mr. Johnson's right about that. But I'm not like them. Honestly." He changed his voice to a gentler tone. "Come on, I'm sorry. Let's head to the barn. Your dad won't know. Bring Gizmo."

Her anxieties settled when she stared into his handsome face and welcoming expression. "It's Gonzo. But listen, you need to learn not to say terrible things about people like you just did. It's not okay."

"I know. It was totally right to call me out." He offered a warm grin and held out his hand. They walked over mowed fields; the cut blades and surrounding vegetation offered a comforting blend of country fragrances.

They entered.

"Wow, this is the nicest barn I've ever seen."

"I love it here. It's where McCloud and I hang out."

"How's John doing? I haven't seen him in weeks."

"He's a camp counselor and gets home on Saturday."

"We think it's funny that the two hottest guys in Eagle Bay are best friends."

"Who's we?"

"'We' is every girl I know."

"None of that matters. I'm just lucky John's my friend." His face appeared frozen in devotion.

"Wow, you said that like you worship him. Do you?" She laughed and roamed around, looking at decades of metal signs covering the walls. She stared up a ladder. "Killer loft. What's up there? It looks too nice to store hay."

"Go on up. Check it out."

The ladder's side rails were smooth, glazed by decades of stress and sweating palms. The middle of each rung was visibly depressed half an inch through a century of heavy steps. Gabriela reached the loft's floor. "Whoa, this would be a killer place to ditch your parents."

"Exactly," Thomas replied. "My secret lair."

"Lair? Your vocabulary cracks me up sometimes. Is a lair a loft?"

"It can be. It can also mean a den for wild animals."

"Are you a wild animal, Thomas Westbrooke?" She laughed.

"Not that I know of." His expression transformed during minutes of idle conversation. "Hey, Gabriela, you want to make out? You're the prettiest girl in homeroom, and I've always liked you." He was excited about having her alone.

"*No way!* You know I like Matt. But even if I didn't, I'd never kiss you."

"Why not?"

"You're not my type. Besides, I'm still mad you called me 'just a Mexican.'"

"Hey, I said I was sorry. Forgive and forget, right?" He reached out and caressed her long hair between his thumb and forefinger. "You're so beautiful."

Gabriela moved away.

Thomas leaned forward and kissed her. She hesitated before stepping backward, tripping and falling to the hardwood floor. Her right arm swung outward and hit a wooden box, which broke open and dumped its contents—pages of colorful drawings swept across the floor. The subject of the illustrations—the strange treasure Thomas had secretly taken from the crate after he and Robert killed the man in the pond the prior year—clunked from the wooden box onto surface planks.

"Oops, sorry, Thomas. I guess that's what you get for trying to kiss me." She studied the illustrations and the small relic now lying on its side. "Wow, you're a crazy-good artist. What is that weird thing you drew?"

He gathered everything and moved with a singular purpose, maniacally. "*Oh shit, oh shit*. Why'd you do that? Don't look!"

"Uh, hello, because you kissed me right after I told you not to. Maybe that's why? You need to chill."

"Huge mistake."

"Wow, Thomas, get a grip. I'm sorry I knocked over your freaky little antique man and the drawings of him. It's your fault, not mine. Don't be a jerk."

"You should've just let me kiss you. None of this would've happened."

"None of what?" she shot back. "Big deal, you had to pick up your stupid drawings and that dumb thing—whatever it is. So what?"

"What are you going to do now? My dad says you're just a beaner." She gaped in disbelief, and Thomas screamed, "Shit! I'm *so* sorry I said that. And my dad's wrong."

"Oh my God! So, you *are* just like your father—an ass! Wait till everyone hears how you went crazy after kissing me and lost it over stupid drawings of your weird little toy man. *Loser!* I'm going home."

He cut off her path. "I can't just let you leave. We need to talk. You don't understand." He bit his lower lip and his brows crumpled. "Really, Gabriela, you don't get it. Sit down and let me explain."

"*You* don't understand, loser. Out of my way, jerk."

"You can't leave. Not until we talk, okay?"

She bolted for the second ladder, and Thomas clutched the back of her shirt. She shouted and flailed. Her puppy ran in circles at the base of the ladder, barking. "*Stop, you ass!* Leave me alone. I'll tell my dad, and he'll call the police. You're in huge trouble. Let me out of here—*let me out!*"

"Please, Gabriela, just listen to what I have to say. That's all. We need to talk things through." She continued thrashing. "*Please, please!* Robert will call the cops and send your family back to Mexico if you don't. But that doesn't have to happen." The words he spouted sickened him but panic short-circuited reason.

"Who's Robert?"

"My father."

"His son's an asshole. Get away, Thomas. Let me down. *Help! Help! Somebody help me!*" Her face turned distorted and flushed.

"I can't, Gabriela. You'll let the secret out."

"What secret? The one about you being a jerk?"

"The secret of the drawings—you'll tell people."

"Yes, I will! I'll tell *everybody* about *everything*. About the drawings, the weird little man, and you kissing me after I said not to. Unless you let me go. *Now!* I mean it."

Thomas spoke in a quieter, monotone voice. "People will try to take what we have." An eerie expression spread across his face. "It's your job to protect the family. To protect the assets."

"You're a freak! What are you saying? Who are you talking to?"

He stood upright with his head tilted downward, keeping a grip on Gabriela. His mouth fell open, and his gaze bore into hers.

"Just let me go!" she shrieked. "You look crazy!" Struggling to escape, she gripped one of the wooden rails at the top of the ladder and swung her body around to descend.

Thomas maintained his grip on her wrist and squeezed. She demanded he release her; instead, he tried to yank her back into the loft. Gabriela simultaneously struck at him with her free hand. As she did, her wrist slipped from Thomas's grasp, and she plunged backward, crashing onto the floor fifteen feet below, her head whiplashing hard against the surface.

She stared into his shocked face and muttered, "Thomas?"

He stood still as blood gushed from the back of her head and pooled across the floor.

"Thom . . .?"

"I didn't mean this, Gabriela. But I had to stop you. You don't understand. I'm sorry. *I'm so sorry.*"

"T . . ." She faded away, her eyes still open.

Tears poured down his cheeks. "Why'd you threaten me? Why, Gabriela, why? You could have just done what I asked." His voice sounded unnatural. After descending the ladder, Gonzo nipped at his ankles. He pushed the dog away with his foot, but the small animal remained unrelenting and continued its attack, biting into his flesh. Thomas kicked him to create space.

Walking in circles, Thomas yelled out Gabriela's name, pleading for her to return to life as Gonzo continued his attack. He kicked the animal again; it curled up. Soon, the puppy recovered and grew even more aggressive, pushing its teeth into his calf.

"*Stop! Stop!*" he yelled at Gonzo. He stood over Gabriela, watching the blood spread, sobbing. "Oh, Gabriela . . . Why?"

Gonzo sustained his attack.

"Damn dog!" With the animal refusing to release its clamped jaws from his calf, Thomas scanned for something to end the assault. He swiped at the animal and limped toward a workbench, where he grabbed the handle of a three-foot-long spaded shovel. He swung it downward, hoping to thrust the dog aside using the flat surface of the spade. Instead, the handle twisted as he swung, and the spade's sharp edge pinned the dog's leg to the wooden floor, severing its limb. Gonzo howled in pain, running from the barn as a crimson path trailed him.

"*No!*" Thomas gazed down at the puppy's detached front leg and the gore covering his whitewashed jeans and tennis shoes. He held his hands up and studied the red on his clothing. He screamed that none of this was supposed to happen and begged, "Please help me. Someone." It struck him that Gabriela had made the same plea.

Splattered red and the motionless body of a beautiful girl lay on the barn's restored wood floor, like a modernist artist's canvas intending to shock the senses.

July 15, 1971

Thomas needed guidance. A plan. He walked to the house searching for his mentor, carefully avoiding Emma. He found Robert in the backyard and approached him.

"Something happened, Robert." Thomas didn't know how to proceed and said nothing more.

Robert turned around, digesting what he'd just heard. He was shocked: Thomas stood slump-shouldered, his face anguished, his pants and shoes awash in blood. "Holy hell. Are you injured? Is that your blood?"

"No, Robert."

"Whose is it?"

"Most of it's from a dog. Some of it's from a girl."

"What? A girl? Where? On our property?"

"Yes. In our barn."

"Is she still there?"

"I think she's dead."

"Dead? What are you talking about?"

"I didn't mean it," he shrieked. "She threatened to expose our secret. I tried to stop her. It was an accident, Robert. She wasn't supposed to die."

"What secret?"

"About the assets! She said she'd tell others."

"But how did she know, Thomas? Damnit." Robert glanced at the house, scanning for any sign of Emma. He grabbed his son and pulled him behind a tall hedge encircling the back patio, quietly saying, "Let's go. Show me."

Walking over a gravel path to the barn, Thomas said, "I stole one of the assets, Robert. The night you showed them to me. The night . . . we hurt that man in our pond." He hesitated to continue.

"We didn't hurt him, Thomas. You drowned him. Killed him. And like I told you that day, it was the right thing to do."

Thomas considered his father's words; it lessened the burden of his current dilemma. "I've been drawing pictures in the loft. Of the asset I took. Gabriela wasn't supposed to see it. She didn't understand. She said she'd tell others."

Robert slapped him. "The assets mean everything to us. You shouldn't have stolen one from me, and I'll beat you if you ever try that again." He opened an eight-foot-tall red door, and they entered the barn. "We can fix this situation, so calm down."

"I just wanted to . . . talk to her." He could never divulge his true intentions. "She saw the asset and said—"

"That asset is priceless. It goes straight back to the vault when we finish here. Understand?"

"Yes, sir."

Robert stopped walking; Gabriela's body now lay before them, looking angelic and hideous. He shook his head, turned to Thomas, and put both hands on his shoulders. "Don't relish what you've done, but never regret it. Do you understand? This is messy, but your primary decision was sound—you focused on protecting the family."

He tried to stop crying. "Yes, Robert. But it's so hard. It was an accident. Gabriela was nice. She fell and died. The dog attacked me. It was terrible." He stood trembling, a wretched silhouette.

"Let it go. We have work to do. Lock all the doors." He pointed at the tool rack. "Grab two of those spaded shovels. Look in the cabinet for a mop." They began digging a hole in the dirt floor of horse stall number one.

Later, as they exited the barn, they wore clothing Robert had snuck from the house. Thomas's bloodied shoes and pants were burning in the incinerator. Robert had bleached the floor and sprayed down his son's body with a hose. No physical evidence remained, minus a beautiful, innocent victim buried in the corner.

The rest of the Westbrooke Estate appeared tranquil.

Communities along the Oregon Coast can be sunny and warm, even hot, during summer, or they can get boxed in by thick fog with temperatures in the forties. The Westbrookes' home was six miles inland as the crow flies; thus, any moist haze blanketing the bay would typically burn off before reaching their acreage. It was a spectacular day on their hilltop perch and the adjoining grounds, a paradise of Northwestern living. But while a cool mist shrouded Eagle Bay, a mystery brewed within the community.

A police cruiser made its way up their meandering drive. Emma assumed an officer was approaching to speak with Robert; her husband would sometimes stop by the precinct to commend the officers.

She wore a straw hat, jeans, leather gloves, and gardening knee pads strapped to each leg. There was typically a legion of landscapers tending to the Westbrookes' acreage. But horticulture was also one of Emma's passions, so she'd often toil away in the mid-morning and late afternoons during warm summer months.

Three weeks into his new career with the Eagle Bay Police Department, an officer stepped from his cruiser. "Hello, ma'am. I'm sorry to bother you on this perfect day. My name is Corporal Boseman, and I'm assisting with the search for—"

Robert approached briskly from behind Emma looking like he'd been doing his own yardwork. He wore boots, jeans, and a long-sleeved shirt with rolled-up sleeves. "Hello, Corporal. Welcome to the law enforcement ranks within our wonderful community." He turned to Emma. "Oh wait, honey, would you mind turning off the gas stove? The burners are on, warming up oil to fry clams. We don't want it to catch fire. I'll help out here."

"What?" Emma stared harshly but stepped away while complaining, "Of course I will. I don't want our house to burn down."

As she departed, Robert reflected on how he'd called her *honey* for years after their wedding; now, he only uttered the label publicly. He assumed it bothered her.

"No, Corporal, my wife and I have been outside all day, and we haven't seen anything unusual. It'd be quite uncommon to see a young girl with a dog walking across our fields, as you can imagine. We're a bit isolated here. I'm sure Farmer Johnson and his crews are concerned, but as a father, I know how kids can needlessly worry parents. The girl will show up later wondering what the big ruckus was about."

"We're all hoping so."

"I'll keep my eyes peeled and fill my wife in on the details. Good luck finding her, and separately, I hope you enjoy a fulfilling career here in Eagle Bay. We have the best law folk in Oregon and live in the country's greatest town. Good day, now." He extended his arm for a handshake.

Before the police officer was halfway down the drive, Emma exited the front door. "Robert, dirt on the floor, dirt on the counter, a pan with oil, and the gas turned too high. What were you thinking?"

"I thought it'd be nice to fry the clam strips. When I saw the police car, it made sense to come on out. Lost my focus."

"We don't even have clam strips. What are you talking about?"

"Sure we do, out in the fridge in the barn. From when we drove to Netarts Bay with Thomas and his buddies."

"So, you started boiling the oil before you had even gotten the clams from the barn?" Emma shook her head. "That makes no sense. Next time, be more careful and less messy. So what's this whole search thing about?"

"It looks like the daughter of one of Johnson's crew is missing," Robert answered. "His farm manager's daughter." Then he lied. "They've got leads from the other side of town, about ten miles south. I hope they pan out."

"It's not Gabriela Mendes, is it?" She sounded pained. "She lives on that farm. Remember her from the Christmas play? Please tell me it's not Gabriela."

"I don't know who Gabriela Mendes is, but unfortunately, I think that's the name he gave me. She disappeared from the side of the road after day camp. Why they'd let her walk out there alone is beyond me. It's irresponsible, and you're asking for trouble, even in this town."

"This breaks my heart. Gabriela's such a pleasant child. I'm surprised you don't remember her. Thomas mentioned her at dinner a couple of times. She played Mary in the Christmas play at the Boys and Girls Club fundraiser." She stared into his annoyed face. "You don't remember her? Really?"

"Emma, enough," he shot back. "I've no idea who she is, and I don't remember seeing her in any damn Christmas play. Okay?"

"That's it." She pulled off her gardening hat and shot back, "Why are you so irritable lately? What's going on? Are you mad about something? It's getting worse—your moods, your words. Even if you don't remember her, be more compassionate about what's happening at the Johnson farm." She tossed her gloves at his feet and stormed into the house.

Minutes passed before a scream exploded from inside their home. Robert ran toward the backyard and found Emma's palm on the mutilated body of a small black-and-white puppy, his fur covered in blood, his eyes open wide and bloodshot, with one leg missing. He was dead.

"Dear Lord, I found him lying right here against the glass door!" Stark purple contrasted the gray patio cement. "He must've been trying to get inside."

Robert extended his arms. "Here, let me pick him up. I should bury him. I don't know what to say."

"Excuse me? *You don't know what to say?* What is this? Call the police, Robert. Only a demented nut case could do something like this. Chop a leg off? Didn't that officer tell you Gabriela was with her dog? Is *this* her dog? Oh God, I hope not, anyone capable of this . . ."

"Maybe it was a tragic accident," he replied. "I can't bear to look at him any longer. I'll bury him and hose off the patio and glass door."

It was seven o'clock and wouldn't be dark for three more hours. Beautiful yellow roses lined the patio, juxtaposing the images of an animal's final struggles.

Thomas walked into the room and saw the lifeless dog he'd inadvertently tortured cradled by Robert.

"Oh, the poor thing's blood is soaking the towel. Thomas, turn away. You'll have nightmares." She ran to the laundry room to grab more towels to wrap the puppy in, yelling while rifling through cabinets, "A disturbed person did this! Someone wicked. It was no farm accident, or someone would've intervened. I hope they find the bastard. This creep is dangerous."

Having taken off her shoes before discovering the dog, she reentered the room on soft feet covered in thick cotton socks. As she rounded the corner, she found Robert lowering his head and speaking in a hushed voice to Thomas outside the glass door. It didn't look right.

"What's going on, Robert? Why the private conversation? Do you know something about this, Thomas?" She peered into his wide eyes. "Well, do you?"

The boy hesitated before shifting his gaze to his father, seeking direction. Robert suppressed complicity that Emma quickly discerned.

She released cries of agony. Emma took another look at the disfigured dog, collapsed to her knees, and begged for a truth she assumed she already knew. Her young son, the extraordinary boy who'd impressed teachers and peers but whose demeanor and temperament had changed over the previous year, had acted out in a way she hoped he never could.

Thomas pleaded, "But Emma, it was an accident!"

Robert screamed, "Enough, Thomas! Shut up and go to your room, *now*."

"Tell her! Tell her it wasn't my fault. It wasn't supposed to happen." He continued, "I hit the dog because he was biting me. The shovel blade turned or something."

"What about Gabriela Mendes?" Emma asked. "Have you seen her today? Do you know what's happened to her?"

Robert slapped Thomas and bellowed, "Damnit, I said go to your room. *Go, now!*"

"Yes, yes, Emma, I saw Gabriela! She threatened to tell people about the secrets. But, but . . ."

Robert struck Thomas so hard that he crumpled to the ground. He bent down, lifted the boy to his feet, and pushed him toward the stairs.

Emma rushed forward. *"Stop, Robert, stop!* What the hell is going on here?" Robert grabbed her as she tried to approach their child.

Thomas halted halfway up the stairs. "Our secret, Robert, it's still our secret. That's what I'm supposed to do, right? No matter what, protect our secret." He walked up to the landing, turned around, and repeated, "It's still our secret."

"What secret, Robert? *What have you done to my son?* Look at what he's become."

Robert glanced at Emma but said nothing.

After sustained quiet, her expression turned defeated. She pivoted and walked to her bedroom. Heavy doors shook the house after getting slammed shut. Robert left her alone.

A day passed. Emma avoided being in the same room as either father or son. The two never attempted to explain away the dog event, which only pushed her to view each of them, even the son she adored, with contempt. She was alone, an island.

As the big news of a missing Gabriela Mendes hit the television and newspaper headlines, Emma wondered if Thomas might have acted out even more despicably than maiming a dog. But, she debated, if he could torture a puppy . . . then harming a girl was at least possible. She shook her lowered head and grimaced agonizingly.

The following day, she pulled herself from the depths of shock and dismay. Snooping around, she entered Thomas's room and checked every drawer, closet, and possible hiding spot. She didn't know what she was looking for until she found a white ribbon with strands of brunette hair tucked between his mattresses. She grew lightheaded and stumbled into the hall, dizzy and despairing. She'd seen Gabriela wear such ribbons in the past—it had to be hers.

She contacted her sister Sharon in Portland from the phone on her nightstand. They agreed to meet secretly in downtown Eagle Bay the following morning to discuss something Emma labeled urgent and troubling. Afterward, Emma decided they'd go to the police to supply information that might lead to her husband and son's arrests. God help us, she thought. Then she hung up the phone.

Seated inside his den, Robert hung up from the same landline. He set down his pipe and silently chastised Emma for believing she could control the unfolding drama and for conspiring to destroy her son's life and the family's future, scoffing at her failure to put the dynasty first. He calculated the harm she could do, and then he planned.

As night fell, Emma rehearsed everything she wanted to divulge to Sharon the next day. Robert knocked on the door of their antique-laden master bedroom, asking to enter with a doctor, insisting that he understood her anguish but that she'd jumped to wildly inaccurate conclusions. The truth was much less dire than she presumed. A little medication would allow her to clear her mind and deal with the situation less emotionally and more correctly. He wanted her to share the specifics of her gruesome discovery of the dog with anyone she chose, *especially* the authorities. In fact, he insisted on it. Her presumptions regarding Gabriela, however, were bizarre. Robert suggested the doctor's medications might help provide much-needed comfort and rest.

Exhausted, she considered taking the pills but silently rebuked herself: *Hell no. Who knows what kinds of drugs you've concocted to give me, you bastard?* She demanded they leave.

Instead, Robert stepped through the door and approached his wife.

"Get out. I mean it." Wearing a stylish pink robe fastened at the waist, she faced them with puffy and red eyes, looking as if she'd aged ten years in less than two days.

"Emma, please, hear me out."

"I told you Thomas needed help," she cried. "I tried, insisted. I begged you. You said I was overreacting." She moaned, "I discovered a ribbon under Thomas's mattress that I'm convinced belonged to Gabriella. I've hidden it and swear to God I'll get it to the authorities. Our son is disturbed, and it's your damn fault. What did you do to him? What have you hidden from me?"

"Let me hold you. I love you, Emma." He stepped forward, securing her.

"Did he hurt Gabriela? Damnit, Robert, tell me the truth."

He hugged her more tightly. "Our son is brilliant. Our family's future. And you want to destroy him."

Repulsed by his response and sensing bad intentions, she pushed against his strengthening embrace. It was hopeless. He muscled her backward and forced her into a seated position on their bed. Dr. Munro entered. She understood what would happen. They were isolated; screaming was futile.

"You'll never get away with this—never. You and this doctor of yours can go to hell. Sharon will figure things out."

"Sharon will never be a concern."

His creepy tone unnerved her. "No, Robert. What are you telling me?"

"Your sister slipped and fell down her hillside steps hours ago. I'm sorry."

"*No!* Is she . . . ?"

He tilted his head and whispered, "She's gone."

Emma wept and exclaimed, "Goddamn you to hell, Robert Westbrooke." She felt lightheaded and weak. "You're going to kill me, too, aren't you?"

"I could never do that, Emma. But we are going to subdue you, sweetheart."

"I hate you. Whomever you really are."

"You've let me down. Let your children down." He tapped on her leg. Dr. Munro injected something into her thigh. As she instantly grew unable to control her body, the two men stared at each other. Robert nodded. A second needle siphoned fluid from a vial. The doctor injected it.

Emma felt no more agony, despair, or contempt.

She felt nothing.

36   **CHAPTER**

S kye had grown weary of the rumor and innuendo surrounding her drug arrest. The press typically presented Thomas as the righteous rock-of-a-man who'd tirelessly supported his family and community, only to be wronged by a pampered wife who'd become bored and made reckless decisions resulting in turmoil. Reporters seemed unaware or disinterested in her wealth management and homemaker achievements—business was thriving, and her kids were great people, accomplished students, and hard workers. Skye believed her challenges paled compared to those confronted by Johnny and Dakota. The siblings had withstood a barrage of harsh condemnation of their mother.

The family had settled in comfortably at the elder McClouds' home. Grandpa still appeared military fit, but Grandma's Parkinson's now restricted her to bed. Skye and eighteen-year-old Johnny had officially reclaimed the McCloud name even before a final divorce settlement, a move mom and son found liberating. Skye burst with pride handing out Hastings & Hawkins business cards printed with "McCloud" in maroon and gold. Dakota considered the name change premature.

Random thoughts swirled through Skye's head as she drove to meet Steve for an update on her case, which had been set for trial in four months. She passed over a small bridge on Highway 101 and appreciated the view of a family digging for geoduck clams in an estuary during low tide. She treasured living in Eagle Bay. The town of one hundred thousand was naturally stunning. Elk, bears, salmon, whales, and soaring bald eagles were familiar sights.

Skye realized Westbrooke Coastal Industries was primarily responsible for many of her town's world-class services and amenities: excellent public schools, highly ranked medical facilities, an ever-expanding road, bridges, and communications infrastructure, and the largest police force per capita of any city in Oregon.

Two publications recently ranked Eagle Bay as one of the best cities in the country for young families. Yes, Skye still considered herself an extremely fortunate woman, despite everything. With that thought, she parked her car and walked inside to meet her lawyer.

After a quick update, Steve set his pen down and said, "Thomas and his lawyers haven't flinched. A few of our lawyers are recommending a plea bargain."

"*Hell no on that!*" she exclaimed. "He wants me to take the fall for something I didn't do. And you need to fire those few lawyers; that's an absurd recommendation."

"Relax. I agree with you. About the absurdity, not the firing. Just sharing opinions."

"Please don't share the stupid ones." She refilled her cup and said, "A part of me still thought he might do the right thing. But he's hell-bent on crushing the kids and me. It's sickening."

"I'm sorry," he said, scratching his hairline with his folded glasses. "Moving on . . . The lab report on your purse arrived last night—*only* ten weeks late."

"And?"

"I haven't even had time to review it."

Skye's phone rang; it was Dakota. She winked at Steve and said, "Sorry, give me a sec." She pressed a button. "Hi, honey, shouldn't you be in class?"

"Mom, I'm in the principal's office," Dakota said. "There's a policeman here who wants to talk to you."

"What? What do you mean, you—" The phone had been passed on. "Mrs. Westbrooke?"

"McCloud. It's Mrs. *McCloud*." Her jaw tightened; it was a voice she recognized. She hated speaking to the hairy sheriff she hoped would be proven a criminal one day. "I've told you that before, Sheriff Boseman. Why are you with my daughter?"

"I'm afraid that during an inspection authorized by Eagle Bay Academy administrators, one of our officers found what appears to be methamphetamine in your daughter's locker. I'm requesting you meet us at juvenile hall." His condescension was unmistakable.

"You scheming farce of a man. It's not enough that you're pursuing a fraudulent case against me, but now you and Thomas have conspired against my daughter? You miserable pig. You'll have your day."

"Mrs. *McCloud*, one of my officers will drive your daughter to the courthouse. She'll be there in twenty minutes." The line went dead.

Skye hurriedly redialed the number. No answer. She grew overcome by vengeful emotion while giving Steve the details.

"Don't jump to any conclusions," Steve said, demanding that he accompany her to the courthouse. "You don't know Thomas was involved. Focus on supporting Dakota, getting her side of the story. We'll go from there. Okay?" He grabbed his briefcase.

"The hell I don't know if Thomas was involved!" Skye glared at him and barked, "I don't need my lawyer buying into his bullshit—thanks."

She was horrified by images of Dakota getting handcuffed and escorted to a police car in front of the Academy student body. Steve and Skye sat in silence on their drive to court.

Dakota entered the processing room wearing dark denim pants and a fiery red button-down, donning a turquoise necklace and bracelet. Mom, daughter, and lawyer sat privately, and Dakota appeared to be holding up better than Skye had expected.

"Honey, I'm disturbed by the charges. They weren't your drugs, right?" She gazed at Steve before fixing her stare on Dakota's green eyes.

Dakota was direct, "No, they weren't."

"I knew it!" Skye exclaimed. She jabbed her thigh with a stiff index finger and set her gaze upon Dakota's face, which appeared to transform into worried, with glassy eyes.

"Can I speak to you alone, Mom?" Dakota stared down at the gray tiled floor.

"Of course, honey." Skye looked at Steve and flicked her chin toward the door; he clutched his briefcase and stepped outside.

"What is it, Dakota? Did the police do something to you? Were you threatened?"

"No, Mom. But I stopped by the nurse's office this morning. I wasn't feeling well, and after I spoke with Nurse Belinda . . . I had one of the seniors buy me a pregnancy test."

"What?"

"Mom, I think I'm pregnant."

Skye felt as if her heart got ripped out of her chest. She released thoughts of Thomas and the meth and embraced a trembling Dakota.

"I'm so sorry," her daughter pleaded.

Skye's head spun. She helped Dakota back into her chair, maintained their clutched hands, and seated herself without breaking eye contact.

"Why?" Skye asked. "Don't answer that. Let me ask, who?" She glanced at Dakota's belly. "How long?"

"His name is Grant. Maybe three months."

Clarity followed. How could Skye not have seen the signs? How could she have gotten so engrossed in her business and drug charges that she'd lost track of her daughter's activities or struggles?

The statuesque teenager's frame hunched over in her chair, hair cascading over her face, both palms hidden under her locks. "People will find out I'm pregnant and think I used meth. I wish I didn't exist."

"I don't care what people will think. You're a special daughter and a wonderful person. We'll get through this."

CHAPTER 37

Being pregnant at Eagle Bay Academy was big news. Being a knocked-up class president surnamed McCloud or Westbrooke was epic fodder for rumor and innuendo.

Dakota remained burdened by the fallout of her parents' very public divorce and the mother-daughter meth developments. Many locals had been quick to disparage Skye publicly, so the news that her sixteen-year-old daughter was pregnant would lead to even harsher judgment of the family. Jealous and callous teens called Dakota fake and a slut for presenting the false image of an accomplished and chaste daughter.

"The people judging you are full of it, total hypocrites," Johnny said, pained by how difficult it was for his sister to deal with the scorn.

Her eyes moistened, but she tried not to cry. "They are just so ruthless. I know I messed up, messed up bad, but I'm not a horrible person." She moved closer to Johnny.

"I don't know how they found out, but it was going to happen eventually, right? Seriously, Dakota, to hell with those people. I respect you. And you made a brave decision about your baby." He smiled and squeezed her arm. "Hold your head up. I want to wring Grant's neck, but we don't need another family member getting arrested. I can see the headline: 'McCloud son murders Grant Stark!'"

"Oh, obviously, it's not only Grant's fault," Dakota replied. "I should've listened to you. Look what happened. I let you down, let myself down, let Mom down, let Dad down." A single tear stretched down her cheek and fell onto light jeans, leaving a dark blemish on the worn cotton enveloping her thigh.

"That's in the past. Things happen. And I'll be an uncle soon, strange but cool." Johnny couldn't imagine Dakota caring for a child alone but acknowledged that Skye and Grandpa McCloud would provide know-how and support.

"I'm still considering adoption," she said. "Sometimes, I don't think I'm ready to raise a baby. I go back and forth."

"You'll figure it out, and Mom will be a great counselor. The baby will have an amazing life either way." He flashed a relaxed grin that warmed her. "And the meth in your locker turned out to be fake, so I guess Mom's the only druggie in the family." He smiled before shaking his head disapprovingly. "The fucking Pillar. He gets Mom arrested for possession and has someone plant fake meth in his daughter's locker."

"You don't know that, Johnny."

"I'd have to be an idiot to think otherwise."

"I think you're wrong. He's been supportive on the phone."

Dead silence.

Johnny despised Thomas's insistence on wanting a close relationship with Dakota. He understood most people would consider it respectable for any father to remain a constant in his daughter's life after her parents' separation or divorce. But those people hadn't witnessed what *this* father could say or do beyond the cameras. "He never calls me anymore," Johnny said. "And you shouldn't talk to him."

"He'd like to speak to you, but he said you stopped returning his messages." She brushed the hair from her face. "He feels bad about how things turned out. He loves you and Mom and says our lives would be easier if we were together." She turned away and added, "He said I wouldn't have gotten pregnant if we had worked things out."

"*What the hell?* Are you stupid, Dakota?"

"Shut up."

"I'm serious. Are. You. Stupid?"

"Shut up, Johnny. I'm serious, too."

"Sorry, but the impostor's such a mind-gamer."

"Still calling Dad 'the impostor?' That's lame and unfair."

"He's not my dad anymore. Listen, Mom got set up by the impostor. So did you. Those things happened *because* he was in our lives." He stared into her eyes, annoyed. "And newsflash, his absence didn't get you pregnant. You did that yourself."

"You ass."

"You'll hate hearing this, but he fills you with joyful family BS to get you on his side. You're the holdout, his last chance. Mom and I have moved on. I don't know how you don't see it, Dakota. He's full of shit."

"*He didn't set Mom and me up, Johnny!* He was our real dad's best friend. He married our mother. He's not the total douche you say he is. It kills me to see what's happened to our family, and I just want things to go back to how they were. What's so bad about that?"

"You're in denial, and Thomas can go to hell," he said, wondering if he was too inciting. "Look, I know it hurts to hear what I'm saying, but—"

"Stop. I get it. You hate him." She peered out to the bay. "Way to go, you're an *awesome* son; be proud of yourself."

"A good husband doesn't choke his wife. Or get her arrested. Right? It'll get clearer. His bullshit has blinded you. You're naive."

"Oh, get real. I've got a 4.23 GPA. I'm not a dumbass. And I'm only eighteen months younger than you. Don't treat me like I'm an idiot."

"You remember the night Mom got arrested, right? And you know he cheated on her multiple times. And that he kicked us out of our house. And on and on. Your GPA is high, but you're acting like a—"

"Give me a break! I only want our family to be a *family* again!"

"It's too late! Why can't you get that? Thomas is a freak. Let it go. The McCloud-Westbrookes are no more, and that's okay—it's much better to be a McCloud. The further away we are from the impostor, the better off we'll all be."

"You think you're so smart. You and Mom gave up too easily. I'm not going to do that when I have my own family. I'm stronger than you two."

"Get real." He inched closer to her. "Hey, I felt the same as you do for much of my life. I hated learning the truth. It crushed me."

As an eagle passed overhead, they stared out to the bay and cape in silence. Waves were splashing high over the ancient formations dotting the shoreline. Comical-looking tufted puffins covered Haystack Rock, their black bodies, white heads, and bright bills easily recognized.

"I'm sorry," Dakota whispered. "I'm struggling with all of this; it's painful."

"I get it. But at some point, you must call Thomas out for what he is, even if he is your father. And even if you've loved him."

"I just haven't been able to," she muttered. "Who wants to believe this about their father?" She rubbed her knees as she spoke.

"I understand," he said. "No one wants to find out their dad's actually someone they don't even know."

"He was a good dad, wasn't he? For years? God, Johnny, what's happened?"

"Everything will be better in the future." He put his arms around her, squeezed, and nodded.

"I hope you're right."

Three pelicans floated by just as the final bell rang. They gathered their books, shared half-smiles, and headed to their classes.

Nirvana blasted off the walls of Johnny's bedroom. Finally hearing the loud banging on his door, he turned down the music and hollered, "Enter, Mom or fair maiden Dakota!"

"Hey, I want to show you stuff I found in a box in the den," Dakota said while waving Polaroids and a white sheet of paper back and forth. "Very cool articles and pics of Dad from high school. And a copy of something to do with our Great-grandpa McCloud I found in a yearbook." She handed everything to him. "Take a look. I need to cram for a test."

"Cool. Thanks. Get out." Johnny smiled, slammed his door shut, and turned off the music. As he lay in bed staring at images of his father from the early '80s, he was struck by how similar they appeared. John McCloud was twenty-two in 1980, six-two and 210 pounds of mostly muscle, with shaggy brown hair, a surfer's tan, and a familiar smile. Johnny was his father's doppelganger. A sense of pride accompanied hurt.

There were two sports snapshots. In John's senior year, Eagle Bay Academy made it to the final of the 1976 Oregon 5A High School football state championships. He was a starting linebacker on a team that beat Jesuit Portland 18-17 in front of 16,000 fans at Civic Stadium. Johnny played the same position today.

The final piece of information didn't regard his father, yet it was extraordinary: a photocopy of an old news clipping of two men appearing to be in their late thirties or early forties in front of Cape Nahteenwa, and between them, a dark-skinned man carrying wound-up rope. The caption gave two of their last names, though that information was unnecessary. The man on the right was undeniably Johnny's relative, likely his great-grandfather. The print said his name was John Abbott McCloud. William Edward Westbrooke was the man on the left, and Johnny felt it had to be Thomas's grandfather; he looked just like him.

Johnny was shocked that no one had informed him prior generations of Westbrookes and McClouds knew each other. According to the copied image:

William Westbrooke was pleased to be in the temporary employ of Citizen John McCloud, a knowledgeable man from Eagle Bay with a passion for history and adventure. We know not of their ultimate ambitions, but we German Portlanders send our neighbors on the coast good tidings. August 28, 1928.

Per the news text, the photo was one of several shots taken by a journalist for a German-American newspaper, the *St. Joséph Blatt*, seventy-one years earlier.

A night of discovery gave way to deep slumber. Johnny awoke with little time to eat, get dressed, and make it to his first class by 7:45 a.m. Dakota had already left the house for a French Club meeting, yet another organization she served as president.

As he whisked himself through the kitchen, Grandpa laughed and commented on the boundless energy of youth. Johnny smiled and prepared to ask him questions—so what if he'd be late for PE.

"Grandpa, how come you never told me your dad knew the Westbrookes? It blows my mind that our families have known each other so long." Johnny expected a direct response; his grandfather typically cut to the chase.

"I'm sorry, son. Loud jets and antiaircraft guns tend to damage your hearing. Compliments of the Korean War," Grandpa McCloud said, flexing one of his massive forearms tattooed with U.S. Navy. "What's your question? Something about the Westbrookes?"

"Yeah. While reading stuff from Dad's past last night, I found a photocopy of your dad and what must be Thomas's grandfather standing together in 1928. I'm surprised no one ever told me they were friends." He poured himself more orange juice.

The fit patriarch appeared visibly confused. "Oh Johnny, that's impossible. My father was mining for gold in Alaska for most of '28 and '29 with his partner, Manuel. He must've enjoyed himself too much in the Great North, or perhaps he became a casualty of the dangers of mining. Either way, he and Manuel never returned home. I was born months after they'd left, and I didn't learn about the Westbrookes until I was in my 20s."

"But Grandpa, one of the men is named McCloud! Another is listed as William Edward *Westbrooke*, and he looks just like Thomas. The third guy looks Hispanic; could that be Manuel?"

"What? Fetch me the photo."

Johnny could only guess which emotions or thoughts were stirring in his hero's mind. "Here it is. It's a copy of old newsprint," Johnny said, winded from the sprint to his bedroom and back. He moved and spoke excitedly, believing he'd discovered something more precious than gold. "You see, there's your dad. That could be Manuel, and there's William *Westbrooke.*" Johnny continued posing questions, trying to build the puzzle.

Grandpa put his glasses on, sat at the table, and studied the photocopy. Finally removing his bifocals, he turned to Johnny's alert eyes and said, "Wait a minute." He squinted. "My mother once told me a man befriended Dad just before he'd left for Alaska. She called him Bill. Said he was nice but mysterious, uncomfortably so."

"Bill is short for William, right? Maybe she was talking about Bill Westbrook? What's it all mean, Grandpa?"

Grandpa stood up, walked around the counter, and sat back down. "Holy hell. *Ominous* and *mysterious*—words I'd use to describe Thomas. Like grandfather, like father, like son? Could it be?" He licked his lower lip. "Where'd you find this, Johnny? How come I've never seen it?"

"Dakota found it in . . . Well, I'm not sure where." He didn't want to rat out his sister for rummaging through the McClouds' closets.

Grandpa scratched his chin with a thumb. "Is it possible? Could my father have been in Oregon that whole time?" He remained silent for two minutes, rubbing his stubbled cheek while staring outside. His breathing grew labored. "Maybe they never went to Alaska. Did they know something? *Did Bill do something?*"

Johnny's expression transformed. "Grandpa, relax. Let me get you water." He filled a glass and returned. "Drink this," he said, nodding up and down.

Grandpa McCloud's face grew pale, his inhaling seemed difficult, and he turned a shade of blue. Johnny crouched next to him, placing a hand on his leg and shoulder. Grandpa released a panicked sound and clutched his chest with both hands. He began quivering. Johnny caught him as he slipped off the side of his chair. He laid him on the weathered maple floor.

"Call for help," Grandpa said faintly.

Now bedridden due to her Parkinson's, Grandma called out, "What's going on?"

"I'm helping Grandpa!" Johnny screamed.

"Grandpa, what's wrong? Please, I didn't mean to upset you."

Grandpa sweated profusely and stared up blankly from his curled position. "Help."

"What's wrong?" Grandma screamed again.

Johnny called 911 and got dispatched to an emergency nurse who provided step-by-step instructions. He performed every task asked of him, mired in disbelief. He waited for someone or something to ease his fears, but the situation grew direr.

Grandma continued calling out from her bedroom, frightened by her grandson's anxious tone.

Grandpa strained and found the strength to mumble, "Bill must've been bad . . . must've done something . . . ," he said, nearly losing consciousness.

The crisis nurse told Johnny the paramedics would arrive in minutes but that he needed to perform CPR immediately. The prospect of failure terrified him.

"Johnny! Please!" Grandma again cried from her confines.

"I'm busy, Grandma!" He prayed his grandfather would stay alive until emergency personnel arrived. He started CPR. Grandpa shook his head slowly and met Johnny's eyes, moving his right hand to his chest. Johnny's face twisted in anguish.

With glassy eyes, Grandpa said, "Love . . . you . . ." His expression faded, and his body went limp.

"Love you too, Grandpa," Johnny said through tears. He restarted the CPR.

The wise septuagenarian, a man Johnny respected more than any other, stopped breathing. In a daze, Johnny clasped Grandpa's weathered hand and offered one last embrace as paramedics rushed into the kitchen.

Minutes later, an officer approached. With eyes puffy and red, Johnny ignored him and walked toward his grandmother's bedroom to present horrifying news. Then he called Skye, interrupting her breakfast meeting with a client.

Skye arrived at a house filled with authorities. She thrust forward a halting palm, moved past those gathered, entered a corner bedroom, and found her son lying next to a grieving widow.

39

As the drama of John McCloud II's death played out, all the Steel River attorneys, except one, filed out of a meeting room. Steve had accepted Thomas's request for a private conversation. They faced each other in dueling gray suits; Steve sported a yellow tie, contrasting Thomas's deep red silk.

"Thomas, you're delusional. I'm eager to prove Skye's innocence. Why would I plea-bargain a case you can't win? Please know I'll never understand your motivations, fabricating a case against an ex-wife you once loved."

"She's still my wife."

"Stay tuned," Steve replied, glaring.

"And I've never stopped loving Skye."

Steve glanced around the room and halls before releasing a condescending chuckle. "You're a callous monster."

"Your emotions diminish your well-earned reputation for professionalism," Thomas said. "And you think you have me all figured out. You don't."

"So you weren't the puppet master for everything that transpired the night of Skye's arrest?" Steve asked with aggressive hostility.

"You've been watching too much TV."

"You never choked her? Never got your shill Sheriff Boseman to arrest her on trumped-up evidence?"

"You haven't changed at all. You were always intelligent, and your confidence has served you well in law. I'm proud of you." Thomas stressed the word *proud* as a father might to a child craving his praise.

Steve placed his cordovan briefcase on the floor. "I don't give a rat's ass about any of your opinions." He felt stupid expressing such machismo, but Thomas tended to bring out the worst in him. "I don't buy into that Pillar of Eagle Bay bullshit. Or the public's adulation of the Westbrookes." He walked to the silver coffee pot, swished the remaining brew in a circular pattern, and refilled his cup.

"Well, it seems you couldn't wait to get that off your chest." He unpuckered his lips and added, "I guess neither of us will be attending the other's retirement party. The Westbrooke legacy's not a bad one, by the way. Just ask around. My father's a great man, as was his father." He winked.

"Let me guess: You'll be judged as great, too," Steve replied while shaking his head and stirring his coffee.

"Not at all. I'm just a hard-working businessman giving back to his community. I'm measured by what I do, not by what I say. Being charitable makes me feel good. Let me ask, Steve, are you giving back to your community?"

"I don't think you need that commentary. Let's get refocused."

"I agree; let's wrap this up," Thomas said. "I'll write a check for ten million, commit twenty thousand per month in alimony, give her the house and horses, and pay for the kids' college."

"One hundred million, forty thousand a month, five hundred thousand for college funds," he countered. "The house and the horses are already hers—you only live there. It's a fair offer. We'll push for more in future negotiations."

"Please. Who's pitiable now? There's no way in hell I'm coughing up one hundred million." He calmly added, "It's not the money—I have plenty of that. It's the principle. Understand?"

"I think you'll settle for the hundred mil. We've uncovered irregular money transfers between your personal accounts, foreign banks, and Westbrooke Coastal Industries. Things aren't adding up. Perhaps the IRS would like to chat with us. You've got two weeks to accept our settlement terms." Steve wondered if he was overplaying his hand.

"I have an IQ of 150-plus. And photographic memory. I graduated summa cum laude from Princeton with a double major in economics and finance and a minor in physics. I'm an intelligent man."

"Seriously, we're both busy. If there's a salient point you wish to make, do it quickly."

"Bear with me. And by effectively managing my family's assets and enterprises, I've amassed what most in society would consider a fortune. So I'm smart, and I have money. Agreed?"

"You can call my assistant to reschedule," Steve said as he walked from the room.

"You've slept with three women in the past six months: Stacy, Veronica, and Lynn." Steve stopped and turned around. "You've got a balance of four hundred thousand held in three accounts at US Bank in Portland. You gave twenty-five hundred to the Democratic Party last year and fifteen hundred to Republicans. You traded in your Chrysler for a BMW fourteen months ago—business must be good. You've met with Skye three times in the past thirty days." Thomas rattled off the information as if reading from a to-do list. It was an impressive display of mental acuity.

"I fail to see the advantage of your having spent any time assembling a dossier." Steve grew unnerved; everything Thomas had just spouted was accurate. Was he being spied on?

"Stop indulging yourself in matters concerning the Westbrooke family or me. That includes our businesses. It's more than a recommendation."

Steve set his drink down, keeping eye contact. "A threat? I'll do what's required to serve my client. You'd be wise to assume that's how lawyers operate."

"Most people would label your pursuit of my wealth as the real threat." He watched Steve take a sip of his brew and narrowed his eyes. "Take my advice to heart. Don't meddle in my family's affairs. I have the resources to protect us legally. And I'm relentless." He added, "Armed with everything necessary to pursue justice . . . or the prize, whatever that might be."

"You had the prize; it was Skye. You lost her. And when justice prevails, you will fall."

"You should rein it in," Thomas said as he invaded Steve's personal space. "You have no idea what I'm capable of."

"No, I don't. But you have our offer and two weeks to consider it." Steve reached for the doorknob to exit the room; his hand trembled slightly. Moving down the corridor to his office, he stepped behind his desk and collected himself, staring at a painting of Portland's St. Johns Bridge. Someone tapped at his door.

Thomas poked his head inside and said, "You forgot your briefcase." He half-smiled and strolled through the Steel River offices.

Steve gazed at the reception desk and watched Thomas flirt with one of the firm's young assistants. It was remarkable to Steve how a man could so effortlessly and convincingly shift personas. After minutes of banter between the Pillar of Eagle Bay and the typically reserved employee, she retreated to Steve's office.

In a star-struck state, she exclaimed, "That Mr. Westbrooke is a charmer!"

CHAPTER 40

She glanced into the rear-view mirror of her idling Land Rover and watched groundskeepers assemble to bury the casket. The faces at her father-in-law's funeral had all been familiar; Skye had seen them at other emotional life events during the past twenty years. Best friends, schoolmates, neighbors, and family. Witnesses to her first wedding, a funeral six years later, and her marriage to Thomas. Today she'd laid to rest John McCloud II.

It seemed impossible that almost forty years had passed. Skye reminisced of playing hide-and-seek in the same weathered St. Michael's Cemetery when she was ten. The day's next gathering would be six miles away.

Sadie had offered to host an old-fashioned Irish wake following the burial. Dozens of cars were parked on both sides of the road adjacent to her property. A more upbeat mood emerged as guests entered through Sadie's front door.

"What would I do without you? I couldn't make it through this day, and I might not have made it through the last twenty years." Skye sometimes wondered if she adequately reciprocated her friendship with Sadie.

Sadie peered into tired eyes and placed one hand on each side of

Skye's face, then nodded and smiled. "There's nothing I wouldn't do for you. Knowing you appreciate me warms my heart. Enough of that. How're you holding up?"

"As well as can be expected, I guess. No, wait, that sounds defeatist—give me a do-over. Here's the rundown: The manner of my father-in-law's death crushed me. It was difficult for Johnny to witness his grandfather's passing. I'll need to move Grandma McCloud into a 24-hour care facility. Dakota's making me proud with her desire to give her child a wonderful life. And finally, regrettably, my drug case is moving to trial." She shook and tilted her head. "I'm convinced Thomas set me up. Thank God we'll be legally divorced in about a month." She raised her fist as if in victory. "Never boring, right?"

Sadie grew animated. "That's my girl—chin up. You're amazing. It'll get easier. It has to." Sadie handed her a glass of lemonade.

"Have any Scotch?" Skye asked, considering hard alcohol a more appropriate veneration that both departed John McClouds would appreciate. She wordlessly caught herself: Due to the recently discovered photocopy of the old newspaper clipping, there were three John McClouds to celebrate tonight if she included the one who disappeared around 1928. She knew firsthand that two of them were exemplary men; she assumed their ancestor, John McCloud I, must have been, too.

"Yep, Scotch is the only worthy drink," Sadie said. "Unfortunately, all I've got is the cheap stuff. There's no Lagavulin in my house. I'll be right back."

Skye stood in a black dress, thankful for the turnout. White canopies erected in her yard helped handle the overflow crowd; their primary purpose—rain protection—was, so far, unnecessary.

Sadie returned with the alcohol, and Skye said, "You know, despite everything going on in my life, all the madness, I'm darn happy. I'll never understand Thomas or his motivations, but here's to the future." They clinked their glasses.

Sadie shook her head. "And to think I would've sworn to the goodness of that man six months ago. I'm still blown away with the stuff your lawyer dug up on him, but he's almost out of the picture." They toasted again.

Sadie wasn't forthright. Thomas had offered her a loan to expand her floral business because she'd gotten herself into a bind. After refinancing her home one year earlier and splurging on a new sports car, Nordstrom apparel, jewelry, and a trip to Hawaii, all the refinance funds got spent. She accepted Thomas's loan, convincing herself it was a financial matter unrelated to her friendship with Skye, but remained conflicted about disclosing the issue. Now certainly wasn't the time.

Cody moved through the home seeking Sadie's attention. The house was packed with mourners, so he jutted and flicked his jaw for her to meet him outside. Sadie worked her way to the canopies and approached him.

"What's up?" she said.

"Johnny just found out Thomas—*the impostor* he now calls him—is looking for a place to park down the street. Skye will explode. Johnny says he's going to punch him in the face. I obviously need to tell Thomas to move on, right? Don't you think this is a ballsy move?"

"Of course," she replied. "Having them in the same room would be a disaster. Thomas can't enter."

"Agreed. I'll tell him 'not tonight.'"

"Exactly. But use discretion, Cody. He's your boss's boss. Please don't get yourself fired over something that's none of our business. His intentions might be reasonable."

"I guess anything's possible, but it feels strange he'd even consider showing up. I'll shoot straight and assume he'll abide. Wish me luck. Or check the classifieds and search for 'logistics jobs.'" Cody flashed a grin and walked out to intercept Thomas.

"Hello, Thomas. It's good to see you, even under these sad circumstances." Cody had reached him just as he'd locked the door of his Jag. He hoped Thomas would be in an easy mood. He caught a whiff of the cologne Thomas was renowned for wearing within WCI.

"Good evening, Cody. The elder McCloud was a fine man, as was his son. And a friend to me. Judging by the size of this gathering, he'd endeared himself to many."

"Yes, the old sailor was loved by half the town." Cody believed that, in truth, the elder McCloud and Thomas had never grown too close. Still, he judged Thomas's comments to be appropriate under the circumstances. He cleared his throat twice. "I'm uncomfortable inserting myself into your personal affairs, but I don't think it'd go over well to have you inside tonight. It'd be best if you paid your respects another time." Though Cody towered over WCI's CEO, he felt intimidated; Thomas was built like and moved like a Secret Service-Russian spy combination.

"It's painful to hear those words. Do you ever wonder how Skye and I arrived at this unhappy place? I often do. I came to pay my respects and alleviate my wife's pain. That's what good men do. I'm sure a decent guy like you appreciates the truth of that statement."

"Yes, Sadie and I wonder how relationships have gotten so strained. That said, we feel it'd be best for you to show your respects another time." Cody again challenged whether Thomas could be the monster Skye so coldly describes.

"Please pass my respects on to Skye. You take care of yourself, Cody. You're a solid individual, like Sadie. By the way, I've received excellent feedback on your proposal for a new distribution strategy. Great work. You figure into our long-term plans, and you'll get rewarded appropriately. Good night." Thomas gave him a handshake, settled into his car, and drove away.

Cody felt guilty. He considered it distasteful that while a good man's life was getting celebrated and his own girlfriend's house filled with grieving guests, he dwelled on the potential ramifications of the praise delivered by the young legend himself. He strode back toward the crowd.

Johnny had isolated himself in a corner of the yard. He'd moved beyond sharing the pain of his grandfather's passing. As people came and went paying their respects, he remained preoccupied with the extraordinary discovery establishing links between the Westbrooke and McCloud families seventy years earlier. It wasn't a trivial finding.

Later that evening, Skye grew perturbed when Johnny implied the Westbrookes had murdered two generations of McClouds. She made it clear Thomas might be many things, but he was no killer. It was the right message to deliver to her son. Privately, she harbored her own suspicions.

41

Skye woke up in a great mood, and her coffee tasted delicious. This would be a momentous day, her first as a divorcee. She and Thomas would sign the documents in four hours. Steve had insisted on meeting her in Eagle Bay for the occasion, even as Skye argued it was unnecessary. While sipping their drinks in a café, she believed she had discovered why Steve made the trip: He had reviewed the late-arriving report regarding Skye's purse. The lab found Sadie's fingerprints on and inside the Gucci bag containing meth.

Skye chuckled sarcastically. "What are you implying, Steve? Are you accusing my best friend of sneaking a big bag of meth into my purse?" She squinted, added sugar to her coffee, and shook her head to emphasize annoyance. "I've told you many times: *Thomas set me up.*" The early-morning crowd bustled around them as Skye simultaneously reviewed the final divorce papers and took a call from the office; she'd become adept at multitasking as her business expanded.

"I'm obligated to tell you what the results were, Skye. You can do what you want with the information." Steve exhaled loudly. "But okay, *yes*. I believe Sadie accessed your purse the night of your arrest."

"Let's get going." She grabbed her coat, knocking over a chair as she yanked it toward her. "I don't mean to argue with you. It's just that

I know Sadie *extremely* well. She could never, ever do that to me. You told me yourself she was a great friend just weeks ago."

"New information," he replied as he picked up the toppled chair.

She looked at her watch and told herself she had twenty minutes to mull the issue before meeting up with Thomas and his lawyer. Stepping through customers to exit, she recalled a picture in her office of Sadie and her holding up belt buckle awards from a competition at the St. Paul Rodeo. No way Sadie could betray her—impossible. Upon the drive with Steve, she'd grown even more convinced.

The settlement talks were less acrimonious than anticipated, though the final signing was still odd. Thomas resigned himself to transferring $60,000,000 to Skye and $300,000 into the kids' college funds. On top of the divorce monies, she had her Hastings & Hawkins income, which would remain high since only one client chose to leave after the drug case drama. She'd already decided to give millions from the settlement to charities; there was no benefit to disclosing that news today.

Skye, Steve, and Thomas stood outside the office where the ink of the signatures had just dried. Thomas said, "My dear Mr. Collins, I seem to recall a heated discussion where I had advised you that a one hundred million disbursement was unlikely to occur. I may have conveyed that opinion more colorfully at the time. It appears your client," he nodded to Skye before continuing, "was more reasonable with her expectations."

Steve smirked. "Yep, sixty mil is *all* we got." He pulled out a Butterfinger and held it up. "My victory cigar."

Skye understood Thomas viewed Steve's celebration as pathetic, which made it more joyous to her lawyer. "Steve, please," Skye interrupted. "You did your job." She turned and said, "Thomas, we're done,

 Ken Cruickshank

right? Time for all of us to move on." She stared into his striking eyes, which now seemed less beautiful, for maybe the last time.

"Can you leave us for a moment, Steve?" Thomas's tone was abruptly conciliatory, and he stared amicably at Skye.

She paused and exhaled, adjusting the purse strap draped over her shoulder. "Go ahead, Steve. I'll catch up with you in the lobby."

Steve glanced at Thomas disdainfully and walked away.

"Why the black dress?" Thomas asked.

"Because I felt like it." She glared. "Are those your final words?" He remained silent, so she squinted and said, "Goodbye."

"No, stop. Please."

She halted, turned around, and removed her sunglasses. "What is it?"

"I've always admired you, Skye. I've never stopped loving you. I should've been a better husband. My deeds exposed the charade of my vows to you. There are depths and complexities to my being that'd be incomprehensible to most. I know that includes you."

"*Wow*. Talk about psychobabble twisted apologies—that was one for the books." Her face contorted. "John and I used to speak so highly of you. He'd be deeply disappointed in what you've become. Instead of helping his family, you grew selfish and frightfully bizarre. And then you turned vindictive."

"I regret that."

"*Ha!* Regret, Thomas? Most people believe you're a brilliant and charitable man. It's all they see; it's all I saw for years. You shouldn't have pursued me after John died. You should've let me move on with my kids. Then perhaps I'd still respect you. You aren't well. I hope you get counseling."

"You say that because I don't conform to society's norms—a society whose judgments mean less and less to me. I can't expect you to understand. I am my father's son."

She released a loud sound of frustration. "Don't pin this all on Robert. Whatever the hell your father did to you, you should've worked to overcome it. He didn't cheat on our fifth anniversary: you did. He didn't choke me: you did."

"I've overcome many of my demons."

"So it's okay to cheat and choke?"

"Those are your words."

"You still have many demons to overcome. I thought you were a good person until this year." She added, "I've discovered you're not."

"We'll go our separate ways. You have your children—plus millions—and I'll soon have my obsession. May both of our futures be brighter."

"You're *so* strange. Your words aren't deep or intriguing. Your obsession? Is that another woman? A new business? What? Don't answer. But what happens when 'your obsession' no longer excites you? You grow weary of the very things you relentlessly pursue, Thomas."

"Perhaps I'll get my poetic justice."

"You will. I wish you no harm, but stay away from my family." She headed for the lobby but returned. "I need to know." She swallowed hard. "Did you do anything bad to John?"

He stared back in what Skye considered an uncomfortable, compassionate stupor and reached for her hand. Appearing almost angelic, he said, "I loved John. I could *never* have hurt him."

The creepy tone of his response unsettled her. Skye stared intensely, yanked her hand back, and twisted away. Thomas gripped her shoulder and strengthened his grasp, preventing any retreat. "Stop!"

she snapped. He didn't let go. She swung her fist at his head, but he dodged the blow.

He released his hold.

"Go to hell!" She walked away, glancing back three times.

He yelled out, "No kiss and goodbye?"

She thought he sounded desperate and continued down the hall toward the lobby.

Almost beyond earshot, Thomas hollered, "How's Sadie?"

She paused but shook it off, glad this day and her saga with him was over. She wondered if her once much-loved and brilliant ex-husband, the icon her community remained enamored with, was moving closer to a mental collapse. *Thank God he's out of our lives.*

Delivering his final barb, Thomas smiled before walking down a hall lined with floor-to-ceiling glass. Passing a shadowed area, he gazed at his image in a tinted window and watched his smile fade before setting his briefcase on the floor. He studied the reflection of his face. Tears meandered down his cheeks.

The doors to a room filled with lawyers and clients opened, and the group filed out for a break, curious about the commotion they'd overhead. They slowed to stare at the handsome executive eying the window, whose tears continued to fall. One of the attorneys grew concerned and asked Thomas if he needed help. Thomas never acknowledged the stranger, and others began to murmur that the man before them was none other than Thomas Westbrooke, The Pillar of Eagle Bay.

Moments later, Thomas picked up his briefcase and walked outside through a fire exit, setting off an alarm. He strode to his Jaguar, fired it up, and raced away.

CHAPTER 42

Johnny grew obsessed with disproving the official report stating his father drowned while swimming for his life in the jaws of the Bear Point Delta. Because the only witness was Thomas, Johnny argued the account was untrue. And this October day, he'd prove it.

Exorcising anxieties, Johnny stared at the tall cliffs standing three hundred feet across the rushing water's surface. Perched atop the bluff was a privileged citizen's castle, a well-crafted Northwestern post and beam timber residence surrounded by acres of open grassland with unobstructed views north and south. He thought it was strange that someone would build such a grand estate and not find the time to enjoy it; he'd never seen anybody inside or outside the structure during his years of fishing on the delta lying below it.

The river was quiet; Johnny saw no anglers, crabbers, or boaters. He'd determined this was the perfect time to seek the truth. The strength of the current, the ocean's temperature, the crashing of the jaws—the present conditions mirrored those recorded the day John McCloud III disappeared.

He watched a bald eagle clutching a small salmon soar over his head and attempt to land on the bare limb of a tilted, weathered pine. The squirming smelt fell onto the rocks between the tree's base and the river's edge. The eagle swept down to reclaim its flexing catch in its claws before flying north over the delta.

As the predator soared away, Johnny disrobed to his trunks. Goosebumps covered his body. He placed his left foot into the cold flow, measuring its effects. He hesitated, then jumped in and reacted to the restricting chill. Embraced by numbing waters, the currents thrust him into the jaws of the even colder Pacific. He prayed for composure and strength.

There was someone inside the stately home perched atop the cliff. In fear, a middle-aged woman called 911 to report what she thought would be the end of an unknown man's life. She pleaded for quick responses that might save someone seemingly intent on dying.

It was the same sensation he'd felt when a massive wave on the island of Kauai slammed him headfirst into the sandy ocean floor. But at this moment, the temperature was spine-tingling cold, and the constant shearing in the confluence of treacherous waters challenged him. He fought to remain composed amidst thundering violence.

Any courage soon disappeared. Intense swells tried to crush Johnny, pushing his struggling body below the surface and further out to sea. He gasped for air, his eyes wide. Frightened, fully overcome, he told himself he was going to die.

He cursed himself while considering the pain he'd cause others if he perished, then gazed upward to a haze-covered sun, got his bearings for the east, and swam as never before. Salt stung his eyes, but emotions bolstered him. The more he considered all he could lose, the stronger his body grew.

Establishing a rhythm, his strokes thrust him toward shore. Either the effort was warming his body, or hypothermia was settling in. He peeked at the shoreline every fifty strokes—the trees were getting larger. He wasn't slowing down; if anything, he was pulling harder, moving faster.

Bam! Pain erupted from his skull; he'd slammed into the sharp spur of a log floating below the swells. Dazed, blood gushed from a deep wound, and he swore he could taste it. Sinking, losing consciousness, he would become a statistic, another victim of reckless youth.

Hallucinations accompanied expectations of death. Thoughts of Dakota and Skye flashed through his mind. A blurry image of his father grew focused . . . he remembered sharing that day with him. They walked hand-in-hand, picked up seashells, and he stared with wonder at starfish on the rocks. He was five or six.

A comforting voice from his youth interrupted his senses. "Don't let this happen, son. You can make it."

The voice was clear and recognized. Was it real? The dreamlike state slowly gave way to acute awareness, and he purged seawater from his lungs as he rose from the murky depths into overcast daylight. Kicking and pulling to the surface, he grew determined to survive. He gasped for air and refilled his lungs with life. Fifteen minutes of effort brought the shoreline within reach. The currents shifted to ease his route.

He promised to uncover the truth of that fateful morning with every stroke. For, if the son could survive this challenge, the stronger and more experienced father would have, too. He pulled toward dry sand armed with a single truth: John McCloud III did not drown.

Nautical sirens and the sounds of powerful engines cascaded upon him. He was one hundred feet from the sands when Eagle Bay Maritime Rescue crafts arrived to drag him from the pounding surf.

"I would've made it," he argued. "I would've made it."

"Yes, son, you would've," a paramedic said. The rescuers were impressed; Johnny's poised demeanor belied someone wishing to end his life. They stripped his trembling body and covered him with blankets and emergency apparel. After cleaning and dressing his gash, they wrapped his head in gauze.

Sheriff Boseman inserted himself again into the midst of yet another McCloud family incident. He approached the teenager lying on a gurney surrounded by paramedics and asked Johnny why he'd tried to kill himself.

"I didn't try to kill myself, you hairy, corrupt bastard. I don't have anything else to say to you."

Medical and maritime personnel remained captivated by the steely resolve of the lean and defiant young man. They wanted to know more.

"I can understand how the unfortunate circumstances within your family might push you to such desperate measures," said the sheriff. "But it's our job to keep troubled citizens safe, despite themselves or the dysfunctional families they belong to."

A female paramedic interrupted, "This isn't the time, sir!" She gritted her teeth and locked eyes with another medic, shaking her head.

Johnny turned away, the front of his once-white forehead bandages now fully absorbed in red. His gaze reflected contempt.

Sheriff Boseman walked to his car, grabbed his cell phone, and dialed Thomas's number.

The next day's headline was front-page sensationalism for the *Eagle Bay Register*: McCloud Son Survives Suicide Attempt.

CHAPTER 43

The family celebrated moving back into the house Thomas had forced them to flee the night he choked Skye. Thomas's lawyers had delayed the inevitable reunion through ridiculous legal ground challenges. Skye unlocked the front door and stepped inside. Walking to the kitchen, she passed the familiar sunflower wall clock that read 1:32.

Dakota followed Skye down the hall and released a "Woohoo!" Johnny high-fived his sister and said, "Westbrooke out, McClouds back in." But it was a different McCloud clan reclaiming their estate; fresh memories of unexpected trials affected each of them. Although lab tests confirmed the substance discovered in Dakota's locker at the Academy was harmless crystallized protein powder, not meth, the experience had hardened her. Upon enduring a year of anxieties triggered by the imposter, Johnny was even more driven to pursue elusive truths regarding John, Thomas, and revelations linking the Westbrooke and McCloud families.

"Please, Mom, let me read Steve's report on Thomas. You're divorced now; he was a terrible husband who lied to all of us. But the truth is important. I'm a grown man and can handle whatever's in it." He insisted that, if granted permission to review the report compiled by

Steel River attorneys, it'd be his final request for information related to Thomas.

Skye doubted that. She was eager to turn the page on the chapter of Johnny's life that included Thomas. She felt his obsession with exposing the paradoxes of the man was an unhealthy pursuit. "We've been through this before. You've got more important things to be focused on: choosing a college, getting a summer job, and most importantly, just enjoying your senior year. Your fixation is uncomfortable for me."

"So we're going to let him get away with murder?" He tossed his hat onto the counter and stared at Skye. "We need to expose that sonofabitch." Johnny was tempted to mention that he hadn't jumped into treacherous waters only to prove that John would have survived the dory accident. He wanted people to start believing Thomas might be a killer. But if he mentioned the river episode, Skye would have pounced and lectured him about what the *Eagle Bay Register*—justifiably, in her mind—termed a death wish.

She stared at Johnny, watched dust float through beams of afternoon light, and shifted her gaze outside. Finally, she said, "Thomas isn't a murderer. He's capable of many cruel things but not of killing, especially not John. Let it go, son; it's painful for me to hear. Understand?"

"I'm not trying to hurt you, Mom. But I'd drop the issue if you let me see the report. I could meet Mr. Collins at his Portland office while visiting Lewis and Clark College and U of P. Say yes."

She'd already talked to Steve about Johnny's preoccupation with reviewing the background dossier prepared for the still-pending drug trial. She yielded and agreed to set up a meeting. Whether Johnny sought retribution or justice might not matter; obsession with Thomas's death interfered with living his life.

Two days later, his visits to Lewis and Clark and the University of Portland went well, though Johnny had already decided to attend the University of Oregon—unbeknownst to Skye. But the school visits had served their purpose; they'd gotten him to Portland in front of Steve Collins.

Pushing the elevator's square brass button for the twenty-third floor of the KOIN Center, he was pleased to share the ride with two attractive professionals. They ignored him. He exited and approached a law firm's thick glass door etched with *SR*. Johnny entered Steel River's offices, where another nice-looking employee greeted him and offered a drink. The teenager could get used to this. He sat on a cushioned seat atop a custom wood bench and waited.

Approaching with a face emphasizing *busy*, Steve nodded and led him to his office. He hoped the teenager wouldn't too greatly interrupt his busy work schedule. Steve grabbed a Coke from an office refrigerator, handed it to Johnny, and pointed to one of the two empty chairs on the other side of his desk.

"Your mother tells me you've got quite an imagination. I suspect much of what you believe comes from experience. We're both trying to complete the puzzle that is Thomas Westbrooke. Let's get started . . ."

Johnny stared out an east-facing window toward Mount Hood, which stood prominently and was still snow-covered, even in late June. Nothing Steve was saying registered as fresh or noteworthy. Johnny rotated his head and observed the northern horizon. He contemplated the tremendous forces required to blow the top off the mountain framed by a thick pane of glass—Mount St. Helens.

"I'm a busy man, Johnny," Steve snapped. "Are you even listening? If you're not engaged, it's a waste of our time."

"Yes, sir. I'm listening. It's just that I knew all that stuff. Doesn't everybody?" He'd arrived with lofty expectations.

"No. You know things or sense things that others don't. You've seen the behavior behind the façade. On the one hand, Thomas is more capable than anyone I've ever met. On the other, he seems to be, as you argue, just not 'right.' The fact that he's hidden his duplicity from the public is remarkable."

"He hid it from our family. From my mom." He lowered his head, chewed the inside of his cheek, and added, "He hid it from me." With his head tilted downward, he rolled his eyes up to Steve's, appearing saddened or victimized.

The "Thomas effect" weighing on Johnny prompted Steve to despise the nemesis even more. "I suspect your mother is more aware than you realize. Never blame her for a seemingly noble husband living a life of deceit. He's uniquely capable of pulling off the pretense." He added, "And don't ever blame yourself for not exposing Thomas earlier or preventing any of his deeds. We were all duped. Even now, much of Oregon believes Thomas is truly," he flashed air quotes, "The Pillar of Eagle Bay."

Johnny nodded affirmatively. "He's not normal. I think he's a psycho. Don't you?"

Steve wondered if Johnny subconsciously hoped he might discover that sickness accounted for Thomas's despicable behavior. Maybe the man had sincerely loved his wife and children once, but psychosis prevented him from being the person he'd wanted to be.

"It's possible Thomas is sick. But he could also simply be wicked. Either way, he's a paradox. He seemed to enjoy observing your mother's anguish as she struggled with the misfortunes he'd inflicted. I can only speculate about what drives him to such malevolence. And he's growing more bizarre." They stared at each other, two men grappling with the enigma.

Johnny stood abruptly and exclaimed, "Thomas Westbrooke murdered my dad! And Thomas's grandfather murdered my great-grandfather. The Westbrookes have been killing the McClouds for generations." He hoped Steve would appreciate the *aha* moment.

"Johnny, please." Steve shook his head with an expression that barely disguised condescension. "I know you're serious, but it's a silly contention. Generations of killing?" He appeared painfully irritated. "You sound like a TA historian referencing the Hatfields and McCoys. Your argument's absurd."

"*You think?*" Johnny stood and exited Steve's office, his face contorted by embarrassment and anger.

"Johnny, stop."

He continued to move down the hall.

Steve jogged through the offices to intercept the rigid teenager at his receptionist's desk.

"Johnny, it's been a long day. It's not an excuse, I know. The outlandish . . . Sorry, the *nature* of your accusations caught me off guard. Come back to my office, and let's discuss this. Accept my apologies?"

His face was still red, but he settled himself. "Okay."

Fifteen minutes into their revived discussion, and after studying the photocopied image from a 1928 newspaper, Steve said, "This is remarkable." He moved the white sheet of paper closer to Johnny and tapped a finger on top of one of the men in the picture. "Even in this copy, this man, this 'William Westbrooke,' as the caption says, looks just like Thomas." Steve jotted a note and affixed it to the copied image. "And you shared this with your mother?"

"Yes, sir. She blew it off. She wants to move ahead. I get it, but it's not the right decision." His face no longer appeared flushed, and he spoke with confidence.

"Where'd you find it?" Steve asked as he refilled his coffee cup.

"Dakota found it in my grandparents' den, in a box of my dad's stuff from high school. Anyway, it gave my grandpa a heart attack, and who knows, maybe it got my dad killed."

"Excuse me. I'm still processing it." Steve swiveled in his desk chair and rotated his pen between his fingers. He stared out his window for a long, silent moment, wondering when John may have copied the photo.

"Also," Johnny continued, "there's no way my dad drowned swimming to shore after the dory boat flipped. Something else happened to him. Thomas did something to him."

"Is that why you risked your life jumping into the river? To test a theory?" He stared at Johnny's fading forehead scar, a remnant of the episode.

"Of course. I knew I'd survive, just as my father would have." He wasn't about to inform Steve that he'd almost died. He continued, "It's another reason I think the impostor killed him."

"That was a perilous stunt, Johnny. And your assumptions were flawed. It'd be impossible to duplicate the exact conditions of the delta and ocean waters the day your father disappeared. Be more sensible in the future." Steve tossed his pen on the table and rolled up his sleeves. "And let me be blunt. I don't think Thomas has killed anybody. My opinion may disappoint you, but while I believe he's capable of inflicting emotional pain on many levels and of being perversely intimidating, no one we've interviewed, and no records we've pored over, suggest he's a murderer."

"You believe that because my mom tells you to. If the shrinks you hired are saying the same thing, you need new shrinks. Check out this record. These were Thomas's exact words the day my dad disappeared." He passed it over the table.

Steve put his glasses back on and asked Johnny to pull the blinds up for better light.

"Read the lines I highlighted in green," Johnny said. "Don't you think that's implicating?"

Steve read the words Thomas had spoken almost thirteen years earlier, focusing on the lines highlighted:

The rough waters ate us up, one huge wave after another, flipping the boat and tossing everything inside, including John's life vest. He insisted it was too warm to wear it, so he took it off, against my advice. I loved the guy, but he could be very stubborn. There was no way for me to see or do anything once the boat flipped. I almost got swept out to sea and barely survived. I knew deep down John was gone.

Johnny watched Steve's eyes narrow. "That was three hours after the make-believe accident. He talked past tense like he knew my dad was dead. Because he probably was. Thomas killed him." He tapped his fingers on Steve's table. "My grandfather said John *never* took his life vest off while dory fishing, but the cops believed Thomas. They had no reason not to. Also, my mom said my dad was *not* stubborn."

Steve scratched his temple with his folded glasses and gazed down at the busy Portland streets. The cacophony of city life relaxed him.

"I've seen this report before, Johnny. Thomas was emotional when he spoke those words. I still don't think he's a killer."

"I don't know why you can't see it. It's *totally* obvious," Johnny said as nervous energy caused his legs to twitch.

"I'll meet with my team to get their opinions on everything you've presented. I'll call you after our discussion." Steve checked his watch.

They shook hands, and Johnny left the building. He walked to the parking garage and hopped into the driver's seat of the green Ford pickup he loved more than any other vehicle.

During the three-hour drive back to Eagle Bay, where the road followed a river through the Oregon Coast Range, he mouthed, "They may not see it yet, but I do. I'm going to get you, you murdering fraud." He blinked to dissipate moisture in his eyes.

Minutes after Johnny departed, Steve and Skye were on the phone discussing the meeting. They dissected the evidence Johnny presented—a copy of the press clipping linking Westbrookes and McClouds and the police report—which Skye considered much more damning than Johnny realized. She'd asked Steve to keep those concerns from her son.

The growing unease led Skye to question what Thomas might ultimately be capable of doing. She informed Steve she'd upgraded the alarm system protecting their home and reacquainted herself with the Ruger in her bedroom.

CHAPTER 44

Skye declined an offer for tea or coffee, which prompted a surprised glance from Sadie. "You sure?" she asked, trying to read her friend's thoughts. "That's a first. Everything okay?"

"I hope so, Sadie. I have an uncomfortable issue to discuss."

"What's wrong?"

Skye sat down and pressed the wrinkles from the skirt enveloping her thighs. She took a cautious breath. "You told Sheriff Boseman, Steve, and me that you'd never touched my new purse the evening I was arrested." She leaned forward from the sofa, licked her upper lip, and gazed back up. "Sadie, your prints were all over it."

Sadie stared into her cup, methodically swirled her tea, then set it down gently. "Seriously? Just what are you implying, Skye? I don't like your tone." After her eyes darted between a window and Skye's face, she continued, "My fingerprints *should* be on your purse; I moved it from one side of the kitchen to the other before you left. So what? I'm shocked by the insinuation and don't know what else to say."

Skye exhaled. "They found your prints inside the purse and on the clasp that opens and closes the pouch where they found the meth." She studied Sadie's indignant expression.

"Oh, my God. So thirty years of friendship are out the window?

You can leave now. I'll never forget this—*ever.*" Sadie rushed to the kitchen and threw her saucer and cup into the sink; shards of broken glass and tea splashed onto the Formica and white shutters.

"Sadie, relax. Just explain things; I'm trying to understand." Her denial had been so absolute, so convincing, that Skye considered she might be innocent.

"I don't have to prove anything to you, but here you go. I borrowed your lipstick as you were talking to Cody and the sheriff. *That's* why my prints are in your purse. You've just torn my heart out. Now please leave."

Could Skye be accusing her best friend of something she hadn't done? Unlikely, she told herself; no one applies lipstick as a sheriff enters their kitchen. "Let's sit down and work this out. I'm as uncomfortable as you are, and I want to believe you."

"You sanctimonious bitch. I've always been a good friend to you. Loyal and honest—it's the only way I know how to be. But it turns out you aren't the friend I thought you were, so goodbye." She extended her arm and slammed the door shut as Skye stepped onto the front porch.

It wasn't the first time someone had called her sanctimonious or a bitch. It *was* the first time Sadie lashed out with such resentment. Skye drove away trying to figure it all out.

CHAPTER 45

All those gathered understood that without the Westbrookes' patronage and Thomas's vision and tireless efforts, there'd be no celebration to attend this day and no cancer center to be proud of tomorrow. Twelve hundred officials and luminaries gathered for the coronation of one of the most advanced cancer facilities in the West.

Thomas spoke to the assembled crowd, "And finally, I want to express the Westbrooke family's gratitude to those who've contributed to our city. Thank you, citizens, for your contributions to the finest community within this great nation. *You* are why Eagle Bay has been ranked one of the Top Ten Towns in America—for three straight years!"

The crowd chanted, "Pillar, Pillar, Pillar!"

Thomas continued, "Let me recognize the legend himself, my wonderful father and committed philanthropist, Robert Westbrooke." The guests roared their approval for the elder statesman of the dynasty, presenting him with a one-minute standing ovation. Robert lowered his pipe and tipped his head to the adoring masses.

The prodigy forged since childhood to be the face of the Westbrookes' enterprises impressed patrons and stirred a sense of collective pride. He continued his gushing admiration of Robert, "It is because of this man that I've been able to expand our business operations and use the benefits of that growth as a resource for advancing the community we all cherish. With sincerity, I say thank you, Dad. Thank you, Robert Westbrooke. You're the noblest man I know." Thomas strode to the patriarch, bent down to meet his seated body, and kissed his forehead. The young maverick, dressed in his William Fioravanti suit, then stood and pivoted to face the group. He bellowed jovially, "Now, let's eat and drink some of Oregon's finest!"

Thomas walked off the stage to meet a group of luminaries at a reserved table for their tête-à-tête. He engaged the governor, mayor, and new president of the Westbrooke Cancer Center. The governor envisioned Thomas on the hustings and hoped (almost audibly so) that he'd never run for the state's top office—the Pillar would win in a landslide.

Robert saw nothing but red flags. His son had just delivered a rousing speech laced with adoration of his father, sentiments Thomas had never publicly displayed (and, privately, only before age twelve). Something was up, something big, and Robert wondered if it was happening in real-time.

Robert had always accepted that he might one day have to battle his son for control of the assets and Westbrooke empire. Was this the pivotal moment Thomas's idle threats grew no longer idle? He considered the timing of his son's performance intriguing. The previous week, Robert had made an astonishing discovery while reconciling his secreted Inca treasures, which validated his unspoken presumption. The riches held in his vault represented only part of what the *Santa Sofia* used as ballast on her journey to the northwestern shores of New Spain. More incredible treasures existed—somewhere.

Robert debated whether Thomas knew the whereabouts of the

remaining riches. Impossible. No one could have accessed Montoya's journal or Robert's notes and translations kept inside his impenetrable vault. No, the patriarch sat convinced his son remained unaware that Capitán Montoya mentioned a second sandstone cavern filled with more Spanish bounty. Robert spent the prior week trying to pinpoint the location of the undiscovered Inca riches, a process he knew would remain daunting.

But Thomas had his own secrets and a plan of action regarding the *known* treasures. Step one: play it cool. Step two: move the A1-A4 assets held in Oregon and abroad. Step three: eliminate his adversary.

Robert and Thomas smiled and shook hands with dignitaries and benefactors as dinner continued. The cuisine was classic Oregonian: fresh oysters, clams, Dungeness crab, and Coho salmon. Seventy-five cases of Oregon's highly regarded St. Innocent pinot noir got served as the event's seafood accompaniment, impressing the crowd and ensuring their mood would remain upbeat.

Emma assumed her role as the unexpressive wife drifting deeper into mental obscurity. The public grew impressed by Robert's attentiveness to a diminished woman he demonstrably cherished. Those Westbrookes were good people.

Thomas apologized for stepping away from his conversation with the table guests. Holding his Motorola flip phone to his ear, he carefully listened before answering the man on the other end. "Yes, go ahead. But remember, flawless execution."

Halfway through the evening's scheduled events, the elder Westbrookes departed in their limo. Minutes later, the driver's phone rang as the chauffeur carrying Robert and Emma rolled to a stop at the intersection of Pine and Willow streets. Billy Platt addressed his perturbed employer as the limo momentarily idle, "Mr. Westbrooke, please excuse the interruption."

"Platt, how many times have I told you to silence that damn contraption before I set foot in this vehicle?" Robert said while lowering the pipe bowl he had been packing with fresh tobacco. "And no one but me is supposed to have your number, you irresponsible son—"

The sound was subtle. It reminded Emma and Billy of the pitch made when a crystal wine glass breaks onto a tiled floor. The bullet entered the right rear passenger window, Robert's temple, and settled inside his brain. His head slumped sideways toward Emma as if he'd merely nodded off.

Deep red oozed from the hole, cascading over his cheek and neck and spreading across the white of his pinpoint oxford. The smell of blood filled the cabin, and cool air flowed in through the shattered window. Billy opened his door and rushed around to pull Robert from his seat, laying his warm body on cold asphalt.

Emma was neither stunned nor panicked by her husband's sudden demise. The years of suffering from his insolence, devious incarceration, and injustices left her unable to grieve for the evil man. She stared out the open door and met Billy's gaze with a nod as he crouched next to Robert. Only Billy understood that Emma Westbrooke sat fully aware of where she was, what time it was, and what had just occurred. Five days earlier, fate had altered her world.

Back at the cancer center, Thomas's phone rang, and he excused himself from the VIP table just as servers delivered warm plates of cedar-plank salmon. He assumed the plan for the evening, a plot he and three others were privy to, had been executed. Answering calmly, he said, "Smooth sailing?"

"No, Mr. Westbrooke. Your father is dead." Antonio Salazar presented the facts bluntly, as Thomas had always required him to.

"Yes, I understand that. Do you have the assets?" The evening's plan had included the murder of Robert but also something far more important to Thomas.

"Your father was killed before he arrived here at the estate. Mrs. Westbrooke and the driver are safe. According to the police radio, it was a single shot to the head five miles from here. How should I proceed?"

"What are you talking about? If this is a misguided ploy to play me, please be assured it will not end well. You know I'm a man of my word." He stood irritated but spoke impassively. He had planned to kill Robert after pilfering the primary assets, A1, from the vault below his parents' residence.

"You have been an ideal employer, Mr. Westbrooke," Antonio replied. "There would be no benefit for me to injure our relationship."

"So you didn't get the codes from my father? Never got access to the assets?" He trusted his Argentine contact, though he'd planned to have him eliminated the following day, framed as Robert's murderer.

Antonio understood the questions were a test. "If someone killed your father before I extracted the codes from him, how could I enter the vault? As I said, someone assassinated him before he made it home. I'm still at your parents' estate. Shall I depart?"

Thomas internalized the developments. "No," he said. "I'll arrive to comfort Mrs. Westbrooke. The police will get there before me, so leave the premises but stay available."

After returning to his dining guests, Thomas measured the options for completing both primary objectives of the evening. Someone had just eliminated Robert—goal number two accomplished. The mystery of who pulled the trigger would get solved later. He still needed the codes to achieve objective number one—control the assets.

Upon informing the notables of an urgent personal matter, Thomas departed the gala with all admirers' eyes upon him. His mind raced while driving his Jag XKE toward his parents' mansion. It was twilight as he ascended roads offering views of the Pacific, and the sparkling ocean appeared closer than usual. He'd already begun analyzing all communications and interactions he'd had over the previous days, trying to determine how Robert's killer planned his very effective strike.

He was more intrigued than concerned. Problems were opportunities, as he'd often said within the halls of WCI. He dissected three essential mysteries regarding the assets. They began with who, what, and how?

CHAPTER 46

It had been a difficult delivery for seventeen-year-old Dakota. Skye and a legion of hospital staff supported her through labor, but she eventually welcomed a son into the family. Dakota had informed Johnny he could join Skye for the birthing, but he'd graciously bowed out, privately mumbling there was *no way in hell* he would watch his sister squeeze out a baby.

"Mom, he's so amazing. The most beautiful thing I've ever seen," Dakota said. The teenager's long and arduous public and private journey had taken its toll, but the glow in her tired face expressed the wonder of a new life.

"Yes, honey, he's perfect." Mom held her daughter's hand as the exhausted teenage mother cuddled her wrapped infant.

Johnny finally entered the delivery room, but only after anything that might unsettle an eighteen-year-old brother got removed or concealed. He exclaimed, "Wow, look at that stellar little dude. Great work, Dakota."

"Say hello to Henry Charles McCloud," his sister replied, beaming with tired yet sparkling eyes.

"Love the name!" Butchering a British accent, he added, "Very regal, m'lady."

"Perfect," she said. "I was seeking a name suggesting power and purpose. Long live King McCloud."

"Slow down," Johnny chuckled. "Let him earn the title of 'toddler' before I start bowing to him."

"I'm hoping he grows up to be like you two," Dakota said as her gaze shifted from mother to brother. "I can't think of any better role models." She stared at Skye and said, "Mom, you're the strongest parent I know. You led us through all the challenging times. I'm so proud to be your daughter."

"Well, I hope Henry grows up to be like you. And you've given me too much credit, honey, but I appreciate the sentiments." Skye pressed one of Dakota's hands between her own.

"Can I interrupt your mother-daughter Hallmark moment and hold him?" Johnny asked.

As he pulled the boy to his chest, his eyes glistened, and the room fell silent. Twenty minutes later, a doctor and two nurses entered and asked Skye and Johnny to exit briefly, so they stepped into the hall, glowing.

Early the previous evening, Skye and Johnny had agreed to turn off their phones to focus entirely on Dakota and the moment; twenty-three hours had since passed. While sitting in a small visitors room across the hall during his sister's delivery, Johnny cheated and tried to connect with his friends, but the reception was too weak. Skye now suggested they run to the cafeteria for a snack and better reception. As they entered the food court, Skye noticed she had three voicemails from Cody. Before listening to any of them, she dialed his number.

"Hey, Skye, I hope everything's good with Dakota and the baby."

"Thank you, Cody; it's a momentous day. Mom and baby are doing great, and Johnny's got a nephew named Henry." She'd noted his initial anxious tone. "Is everything okay?"

"Well . . . not exactly. You haven't heard, obviously. Someone murdered Robert Westbrooke last night."

"What?"

"A few miles from their place," he said. "The whole town's going nuts. I'm sorry for dropping this bomb on you, but I thought it best to hold off until Dakota had delivered her baby—Henry."

"Murdered?" Skye audibly questioned while digesting the news. *"Murdered?* I'm stunned."

Cody added, "Their chauffeur was driving them home from the Cancer Center christening. Someone fired a shot through the limo window. Despite all the recent drama he's directed, I feel bad for Thomas. It's tragic news all the way around." He informed her of everything he knew and inadvertently called Skye "Sadie."

Skye paused. "Cody, have you heard anything from her?" Sadie had gone quiet two days earlier and wasn't returning his calls. She'd given no warning, explanation, or clues.

"Nothing."

Her absence didn't feel ominous to Cody; he convinced himself she'd show up at any moment. Earlier in the week, he'd told Skye he didn't believe Sadie was guilty of slipping meth into her purse the night of her arrest. But he harbored no ill will toward Skye for seeking clarification from his girlfriend—there were some loose ends.

Skye shared Cody's big news with Johnny as they walked back to Dakota's hospital room. She contemplated the sometimes-ironic circle of life. A man who helped transform Eagle Bay, the esteemed Robert Westbrooke, lay dead in a morgue. Hours later, a new son was born into the family of his one-time daughter-in-law, Skye McCloud. Two prominent names simultaneously confront momentous events. One year earlier, they considered themselves branches of the same family tree.

CHAPTER 47

Thomas wondered if the dichotomies of his life had grown glaring. Uncomfortably, he realized many of his unspoken thoughts were bizarre or disturbing. If people could measure the depths of his psychosis, they'd be frightened. Hell, even he was worried. But nothing and no one could supplant the single thing dominating his psyche—the assets. His pursuit of them had turned manic. They were remarkable, and he was their rightful heir. He'd earned them.

The morning after Robert's demise, Thomas's first call was to America West Security, specialists at installing and accessing bank and private vaults. Because only Robert's mind possessed all the codes necessary to claim the assets, Thomas believed it was ninety-five percent probable there'd been no breach. But it was in his DNA to be thorough when it mattered most; five percent uncertainty was too much, given the prize. He presumed Robert's killers knew about the gems, gold, and Inca treasures.

"Mr. Westbrooke, our legal team has reviewed the power of attorney you supplied, and we have the green light to gain access," said Mr. Johnson, owner of America West Security. "Whoever designed this guaranteed there'd be no breach. We'll need to employ military-grade explosives because we're dealing with twenty-inch cement walls encased in three-inch-thick, flame-resistant steel plates comprised of the highest-grade metal I've ever tested. Your father had someone build an impressive fortress. The grid-locking door is damn near impenetrable. That's the good news for whatever he wanted to protect. The bad news is that we're not getting inside without using something sophisticated. I'm thinking C4, precision-targeted at the hinges and rods."

"I've already told you to do whatever's necessary. The sooner this gets done, the better."

"I understand," Mr. Johnson replied. "We'll be ready to detonate in two more hours."

"Inform your men I have armed security on the grounds. A precaution," Thomas said. He pursed his lips, pivoted, and ascended the cherry wood stairs.

"I'll spread the word," Mr. Johnson replied. "One last thing—you can't be down here during detonation."

"Now you're frustrating me. Know that I'll be close by but safe during the blast. It'll be our dirty little secret. Or we can wrap this up, and you can get off the property. Your call, Mr. Johnson."

Moments passed. "Okay, I'll see you in a bit." The money was too good—state laws and safety protocols be damned.

Thomas moved upstairs and advised people to assemble outside the patios and gazebos. He warned his three Argentine heavies to prepare for the remote possibility of intruders attempting to force their way to the assets, then he winked at Antonio Salazar.

An hour later, Thomas was about to descend the stairs to the vault when an unexpected voice startled him. He hadn't seen his Bostonian sister Sarah in over three years and instantly turned suspicious. "You flew from New York to PDX and drove here, all in less than ten hours?" He watched her jaw drop, then told himself to dial back his belligerence.

Sarah frowned. "It's good to see you, too, Thomas. Our father just died; maybe a hug and some comforting words would make sense." She stepped forward, peered into his expressionless face, and awkwardly embraced him. "It's a horrible day. I'm trying to catch up with the facts."

"Yes, it's tragic," he said as he rubbed his chin, quietly unsettled by her presence. "What do you mean by 'facts?'"

"What happened at the cancer center ceremony?"

"What's that supposed to mean?"

"Something happened between you and Robert."

"According to whom, Sarah?"

"According to Robert. He called me right after you'd finished delivering a speech last night. He told me to hop on a red-eye, and here I am. *That's* how I got here so quickly." She replayed her short conversation with Robert, which had transpired just as he and Emma departed the cancer center christening.

Thomas said, "I don't believe you." So much for toning down his belligerence.

"*He told me to rush home!* So I did, only to find out someone *killed him* during my flight." She didn't inform Thomas that Robert provided her with three pieces of confidential information. She had no idea why he had but was determined to find out. "What the hell happened last night?"

"Nothing happened. What do you want from me?"

"The truth. You weren't involved, right?"

"Involved in . . . what?" He projected hurt.

She didn't respond.

"Sarah, I won't grieve as you will, but I could never harm my father. I'm disturbed you could even consider the question."

She studied him and ceased what suddenly felt like pointless interrogation. "Sorry. I'm frazzled, and this insane news is beyond distressing. Dad put immense pressure on you during his life, and I thought you two had argued or . . . something. I didn't mean to infer anything dreadful."

"I understand." He held her hand sincerely. "We had a wonderful evening. Some as-yet-unknown shooter murdered him on the way home. I was still at the ceremony when it happened and remain as perplexed as you."

Sarah pressed his wrist while dissecting her earlier conversation with Robert, concurrently scrutinizing everything she'd observed since her arrival. Sadly, she felt Thomas's compassion appeared somewhat contrived. Something was wrong.

"Emma's in the garden room; it would be great if you could check on her," Thomas said. "She appears to be her normal passive self, but events have interrupted her routine." As if it were unimportant, he added, "The vault's going to get accessed with explosives. We'll talk in a bit."

"Explosives? For access?" she shot back. "Oh, Thomas, that's ridiculous. I'll open it. But first, tell me what you're looking for."

Thomas's forehead creased, and he projected disdain that unsettled Sarah anew. *I will open it? Impossible*, Thomas thought. He judged it a sibling provocation and was in no mood for ruses or complications.

"Sarah, you don't know the codes to the vault. I would've been aware of that development *before* Robert delivered them. So please, no games."

"Well, then, surprise. Robert passed them to me last night. Why do you think that was? I'm surprised you don't have them. There must be reasons for all of this." She moved downstairs and barked at the men wiring the C4, *"Stop!* We're not blowing anything up today. Thanks, but please pack up and leave."

The company president directed his surprise toward Thomas, who slowly nodded and motioned for the crew to depart. At least for now, he thought. The owner commented that a large bill would still be forthcoming, based on Thomas's urgent request and the painstaking nature of the work his crew had just completed.

Sarah requested his business card, wrote something on it, and handed it back. "I'll make sure you get paid."

Thomas observed Sarah speaking with confidence and authority; he was impressed. Her intelligence, articulate dialogue, and general presence suggested "leader." No wonder she'd reached the executive ranks. But she was no match for the Pillar. He'd recognized these same displays of determination during their years under the same roof, which he respected then as now. But while sensing that Sarah honestly believed she could access the vault, he surmised she *had* to be bluffing. "You're a real work of art, but I'll play along with your theater."

Standing next to the vault, Sarah located three electronic touch-pads paired with manual combination dials; she would have to enter six sets of numbers to unlock the imposing door. After tapping the codes on the first touchpad, she spun the second set of numbers on the corresponding rotary dial: right, left, right, left, right. *Click.*

Thomas stared at her with an expression he hoped was emotionless. Could she detect his sudden anxiety that he was now only *assuming* versus *knowing* she wouldn't be able to enter the vault?

She moved to the second touchpad and entered a set of numbers, followed by a manual spin of another rotary dial. *Click.*

He transitioned to slightly neurotic.

Sarah shielded his view and entered the final set of numbers. Whoever entered the six sets correctly would detect the whirring sounds of eight titanium hydraulic shafts receding into the walls, allowing the vault door to open with a push inward. She tapped the touchpad and turned the dial using the last set of numbers. Dead silence.

Denied after all! Thomas thought, shaking his head gratifyingly. For effect, he derisively mumbled, "Hmm . . ." But seconds later, a humming emanated from inside the wood-paneled metal door. The hydraulic rods vibrated as they receded. Thomas stood incredulous and dazed. "You've got to be bloody kidding me." He listened for twelve seconds until the sounds of movement ceased.

"Dad wanted me to control access for a reason, Thomas. I'm assuming you've been inside before. Now that it's unlocked, tell me why you're so determined to get inside."

He pushed her aside and stepped forward, flipping on switches as he entered; brilliant white flooded the room from lighting adhered to the cement walls and ceiling. Ten metal cases dominated the vault, identical six-foot cubes of polished steel lettered A–J on top and side panels. A single handle adorned the lid atop each case.

Sarah hurried to open the case labeled A, declaring, "Pardon my intrigue."

Thomas debated preventing her from viewing the contents, but too many people were on the property to intervene if he created a scene. Instead, the siblings would share the astonishment of extraordinary wealth and history. Later, he might need to eliminate the sister he still loved; killing in the name of his obsession had grown justifiable—she'd forced his hand by inserting herself into his affairs.

The first case was empty.

They stared at each other, puzzled. Thomas's expression morphed into hostility. He rushed from container to container, grabbing and lifting the handles on top of those labeled B through I. Each was empty. Only J remained unopened, so he raised its lid. Something lay inside, a small manila envelope with *Thomas* written across it. Each container included an access door, and he opened the three-foot-wide entry to grab the envelope. Sarah darted forward, but he shoved her away and opened the envelope in a corner of the vault. Two four-inch by six-inch photos were inside.

"What? This can't be."

"What is it?" Sarah demanded. "What's it say? Why are the cases empty? What was in them?"

Thomas realized Sarah appeared genuinely bewildered and confused. *But she has to know—about everything.*

"Stop the charade. You know damn well what was in these containers and this envelope. Enough of the deer-in-headlights facade. You can't pull this off, you painfully naive bitch. Tell me where it all is. Screw with me, and I'll ruin your life."

His words frightened her, but she responded aggressively, "I'd never seen these containers! Show me what's in the envelope. *Now!* What are you hiding?"

She was visibly flustered and struggled to express strength. "Is this how you're going to play it?" Thomas pushed her into the corner and pinned her body against the bright steel, leering. "I have no patience for your games. Please know that. Tell me where the assets are."

"Dear God, Thomas, what's happened to you? What have you done? And what do you mean, assets?"

"You're making a huge mistake, little sister." He exited the chamber clutching the envelope, his face strained and jaw clenched.

"Show me what's inside," she again demanded. "You owe me the truth. It's not right what you're doing."

He halted his ascent into Robert's office. "Photos of a cuff," he shouted down the stairwell. "A brass cuff."

He regretted giving her any insight or clue, but it was too late to retract the words. Besides, Sarah seemed truly befuddled. Was he being duped? There were high odds of that, he thought. Nearing the top of the stairs, he peered into the envelope again, asking himself, how? He mouthed the words etched onto the manacle: *John, With Love, Skye.*

Thomas recalled the night he removed John's most precious possession from his lifeless body.

CHAPTER 48

There were too many unanswered questions.

Tensions between brother and sister had grown thick and destructive. Sarah grew appalled by the absence of empathy Thomas showed Emma since Robert's assassination. She'd managed every aspect of their father's funeral and memorial, which Thomas attended only because it would have been bad publicity to be absent. He refused to speak at either observance, feigning heartbreak and despair. In truth, Thomas remained preoccupied with a single pressing matter: Where were the assets?

Sarah insisted she knew nothing about the contents of the containers in the vault, but Thomas found that impossible to accept. He grew less interested in and more unencumbered by expectations of civilized social interaction. Robert had schooled him from an early age never to forget the *rules of engagement* when under suspicion or interrogation: *Deny, deny, when caught in a lie. And when all else fails—deny again.* He assumed Robert imparted that same convoluted wisdom to Sarah, who was now playing him for a fool, which infuriated and impressed him.

The Westbrookes' Oregon-based physical wealth served as collateral for private lenders in the US, Europe, and South America. The unique capital funded the family empire's business interests and lifestyle. But

A1 had vanished, and Thomas needed to find it himself; turning to the authorities could reveal the Pandora's box that was his family's sordid history. Scrutiny was always the family's greatest threat. Regardless of what his sister knew or didn't know, he devised options for dealing with the "Sarah problem."

Before World War II, William Westbrooke, Thomas and Sarah's grandfather and the killer of John McCloud I, funneled the family's incredible riches through multiple illegitimate organizations whose tentacles reached legitimate banks in Argentina, France, and Switzerland. In the 1920s, William's international relationships helped conceal the nature and magnitude of the assets in the not-yet-dynastic family's possession. Over the ensuing decades, low percentages of Westbrooke wealth—the assets—were relocated overseas in stages. With Robert dead, only Thomas understood those crucial details.

Criminal enterprises, essentially Mafia groups, managed relationships with respected banks in exchange for fees paid by the Westbrookes whenever assets in the US got transferred and sheltered abroad. Every person and group involved in converting the physical wealth into tradable currencies benefited—none more than the Westbrookes. The model evolved into a complicated money flow for the uninitiated, but Thomas handled it effortlessly and precisely. Robert and his father, William, never considered dealing exclusively with legitimate institutions; having Mafiosos' well-educated sons and daughters act as intermediaries lessened their exposure.

Because the Americans handsomely rewarded their European partners, those parties never grew preoccupied with how the Oregon family initially possessed gold, silver, and remarkable Inca artifacts. None of the shadow organizations would have guessed that the bulk of the assets rested in a vault beneath Robert Westbrooke's residence in Eagle Bay. Thomas and Robert were careful never to divulge the A1 assets' history, scale, or location. And yet, Thomas frustratingly acknowledged, someone had discovered that information.

Though they had behaved as committed partners for decades, Robert sometimes cautioned Thomas not to underestimate the Mafia's power and zeal. The family's business model only functioned properly when the possessions—A1 in Oregon, A2 in Buenos Aires, A3 in Lyon, and A4 in Geneva—were transported and managed judiciously and in line with stakeholders' expectations. Thomas deemed it a risk that godfathers and patriarchs had lived extravagant lifestyles for six decades through dealings with Westbrooke patriarchs. He agreed there were dangers when getting in bed with the devil, but he just needed to sustain the model a bit longer—until the day he and the assets would disappear.

That prospect exhilarated him. Somehow, he'd soon gain control of the single thing dominating his psyche since childhood. The assets were a worthy pursuit, an aspiration borne of Robert's twisted tutelage. *Of course I deserve them. Are you turning in your grave, Robert?*

He'd become impatient with the pace of locating his obsession. It was time to accelerate matters.

49

CHAPTER

Emma sat in her hand-crafted wingback chair and listened. That was the remarkable truth: *She was listening. Understanding.* Ever since the day Gabriela Mendes disappeared when Thomas was thirteen, Emma Westbrooke had become little more than an ornament in her home, a victim of extreme sedation with illegally prescribed antipsychotic drugs. And then it all changed, a secret she continued to guard.

Days before Robert's assassination, she'd stopped taking the medications that would, as Dr. Munro had explained to the Westbrooke family, help Emma function after her "complete mental breakdown." The doctor's agreement with Robert had kept her in a two-decades-long compromised state, leaving her unable to understand complex issues, express normal emotions, or make even mundane decisions.

Dr. Munro's sudden demise from a brain aneurysm triggered momentous changes. The nurses assigned to treat Emma continued drugging her as the now-dead Dr. Munro had instructed for years. Unbeknownst to the RNs, the medications administered to Emma since her concocted "mental breakdown" were highly debilitating, dangerous elixirs personally fashioned by Dr. Munro, like a mad scientist mixing potions in his lab. Thus, the nurses had unwittingly maintained Emma's stupor.

Upon Dr. Munro's death, Robert searched for and found another sketchy doctor he could buy off to continue Emma's contrived treatment for acute mental illness. But just before the new routine got executed, the unknown assassin murdered Robert. Thomas was granted medical power of attorney over Emma through Robert's will. When nurses called him inquiring how to proceed with his mother's care, he located a competent physician to monitor her condition and prescribe medications. Thomas lived unaware that Robert had plotted and sustained Emma's mental stupor.

On the fourth day of being administered the weaker drugs, Emma stopped swallowing any pills, spitting and flushing them away upon her nurse's departure. As her mind slowly recovered, she took a huge gamble and confided in Billy Platt, the ex-Army Ranger Robert had hired for protection under the guise of "limo driver." Emma judged Billy as ethical and needed an ally to pull off her renaissance.

The middle-aged patient grew more coherent every day and eventually fully liberated herself. Proactive and articulate thought returned, as did memories. Emma Westbrooke had reawakened, though friends and family remained unaware. Having missed much of her children's adolescent development and adult lives, she told herself to observe and learn before judging or acting.

Sarah perceived a minor change in Emma, but it would have been impossible for anyone to realize the extent of her rebirth. Thomas scarcely interacted with Emma since Robert's assassination; she remained the passive and distant mother he'd known since that day Gabriela disappeared, and the mutilated puppy died on their back patio.

Brother and sister were locked in a testy exchange. Emma remained seated in the background, as she'd done for too many years of oblivion. But this evening, she compiled copious mental notes, carefully assessing the siblings. Sarah displayed signs of what Emma perceived to be genuine decency, so much so that she yearned to embrace her daughter and engage in conversation as her now-cogent mother. That would have to wait.

Thomas appeared sick or evil. She'd feared it since he was thirteen and assumed her dead husband was at least partially responsible. Robert had insisted on terminating Thomas's psychological evaluations during that time, overriding Emma's pleas that the once cheerful boy needed help. During the past week, it hurt to observe the actions of a gifted man who once possessed the limitless potential for good. She grew horrified assessing his calculated deceptions and treatment of Sarah, and guilt burdened every inch of her soul.

While her newfound clarity prompted competing emotions, she vowed to keep those feelings corralled until she'd uncovered the evidence necessary to seek justice for people harmed by her husband and son. She believed she was on the verge of crucial revelations that she could deliver to authorities.

Sarah said, "You sound like you're losing your mind, Thomas. You don't trust me and treat your parents terribly—the living and the dead. And no, I have no idea what was in those containers in the vault. Or where their contents might be."

"I don't believe that because Robert granted you the codes. Pretending you're clueless is ridiculous. Ignorance is not bliss; it's unbecoming and dangerous. No more wasting time with your contrived bullshit. Understand? I want the assets, and you know where they are. Continuing this pretense could eventually drive WCI into the ground, and I won't let you do that."

"What?" Sarah replied. "Drive the company into the ground? You're delusional."

"I'm responsible for making our companies grow and prosper while you play fashionista back east," he replied. "I've done a fine job, and you're a beneficiary of that success. The assets make everything possible. But managing our little dynasty is becoming a less rewarding pursuit for me."

"You're impossible to follow. Why can't you tell me what these assets you keep referring to are?"

"I still have Robert's lecture memorized. 'Don't ever describe them in real terms, ever. You're to refer to them *only* as the assets whenever we discuss them.' I was twelve. They're all that matters, Sarah. You *know* that. It appears Robert decided to entrust them to you before meeting his end. And now you've hidden them."

She expressed annoyance and confusion. "Go away. I can't decide if you're pretending to be confused or are genuinely mentally ill."

He smiled devilishly as dark thoughts stirred and emotions strained the vestiges of any rational thought. Controlling his thoughts grew difficult. "I've done horrible things to protect the assets, to protect us," he said. "Robert owed me. Now *you* owe me. I've reached the end of my rope and think I might be melting down." He stared out a window to the valley below and muttered, "You're playing with fire. You're playing with fire. You're playing with fire . . ." Thomas turned and stood at attention like a soldier, repeating the words, "You're playing with fire . . ."

"Oh, dear God," Sarah said, her voice cracking.

He raised his voice but remained rigidly upright, sounding like a broken record. "You're playing with fire . . ."

Sarah looked as if she were about to speak but said nothing as tears cascaded down her cheeks.

Thomas stopped his incessant chirping. Expressing nothingness, he strode up to Sarah's side, and with their faces separated by inches, he tilted his head eerily left and right. Upon inspecting her features for seconds that felt like minutes, he spoke in a threatening tone.

"I want to hurt you."

"You're disgusting. *Get out!*"

"No, seriously, I want to hurt you. Tie you up to a beam and torture you. Take gardening shears and clip off your pinky. Your left pinky. *Clip!* Listen carefully. *Clip!* Can you imagine that? I can. And after the *clip clip* I want to observe your reactions, your agony. Yes, yes, yes! *Clip clip!*"

She stood, unable to reply.

"You have the information I need, Sarah. You're trying to play me like a damn fiddle, but you'll tell me where the assets are. I promise. Double-pinky promise." He reached out, clutched her body tightly, and kissed her on the cheek. "And then you might die, *bitch*." He roared with laughter.

"You're insane."

CHAPTER 50

It was bound to happen eventually. The priest on St. Croix warned Thomas to seek redemption or risk succumbing to his demons. But he'd repressed his urges too long, and it felt good threatening Sarah; he anticipated the euphoria of following through.

She darted from his clutches. "I'm calling the police. You need help." Struggling to maintain composure, she hoped to appear steadfast and convincing. His expression told her she failed as an actor.

Smiling while lifting his brows and arms, Thomas said, "Let's hike over to the famous Westbrooke Century Barn. There's a whole lotta rope out there to tie you up with, and then I'll find the garden shears. *Clip! Clip!*" He released a guttural hoot. Deep troughs lay etched across his forehead. "Come on, fashionista, let's do this! Good times!"

His face and body movements grew more expressive. Rapidly nodding, he mimicked the motions of tying Sarah up and squeezing clippers as if participating in a game of charades for the mentally deranged.

Sarah hurried to the antique hall stand and grabbed the phone atop its marble base to dial 911. "This is Sarah Westbrooke at the Westbrooke estate on Osprey Drive. I need help; my brother has turned deranged and is threatening to cut off my finger. *Please hurry!*"

Thomas grinned as he walked toward her, circling her body like a quiet, preying intruder, whispering, "Deny, deny, when caught in a lie . . ." Only Sarah could hear him, not the emergency dispatcher.

She glared and jabbed twice at his shoulder with an open palm, then yelled into the phone, "Get the police over here—now!"

Placing his arms around her midsection, he hugged her tense body. She tightened her grip on a phone she considered her only link to safety. "He appears disconnected from reality. I think he's going to hurt me."

The siblings sensed movement across the room and turned in that direction. Emma stepped forward with an angry face, and they froze. "*Stop it, Thomas!*" she commanded.

Emma spoke lucidly for the first time in their adult lives. With eyes glassy from regret but with steely resolve, she grabbed Sarah's wrist and sneered at the man she had given birth to almost forty years earlier. "I know what you're capable of, Thomas. Your sister's right—you need help. Leave her alone. It's over." She yanked Sarah from his side.

Thomas stiffened, gathered himself, and responded in a voice still too soft to be heard by the operator. "My goodness. Stunning news: Mommy nut case has temporarily snapped out of her stupor. Welcome back, Mrs. Westbrooke. What's up?" He turned to Sarah and rambled, "Deny, deny, when caught in a lie."

"What's happening?" Sarah said as she shifted her gaze from Thomas to Emma. One urgent issue at a time, she told herself. "They're on their way, Thomas. Enough of your madness. Sit down and get a hold of yourself. *Stop threatening me!*" Her brother had devolved into a remnant of the once-loving sibling who'd shared her childhood. And Emma, at least momentarily, no longer resembled the diminished mother of the past two decades. Her world had been wholly upended.

Thomas stepped away and began ballroom dancing solo across

the black and ivory checkerboard floor. He moved with his arms clasped before him and his feet gliding gracefully as if enjoying an intimate moment with an invisible lover. The sounds of tapping heels and sliding leather soles were oddly serene. Every few elegant movements, he'd repeat the words, "Deny, deny, when caught in a lie."

Interred as a wallflower for years, Emma spoke of the events prompting her imprisonment. "I remember that day, Thomas. You knew something about Gabriela Mendes vanishing. I think you did something terrible, and I swear people will know the truth before I die."

He stopped twirling and stood slump-shouldered, appearing angelic. "Before you die? You mean, like, tonight?" He cocked his head.

"Your father did great harm mentoring and shielding you. By introducing you to evil, he let you live guilty of conscience but free of repercussions."

"You're right," he replied. "I haven't had a conscience for twenty years."

The wonder of her mother's shocking revival contrasted with her brother's meltdown. "Mother? Are you . . . actually okay? I mean . . ." She dropped the phone and ran to Emma.

Thomas strode to the phone and set it back upon its base, killing the connection. He glowered. "Your mother isn't well, Sarah. She needs help. She speaks coherently, but she's batty. Aren't you, Mommy nut job?"

"I'm quite well and have been for weeks. I've been reborn—enlightened, if you will—and I'll set things right. I'm not afraid of your wickedness and threats, Thomas."

Thomas squinted with crow's feet stretching to his temples. He drew back his shoulders and neck. "Who do you think you are? If I'm evil, I hope you're burdened eternally with images of birthing me."

Sarah's face tightened, and she shouted, "Listen to you! You sound like the devil. Get out of here."

"It gets worse. I'm convinced your brother killed John McCloud."

"*What?*" Sarah yelled. "*No!* Thomas, tell me that's not true."

Emma proceeded unwaveringly. "He killed his best friend. I'd been snooping around the guesthouse and found an engraved cuff Skye had gifted John atop a shelf in a closet." She stepped away from Sarah and approached Thomas aggressively, stopping to peer with furious eyes, projecting contempt. "How could you do that? You're appalling."

"Christ, poor Skye! And then you *married* her, Thomas? Raised Johnny and Dakota as your own? I can't . . . What are you?" Sarah grabbed a seventeenth-century Japanese vase and threw it at his head. He ducked it.

Beams of light from approaching EBPD cruisers swept through windows and across rare paintings decorating interior walls. Urgent sounds and slamming car doors echoed, anxious voices called out, and heavy legs rushed through the grounds.

"Yes, your brother is responsible for John's murder. I'm guessing it happened in our barn. Now we know the truth, Thomas, and—" She halted as multiple police officers charged into the room through every entrance.

"Thank God you've arrived, Sheriff," Thomas lucidly exclaimed. "My mother has experienced another psychotic episode. I've tried to comfort her, to no avail."

"*You liar!* Comfort? My brother's snapped. He's threatening me and acting like a demented patient in the psych ward. And I've just been told he committed terrible crimes against people in Eagle Bay. A young girl and John McCloud! You remember John, right, Sheriff? My mother has damning proof Thomas killed him."

"I'm sorry, Sheriff," Thomas said. "As you'll quickly discern, I'm quite coherent this evening, not the mentally imbalanced person Sarah claims." He held his arm out to his mother and sister. "My heart aches for these women; I love them very much. But we've had problems with Mrs. Westbrooke's medicating, resulting in frightening hallucinogenic episodes. Tonight's is the latest of several episodes I've dealt with recently."

"He's lying again!" Sarah argued. "He's going crazy, threatening both of us." Stepping closer, she held an accusing finger inches from Thomas's face. "Tell the truth, damnit."

"Sarah," Thomas said, "I love you. We'll get through this."

"Mom, tell them!" Sarah demanded.

Thomas interrupted. "I've got a power-of-attorney assigning me as sole legal authority for all issues regarding Emma Westbrooke. Could you please have an ambulance delivered to the property? I want to ensure she gets the care she deserves." He expressed genuine concern, portraying the honorable man everyone had read about, the business icon and community benefactor with exemplary character. The Pillar of Eagle Bay.

Sarah persisted in making her case, demanding her statements get written down. The realization of what was happening pushed her to extreme behavior. The authorities' faces conveyed compassion for the distraught sister, but their collective expressions reflected a shared judgment: At this moment, Sarah was the irrational Westbrooke.

"You're not listening to me! My brother's playing all of you for morons. Five minutes ago, he threatened to cut off my fingers while chirping the words 'deny, deny, when caught in a lie.' Now he's orchestrating your every move. Why can't you see through it?" She shook her head while measuring each doubting face, her mouth agape.

"I'd deny the statements if they weren't so patently absurd. Sheriff Boseman, let me know what you need from me. I'd hoped my sister's troubled 911 pleas would result in your arrival. It seemed prudent for me to let her drone on with her absurd claims rather than physically intervene." He pointed at the floor. "She threw that priceless vase in a fit of despair. She's a wonderful woman, but we're all struggling with the implications of a future without our father."

Emma surveyed the room before speaking loudly, "Are you a fool, Sheriff Boseman? Or a pawn, perhaps? Why haven't you considered that my son is indeed orchestrating his way out of a terrifying episode that *I also witnessed?* How about you other officers?" She waved her arm at the gathered police force. "Don't you sense something wrong here? My son's a chameleon, and he's lying through his teeth."

Sheriff Boseman appeared stunned by her strong voice, cogent demeanor, and articulate questioning. "I'm sorry, Mrs. Westbrooke, I didn't realize . . . Well, I didn't know—"

Emma interrupted the stumbling officer. "Didn't know I was a capable and sane human being, Sheriff? *Well, indeed I am!* And my daughter just told you the damn truth, that my son was acting terrifyingly crazy. She's correct about his involvement in the murder of John McCloud and probably Gabriela Mendes, who went missing when Thomas was thirteen. Remember that day, Sheriff? You visited me on our estate. I can supply incriminating proof, so I suggest—"

"Sheriff, my mother's compromised and needs care. Psychotic people are a danger to themselves and others—agreed? As her son and legal guardian, I request that you immediately transport her to the Chinook Psychiatric Clinic for evaluation." *You sonofabitch*, Thomas thought, *we've been paying you off for years. Earn your damn money.*

The room fell quiet, and the Sheriff cleared his throat. "I'm very concerned about your mother," he said with an easily noted absence of his typical bravado. "I agree; it's prudent to transport Mrs. Westbrooke for assessment."

Officers shot gazes at each other, clearly perturbed by Thomas's tone and their sheriff's acquiescence.

"*No way!* There's nothing wrong with my mother, you idiots. Handcuff my psychotic brother, or did my 911 call fall on deaf ears? This is all suspect, and my mother goes *nowhere* until I contact my lawyer. She doesn't need a damn doctor; that's ridiculous" She seethed with intensity but also appeared on the edge of reason.

The sheriff motioned to one of his officers. "Ensure Mrs. Westbrooke gets escorted to an ambulance and delivered to the Chinook facility. Call me after her admittance." A young sergeant nodded and motioned for Emma to follow him outside.

Sarah remained disbelieving of her inability to affect the drama playing out. She rushed forward. "*Stop!* Get your hands off my mother! Sheriff, I want you and your men out of our house. *Now!* Understand? Get the hell out! I called for help, not to be bullied. *Arrest my fucking brother!*"

After Sarah sprinted into the hall to grab her mother's arm, the officer escorting Emma glanced at the sheriff. With a flick of his chin, Sheriff Boseman ordered the officer to continue to the ambulance winding up the cobblestone drive. Sarah slapped the ushering sergeant so hard that her fingernail sliced his cheek. Blood trailed down his square jaw. Boseman ordered officers to restrain Sarah, who continued with a barrage of violent outbursts. The dazed fashion executive was handcuffed and led to a police cruiser for transport to the Eagle Bay precinct.

Settled into the back seat of a patrol car, Sarah exhaled with resignation. "You're arresting the person who made the 911 call. Does that make sense to you? Your sheriff behaves as if he *works for my brother.* Doesn't anyone else consider this bizarre?" She lowered her head as the door of the cruiser was shut.

With the commotion waning, Thomas ensured each public servant on the property received a personal thank you. Two of the officers refused to shake hands. Regardless, Thomas reminded them to be proud representatives of their idyllic community.

Thomas moved through the dim light to the ambulance. Before a paramedic slammed the rear door shut, he inserted himself to transfer information regarding Emma's care, then leaned forward and placed one hand on her leg. "Love you, Mom. Everything will be okay."

As he pulled his shoulders away from the vehicle bay, and with his body doused in the red glare of brake lights, she replied, "I'll be fine, Thomas. But don't you worry about the assets, son. They're in good hands, just like the cuff."

He stood halted by her words and stared into her face. With the significance of the statements fully absorbed, he narrowed his eyes.

Emma winked.

Soon, the family matriarch felt her body get poked with needles connected to translucent lines dripping intravenous fluids. She had no idea how this evening, tomorrow, or the next week would unfold.

But she took solace in recounting a critical development: The cat was now out of the bag; she and Sarah had vigorously challenged Thomas's glorious reputation in front of a room full of seasoned police officers. Perhaps one or more of them might doubt her son's character. After all, John McCloud and Gabriela Mendes still awaited justice served.

As the last officer departed, Thomas walked downstairs to the vault. Standing under bright lights among empty metal containers, he released a barrage of agonized screams while flashing intense rage. He found no solace.

51

CHAPTER

Skye savored a steaming cup of her favorite home-roasted brew made with Bolivian mountaintop coffee beans. She stared out to a picturesque and chilly Oregon Coast morning. Seated at the round kitchen table, she watched the deer, raccoons, and coyotes make their morning retreats into the misty forest adjoining their property.

Dakota glowed from the emotions of having Henry in her life. While she sometimes contemplated the experiences missed by not being in school, she also knew she'd be able to resume her studies and walk with her Eagle Bay Academy graduating class. She was determined to attend college, even if the thought of doing so as a single mom felt daunting. Despite the uncertainties, Dakota believed she'd been born with a special purpose and deemed her future to be exhilarating in its possibilities.

"Morning, Mom." Dakota flashed her exceptional smile that improved Skye's day even more than Bolivian mountaintop coffee.

"Hi, sweetie. Did you get more rest last night?"

"Yeah, thank God. Henry slept through the night; unless you consider 5 a.m. nighttime like I did not too long ago." She'd already mastered pouring a drink with one arm while holding her squirming son with the other. While stepping through the screen door to join her mother on the porch, a truck towing a colossal flatbed trailer laden with bales of hay rambled up their winding drive toward the barn. "Wow, the horses must be getting fat. That's more hay than I've ever seen delivered here."

"You're right. That's three or four times the usual load. Diego knows what he's doing, so no worries. We are blessed to have him back, Dakota. Your father would be pleased." She watched the horses trot through green fields. "It's terrible that Thomas threatened him, shot out his window, and then fired him. Just another crazy Thomas moment." Skye paused and shook her head. "Amazing, Diego's banishment happened over ten years ago. I'm getting old."

"Mom, why do you think Thomas is so messed up?"

"No idea, honey." Skye stared into her coffee. "He put us through hell with his secret life, lies, and disruptive behavior. Strangely, I think he may have loved us all once, but after the choking . . . Anyway, enough of that. We've persevered and are marching into a bright future." She offered a tender smile.

"You led the way, Mom. Johnny and I are so proud of your strength and commitment to us. You're amazing." Dakota walked around the table, and they hugged.

The phone rang. Skye stood up to grab it with one hand while tickling the wet chin of her grandson with the other. "Hello?"

"Skye, it's Steve. You alone?"

"Uh, hold on a sec." She turned to Dakota and motioned her and Henry to the family room. "Okay, I am now. Everything alright?"

"I'm afraid not. It's been an eventful first hour in my office. When I arrived, a gentleman was waiting with a package from Emma

Westbrooke, and its contents are remarkable. I've just discovered she was placed in the psych ward late last night after a confrontation between Thomas, Sarah, and her. Sarah was handcuffed and taken to jail by the EBPD; she'll get released soon. According to Emma, Thomas had a terrifying psychotic episode. We've both seen your ex transform before our eyes."

"But the package is from Emma?" Skye asked. "I don't think she'd be capable of sending you anything. She's not all there if you know what I mean."

"Her letter is quite clear, and she included evidence—a white ribbon with dark hair strands."

"Evidence of what?"

"Bear with me. It says here in my note that your package will clarify everything, but it will also break your heart. Have you received it?"

Skye's mind processed all the possibilities, and she remained silent.

"*Talk to me!* This is pressing, serious stuff."

"Relax, Steve. No, I didn't get a package. Let me—"

A smiling Johnny interrupted her by tossing a thick folder onto the table. "I've got to go, Mom. A courier dude dropped this off while you were in the shower. *Ciao.*"

"Skye, answer me. Did you—"

"*Yes.* I'm setting the phone down to open it. Hold on."

"*No!* Stay on the phone with me."

She'd already placed the receiver on its side atop the table. Skye walked to her drawer to grab scissors, eyed Dakota and Henry in the adjoining room, and sat back down to open the parcel. Inside was a letter and a second, smaller package. She began to read:

Dear Skye,

Please know I am more cogent than at any time since your childhood as I write this letter. Enclosed is a possession belonging to John that I recently discovered. My Thomas was responsible for your husband's murder and disappearance. This evidence corroborates other damning information collected. I suspected Thomas might be capable of disturbing behavior as far back as his adolescence, but my late husband refused my pleas to get him counseling. Robert and a criminal doctor drugged me into submission and irrelevancy for the past twenty-five years. This must undoubtedly sound preposterous, but it's the truth. I have assembled extensive documentation regarding my accusations against Thomas and sent it to Steve Collins. I have contacted no authorities because I'm convinced at least one senior member of the EBPD is in cahoots with my son. I don't know whom to trust yet. Your lawyer will be able to protect my original statements and begin an independent investigation. I have insisted it involve the FBI. I am saddened and horrified by the burdens my family has laid upon you and your children and pray that you might forgive me one day.

Sincerely,

Emma Westbrooke

Upon clutching a smaller package tucked inside the first, Skye fully envisioned its contents, which provoked a soft, hurting sound to emanate from within. Her stomach convulsed as she sat and swayed to and fro. Tears flowed in volumes that drenched her shirt and jeans. She moaned, "Dear John, oh my dear John."

Dakota entered the kitchen. "Mom, what's wrong? Why're you crying? What's going on?"

"*Skye, Dakota, please pick up the phone!*" Steve turned frantic with his inability to affect any of the unfolding drama.

"Someone's yelling through the phone." Dakota grabbed the receiver. "Who is this?"

"Dakota, it's Steve Collins. Put your mother on the phone."

"Mr. Collins, I'm frightened; she's swaying back and forth as if in a trance." She lowered the phone. "Mom? *Mom!*" There was no response. "What should I do? Call 911?"

"*No!* Do *not* do that! Put the damn receiver in her ear right now."

"*Stop yelling at me, Mr. Collins!* What's happening to my mom? I'm frightened."

"I'm sorry. Everything is going to be okay, but it's imperative that you physically grab your mother's head and stick the phone to her ear, Dakota. Please do that for me. *Now.* Thank you."

Skye opened the smaller package. Her expression transformed when she pulled out the oval cuff she'd had custom-made for John almost twenty years earlier. Someone had cut and bent a portion to remove it from a dead man's wrist. She mouthed the words inscribed: *John, With Love, Skye.*

Steve continued to yell through the phone. Skye grabbed it from Dakota and spoke. "Emma sent me a cuff I had made for John early in our marriage. She'd found it in the Westbrookes' guesthouse." She screamed, "*That monster killed my husband!*"

"My letter from Emma informs me of the cuff details," Steve said. "I'm very sorry, Skye, but now you must act on my urgent instructions."

"This news is ripping my heart out. Dear God. Okay, what should we do?" She motioned with her free arm for a still-confused Dakota to move closer.

"Do not panic, but you may be in danger."

"Keep going." Her voice grew more assertive.

"I need you to gather the kids and drive to an address I'll give you in a moment. A man named Martin will meet you there. He'll protect you in the unlikely event that it's necessary. This dossier on Thomas is more disturbing than you or I could have imagined. It makes sense to take extra precautions."

"I get it. We'll be out of here in minutes, and I'll call Johnny at school from the car. Give me the address." Hanging up the phone, she barked orders at Dakota to get packed and into the SUV with Henry.

A bright blue sports car raced up their long driveway. Sarah Westbrooke sprinted from the car after screeching to a halt just beyond the front porch, appearing tense and harried. They met on the front steps. "Skye, I'm so glad I caught you. Thomas and I had a frightening blowup last night, and I learned horrifying things. We need to talk."

"Your mother sent me John's cuff this morning. I understand the implications. *Your twisted brother killed John!* Now's not a good time to discuss your screwed-up family's issues. We're leaving."

"Mom, I thought we needed to get out of here?" Dakota looked exasperated after running back inside from the SUV.

"Are you fleeing from Thomas?" Sarah asked Skye. "I was going to recommend you relocate for a while. I wanted to call the police, but—"

Skye unclenched her jaw. "Yeah, I know, they're crooked like your family. You need to leave, Sarah. I don't know whom to trust anymore, and that includes you."

The women twisted around to watch a white sedan with its revved engine speeding toward the house with reckless abandon, clipping corners of the tarred drive and bouncing over small landscaping rocks lining its path. It was an unfriendly approach.

"Damnit, Sarah, curse you to hell! If you've led Thomas here, I'll never forgive you. Dakota, grab Henry and run inside and lock yourself in my room. Get the Ruger from my nightstand safe, and don't be afraid to use it. The combination is 7–4–6. I'll intercept Thomas or whoever this is."

"No, Mom, come with me!"

"Go, now! I mean it, damnit! 7–4–6."

Dakota was halfway to Skye's bedroom when the sedan slid to a halt between Sarah's car and the front steps. Two foreigners jumped out with large firearms trained on the women. "On the ground! *Now!* Don't run, or you're dead!"

The two assailants exchanged words in Spanish, and as one stood over the pair wielding his imposing weapon, the other rushed inside toward Dakota and Henry. He searched each room, making his way down the hall to the only closed door, shielding his body from behind the wall adjoining the door's hinges.

Dakota had just dialed Johnny's number on her cell phone and could see the intruder's shadow through the light at the base of the door. She was too afraid to speak and slid the phone under the bed before gripping the pistol with both hands.

As the gunman extended his left arm, slowly turning the horizontal brass handle, Dakota blasted eight 9mm holes through the wood-paneled entry. One of the bullets exploded the Argentine's left elbow.

Enraged, the wounded man kicked in the door and rushed to Dakota, aiming at her head. Henry screamed from the bathroom, where his mother had wrapped and laid him in the bathtub moments before. Dakota appeared ghost white with Skye's Ruger still gripped, crazily pulling the trigger while aiming at the man's chest, but the ammo clip held no more rounds.

"You American bitch!" he screamed as blood spilled off his elbow and onto the cream-colored carpet.

Skye shrieked during the commotion and attempted to raise herself off the ground. She was kicked in the head by a steel-tipped boot; the laceration across her cheekbone instantly swelled.

From the front of the home, the second man demanded in Spanish that his injured comrade not kill Dakota. Not yet.

Skye lay rigidly, one cheek pressed against the dirt, her warm blood seeping into the ground. She and Sarah shared gazes from their prone positions. Fluent in Spanish, Skye hoped to hear something that might offer hope.

52 CHAPTER

While the drama unfolded on the McCloud Estate, Steve presented allegations of murder against one of Oregon's most esteemed citizens. State authorities found the initial evidence compelling enough to act swiftly, justifying the protection of McCloud and Westbrooke family members. Bureaucracy delayed a coordinated inter-agency response, which Steve argued was essential due to clear evidence of corrupt officials in Eagle Bay and perhaps elsewhere.

While standing in front of Steel River's downtown Portland office building, Steve's assistant rushed to his side with his phone pressed to his chest. "The FBI needs to talk to you again." He handed the phone to his boss.

Steve ended the call and turned to his associate. "Feds are on it. They'll be interviewing Thomas Westbrooke today."

Clandestinely, amidst the developing chaos, Thomas requested a $10,000,000 transfer from WCI to a bank in the Caymans. He convinced a junior controller that an opportunity the board had been negotiating needed prompt funding and would net the company millions in investment returns. The controller had no idea the receiving account was a Caribbean entity tied to shady banking practices. Thomas reminded the employee he'd never put his stamp on a deal resulting in a poor investment return for the company and that the controller's boss, WCI's CFO, would expect him to execute the request if he weren't currently in Beijing on business.

"Scott, your quick advancement in the firm has been impressive. I've wanted to discuss your future at WCI for months, so why don't you schedule a one-on-one for Friday morning."

"Thank you, Mr. Westbrooke. You're an inspiring leader, and it's an honor working for you." Thomas's compliment removed the subordinate's last instinct of caution; Scott initiated the transaction.

Thomas had ensured the funds would be re-directed through a complicated maze of legitimate banks and illicit shell institutions within thirty minutes of the transfer. The money would become for-ever irretrievable.

He walked from his fabled company's headquarters for what he understood was the last time. The charade of the Pillar of Eagle Bay was over—he'd be a wanted felon before the end of the day. After the previous evening's drama with Emma, Sarah, and the police, he was surprised he'd made it this far without interference from authorities.

Thomas dialed Antonio Salazar while speeding toward the Chinook Psychiatric Clinic. "Are the assets ready for transfer?" The men had devised a plan to transfer the A2 assets in Buenos Aires. Thomas had likewise coordinated transfers with Antonio's Italian counterpart man-aging the assets in Geneva and Lyon, a Sicilian named Luigi Bucaso. The final step of their plot was an old-school *mano-a-mano* exchange on the outskirts of three foreign cities.

"Sí. All good."

"Sarah and Skye in the McCloud barn?"

"Sí. And the girl. The baby is in the house. We do not know where the son is."

"Doesn't matter. We have the people we need to get answers. I'll be in touch." He hung up.

Thomas grew invigorated by not knowing how each page of his new story would get written; he even saw himself smiling in the car mirror's reflection. It was gratifying not being in absolute control of every outcome, a lifelong routine he now considered unfulfilling. Pursuing the missing A1 assets remained the only goal that mattered, and he needed to swiftly eradicate any obstructions to securing them.

The sights of the open land between WCI and the Chinook treatment center holding Emma enthralled him. It was a clear day offering Oregon's natural beauty in sharp focus; the mountains to the east looked close enough to touch. He contemplated how bemused the state of Oregon, Wall Street, and journalists would become following news updates of The Pillar's final day as a respected man. Minutes later, he rolled into a parking spot, stepped from his Jag, and tucked his Sig Sauer Luger into the shoulder holster under his suit coat. Striding through the dark glass entry door, he slipped his sunglasses into his jacket pocket as he approached the front desk.

"Hello beautiful, I'm here to take Emma Westbrooke to a dental appointment." He smiled and winked, prompting the young lady to blush from the attention of a handsome man. She returned a flirtatious grin.

"Yes, sir. Oh, wait a minute. She's talking to a couple of men in the cafeteria right now. You can head down that hall to meet them. Is that okay?"

"Two men, you say? Are they in uniforms?"

"No, sir, just white shirts, dark pants, and sunglasses. Kind of boring looking, unlike you." She giggled.

FBI. Emma had triggered events. She was indeed much more coherent than he ever could have guessed. *Touché, mommy dearest.* He must've barely missed the agents at his office or on the road and realized his window of opportunity was quickly closing. A brazen act was his only option.

As he stepped away, he placed his hand on the young woman's and flashed another flirtatious smile. "You've been a great help, thank you. I see you're not wearing a wedding ring—I can't understand that. Goodbye now."

She bit her lower lip.

Walking through the hall unassumingly, the reeking odors of bleach and sterility overwhelmed his senses. The gray walls smelled of fresh paint. As he entered the cafeteria, he had already reached for his Sig when Emma spotted him. She urgently warned the agents her dangerous son had entered and was approaching; then she shook her head at Thomas in a futile attempt to get him to stop.

Thomas's adrenaline flowed; he was excited. Over the previous six months, he'd practiced shooting his pistol by firing over two thousand rounds at the Northwest Gunnery range in Yachats. The seasoned agents were no match for the expert marksman possessing rattlesnake reflexes and who was also unafraid to die. A single shot to the forehead killed each of the agents. Screaming and pandemonium erupted as employees and visitors joined the mentally impaired in scattering like spooked deer during hunting season.

Emma reasonably assumed her death was near.

"Hello, my coherent Emma. I'm so proud of you, *Mom.* Why don't we go for a drive?" By the time security had arrived at the cafeteria, mother and son were far removed and speeding toward the McCloud Estate inside a blue Jag.

"How long have you been cured, Emma?"

""Long enough. I never needed to be cured, just unshackled."

"And what's that supposed to mean?"

"It means I'm no longer drugged. What you and your father did to me was evil, stealing twenty-five years of my life." He flashed expressions any mother could decipher. "You didn't know . . ." She was astonished but relentless. "Your father locked me away in my own body with drugs, and I assumed you helped him."

He squinted.

"You don't have to do this, Thomas."

Seconds passed. "Where are the assets? You'd be wise to tell me now."

She remained silent and turned to the ocean.

"Who killed Robert, Emma? I think you know. I wanted to but didn't have the privilege. So who shot him?"

"I have no idea."

"Taking it to your grave? As you wish."

Emma gazed at a herd of elk grazing on a plot of unworked farmland. The peaceful image contrasted anxieties for whatever lay ahead. Thomas assumed she was thinking about Sarah and Skye, wondering if they'd gotten caught up in the day's events.

"Why'd you put the photo of John's cuff in the vault?" he asked.

"To let you know you're no longer in control of terrorizing innocent people. That your secrets will no longer be so. By now, Steve Collins and the authorities know about you torturing Gabriela Mendes's puppy.

I'll never forget the image of it lying dead at our door. And I remain convinced you harmed Gabriela."

"Harmed? I guess so. She's dead." He added, "I never meant to kill Gabriela; it was a horrible accident, as was clipping the puppy's leg off with the garden spade."

"I don't believe you."

"I always feared you wouldn't."

She shook her head while staring ahead absently. "You liked her so much. She was so kind and lovely. Why hurt her?"

He turned and glared. "I'm telling you the truth; I never meant to hurt Gabriella. She threatened to expose information about the assets and mocked me instead of heeding my warnings. Robert thanked me later, telling me her death protected our family. How messed up is that? I guess none of that matters now."

She pushed a strange sound from her lungs. "You were such a good little boy. So loving and sweet. What happened?"

"Are you serious, Emma? Acting as if you're not complicit? My parents happened, that's what." He shuffled in his seat. "Robert forced me to kill a man when I was twelve years old. *Twelve!* To protect Sarah, you, the assets." Moments later, he added, "His body's at the bottom of your pond."

"Dear God."

"It's a little late for your god." He pointed spitefully. "I almost killed myself when I was thirteen. I couldn't cope. Nobody gave a shit. Where the hell were you when I needed you, Emma?"

"I tried to get you more counseling. Robert resisted. I had no idea what he was doing to you. No wife believes her husband is capable of *teaching her son to kill.* He was too good at concealing the truth, just as you've become."

"Blaming it on your dead husband." He mumbled something inaudibly.

"We were both victims. And I did what I could."

"You didn't do enough. Now you've got a powerful and despicable son who'll do anything to get what he wants."

"*Stop blaming others for your evil!* None of my failures to intervene, or Robert's insane tutelage, justifies you harming others today. You know this is all very wrong. And those assets, as you call them, they'll mean nothing in the end. Stop and let me help you."

"Too damn late. I'm devoid of decency, even when I don't want to be. A capable man without a conscience. The way to fix me is to kill me." He studied his reflection in the rearview mirror. "As I've killed others."

Time seemed to slow down. "What happened to John McCloud?" It was likely her last chance for a confession.

"I killed John, who learned too much about the Westbrookes' secrets—secrets that your dead husband and tortured son spent their lives protecting while you and Sarah lived obliviously. John was a good man who made bad decisions at the wrong time." He scanned the streets for the authorities. "I miss him. Ponder that statement. Even though I killed him, married his wife, and traumatized his family—I miss him." He laughed, then stopped and leered. *"That's my legacy."*

Emma sat burdened with guilt and regret, tormented but now armed with the truth. She remained silent for the rest of the drive, staring out her window to the skies, her lips moving in silence.

"We're approaching the finale, Emma. You can make it easier for everyone by telling me where the assets are. Last night you said they were in good hands, and today, disclosing their location might save your daughter's life."

53

CHAPTER

Antonio Salazar arrived at the McCloud property, joining his two compatriots. He helped his uninjured countryman tie Sarah, Skye, and Dakota to the interior walls of the barn. Moments later, Thomas drove inside and hopped out, pointing at Emma. He instructed the men to rope his mother up with the others.

"You'd all be well advised to give me quick answers." Thomas's gaze terrified Sarah and Dakota.

"Thomas, settle down," Sarah said. "It's not too late to stop. There's nothing we have that you want. None of us knows anything about the assets. And none of us deserves to be hurt."

"*Au contraire*, on both fronts. Emma knows where the assets are. She's full of surprises." His laugh sounded demented. "You know what must now come to pass, sis. Remember our conversation from last night?"

"You're not well," Sarah pleaded. "Let us help you."

Thomas commanded Antonio to hold Sarah's left hand against a post, and he walked to where he remembered the McClouds kept their gardening shears. He rummaged around a workbench and returned.

"Robert would be proud, Sarah." He stepped closer with one arm behind his back, concealing the blade. "*Deny, deny, when caught in a lie.* I think you know about the assets. I know Emma does. The good news is I know how to extract the truth from you. I wasn't kidding last night." He revealed the shears.

"*No, Thomas!* You can't mean this!"

"Sure I can, sis. I've killed two FBI agents in the last thirty minutes. And you told the police I was a deranged nutcase last night, so these events will make you a prophet. I'm going to watch you bleed."

"Why are you doing this? *Why?*" Dakota cried.

Thomas studied her and shook his head. "Don't be naive like your mother."

Skye exploded. "I'm not naive, you monster. And leave your sister alone. The police will be storming this place any moment."

He stepped from Sarah and stood facing Skye. "It'll be a while before they figure out we're here." He brushed the hair away from her face and stroked the uninjured side of her head.

Kissing the blades of the shears, he returned to Sarah and winked. Then his face transformed. Anticipating evil, all four women shrieked for him to stop.

Skye turned to Dakota, demanded the young mother gaze into her swollen face, and whispered, "I love you. Close your eyes. We'll be okay." She wanted to say more. Paralyzed by fear, she questioned whether Thomas could actually kill an innocent daughter.

Thomas inspected Sarah's eyes; their noses nearly touched. The fingers of his free hand twisted an eyebrow. He asked, "Where are they?"

"Thomas, honestly, I don't know anything," Sarah begged. "Robert gave me the six codes and asked me to help coordinate moving everything in the vault without your knowledge. He said you could no longer be trusted. That's everything he told me. I swear. Please believe me."

"I don't," he said. "You're a lying bitch." He slid the blades gently across her cheek.

Emma screamed, "*Stop, Thomas!* I know where the assets are, and Sarah has no idea they even exist. I've removed and secured everything, including Montoya's journal. I'll give you their location if you let them all go. If you don't, you'll never see them."

"This isn't a negotiation! And lying has consequences, *Mommy!*" He turned to Antonio. "Shut her up and make her watch." The Argentine pressed his palm against Emma's mouth, forcing her head sideways to view Sarah.

Thomas grabbed his sister's wrist. "Deny, deny, Sarah." He turned to Emma. "You own this, Mother." With Sarah's arm outstretched and her left hand pressed against the thick post, he placed her pinky between the gardening shear's two blades as her face contorted with expressions of contempt and fear. Preparing to clip off her finger, he glared into her distorted face.

Sarah accepted it would all be over soon.

"Pain is justice, Sarah. Robert taught me that."

Squeezing the blades so that they penetrated the first layers of skin, Thomas whispered, "Give me answers, and you'll be free to go."

No one believed him.

No longer able to remain silent, the Argentine that Dakota shot through the bedroom door grimaced and yelled out in pain, blood from his arm dripping onto the floor. Thomas leered at the injured man. "When is this guy going to remember I'm fluent in Spanish? He wants you to rush him to a doctor or he'll talk to the authorities? I have bad news." He pulled out his 9mm Sig Sauer and shot the wounded accomplice in the head. Dakota screamed.

Skye yelled, "*Thomas, no more! Pull yourself together*! Stop and think about what you're doing. Just take cash and flee the country. What do you gain by staying here? Or hurting us?"

Thomas stared at her. "Don't be an idiot. I gain the assets." He remained still, saying nothing for a long pause. His co-conspirators glanced at each other, confused. Thomas stepped toward Skye and placed his gun's barrel against her temple. "Five, four, three, two, one."

He didn't fire.

Dakota fainted; her limp body resembled a rag doll suspended by the ropes around her wrists and midsection.

Skye moaned with a swollen and moist face, "You're evil. A murdering devil."

He moved closer. "Can't be that terrible. You married me."

"I married a betraying fraud." She spit in his face.

He wiped it away. "I killed John."

"I know that. I hate you." She spit in his face again.

Thomas slapped her. Dried blood that had oozed down from her forehead gash earlier stuck to his palm; he rubbed it on his pants.

Skye turned and thanked God that Dakota remained unconscious.

Thomas stepped back. "The assets—*and* the journal—are all that matter, people. Astonishingly, it appears Emma may be the only one aware of them. So, dear Mother, tell me where you've hidden them, or I swear I'll put a hole in each one of their precious little heads."

"*Let them go!*" Emma screamed. She feared Thomas would kill them all despite any information provided.

"No more delays. Tell me now, or I'll shoot new mommy in the head, then Sarah, and then you, Mom." He gazed into each of their eyes. "I'll save my wife for the encore."

"I'm not your wife, you sick bastard! You've taken too much from us! You're a psychopath! A weak and heartless man!"

He lifted his pistol barrel to Dakota's limp body. "Say goodnight to your sleeping little princess."

Johnny stepped from behind the hay truck with Skye's reloaded Ruger drawn. His extended arms kept his target in sight. The criminals could scarcely internalize the image of a teenager bearing down on them with the demeanor of a trained assassin. Johnny's first shot from the Ruger ripped a hole through Antonio's right shoulder; he collapsed to the ground, squealing in pain.

Still armed, Antonio fired back at Johnny from the floor, nicking his hand and knocking the weapon under the trailer stacked with hay. Johnny knew retrieving the gun was the only way to save his family; failure meant death. He never got the chance. The teenager froze and stared into another shooter's eyes, a man he once called dad.

Pop! Pop! Pop! The shots rang out from the shadows in a corner of the barn. Two bullets entered the back of another Argentine, blasting a hole through his heart. Two of the four assailants now lay dead, leaving just the ailing Antonio and armed Thomas. The third shot from the unknown gunman flew past Thomas's head, and he scurried behind the hay truck, assessing the situation and searching for the shooter.

Diego, the loyal vaquero who'd been exiled and threatened by Thomas years earlier, was the hidden triggerman. Having stumbled upon the chaos after a day toiling around the McCloud's property, the quiet man had rushed to his pickup to grab a gun he'd owned for twelve years but never fired at a living thing. Diego snapped off two more shots through a corner of the hay stacked upon the flat trailer, hoping to strike Thomas with a crippling blow.

A minute passed. As the victims wondered if Thomas had perhaps fled, his arm extended from around the trailer. Diego squeezed his trigger and sent two more shots in the direction of a man he considered biblically wicked.

While Thomas took cover amidst Diego's assault, Johnny used a knife to slice through the ropes restraining Skye, and she grabbed one of the dead men's Beretta semi-automatic handguns. Then she, Diego, and Johnny scampered behind farm equipment.

"I've got to untie Sarah and the others. They're sitting ducks," Johnny said to his mother and her farmhand. "Cover me."

Diego whispered, "No, not yet. I can't see Mr. Thomas."

"I'll untie them," Skye said. "You stay with Diego."

Too late. Johnny rushed toward the three bound women. Dakota remained unconscious. Sarah still had her finger but expected Thomas to step forward any second and shoot them all. Emma's eyes darted about the barn.

"Leave me, Johnny!" Emma demanded. "Protect yourself. Help your mother."

But Skye and Diego arrived just steps behind Johnny and the bound women. Each of them understood Thomas could be anywhere, aiming at their heads. Skye and Diego sporadically fired rounds toward Thomas's likely positions.

Thomas had circled the trailer and now stood undetected behind them. "I killed your father, Johnny. It's time to kill you," he said after stepping from one side of the diesel cab connected to the trailer. Diego and Skye would have to pivot around and shoot him before he killed the teenager.

Pop! Thomas's shot whizzed past Skye's head, striking Johnny in his shoulder joint. An expert marksman, he questioned why he hadn't killed his adopted son as he'd threatened to do. With Johnny agonizing on the ground, Thomas shifted his aim between Diego and Skye, then at Johnny's head, preparing to finish him off. But once again, he hesitated.

Antonio tried to cover Thomas but was too slow to lift his handgun because of injuries, giving Diego time to kick him in the head and yank the Argentine's weapon away. The McCloud's loyal vaquero turned around to find Skye frozen in a shooting position.

Pop! Skye pulled her trigger. A bullet struck Thomas in the chest, exiting his back and thrusting him to the ground. She ran and stood over him, glowering, before grabbing his Sig Sauer and tucking it inside her waistband. She told Diego to guard Thomas and rushed to Johnny's side.

The farmhand stared down disgustedly at the powerful man who'd once threatened to kill him. He believed Thomas would survive, so he pointed his barrel at his heart, wordlessly demanding compliance.

Lying on the dirty wooden floor, Thomas peered up. "You . . . you," he said with scorn.

The ranch hand bent down, their faces nearly touching. "Yes, it is me, Diego. It has been ten years, Mr. Thomas. You are what my American friends call a sick sonofabitch. I call you *el mal gringo.*" Thinking back to their intense exchange years earlier, he added, "You *comprende?*"

"Shoot him again!" Emma screamed at Diego, a man she'd never met. "Please. He's wicked and capable."

Diego looked to Skye, who remained preoccupied. She'd already torn Johnny's shirt open to inspect his injury. "Untie the women, Diego," Skye yelled. "Call 911. Keep an eye on Thomas. If he moves, kill him." She stroked Johnny's head, feeling confident he'd survive after inspecting the wound.

Emma untied Dakota and slapped her back into the moment. "We need to get inside, Dakota. Show me where your medical supplies are kept."

Dakota scanned dead bodies and a bleeding Johnny. *"Oh my God! Johnny! Mom, don't let him die!"*

"Dakota, now!" Emma yelled. "We need clean towels, gauze, and a tourniquet. Show me the way."

Dakota grabbed Emma's hand to lead her and Sarah inside. After pointing to the laundry room and medicine cabinets, Dakota ran to check on Henry, who was red and shrieking but otherwise fine.

Thomas and Antonio were still very much alive. The scene remained tense. Thomas turned his head to Johnny. "You win, thanks to your favorite Mexican."

"Listen to you," Skye said as she applied pressure to Johnny's shattered bone. "So despicable. I hope you die."

"But I won't, Skye," Thomas strained to say. "How's my son doing?" He nodded in Johnny's direction.

"I'm not your son, you freak," Johnny said, struggling to overcome his pain. "You killed my dad. Tried to torture your sister."

Skye thought Johnny appeared to be in shock. In a soft voice, she told him, "Stop talking. Don't give him the satisfaction."

Sirens blared in the valley below. Thomas glanced at every actor in the drama before locking onto Skye. "You McClouds, always so goddamn noble." He added, "No matter. Dead father like dying son."

Skye halted and stared outside through open barn doors. She picked up her pistol, walked over to Thomas, and aimed steadily at his heart.

Barely able to speak through the pain, Johnny said, "No, Mom. Don't. Please don't."

Skye studied Johnny for seconds without expression. Memories and concerns flashed through her mind, similar to when people anticipate catastrophe. Resigned to her decision, she stood over Thomas's head and glared into striking blue eyes. "Burn in hell." She extended her arm with a tight grip on the gun and pulled the trigger. *Click.* There were no more bullets. She tossed the weapon aside, grabbed Thomas's Sig Sauer still tucked in the waist of her jeans, and readied her aim a second time.

Johnny nearly passed out but uttered, "No, Mom . . . Please."

"*Stop!* Drop your weapons, or I'll kill your son." Antonio glanced at Skye but kept his barrel trained on Johnny. The Argentine had been toting a second gun, a .36 caliber pistol holstered above his ankle. He stood hunched over, blood drenching his clothing, one arm dangling.

Skye froze. Her finger twitched against the handgun's trigger. Years of deceit and wickedness filled her head, but her family's survival was all that mattered.

"Drop them. *Now!* Both of you," commanded Antonio a second time. Diego remained close by with his gun pointed at Thomas's head.

Skye and Diego glanced at each other. The protective mother felt trapped and said, "Do as he says." They set their weapons on the floor, hoping they wouldn't all get killed regardless.

The cacophony of sirens grew louder.

Blood poured from Thomas's chest, but he was able to stand. "You should've killed me, Skye." He bent over to pick up the loaded pistol Skye had placed on the ground. "I've temporarily lost the assets, but you're about to lose John's son permanently." He peered into Johnny's eyes. "I'm sorry. This is it, Johnny. I know you could never understand, but I'm simply wicked and can no longer rein it in."

Antonio fired a shot at Thomas's feet, causing him to straighten up and glare at his partner. "What the hell are you doing?"

"The police are almost here. I'm too injured to drive, and we must flee—*now*." Antonio aimed the gun back at Johnny to freeze Skye and Diego while speaking to his boss. "I am saving us both. Let's go." Antonio silently questioned how Thomas could contemplate killing his son.

Thomas glared as he reached into his jacket, grabbed his keys, and limped toward his car. He twisted around. "This isn't over, Skye. Pass that on to Emma and Sarah."

"How can you live with yourself?"

"I can't. This is what happens to men like me."

Antonio shifted his aim between Skye and Diego, commanding them to move back. He grimaced in pain while bending to pick up Diego's weapon. Moments later, the armed assailants sped away in Thomas's Jag.

Skye tended to Johnny, who lay with a contorted face expressing agony. How could he not, Skye thought to herself—the father he once loved and respected just shot and threatened to kill him. Emma reentered the barn with medical supplies as the police arrived at the property. Paramedics rolled Johnny into the first ambulance on the scene.

CHAPTER 54

Thomas's murders today and years prior, and his brutal accosting in the McCloud's barn, resulted in a sweeping manhunt.

Sheriff Boseman sat in an SUV off an old lumber mill route in the coastal hills south of Yachats. Over an untraceable line, the sheriff proclaimed that this favor for Thomas was to be his last. He wanted out.

"Careful not to cut off the hand that feeds you, Sheriff. I'd advise you to employ a more measured tone. You've been paid very well for your services, but now the house of cards is falling. You may need me." Thomas recognized that the crooked cop didn't possess the mental faculties required to protect himself from the torrent of charges he'd soon face. So be it. He killed the line.

Antonio said, "So, the American physician will fly with us to Buenos Aires, sí?" He turned his head and tried to flash a slight grin.

Thomas had grudgingly accepted that Antonio's ultimatum to flee was prudent. "I'd smile but driving with a bullet hole in my rib cage is uncomfortable. Though, it's a pain that exhilarates. When the final chapter gets written, we'll be living luxuriant lives, my friend."

Antonio nodded, reflecting that Thomas had never before called him a friend. He asked, "What is the range of our plane?"

"Forty-five hundred miles. We'll refuel in Bogotá. Everything's confirmed." Thomas arranged for a Gulfstream G3 jet to be prepped for immediate departure from Southwest Regional Airport in North Bend. Six large, heavy wooden crates were loaded into the aircraft's belly. He pondered the fortunate reality that people with money could synchronize complex activities on short notice, with few or no questions asked.

Yes, money meant power. But the sway associated with being a business icon and pretend humanitarian would soon be a fading contemplation. Possession of the Westbrooke dynasty's great secret would be his ultimate gratification. His reward for a lifetime of perverted loyalty. It was time to reclaim the prize stolen from his father's vault.

Dr. Stan Braswell sat aboard the jet as Thomas and Antonio entered the hangar. $200,000 had been delivered to the surgeon's home inside a leather briefcase thirty minutes earlier. He understood he would attend to medical emergencies while flying to Buenos Aires. Hours after arriving in Argentina, the same plane would shuttle him back to Oregon.

The pilot, Frank Washington, was ex-CIA; he was well-versed in the world of covert operations. He asked no questions and would behave obliviously in return for insanely good pay.

Thomas dropped Antonio off at the steps leading into the jet before driving to the small terminal he'd walked through many times during his life. With his bleeding slowed, he stopped to purchase drinks and snacks, even though he knew the Gulfstream had already been well-stocked. The intimidated cashier stared uneasily at his injuries, put his goods into a plastic bag, and received a wink from the wounded stranger. The young man watched Thomas drive off in the SUV; he was now a witness.

It was a dark evening along the Oregon Coast. A shroud of mist moved through the airport, and Thomas flicked the truck's wipers. Entering the hangar, he rechecked the cargo bay and its large containers. They appeared to have gotten loaded precisely as instructed.

Rounding the tail section of the Gulfstream jet and ducking his head for clearance, Thomas caught three minutes of Antonio's hurried cell phone conversation spoken in a Sicilian dialect. When Thomas entered the plane, the Argentine concealed his phone. Thomas noted Antonio's condition appeared much improved since leaving the McCloud's barn. Minutes later, Dr. Braswell sterilized Antonio's wounds, sutured him up, and directed him to swallow six white pills with water.

Thomas had important matters to attend to. He asked the doctor for privacy, and the confused physician moved to the back of the plane. Thomas commented on the cool and damp weather, saying it should be better in Buenos Aires. He noted in Sicilian, "You never told me you spoke Sicilian, Antonio."

Antonio shrugged and said nothing.

Thomas discerned a touch of unease. "I'm intrigued. I've known you for years without fully appreciating your linguistic skills," Thomas said. "Your knowledge of our asset management systems, coupled with your impeccable Sicilian, would make you a valuable resource to many."

Antonio didn't flinch.

"Are you aware that my most trusted European confidante is Sicilian? Manages Westbrooke affairs on the continent. Lives in Palermo and goes by Luigi Bucaso. Perhaps Robert had mentioned him to you?"

Still no reaction.

"A principled man. Non-violent. Prefers others to do the unpleasant things—like kill people."

Antonio replied in English. "Mr. Westbrooke, we are both exhausted. Lucky to be breathing. Yet you have the energy to question my allegiance to you? I am not offended, only disappointed. I have Italian and Spanish heritage, so it makes sense that I speak both languages well."

"But you speak a rarer regional Sicilian. It's not important, of course. But you are a man of startling dimension, Antonio." His mind in constant motion, the Pillar on the Run had concluded there were now two viable masterminds, or pawns, regarding Robert's assassination. Emma, the lucid matriarch who may have struck back against her deceiving husband, a man responsible for twenty-five years of her mental incarceration, and Antonio Salazar, a despised yet heretofore necessary and trusted co-conspirator, a traitor to Robert Westbrooke, and a man whose own desires for the assets may have pushed him to engage in another round of double-crossing by aligning with Thomas's associate, Luigi Bucaso. Did Antonio or Luigi now possess the A1 assets? Thomas would spend the coming days solving that mystery.

Staring at the Argentine, he said, "You've always been loyal, Antonio. I value that. Let's complete the transfer of A2 through A4. You're confident the men making the exchanges are the only ones aware of the plan?"

Antonio visibly relaxed. "Sí, Mr. Westbrooke, that is correct. Plus me, plus you."

Thomas doubted that, but he had a workaround. "Okay then, let's get this done, amigo."

"Sí, Mr. Westbrooke."

Over the next few minutes, Antonio called Buenos Aires, and Thomas connected with individuals in Geneva and Lyon. They instructed three different men on the outskirts of each city to rendezvous with three strangers and to transfer cargo from one SUV to the other. Each of the three vehicles driven away would hold a single metal container in its rear compartment, measuring seven feet in length, four feet in width, and thirty inches in height.

Antonio was unaware that the three men driving the heavily laden SUVs from the exchange points had previously been assigned one final task by Thomas: Put bullets into the heads of the other three men.

So, the foreign assets were about to be controlled by Thomas's new cadre of associates. Antonio had no connections to the men securing the bounty, making him expendable.

Thomas valued the A2-A4 assets at about $140,000,000, though he'd never sell them. Added to the $10,000,000 transfer executed by the WCI controller hours earlier, the soon-to-be felon was worth approximately $150,000,000 in untraceable wealth. The valuation wasn't critical to him, but possession of Inca history was. With the authorities in hot pursuit and with nefarious families unexpectedly removed from the seventy-year-old financial model they'd benefited from, Thomas realized his primary challenges moving forward would be to remain invisible and alive.

Thomas called Dr. Braswell back. The surgeon confirmed that the bullet entered and exited Thomas without hitting vital organs and arteries. Still, as he cleaned and sterilized the flesh and tissue surrounding the 9mm round's entry and exit points, he told himself his patient was lucky to be alive.

Antonio grew annoyed by yet another delay, considering it an unnecessary risk. He presumed federal agents must have expanded their search perimeter further south along the coast.

The doctor finished suturing and dressing Thomas's wounds.

Support personnel in the hangar gave the pilot thumbs-up, and the Gulfstream made its way from the tarmac to the runways. The two villains faced each other in reclined seats, sharing blank expressions and immersed in very different thoughts.

Antonio rested at ease despite his painful injury. Thomas's mind stirred with malice because of the conversation he'd overheard between Antonio and Luigi Bucaso. Listening to the Italian and Argentine further strategize their double-crossing was infuriating, but it wouldn't alter Thomas's plans.

The Argentine and Italian had aligned on a ploy to seize the A1-A4 assets and eliminate Thomas. He learned their conversations had begun before Robert's death and that one of Bucaso's assassins flew to Oregon to kill the Westbrooke patriarch. But then, the acquaintances turned adversaries—Thomas, Antonio, and Luigi Bucaso—learned almost simultaneously that the assets were missing from the vault under the Westbrooke estate.

Thomas's newfound adversaries had agreed to equally divide the A1 assets upon extracting them from the Westbrooke Estate. Antonio accepted the deal without hesitation or qualms; he would be rich beyond his wildest dreams. More importantly, the Italian mafioso wouldn't order his henchmen to hunt down and kill the Argentine for rejecting the proposal. But when the A1 assets seemingly vanished, everything changed for those with eyes on the prize.

Thomas and his new rivals shook their heads with astonishment upon realizing Emma Westbrooke apparently knew where the A1 assets were. The men wondered if she understood how precarious and finite her future would be.

The day's developments prompted Antonio's earlier call to Bucaso to modify the foreign co-conspirator's plan. The update called for Thomas and Dr. Braswell to get executed within minutes of arriving in Buenos Aires. Later, teams of Bucaso and Antonio's men would depart from Italy and Argentina, joining up in Oregon.

The plan was to round up and torture the surviving Westbrooke and McCloud family members until one of them divulged the assets' whereabouts. Italian and Argentine thugs would seize the prized bounty, split it up, and ship it abroad to convert to fiat currencies. The Italian mafioso would then order his men to eliminate any remaining McClouds and Westbrookes.

Now nearing takeoff, Thomas winked at Antonio.

The Argentine winked back.

The pilot contacted the control tower. "Southwest Oregon ground control, this is Gulfstream 63127, Northwest Aviation, taxi with kilo."

"Roger that, Gulfstream 63127. Runway 022 cleared for takeoff."

"Roger that."

The plane lifted off and turned northwest before veering southwest, passing over the airport and Coos Bay, one mile west of the shoreline. Thomas reflected on the day's events, disappointed he hadn't yet discovered and secured his obsession—a future opportunity. He felt his body fill with adrenaline, his mind grow acutely aware, and his internal clock tick.

Loud as a sonic boom, the explosion was catastrophic, decimating the aircraft Thomas and Antonio had climbed aboard. A great ball of fire turned artistic through its colors-of-fire juxtaposition against a pitch-dark sky enveloped in light coastal fog. Witnesses described the shifting tints of the intense reflected colors as similar to the images viewed through a kaleidoscope on a sunny day. Tentacles of multi-colored intensity reached down from the sky for several minutes, followed by a dark emptiness.

Recovery crews would locate no piece of the fuselage larger than a pizza tray.

Authorities later announced that no one could have survived.

CHAPTER 55

The McClouds' guesthouse became a command center for the FBI. Two of its agents were murdered in cold blood at the Chinook Psychiatric Clinic. Thomas met his end in an explosion that obliterated the Gulfstream jet multiple witnesses at the airport had placed him aboard.

A live television report from Oregon's state capital caught the room's attention. "We're focused on gathering clues that might explain the blast. We have determined that at least two local men were aboard the plane. One is a well-recognized Oregon businessman and philanthropist from a notable family. The second is an ex-Navy pilot once employed by Evergreen Airlines and the CIA. After being apprised by the FAA, FBI, and state law enforcement, I will provide further updates. We offer our heartfelt condolences to the families dealing with this tragedy." The governor looked shaken as his top campaign contributor—and a good man by his measure—seemingly experienced a mental breakdown before masterminding a grisly terror spree, only to meet his dramatic end.

"He shouldn't have died that easily," Johnny muttered from his hospital bed. His comment drew a bemused glance from the FBI agent interviewing him and an agreeing nod from Skye. "It would have been fairer for that evil prick to have spent the rest of his life in jail."

The agent declared, "Based on what I've learned in the past ten hours, Mr. McCloud, I'd agree. By the way, sir, congratulations on your heroism. And your mother's. You both have much to be proud of."

The agent's remark struck an emotional chord when he addressed him as Mr. McCloud. Later, when mother and son were alone, Johnny glanced at Skye but said nothing. His thoughts drifted to his father, John III. He watched the moon rise outside his window and whispered, "I always tried to protect Dakota and Mom. I swear I did."

"Who are you talking to, Johnny?"

Johnny floated in and out of coherence due to the drugs infused after a successful surgery. "Dad," he answered. When his eyes moistened, he turned away.

With Johnny needing rest and being well attended to by doctors and the nursing staff, Skye returned home.

The information the McCloud and Westbrooke families provided Steve Collins, state law enforcement officials, and the FBI proved invaluable. The list of known or suspected victims of Thomas continued to grow. The oldest case required draining a pond on the Westbrooke estate to determine if Thomas's claim of drowning an intruder at Robert's behest was valid. The ensuing investigation involved thirteen-year-old Gabriela Mendes, who was last seen twenty-five years earlier on the Westbrooke estate by two witnesses. The latest cases involved the witnessed killings of two FBI agents and an injured Argentine co-conspirator Thomas executed in the barn.

Investigators concluded John McCloud had likely gotten buried inside or just outside of the Westbrookes' Century Barn, based on information gleaned from a conversation between Robert and Thomas that Emma partially overheard and somehow registered during the slow recovery from her induced stupor. The discovery of John's oval cuff added credence to Emma's allegations.

Despite Skye's unease regarding Sarah and Emma's connection to her life, she felt compelled to call Sarah after Thomas's unhinged threats in the barn. All the women had difficulty reconciling the psychotic behavior they witnessed. "Anyway, Sarah, I'm heartbroken over what your brother subjected you to. And thankful he didn't hurt you as he threatened. That's all I wanted to say. I'm relieved you're physically okay—that we all are." There was no response, so she said, "Goodbye now."

"Wait, Skye, hold on. Please. All these events were a horrifying impetus for reconnecting us, but perhaps it was fate. I want you to know I'm sorry for everything our family put you and your children through. I hope Johnny heals well and that you'll give Emma and me a chance to regain your trust and friendship."

Skye told herself to be cautious with her response. Marrying into the Westbrooke family had ultimately delivered nothing but pain and hell, but she pushed those truths aside. "Thank you. We'll talk again, Sarah. I should go."

Just as Skye hung up, the phone rang again. She hesitated to answer due to the overwhelming barrage of calls from family, friends, and strangers connecting with good intentions. But on the fourth ring, she reached for the receiver.

"Mrs. McCloud, this is FBI Special Agent-in-Charge Quincy Armstrong. Because the media tends to report field developments more quickly than we, hmm, appreciate, I thought I'd call you myself. We've uncovered a grave beneath a cement slab poured conspicuously in what used to be a horse stall in the Westbrookes' barn. Our cadaver hounds picked up a weak human scent. We've unearthed a deep burial pit, and three sets of human remains laid one on top of the other, each separated by about two feet of dirt. While DNA testing will provide absolutes, we believe one set of remains is your husband's. He appears to have two gunshot wounds. Excuse me for being so graphic; this must be overwhelming." He waited for a response.

Skye suppressed strong emotions.

"It's busy here, Mrs. McCloud, so I must press on. I'm asking you to keep everything I'm telling you confidential. The remains placed below the person we suspect to be your husband are of a young girl and what appears to be a small dog and, hmm, that very well could be Gabriela Mendes."

Skye had expected investigators to find John's body, but the image of a little girl filled her head. She stared at Dakota and Henry, thought about Johnny, and realized how fortunate she was. "That poor child. My heart goes out to her parents and family."

"Of course," Agent Armstrong said. "Surprisingly, buried below the child's remains are the bones of another adult, a man we believe has been dead for at least many decades."

"Strange." Skye scratched her forehead and stared out a dirty window. *"Wait!* I think I know who that might be." She hesitated. "Incredible."

"What?" the agent asked.

"Your DNA testing should prove it, but I think it might be my first husband's grandfather. My children's great-grandfather, John McCloud I. It suddenly all seems plausible."

"Based on what, ma'am?"

"Pictures, newsprint, family histories. It's a long story. We have the information in a law firm's vault. I'll request it for you." She paused to watch horses trot through their pasture and asked herself: *Why would a Westbrooke have killed the first John McCloud?*

"Hmm, I look forward to reviewing what you have. It's an intriguing claim. I'm sorry for any anguish discovering your husband's remains might cause. Excuse me, but I must go now."

For three decades, Sadie was the friend who'd served as a voice of calm, encouragement, and emotional support for Skye. She remained convinced Sadie helped Thomas get her arrested on meth possession charges; she had no idea why. Thomas wasn't who he appeared to be, and ditto for Sadie, she now knew.

Cody paid the highest price for Sadie's inexplicable departure; he truly loved her. Her vanishing act was cruel, but he remained adamant she'd return. She'd disappeared in the past, needing time to "get her head straight." Skye wondered whether Thomas might have killed her, but she couldn't answer why he would have.

Cody recently left on a WCI business trip to China. He'd warned Skye that phone and internet access in parts of China were not yet reliable, thus, not to expect any contact. Skye anxiously awaited his return; he'd always been a good man, and they provided each other stability. Steve was a great source of comfort to her, but nothing soothes like an old friend.

Skye realized she'd grown stronger and more independent through her marriage to Thomas. She almost laughed out loud upon the reflection, knowing that growing stronger was scant benefit for the hell she and her family endured. Yes, she could now handle anything, but she desperately wanted life to settle into a more conventional routine.

FBI agents departed the McCloud property late that afternoon. Skye's generosity had allowed them to set up operations in the guesthouse, which lay feet away from a primary crime scene—the barn. Eagle Bay's police force would have ordinarily participated in most aspects of a case within its jurisdiction, but Oregon's district attorney suspended Sheriff Boseman and the Sea Cliff County chief of police based on convincing allegations of misconduct. The FBI collected incriminating testimonies within the EBPD related to Skye's drug arrest and Sarah's 911 call the night of Thomas's meltdown. Those revelations were the first steps toward what Skye believed would be the sheriff's downfall and imprisonment.

An evening of the McCloud family settling their emotions gave way to a pristine morning. Still dazed but less exhausted, Dakota, Henry, and Skye conveyed an air of normalcy during breakfast. Dakota recovered impressively from the mental trauma of watching her father torment Sarah and shoot Johnny. Henry was smiling and cooing as if nothing unusual had happened during the week. Doctors authorized Johnny's release from the hospital in three days.

A knock on the front door echoed.

Upon answering, Emma Westbrooke's personal driver, Billy Platt, asked to speak privately with Skye. She complied and joined him on the porch. He explained that Emma Westbrooke had requested that he relocate something vital to her barn with utmost urgency hours before Thomas's meltdown. Billy nodded at two fit men standing on the driveway. They approached, and together the group ambled over a stone path toward the barn.

Skye grew captivated but remained confused.

Upon entering the barn, Billy asked his two associates with military tattoos to remove hay bales from the flatbed trailer parked in the middle of the floor. Diego had ordered the feed from WCI's agricultural division, just as he had many times before. But this time, the Ag Division "sales rep" Diego had spoken with was actually Billy Platt, who convinced Diego to purchase three times his usual order by offering a discounted price the farmhand and stables manager couldn't refuse.

Skye stood perplexed as bales were lifted from the trailer and stacked on dirt. Eventually, a series of large wooden crates were exposed. Helped onto the trailer's bed, and now standing next to the first wood container, she remained puzzled. It was pried open with a crowbar.

"What the heck? Is that stuff real?"

"Yes, it is, Mrs. McCloud. And every container is filled with similar treasures. Emma Westbrooke would like to meet with you regarding the proper storage, security, and insurance required for everything you see."

"I don't understand. At all." She picked up and examined random pieces. "So strange. So incredible. It's hers?"

"Yes, ma'am, it belongs to Emma Westbrooke."

"It doesn't make sense. I'm lost. Why's it here, in a darn barn? *My* barn?"

"That's a long and complicated story. She wants to tell it to you personally."

"Why would Emma Westbrooke want to talk with me about anything related to something so random and precious? That belongs *to her?*"

He grinned. "Because she's going to give all of this to you, Mrs. McCloud." He'd been excited to measure her reaction to the disclosure.

"What? Are you . . . ? Why? I have money. This stuff must be . . . priceless." She laughed nervously, moving her eyes from man to man, wrinkling her forehead, awaiting a response.

"You'll have to ask Mrs. Westbrooke. But I don't think it's about money."

Lightning struck. "*Wait a minute!* Are these the assets?"

"Yes, ma'am, they are."

CHAPTER 58

The relaxed air would change.

Emma, Skye, Johnny, and Dakota sat around a dark oval table in Steel River's headquarters. Billy Platt sat in the corner of the room, looking highly attentive. Hot coffee, iced tea, and lemonade lay in the middle of the table, along with a platter of donuts.

Centered on one wall was a Karen Busch original abstract painting. A massive window of thick glass offered unobstructed views south and east. White jet contrails streaked across blue skies, and the Willamette River below them was filled with boaters and sunbathers enjoying a perfect City of Roses day.

Steve Collins entered the room with two strangers who smiled and appeared excited. Johnny thought one looked like the generalized Hollywood archeologist adventurer, all the way down to his brimmed khaki hat and scruffy facial hair. His associate looked half outdoorswoman and half librarian, wearing a ponytail and black glasses.

"Everyone take a deep breath," Steve said. He shifted his eyes from person to person, carefully peering into each face. Looking at Skye and the mystery guests and back to the teenagers, Steve's face lit up. "What you're about to hear will be one of the more fascinating moments of your life. I want you to focus on everything said, to appreciate this experience forever."

"Whoa," Johnny said as he turned to Dakota and put a hand on her shoulder. "You think we can handle this, sis?"

"I sure hope so," Dakota replied with a chuckle. "But I don't know; it sounds like a *pretty . . . big . . . deal*." She swallowed a sip of lemonade and turned to Skye. "You didn't tell us this day would change our lives, Mom." Dakota grinned, judging Steve's set-up to have been melodramatic.

Skye winked. "Pay attention. I can promise that you have no idea where this is going."

"Our guests are Pierre Lafitte and Elizabeth Cohen," Steve began, "from the Smithsonian Institute. Pierre is an archaeologist with a Ph.D. from Cornell. His expertise is in Latin American history. Elizabeth has a degree in art history from the University of Oregon and a Ph.D. in history from Harvard. She is also the curator of Ancient American Civilizations at the Smithsonian Institute Museum." Steve measured every face in the room, speaking more excitedly as he built the puzzle. He nodded to Elizabeth, sat down, and pulled out a Butterfinger.

"Hi, everyone. It's good to be back home—I grew up in Lake Oswego." Elizabeth cleared her throat. "This is an extraordinary day." She gazed at Dakota, emphasizing the point. "What I'm going to reveal has only been discussed with three executives at the Smithsonian; that's how privileged you all are. The Institute agreed to Steve's confidentiality demands on behalf of both families, that we not share any images or publish our findings publicly until he, Emma, and Skye say it's okay." She could sense the teenagers' minds spinning, so she paused to let their imaginations run wild.

Elizabeth continued, "We were skeptical about the information initially provided—it just didn't seem possible. So we flew out west, and we nearly fainted." She eyed Pierre. "We've researched and confirmed our conclusions, which may still be controversial. Years of cataloging stand before us—regardless of where everything is headed." She shot another glance at Skye, raised her brows, and pressed her hands in hopeful prayer. "We're ready to announce our findings." She was nearly hyperventilating and visibly forced herself to relax. She took a swig from her clear water bottle. "Pierre and I are now *believers*. You will read about this in every newspaper in America and worldwide when we announce it publicly."

The room remained still as a painting—the grins of teenage annoyance replaced by anticipation. Johnny's leg tapped from under the table, adding a soft cadence reverberating between the walls. Dakota looked like an awestruck teenager, unconsciously turning the bracelet on her wrist. Elizabeth's comrade, Indiana Jones, smiled and nodded while holding his unshaven chin in his hand.

"We've all heard about the great Inca civilization," Elizabeth said. "And we've all seen photos of Machu Picchu. I understand Pierre and I are the only two in this room to have visited the remarkable city. Johnny and Dakota, are you familiar with Inca history?"

"Well, I know their empire spanned the Western portion of South America," Dakota blurted out. "And I think their reign spanned the thirteenth century until the Spanish arrived in fifteen hundred and something."

"They got ripped off by the conquistadors, didn't they?" Johnny asked. "At least, that's what I thought after discussing it in AP history."

"It was a difficult end for the Inca Empire," Elizabeth said, with

Pierre nodding in agreement. "Many would argue it was inevitable. Some might term it the spoils of war. But let's focus on your comment about them getting 'ripped off.' I'm assuming you're talking about the conquerors taking the empire's gold and silver. Am I right?"

Johnny and Dakota both agreed.

"As archaeologists, historians, and art lovers, people like Pierre and I find it tragic that the bulk of Inca artifacts are considered gone forever. Most of the Inca gold and silver relics discovered by the Spanish got destroyed. Christian Europeans considered the religious and artistic expressions of the civilization's people unworthy. Few exist today."

"I know historians still believe there are Inca treasures hidden somewhere in Peru," Johnny said. "Are you going to tell us you found a map or something?"

Steve, Pierre, and Elizabeth chuckled. "Or something," said the weathered Frenchman in his heavy accent.

Elizabeth took a deep breath. "Everything has changed." She pressed her lips and raised her brows before repeating, "*Everything* has changed."

Johnny shot a gaze at Skye and back to Elizabeth. He said, "Okay . . . and?"

"*The Lost Treasures of the Inca are lost no more,*" she announced in a melodic cadence. "I repeat: The Lost Treasures of the Inca are lost no more." She turned to Pierre; the Frenchman stood up and hugged her. Shrouded in her fervor, Elizabeth turned to Skye and Emma and beamed like a flighty groupie.

Emma clutched Skye's hand, both women shaking their heads. Dakota and Johnny weren't sure what to make of the declaration; they studied each other through squinted eyes with mouths agape. They peered up at Elizabeth, wanting—*needing*—more information.

Elizabeth said, "We have seen them. We have held them in our hands: gold, silver, and spectacular gems. Many historians assume the Inca hid the bulk of their vast riches from the conquistadors. Over the centuries, the mythic treasures would reportedly be discovered or rediscovered, but none of those claims proved true. Most modern-day historians presumed they were lost forever. But somehow, incredibly, likely centuries ago, they made their way to Eagle Bay, Oregon!"

"Wow," Dakota said, grabbing her brother's arm. "Can we see this stuff, Mom?"

"Soon, honey."

"Six thousand pounds of ancient religious icons and artwork. Roughly 160,000 ounces of gold and silver that, priced by weight alone, are worth over $19,000,000. Valued as the priceless history they represent, well, hundreds of millions of dollars—probably more. Four hundred pounds of gems, including, we think, twelve of the twenty largest emeralds known to exist. It's all beyond incredible. Three life-sized bodies of pure gold. What we believe might be the busts of three emperors . . . *in* . . . *pure* . . . *gold.* Inca gods crafted with precious metals with inlaid gems. Our understanding of the reign of the Inca civilization just got altered forever. For Pierre and me, this is like finding King Tut's and Cleopatra's tomb and treasures—*all at once.*"

"Unbelievable," Johnny kept repeating. Recollecting the past, he blurted out, "That's what Thomas had been drawing in the garage, Mom. Maybe he got hypnotized by all this stuff." Moments later, he asked, "How'd it get here?"

"A million-dollar question," Pierre replied.

Everyone remained silent for a long moment, letting it all soak in.

"*Holy crap!*" Johnny bellowed while jumping to his feet. "Holy crap!" He placed his hands on top of his head. "Incredible."

"What, Johnny, what? Stop freaking out. Just tell us," Dakota demanded.

"Don't you get it? Doesn't anyone understand?" he implored, scanning faces around the table.

Elizabeth and Pierre acted confused. Dakota waited for more information. Billy sat calmly. Emma and Skye shared knowing glances.

"*Our family once owned this shit!* Our great-grandfather McCloud was killed over these treasures! This must have been what started the entire *thing* between our families." His eyes were wide, and his arms extended.

"Oh, wow," Dakota said, quickly internalizing the ramifications. "Is that possible? Scratch that; I've learned anything's possible. But, but . . . Emma?" Dakota looked at Emma, uncomfortable with accusing her of being an accessory to perhaps the greatest heist in history.

Skye placed her hand on Emma's. "We think you *may* be right, Johnny," she said. "But Emma had no idea, kids. It was Robert and Thomas's great secret. They took it to their graves." She half-smiled. "Now there's a great mystery to unravel. It appears three generations of Westbrooke men spent their lives protecting the secret. My guess is McCloud ancestors owned or discovered all of this and that something terrible happened. And if the Westbrookes stole the riches, they'd need to keep everything hush, hush to minimize risks of their claims getting scrutinized. They would have done whatever it took to protect their ownership. I have a hunch the WCI empire grew using the treasures as business capital. So, let's hope all the blanks get filled in eventually."

"What are you going to do with it?" Johnny asked.

"I'm not sure yet." Skye glanced at Elizabeth. "The Smithsonian is very interested, of course. But it's part of Peruvian history, so I feel strongly their citizens need to share in the discovery. Based on a 400-year-old journal in my possession I'm trying to decipher, appears very possible the treasures were not stolen but rewarded to an extraordinary conquistador named Juan Francisco Montoya. We'll discuss that later."

"Where's it all kept?" Dakota asked.

Skye tipped her head to Billy Platt.

"Hidden and protected," Emma's "chauffeur" replied, looking quite capable of hiding and protecting.

CHAPTER 59

Skye awoke early and sat at her home-office desk, enjoying dark coffee as beams of sunshine shot through the adjoining forest. She held the journal once belonging to Capitán Juan Francisco Montoya, which she'd been scouring for months. Only twenty pages of the fascinating narrative remained unread. Even with Robert's notes and translations, reviewing each page was laborious. She wondered if the manuscript's final entries would deliver any surprises.

Opening a vault built into the wall, she laid Montoya's writings inside and closed its steel door. The assets were kept in an undisclosed Fort Knox six miles away, protected by Billy and three of his ex-military comrades that Emma and Skye had interviewed and had vetted by Steve's legal team at Steel River.

She wandered into the great room and relaxed on a sofa offering views of the corrals and horses. Reading Montoya's account had prompted thoughts of the two Westbrooke women. Skye now accepted that Emma and Sarah were admirable people victimized by the charlatan—just as her family had been. She realized it must be difficult for them to reconcile all the horrors witnessed or attributed to Thomas.

As the late afternoon sun settled, two McClouds, two Westbrookes, Steve Collins, and Diego gathered for a home-cooked meal. The kitchen buzzed with eager conversations about dreams and happenings in their lives. The aftertaste of St. Innocent pinot noir lasted well after Skye set her glass on the gray slate kitchen counter. Glancing at the hands on the sunflower wall clock, she grew annoyed and reached to turn down the stove's gas burners. "Where's your sister, Johnny? Dinner's ready."

"Want to guess? At the shooting range. Where else?"

Dakota burst into the room. "Sorry, guys! *Sorry.*" She beamed, sauntered to the table, and tossed four targets to Johnny, each displaying ten holes. "Forty shots. Forty bull's eyes. One hundred feet."

Johnny laughed. "Amazing. Seriously, that's pretty impressive."

"The imposter is damn lucky he's already dead!" Dakota had adopted Johnny's disrespecting moniker.

Skye grimaced. "Honey, we have company. This might not be the best time to voice your scorn." Skye turned to Steve, who lifted his shoulders and provided no protest. She shifted her gaze to Emma.

Emma shook her head slowly. "Please, Dakota's right. My son deserves only contempt for what he put you all through." The Westbrooke matriarch lifted her glass. "To Dakota! Slayer of the ghost of a wicked man!"

Everyone acted surprised by Emma's candor. Steve put his arm around Skye and squeezed, wishing he had a celebratory candy bar. Dakota stared at Emma, expressing solidarity. Diego smiled, lifted his brows, and tipped his cowboy hat. They clutched the closest glasses, raised them, and toasted to a young lady's wistful vengeance.

"*To Dakota!*"

60 CHAPTER

The meal was delicious. After cleaning the kitchen, they walked up an ashwood staircase. Temperatures barely dropped as the sun set below a colorful horizon.

"Oops, I forgot dessert," she said. "Be right back." Her skin had tanned, and her hair had lightened a few shades.

He winked and walked across the teak deck of the yacht, appreciating the views of the Caribbean Sea and St. Johns Island. Moments later, she returned and filled two crystal glasses with port.

"Here you go, my darling man."

His lips formed into a relaxed smile. "You're the girl of my dreams."

Sadie kissed him passionately.

Still embraced, Thomas said, "It's time to fulfill my destiny. We leave for Oregon in two days."

ACKNOWLEDGMENTS

To the early readers of *Eagle Bay:*

Karen Cruickshank, J. Ken Cruickshank, Caitlin Cruickshank, Bre Cruickshank, Will Sutherland, Chet Morgan, Bob Cruickshank, Robert Cruickshank, Celia Fraser, Beth Flanagan, Fran Killen, Peg Schuetz, John Busch, Mike Busch, Kris Curry, Kirk Rozman, Kevin Luby, Ron Cannady, Beth Groshans, Dan Groshans, Parmi Van Dyke, Nance Case, Lesley Heinrich, Jennifer Ciacci, Pete Beucke, Paul Younkin, Chris Leicester, Yvonne Myette, Doug Jackson, Doug Franklin, Carol Franklin, Mark Busch, David Aretha, Karen Azinger, Cynthia Whitcomb, Mark Marcantonio, Charlie Sutherland

Thank you.

AUTHOR BIO

Due to multiple sclerosis and an accident, Ken Cruickshank uses speech-to-text software to write groundbreaking thrillers, historical fiction, and memoirs. *Eagle Bay* is Ken's debut novel. A second thriller, *The Emerald Cross*, is scheduled for release in the summer of 2023. Both stories take readers on unexpected journeys, and their endings are unguessable. *Stand Up: a memoir of disease, family, faith & hope* was his debut memoir. Ken appreciates every reader who commits precious leisure time to his books. After thirty years in Oregon, he and his artist wife, Karen, now call Arizona home.

Visit Ken online at:
www.kencruickshank.com
www.instagram.com/authorkencruickshank
www.facebook.com/KenCruickshankAuthor/